Eugene Vesey was born in Manchester. He was educated at a R' ...mar school in Manchester, a Roman ... English Lake District, at the Univers... ...d English Language and Literatur... ...ity of Liverpool, where he obtaine... ...ves and works in London, where he ...s a Foreign Language at Colleges of ... forty years. His novel **GHOSTERS** is a ... **OSITE WORLDS**. Both novels are available from

Also by Eugene Vesey

Ghosters (Novel)

Venice and Other Poems

OPPOSITE WORLDS

Eugene Vesey

First published 2011
This edition October 2012

All characters in this publication are fictitious and any resemblance to real persons, living or dead, is purely coincidental.

ISBN: 1461075874
ISBN-13: 9781461075875

for

Xiaoqian

again

CHAPTER ONE

'I can to speak weeth you?'

'Sure,' he said, only too pleased – she was a gorgeous Greek girl, who had stayed behind at the end of the lesson.

'We can to go somewhere?' she asked, in her sexy, husky voice.

'Would you like to go for a coffee?' he suggested, secretly excited – she looked like a model, with long, jet-black hair, a tanned if slightly rough complexion and a voluptuous figure. She was wearing a tight red sweater, which accentuated her already big breasts, and tight black, velvet trousers, which did the same for her hips. A slightly upturned nose added a certain pertness to her features. She had a leopard-skin coat draped around her shoulders and, as always, a pair of sunglasses on top of her head, even though it was winter.

'You are sure you have the time?' she asked.

'Well, I've got some time,' he said, checking his watch, suddenly feeling nervous. She wasn't trying to pick him up, was she? She couldn't be – she was far too glamorous to be interested in *him*, a humble EFL teacher in a back-street private English school in Soho!

He had noticed her before, because she always sat at the very front of the class, staring at him. He found it difficult not to ogle her during lessons – especially those tantalising boobs– and often fantasised about fondling them, but had never expected it to come true, still didn't. She couldn't possibly fancy him, could she? She probably only wanted to ask him for help with her visa or some such mundane matter, as students often did.

'Let's go, then,' he said, picking up the plastic bag he used as a briefcase and ushering her towards the door. '*You and I*,' he added to himself silently, quoting from the poem by habit.

As she went down the narrow wooden stairs of the school ahead of him, leopard-skin coat draped over her shoulders, sunglasses on her head, he couldn't help noticing what a sexy bum she had too. God, she was gorgeous! He fancied her like mad, felt himself getting aroused, but tried to suppress it. She couldn't possibly fancy him, he was sure, so it was better not to raise his expectations. *If you'll pardon the pun*, he remarked wryly to himself, following her out.

They went to a coffee bar just along the street from the school. Being in Soho, it was surrounded by strip clubs, sex shops and porn cinemas, as well as restaurants and pubs. He found the area stimulating, in a sleazy sort of way – not that he had ever availed himself of any of the services, lonely and frustrated as he was. He would be too embarrassed, even to go into one of the cinemas! The films looked crass anyway. He was curious about the strip clubs, but was put off by the shady-looking doormen, didn't fancy being surrounded by lecherous German, Scandinavian and Japanese businessmen and was afraid of being ripped off. As for the prostitutes who advertised in doorways – he would never have the nerve to try one, even if he wasn't afraid of catching some gruesome disease.

Anyway, maybe he could get off with this Greek girl. No, he was kidding himself. He had no chance! She was far too glamorous for him. He wasn't bad-looking, he supposed, and had quite a good figure – he was tall and slim, a bit lanky perhaps – but he was no film star or model. He was definitely not in *her* league!

What did she make of Soho, he wondered? He felt a bit embarrassed by it, but she didn't seem bothered at all. Maybe it was just him, because of his background, he reflected uncomfortably. After all, he wasn't just an ex-Catholic, but an ex-seminarian, too. 'From Seminary to Soho' – it'd make a good title for a novel, he chuckled to himself. It wasn't funny really though. He was screwed-up, he supposed, but there was no use moping about it. The thing was to *do* something about it. That was why he had come here to London. All he needed was a girlfriend. Like this one maybe …

'Sorry, what's your name again?' he asked, sitting next to her in the coffee bar.

'Kalli,' she said, offering him a cigarette, which he declined, and lighting up herself. She had long fingernails varnished red, he noticed, with a ripple of excitement.

'Is that from 'kalos', meaning 'beautiful'?' he asked. *Very appropriate, too,* he thought, wondering if he dared say so.

'No. 'Kalos' ees mean 'good'. 'Beautiful' ees 'omorfi'.'

'Oh. That must be Modern Greek. In Ancient Greek 'kalos' means 'beautiful'. As in 'kaleidoscope' – 'kalos, beautiful, eidos, sight, skopeein, to look'.'

'You speak Greek?' she exhaled, neatly-pencilled eyebrows raised.

'No,' he laughed. 'I learnt Ancient Greek at school, that's all.' Little did he think, all those years ago in the junior seminary, that one day it would come in useful for chatting up an attractive Greek girl in a coffee bar in Soho! What would Father Percival, the classics teacher, make of it, he wondered? He might be chatting up a girl somewhere himself – several of the priests who had taught him had also left, from what he had heard. No doubt they too had seen what a nonsensical way of life it was. But no, not Father Percival – he was far too prim and proper, positively priggish. He wouldn't survive for five minutes in the real world!

'Really?' she asked, impressed.

'Yes,' he said, pleased with himself. 'So, you see, I think your name means 'beautiful'.'

'I don't think so. Ees just name,' she exhaled.

'Well, it's a beautiful name and it suits you, anyway,' he said, surprised at his own nerve.

'Thank you,' she exhaled again.

God, she was so sexy, he thought, trying to suppress his growing excitement! She couldn't really fancy him, could she?

'So what did you want to speak to me about?' he asked, deciding to get to the point, since he didn't have much time before his evening class.

'Nothing special. I am just find you interesting,' she said, in her sultry voice.

'Oh, well, thank you,' he laughed, flattered.

'I can to ask you something personal?'

'I suppose so,' he said, intrigued.

'You are married?'

'No, why?' he laughed, blushing.

'I just wondered,' she shrugged her sexy shoulders. 'You have girlfriend?'

Blimey, he thought, she was nothing if not direct! 'Not at the moment,' he said, trying not to blush again, and not to think of Marina, who had left him and gone back to Yugoslavia only a few, lonely weeks ago. 'Why?'

'Nothing. I am sorry. Ees not my business.'

'It's all right, I don't mind,' he said, actually rather pleased to be discussing such intimate matters with her. 'What about you? You're not married or anything, are you?' She had a ring on her wedding finger, he noticed, but one on almost every other finger as well. She was obviously into jewellery.

'I would not be here, if I would be married,' she smiled archly.

'No, I suppose not,' he laughed, resisting the impulse to give her a quick lesson on the second conditional and wondering whether she meant 'here' with him or in Britain. 'How long have you been here?' he asked.

'Six months.'

'And what else do you do, apart from learning English?'

'I am singer.'

'You're a singer?'

'Yes. I sing in the restaurants. The Greek restaurants.'

'I see.' He was impressed. 'Is that what you did in Greece?'

'Yes, but in the Greece I was actress, too.'

'An actress? What kind of actress?'

'On television. How you call it – 'soap'?'

'Soap opera, yes. I see. So you were famous, were you?'

'A little bit. I was also model.'

'Really?' He was surprised, though it wasn't surprising, considering her looks.

'Yes. I can to show you photograph, if you like.' She searched in her handbag.

'Yes, if you've got one,' he said, becoming more infatuated with her every minute.

She took out a large, black and white photo and passed it to him. It was obviously professional and showed a sexy-looking girl posing with one hand on her hip and one behind her head, in a short, patterned dress with a shiny-black belt around her waist and shiny-black, knee-length boots. God, she was not only good-looking, but talented as well, he thought, trying to stop himself falling any further in love with her, since he still couldn't believe he had any chance.

'It's very good,' he commented, handing the photo back to her.

'You can to keep if you want,' she said, exhaling.

'Are you sure?'

'Please,' she said. 'I have more.'

'Well, OK, thanks,' he said, putting it in his 'briefcase' and wondering why she should be giving him a photo of herself. Did it mean something? *No! Don't count your chickens, Frankie boy!*

'So, er, why did you leave Greece?'

'You know situation in the Greece eet ees very bad?'

'You mean politically?'

'Yes.'

'I know – the Colonels.' It was ironic – the country that had given democracy to the world under a military dictatorship! 'Was that why you left?'

'Yes.' She didn't seem keen to talk about it.

'You had problems?' he pursued anyway.

'Yes. And now I have any problems here.' It sounded like 'proplems'.

'You mean 'some' problems,' he corrected her.

'Thank you,' she exhaled.

He wondered what kind of problems, but didn't want to probe too much.

'Ees why I want speak weeth you,' she said. 'I want ask you make me favour.'

She was gazing at him, her big brown eyes, complete with false lashes, pleading. She looked as if she might be about to cry. His heart went out to her. He wanted to throw his arms around her and hug her. He wanted to do more than hug her! 'What favour?' he asked.

'You will?'

'Yes, of course, if I can,' he shrugged, his voice sticking in his throat.

'I like you, Francis,' she murmured, her eyes gazing into his. They seemed to have a hypnotic quality that drew him closer and closer. The smell of her perfume made his senses swim. Then suddenly, to his amazement, their arms were around each other and their lips met in a long, intimate kiss ...

'I like you, too, Kalli,' he whispered into her ear, caressing her face tenderly with his fingertips, stroking her long, jet-black hair, holding her close so that he could feel her breasts pressed against his chest, giving him a huge hard-on. He could hardly believe this was happening!

'What do you want me to do for you?' he whispered. At that moment though, the waitress, to his annoyance, came to take away their cups, so they let go of each other.

'I prefer not speak about eet yet – I want know you first,' she said. 'You will to come to restaurant tonight?'

'Which restaurant?' he asked, wondering why she was being so mysterious.

'Restaurant where I sing. Ees called 'Acropolis'. Ees in Charlotte Street, not far from here.' She reached into her bag again, pulled out a card and gave it to him. 'You will to come?'

'What time?' He suddenly felt nervous again.

'I start to sing at ten, but you can to come before.'

'Are you sure it's all right?'

'Ees no proplem.'

'All right.' What the hell, he thought, checking his watch – it wasn't every day you were invited by a sexy-looking girl to go and hear her sing. 'I'd better go,' he said. 'I've got another class.'

They stood up and went out into the busy Soho street. 'I'll see you later, then,' he said, awkwardly.

'Thank you,' she said, giving him a peck on the cheek and sashaying off sexily, to be swallowed up in the throng of tourists and commuters.

He hurried back to the Shakespeare School of English, hardly able to contain his excitement at the prospect of seeing her again later, hardly able to wait for the next few hours to pass, hardly able to believe he had kissed her, she liked him, she had invited him to see her! But what was this favour she wanted? She hadn't actually said. It didn't matter, he told himself – he fancied her like mad. He'd do anything she wanted!

The restaurant was nearly full, mostly of Greek men. It was small, with just a few tables, and pictures of the Parthenon on the walls. In one corner, on a tiny stage, a musician in a red shirt was playing a bouzouki, accompanied by a drum machine.

'You would like table, sir?' asked a man who looked like Aristotle Onassis, only even uglier.

'Er – I've come to see Kalli, please,' he said, uncomfortably. Onassis gave him a suspicious glance, then waddled off through a door beside the stage.

A few moments later Kalli came out, said hello and led him to a table at the back. 'Who's that?' he asked, sitting opposite her.

'Plato. He ees owner,' she said, asking a waiter for a menu.

'I don't want to eat,' he said quickly. He was hungry, but didn't have much money on him. Anyway, he was too nervous to eat.

'You must to eat something,' she insisted, looking at the menu. 'What you would like?'

'Anything,' he said. 'Just something small though.' Who was going to pay, he wondered?

She ordered something from the waiter, who went off. 'You shouldn't,' he said to her.

'No proplem,' she said.

'Aren't you eating?' he asked.

'No. I must to go and change. I eat later.'

'Oh,' he said, disappointed. 'Are you going to sing now?'

'Yes. See you later.' She stood up.

'OK. Sorry – endaxi,' he added, practising his Greek.

She disappeared backstage. He sat listening to the bouzouki, enjoying the sound, but still feeling uncomfortable, sitting there on his own. After a few minutes, the waiter came back and put some food on the table, with a bottle of wine, from which he poured him a glass. 'Efharisto,' he said, self-consciously, tasting it.

'Endaxi,' the waiter smiled and left him.

He drank some wine and nibbled the food – 'dolmades' Kalli told him later – while waiting. He felt self-conscious, sitting there on his own, but excited, too. It was certainly better than being on his own in his bed-sit in Clapton!

Suddenly, the lights dimmed, the bouzouki player stopped playing and announced in Greek, then English: 'Ladies and Gentlemen, here to sing for you, the beautiful Kalli!' A spotlight switched on and a glamorous-looking diva stepped into it. Her hair was coiled up on top of her head, she was wearing a long, red, low-cut evening gown that revealed a voluptuous cleavage, and was dripping with jewellery. For a few moments he couldn't quite believe it was Kalli – it looked more like Shirley Bassey. But it *was* Kalli!

She picked up the microphone, the bouzouki player struck up and she started to sing in Greek. He was impressed – she not only looked, but sounded, like Shirley Bassey! As she sang, she swayed sensuously to the rhythm, sometimes playing a tambourine. God, he thought, not only was she great-looking, she had a great voice, too! He couldn't help feeling excited at the thought that he had *kissed* her. What would it be like to go to bed with her? *No, better not think about that …*

'I would like sing next song for somebody special. He ees sit at back,' she suddenly announced into the mike, after she had done a few numbers to enthusiastic applause.

The other diners looked around and so did he, but then he realised she was talking about *him*! Embarrassed but flattered, he listened to her sing, in Greek, what sounded like a big, romantic ballad, followed by several more numbers.

'You're very good,' he told her, when she came to join him during her break, enjoying the jealous glances of the other men in the room.

'Thank you,' she said, exhaling a cigarette. 'You like the Greek music?'

'Yes, I do. Especially when you're singing.'

'You like food, too?'

'Yes. It's delicious. And the wine. You don't have to pay for it, do you?'

'Ees from Plato.'

'Is he actually the owner or just the manager?'

'He ees owner.'

'What's he like?'

'I don't like him, but he pay me,' she shrugged, sexily.

'Why don't you like him? Doesn't he pay you enough?'

'He pay enough, but he want sleep with me, too.'

'Oh, I see,' he said, shocked. The lecherous bastard! But he'd like to sleep with her himself, so he couldn't be too judgemental, could he?

'I don't think he will keep me if I won't to sleep with him.'

'You mean, you'll lose your job?' He was even more shocked.

'Yes. He told me.'

'The bastard!'

'Ees everything OK?' Plato asked smarmily, suddenly sliding up to their table. *Speak of the devil!*

'Lovely, thanks,' he forced himself to smile. 'It's very kind of you.' *You lecherous bastard!*

Plato looked at Kalli, tapping a chunky gold watch on his hirsute wrist, and said something in Greek.

'One minute,' Kalli said, exhaling. Plato glanced from her to him and waddled off.

'You wouldn't sleep with him, would you?' he asked her and immediately realised he had put his foot in it.

'You think I am prostitute?' she asked, offended.

'No, of course not. I'm sorry,' he said, blushing. *What a bloody stupid thing to say!*

'I better go back,' she said, stubbing out her fag and standing up.

'Shall I stay?'

'You want leave now?'

'No, not at all. I'm enjoying myself,' he said quickly, realising he had struck another wrong note.

'I see you later then,' she said, to his relief, going back to sing again.

'What you want do now?' she asked, rejoining him when she had finished singing and changed back into her everyday clothes – tight red sweater and black velvet trousers. She had left her hair up, though, which made her look even more sexy and sophisticated.

'I'd better go home,' he said, looking at his watch – it was nearly two in the morning. Not that he wanted to!

'You live far?'

'It's about half an hour on the bus. If there is a bus. I'll have to get the night bus, I suppose. What about you?'

'I go with minicab.'

'How long does it take?'

'Half an hour.'

'That must be expensive.'

'Ees OK – Plato pay it.'

'I see. Well, I'd better go, I suppose,' he said, starting to get up.

'I can to go weeth you, Francis?' she suddenly asked, putting her hand on his arm to stop him.

'You mean – ?' Did she mean what he thought she meant? He could see from her eyes that she did! A current of excitement went through him. 'Yes, of course,' he said, taking hold of her hand.

'I call cab,' she said, getting up and going over to the payphone near the door.

In the back of the minicab, she sat so close to him that their thighs touched, sending an even bigger current of excitement through him. Almost instantly, they were in each other's arms and kissing, tongues eagerly exploring each other's mouth, hands eagerly exploring each other's body. He put his hand on one of her breasts and started to fondle it, when she suddenly grabbed hold of his wrist. For a moment he thought she was going to stop him because he had gone too far, but instead she pushed his hand under her sweater! Then, with a shock of delight, he felt her hand slip down to his crotch and begin rubbing his already huge erection. This excited him so much though that he had to stop her, because she was almost making him come. Besides, he noticed the taxi driver glancing surreptitiously at them in his mirror.

As soon as they got into his room though, they pulled each other's clothes off impatiently and made frantic love, first on the floor, then on the single bed. She made love with an abandon that both shocked and excited him, so he quickly lost all his own inhibitions. It was so much easier than with Marina, his Yugoslav girlfriend, who had been so terrified of getting pregnant she would never let him actually do it properly with her, not even with a condom.

Kalli, by contrast, was obviously experienced. He hoped she didn't notice how inexperienced he was – it was actually the first time he had ever made love properly, so technically he was still a virgin! It wasn't too difficult to hide though, because she was so passionate. They made love in a whole variety of positions, like actors in a porn movie. Her favourite position seemed to be sitting on top of him, with him inside her, bouncing up and down as if she was riding a horse, her head thrown back, her hair down her back, her boobs bouncing up and down, panting and gasping, groaning and moaning with pleasure.

She didn't seem to be worried about getting pregnant, so he presumed she was on the pill and, when he couldn't hold it back any longer, came inside her. Later, she came with him on top, crying his name out over and over again, faster and faster, louder and louder, until she finally came in a long, violent convulsion of ecstasy. Afterwards, they rested for a while, then carried on, again and again and again, until they were both exhausted and fell asleep in each other's arms.

He went to the Acropolis – and a Turkish restaurant where she worked as a belly-dancer – every weekend. Afterwards, they went back to his room by minicab and made love. He enjoyed wining and dining for free, while he watched her singing or dancing. He enjoyed seeing other men ogling her lecherously or trying to chat her up, knowing she was *his*, it was *he* who would soon be making love with her and not them! Making love with her was what he enjoyed most of all and yet – there was something missing, something wrong. He couldn't quite work out what though.

Why did he always feel guilty afterwards? Was it just the usual Catholic guilt about sex? After all, according to Catholicism, sex was a sin, a *mortal* sin – except in marriage and for the purpose of procreation. You could go to HELL for it! That was what he had been brought up to believe, like most Catholics – like most Irish Catholics, anyway. Not that he believed in Hell – or for that matter any of it – any more. Catholicism – indeed Christianity and all religion – was a load of superstitious nonsense as far as he was concerned now.

In his case though, there was more than the usual Catholic guilt about sex. There was something else wrong. Was it something to do with the Ghosters? With the fact that for nine years, from the age of twelve to twenty-one, he had been brainwashed by a bunch of black-frocked celibates against women? With the fact that one of them had –

No, he didn't even want to think about *that*. He refused to think he might not be normal. That would mean they – the Ghosters – had won. That was unthinkable! He *was* normal! And he was determined to prove it to himself by fucking Kalli as often as possible – and enjoying it!

He couldn't quite shake off the feeling that there was something wrong though, no matter how much he tried to analyse and rationalise it. He wondered if it had something to do with the 'favour' Kalli had said she wanted to ask him for, with the fact that she wouldn't tell him what it was, kept stalling whenever he mentioned it. 'Why are you so cryptic about it?' he asked her one night in bed, after making love, when she avoided answering yet again.

'What does mean 'cryptic'?' she asked, exhaling a puff of smoke, post-coital cigarette held elegantly between long, brown, be-ringed fingers, fingernails painted bright red.

'You should know – it's Greek!' he said and explained the etymology of the word to her, but she still managed to evade the question.

Her evasiveness had started to bug him though. He was determined to get it out of her the next time he saw her!

'So, come on, what's the big favour you want me to do for you ?' he demanded, taking a first sup of his Guinness with a small gasp of pleasure and licking the froth from his moustache.

They had gone for a drink in Soho and she had promised to tell him what it was, having put him off for several weeks. She wiped more of the froth from his moustache with a tissue, a gesture he found erotic, because it reminded him of how she used a tissue to dry him off after sex. She took a sip of her wine.

'You will marry me, Francis?' she asked, taking another drag on her fag and blowing the smoke out sideways, but keeping her big brown eyes fixed on him.

'Marry you?' he laughed, spluttering as he took another sup of Guinness. She must be joking. He had never thought of that!

'Yes,' she said, serious.

'Why?' He took a slug of Guinness to fortify himself.

'I want stay here, so I need to marry British citizen.'

He had been vaguely hoping she might say, 'Because I love you'!

'You mean, you want a "marriage of convenience"?' he asked, shocked, as it dawned on him that she was deadly serious.

She nodded. 'Why you look so shocked?'

'I'm not shocked,' he fibbed. 'It's just that – well, I thought you might say, 'Because I love you'.' He laughed ironically.

She put her hand on his, rings glittering. 'But I do love you, Francis – you already know that, don't you?'

Did she, he wondered, scrutinizing her? 'But you just want a "marriage of convenience"?' he asked.

'I don't want – what you say – tie you up?'

'Oh, you can tie me up if you want!' he joked, trying to evade the question himself now, trying to think of what to say.

'Why you laugh?'

'It's a joke!' he explained. ''Tie up' means like this.' He crossed his wrists. 'Some people think it's quite sexy! You mean, 'Tie down'.'

'I don't want tie you down,' she said, still serious. 'After one year, two year, we can make divorce, if you want be free again.'

He took another swig of Guinness, trying to think.

'You will do eet for me, Francis?' she cajoled, in her sexiest, huskiest voice, holding his hand tightly.

'I don't know, Kalli,' he said. 'I'll have to think about it.'

It wasn't the answer she wanted, he knew, but for some reason the idea scared him – he couldn't quite work out why. Marina, his Yugoslav girlfriend, had jilted him at the altar – well, at the register office – but it wasn't just that. Here was a gorgeous, sexy, talented Greek girl, asking him to marry her, even if only for "convenience", and he was hesitating! How ironic! He ought to be thrilled, ought to declare, 'Yes, of course I'll marry you'. Yet somehow he couldn't bring himself to do so.

'You promise, Francis?' she implored, clasping his hand with both of hers, having stubbed out her cigarette in the ashtray.

'Yes, I'll think about it, I promise,' he assured her, taking another slug of Guinness.

The more he thought about it though, the more nervous he felt. He still couldn't quite understand why – it wasn't such a big deal. What was he afraid of? Was he afraid of being trapped? Yes. Was he afraid of doing something illegal? Yes. Was he reluctant to take part in a charade? Yes. It was all those things. But there was something else. It was a horrible thought, but he couldn't help thinking it: Had she just been using him all along?

'I can't do it, Kalli,' he told her, during her break in the restaurant one evening.

'Why not?' she asked, hurt.

'I just can't,' he said, choking. He still wasn't completely sure why not himself.

'I pay you,' she said.

'Kalli, please.' He was shocked. 'It's not a question of money. I just can't do it.'

'Why not, Francis?'

'I don't know. It just doesn't feel right.'

'Please help me, Francis,' she grabbed his hand, tears in her eyes.

'Kalli, I'm sorry. I can't. I'll do anything to help you, but – '

To his relief, because he was almost in tears himself, Plato, the proprietor, signalled her to go and sing again. She dried her eyes and went back. It made his heart bleed, listening to her sing and knowing how she must be feeling. He knew it might mean the end of their relationship, but still couldn't bring himself to do it.

'I go home alone tonight,' she said ominously, when she had finished singing, changed and re-joined him at his table.

'Why?' he asked, alarmed – they always went back to his room and slept together.

'I am tired.'

'You can sleep at my place.' He knew it was useless, he was only trying to stall the inevitable.

'Really, Francis, I am too tired tonight,' she sighed.

'Are you upset?'

'Of course I am upset.'

'I'm sorry,' he said, feebly.

The minicab came, they went outside and she got in alone. 'Are you sure?' he asked, in a last-ditch effort to make her change her mind.

'Yes, I am sure.' She gave the driver her own address and he realised he had never been to her place, now maybe never would.

'Good night,' he said, choking.

'Goodbye, Francis,' she said, with a chilling finality.

He walked home, which took him over an hour, feeling more and more dejected with every step. He had lost her, he knew – it was over. The end. Finito. Kaput. He was on his own again. He felt loneliness wrap itself around him like a shroud. There was only one escape – when he arrived home, he put on 'Blonde on Blonde', took out the bottle of Jameson's he kept for such moments and poured himself a large one.

The following week, as he had feared, she didn't come to class. He phoned her, but she never answered. He went to the Acropolis, but Plato told him she didn't work there any more. The bastard had probably sacked her! He did several tours of other Greek restaurants, but never found her. After a few weeks, he accepted the inevitable and gave up.

There were other girls at the school, but he wasn't interested in them. He missed her too much – and not just in bed. God, he thought, he had really loved her! The question was, had she really loved him? He often gazed at the photo she had given him at that first meeting in the coffee bar and asked himself the question, but realised he would probably never know.

CHAPTER TWO

The address of the college was 'Dove Road', which was a good omen, he thought, as he made his way there, A-Z in hand. It was a college of further education, where he had applied for a job – he had had enough of working in a private school, teaching thirty hours a week for peanuts, with no holidays or sick pay.

When he arrived though, he wasn't so sure. It was actually just an annexe of the main college, a rather grim-looking, Victorian ex-primary school, just off the junction of Essex Road and Balls Pond Road in Islington, surrounded by small 'fashion' factories – in other words 'sweat shops' – and drab terraced houses. Oh well, he might as well give it a try, he supposed, going in. At least it would be better paid, more secure and he wouldn't have so far to travel.

He passed through the empty playground, where the ghosts of thousands of kids still hovered, and entered the building. There was no one around on the ground floor, so he made his way upstairs, wondering if he had come to the wrong place, and through a pair of swing doors into a parquet-floored corridor. It reminded him of the study hall at the junior seminary – which wasn't such a good omen. Half way along the corridor, a man was talking animatedly to a couple of girls.

He supposed the man must be a teacher, but as he approached, he started to wonder – he looked more like a vagabond who had wondered in off the street. He was wearing a T-shirt, cord trousers and sandals on bare feet, had long, straggly, grey hair, though he was as bald as a monk on top, and had a battered duffel bag slung over one shoulder. He looked about fifty. The girls, in contrast, obviously foreign, looked considerably younger and prettier.

'Excuse me,' he said, interrupting as politely as possible.

The man reluctantly finished what he was saying to the two girls and turned towards him. 'Can I help you?' he enquired, in a high-pitched, RP voice. Frank noticed he had a florid complexion, watery blue eyes and the most derelict teeth he had ever seen. He also caught a whiff of halitosis.

'Sorry to interrupt. Are you a member of staff?' he asked, shifting back slightly, trying not to look at the disastrous dentures.

'*I* am, yes, but these two aren't,' the man said. He seemed to think this was very funny, because he put his hand over his mouth and giggled like a schoolgirl.

'Could you tell me where the office is, please?' he asked, smiling.

'Oh – are you looking for Mrs. Smythe?' the man asked, in his Oxford voice, which made him secretly wince and think of the D. H. Lawrence poem.

'Is she the – er – person in charge of English as Foreign Language?'

'Yes, that's right. But there's no office as such. You'll probably find her in the classroom at the end of the corridor.'

The man turned back to the two foreign girls and resumed chatting to them, obviously more interested in them than him, for which he could hardly blame him – they were both rather attractive, South American by the look of them.

'Thanks,' he said, going down the corridor and knocking on the open classroom door at the end, trying not to be reminded of the junior seminary.

'Come in,' a tall, red-haired woman standing behind the teacher's desk said, peering over a pair of gold-rimmed specs at him.

'Hello,' he said, going in and offering his hand. 'I'm Francis Walsh. I've come about the teaching post.'

She shook his hand and introduced herself as Janet Smythe. He expected her to invite him to sit down, while she interviewed him – he had mentally rehearsed his answers to the questions he expected about his qualifications and experience as a teacher of English as a Foreign Language – but she didn't.

'Have you got a degree?' she asked, straightaway.

'Yes,' he replied, taken aback by her directness.

'In what?'

'English language and literature.' Thank goodness he had somehow managed to get a degree, he thought, despite being in a state of severe mental depression for the three years of the course and when he did his Finals. He got ready to be grilled.

'Good,' she said, scrutinizing him over her specs. 'That's all I need to know. I like the look of you. Can you start this morning?'

'This morning?' He was truly taken aback now!

'Yes. In about five minutes to be exact. We've got four groups but only three teachers. Could you manage a Proficiency class?'

'Yes, of course.'

It was the easiest interview he had ever had! No questions about methodology, materials, grammar …? No demand for a CV or even proof that he had a degree? It was incredible, but he wasn't complaining – it was the way he preferred it, informal and relaxed.

He started there and then. He enjoyed it, because there were only about twelve students in the group, with a good mix of nationalities: French, German, Spanish, Polish, Italian, Greek, Malaysian, Brazilian. And most of them were girls!

It was a three-hour lesson and in the middle they had a coffee break, during which he met the other teachers. The man he had met in the corridor was called Roger and turned out to be a writer, like himself. Well, at least he himself was a would-be writer.

'What do you write?' he asked Roger.

'Oh, biographies mostly, and a bit of poetry, you know,' he said, in his fluty Oxford voice.

'Are you working on anything at the moment?'

'Oh, yes, acksherly, something on the Earl of Rochester.'

'The Earl of Rochester?' He scanned his memory bank but drew a blank.

'You haven't heard of him?'

'I'm afraid not,' he said, shaking his head, embarrassed.

'Oh, you don't need to apologise!' Roger laughed, putting his hand over his mouth. 'Why should you? He *is* a somewhat obscure figure. He was a restoration poet and libertine who wrote a lot of very funny satirical and bawdy stuff, died at the age of thirty-two and repented of his wicked ways on his deathbed.'

'He sounds interesting!'

'Oh, he's a fascinating character! I'll give you a copy when it comes out.'

'Thanks. I'll look forward to reading it.'

'Do you write yourself, by any chance?'

'Yes. I'm – er – trying to write a novel.'

'I see. May I ask what it's about? You don't have to answer!'

'Er – it's about a boy growing up,' he said, vaguely – he didn't really like talking about it. Luckily, he didn't have to, because at that moment the other teacher, a young woman wearing a denim dress, came in.

'Ah, here's Melanie!' Roger declared. 'Have you met?'

'No. Hello,' he said, shaking hands with her. 'Frank Walsh.'

She said hello and introduced herself. She had a very RP voice, too, but he liked her immediately, because she seemed friendly and down-to-earth. She was also attractive – slim, with long, black hair, delicate features and fair skin. She was obviously very political, because she sold him one of the Socialist Worker newspapers she was carrying in a large satchel and invited him to a meeting. He wasn't very political, but he accepted, because he was curious – and because he fancied her.

Since Kalli had left him, he had been feeling lonely and frustrated. There were lots of girls at the college and he fancied a few of them, but not enough to ask out – he didn't just want sex, he wanted love as well. He also wanted to be able to have an intelligent conversation! There was a Spanish girl called Dolores he really fancied, but she had a boyfriend. There was also a Greek-Cypriot girl called Flora, who was as pretty and charming as her name. He liked her and she seemed to like him, but she was only sixteen – and she lived with an uncle. He had visions of being chased away by an irate, moustachioed Greek brandishing a kebab cleaver, so kept his distance.

Anyway, he was fed up with foreign girls. He had had two international girlfriends now – Marina from Yugoslavia and Kalli from Greece – and they had both let him down. Where else was he going to find a girlfriend though? There were discos, but he hated them – they were too crowded, noisy and expensive, and besides, he didn't like either disco music or dancing. The only other place was the pub, where he usually went on Saturday evenings. A few pints of Guinness helped to alleviate his loneliness, even if he didn't meet anyone. Afterwards, he would go back to his bed-sit, put some music on – Bob Dylan, Van Morrison or maybe some

Irish music – and finish the job off with whiskey ...

What he needed to find, he decided, was a pub with some live Irish music – it was a long time since he had heard any. There had been a good pub in Manchester, which he used to go to while he was a student, with his brother, Kevin. It was called the 'Exile of Erin', a tiny shebeen hidden away in the back streets of central Manchester. You could listen to live traditional music there – and knock back pints of Guinness – till five or six in the morning. It was illegal, of course, but it was good craic! If only he could find somewhere like that in London, he thought – he might even meet a girl there. Camden Town seemed to be the best area for Irish pubs, so one Saturday he decided to go prospecting.

The first pub he went into was called the 'Dublin Castle'. The name sounded promising, he told himself, but he couldn't have been more wrong – it was full of men, but not an Irish navvy among them. It didn't take him long to realise it was a gay pub! Out of morbid curiosity, he decided to stay for a pint anyway. A singer in drag was belting out bawdy ballads to the accompaniment of an organist and drummer, ballads with titles like, 'Do It Again' and 'Look Like An Angel, Think Like A Marine', at the same time miming masturbation, copulation and orgasm in the most grotesquely obscene way.

The audience were laughing their pretty heads off and singing along. Between songs, the performer told jokes, such as: 'My friend told me he went to Egypt for his holiday last year. He said they just walk up to you and put it in. That's nothing, I said. I went to Turkey. There they put it in and walk up to you!' The audience laughed like drains. Revolted, he finished his pint quickly, especially as one or two of the punters were giving him the eye, and made his escape.

He tried a couple of other places, which were no good, then one where a band called 'Cyril and the Rhythm Boys' were advertised as playing 'Irish Favourites'. Cyril turned out to be not from County Galway or Kerry, but from the 'County Caribbean'. He was 'as black as coal' – as it said in the Dubliners' song – and sang and played the saxophone, accompanied by a lead guitar, bass guitar and drummer. It wasn't exactly Planxty, but he ordered a pint and listened, fascinated, as Cyril introduced the next number: 'Ah've had a request to do 'De Ol' Bog Road'. But fust ahm gonna sing for you, 'For Dese Are Mah Mountins''. As he sang, he rolled his eyes and fluttered his hand like Louis Armstrong. It was hilarious, but he stayed for another pint, because Cyril was quite good, in a bizarre way. It was far from the traditional music he preferred, but he had a weakness for the old sentimental stuff, especially when he was a bit drunk, as he was by then. Besides, it was nearly closing time and he didn't feel like going anywhere else.

When the bell for closing time rang – that most sorrowful of sounds – Cyril said in his gravelly voice into the mike: 'Now ahm gonna ask you to give a big round of applause for de Rydm Boys here. Thank you. And now ahm gonna say goodnight to all you good folk and thank you once again for coming. God bless your dear hearts.'

Having had enough of this Irish-West Indian fusion by now, he slipped out and got the bus home feeling doubly frustrated – he had found neither the music nor the companionship he was looking for. Back in the solitude of his bed-sit, he put on a Fureys record, poured himself a large glass of Jameson's and, to the strains of 'The Green Fields of France', 'Shipyard Slips' and others, drank himself into oblivion.

One afternoon shortly afterwards, he decided to walk home from work along the Balls Pond Road, instead of taking a bus as usual. The Balls Pond Road was a rather scruffy main road with little or nothing of interest on it, architecturally or otherwise – just a few shabby shops and grimy Georgian houses.

On one corner, however, there was a small pub called 'The Duke of Wellington'. He had never taken much notice of it before, since it didn't look particularly prepossessing and was hardly likely to be an Irish pub, with a name like that. Stopping to look at it now though, he noticed there was an extension at the back with the name 'The Sugawn Kitchen' on it in Celtic lettering.

Intrigued, he approached the door, on which there were some notices advertising not only 'Irish Folk Music' at weekends, but also Irish theatre. It was incredible, because it sounded like exactly what he was looking for, and he had passed it on the bus every day for weeks on his way to and from work! He was tempted to pop in for a pint, but resisted – it was his rule never to drink during the day, since he wanted to go home and write. Besides, he didn't want to become an alcoholic! He would definitely go this Saturday though, he promised himself, already looking forward to it.

On Saturday, as soon as he went into the 'Sugawn Kitchen', he felt at home. It was an old billiard room at the back of the pub, lit by imitation oil lamps. The walls were painted black and plastered with posters and notices about Ireland and Irish events. There were benches around the sides and tables with straw chairs – 'sugawns' – in the middle. At the front there was a small stage, backed by a big open fireplace, complete with black kettle hanging from a hob, just like the ones he remembered from childhood summer holidays in Ireland. The room was packed with people drinking, talking and laughing merrily. On the stage a group of musicians – two guitars, banjo and fiddle – were playing and singing. He stood at the back, imbibing both a pint of Guinness and the atmosphere, like a man lost in the desert who had just stumbled into an oasis.

After about an hour, the group had a break, during which the MC invited people from the audience up to play or sing. One of them was a girl called Mary, who sang unaccompanied in a very clear, sweet, high voice, in a somewhat nervous manner, a song called 'The Wild Rapparee'. He listened and looked at her with special interest. She was petite and pretty, with a wan face and waist-length, blond hair. She was wearing an Aran cardigan over a cream blouse and black skirt. She sang two songs, the second of which, 'Carrickfergus', was one of his favourites, to enthusiastic applause from the audience, after which she went back to sit down with her friends.

He kept an eye on her for the rest of the evening. She was not only pretty, but seemed to have a pleasant personality too, from the way she chatted and laughed with the people in her group. She certainly had a good voice. If only he could meet her! He'd definitely have to come back next week, he decided. He'd come back anyway. The place was – almost literally – right up his street.

He went to the Sugawn every Saturday and soon got to know people, including the landlord, theatre members and musicians. The landlord, Jim, was from Limerick, and used to be a quantity surveyor, but now ran the pub and wrote plays and novels. The theatre director, Seamus, a Corkman, was a wiry little leprechaun of a fellow with a black goatee beard. He was an artist as well and some of his paintings were for sale on the walls. He quickly roped him into the theatre group and cast him as an 'irregular' in the forthcoming production of 'Juno and the Paycock' by Sean O'Casey.

Juno herself was being played by a plump, red-haired, middle-aged primary school teacher called Maggy. She was infatuated with Seamus, even though she was married with two children and even though Seamus was gay – his 'boyfriend', Perry, ran the theatre with him. Other members of the group were Pat O'Keefe, a young Irish-American from Chicago, tall, gaunt, ethereal, another would-be writer; his girlfriend, Peggy, from the Aran Islands; Gerry, a crane driver from Dublin, genial and surprisingly well-read, who made the stage sets; and last but not least, Mary, the girl he had seen singing that first night and taken a fancy to.

Mary was his main motive for joining the group, though he fancied doing a bit of acting as well. She was playing the part of Mary Boyle, Juno's daughter. He couldn't help feeling slightly jealous of Pat, who was playing the part of Jerry Devine, the young schoolteacher who falls in love with her, but he soon got to know her. She came from a large London-Irish family of seven children. Her father was a bus inspector and her mother worked as a care assistant in an Old People's Home, as she did herself. He could tell she liked him, so after a few weeks, he invited her out and she eagerly accepted. He took her to the Victoria, a pub he had found on Holloway Road, to hear some Irish traditional music.

'What would you like to drink?' he asked her, after they had found a seat.

'Just an orange juice, please,' she said.

'Are you sure? Nothing stronger?'

'I'm not allowed.'

'Why not?'

'I'm on medication.' Her accent was a slightly strange hybrid of Cockney and Irish.

'Medication? What for?'

'I'll tell you later.'

He went to the bar to get the drinks, wondering what she could be on medication for, brought them back and sat down beside her. She had taken off her duffel coat and was wearing a pink blouse with a black skirt. She was very slight, even delicate, with small breasts, but that didn't bother him, because he liked her. He noticed she had put a little make-up on – lipstick and mascara – which brightened up her otherwise rather wan, freckly face, so that she looked positively pretty. Her best feature, he decided, was her waist-length, blond hair, on which she was wearing a maroon alice band. He felt an almost irresistible desire to stroke it!

'So, what are you on medication for?' he asked, taking a sup of his Guinness.

'Tell me about you first. We can talk about me later.'

'What's the big secret? You haven't got some fatal disease, have you?' he joked.

'No. I just don't want to talk about it now. What about you?'

'I'm not very interesting. What do you want to know?'

'You're a teacher, aren't you?'

'Yes.'

'Which school do you teach in?'

'It's not a school. It's a college of further education.'

'What subject do you teach?'

'English as a foreign language.'

'Did you go to university then?'

'Yes.'

'So you've got a degree?'

'Yes.'

'In what subject?

'English language and literature.'

'And a teaching qualification?'

'Yes. A Cert. Ed. as it's called. Is this an interview?' he laughed.

'I wish I could've gone to university.'

'Didn't you?'

'I wouldn't be working in an Old People's Home if I had, would I?' she said caustically, to his surprise.

'Academic qualifications aren't everything,' he shrugged.

'It's all right for you to say that,' she retorted. 'You've got them.

I haven't even got O-levels.'

'Why not?' he asked, realising he had touched a raw nerve.

'They wouldn't let me do them when I was at school.'

'Why not?' he asked, shaking his head. 'You seem bright enough.'

'Because of my drugs. They said exams would be too much for me.' She sounded bitter. He really had touched a raw nerve!

He was curious to know what these 'drugs' were, but hesitated to ask – she seemed very sensitive about it. He didn't want to alienate her before they had even got started.

'It's not too late,' he said, suddenly feeling sorry for her. 'You can still study. I'll help you if you want.' That was a good chat-up line, he thought to himself – he was getting better at this!

She was blushing – maybe he had been too forward. But he didn't care – he liked her. She was attractive and there was something appealing about her self-diffidence that brought out his protective instincts.

'Anyway,' he carried on regardless, emboldened by alcohol now, 'what are these drugs you're on?'

She looked away, embarrassed, and he regretted pushing it. 'I'm sorry,' he said. 'You don't have to tell me, if you don't want to.'

'It's all right,' she said, turning back to him. 'I don't mind. You have to know, sooner or later, so you might as well know now, before we go any further.'

God, he thought in alarm, maybe she really did have some terrible, terminal disease! He didn't care though – it wouldn't stop him liking her, or even falling in love with her. In fact, he had already started to fall in love with her. He *wanted* to 'go further', as she put it!

'Go on, then, tell me,' he encouraged her.

'Haven't you noticed anything about me?' she asked.

'Only that you're very pretty,' he grinned, scanning her face.

'Oh, now you're making fun of me. I'm not pretty,' she protested.

'I'm not making fun of you! I think you *are* pretty!'

'Do you? I'm not as pretty as some of the other girls here, am I?'

He glanced around the pub. There were a few good-looking girls in the audience, all dolled up for a night out, but none he found as attractive as her.

'I think you're the prettiest girl in the place,' he declared.

'Don't talk rot,' she retorted, blushing again, but he could see she was flattered.

'I mean it!' he laughed. 'Anyway, what am I supposed to have noticed about you?'

'Haven't you noticed anything about my eyes?'

'They're made of glass?' he joked, grabbing the excuse to gaze straight into them. In fact, they did have a glazed look, but the most noticeable thing about them was that they were a bit bulging, with a staring quality. As he gazed into her eyes, he caught an enticing whiff of perfume.

'Don't be so horrible!' she laughed. 'Seriously, are my pupils dilated?'

'I didn't know you were a teacher, too!' he quipped, the Guinness making him facetious.

'Seriously, are they?' she insisted, smacking his wrist playfully.

'A bit, I suppose, but that's because it's dark in here.'

'It's because of the drugs.'

'Because of the drugs? You don't look like a junkie!'

'Medical drugs, silly. I have to take them three times a day.'

'What for?'

'I've got petit mal.'

'Oh. I see.' Was that all? It didn't sound too serious!

'Do you know what that is?'

'It's a kind of minor form of epilepsy, isn't it?'

'Yes. I'm a bit of a crock, I'm afraid.'

'You shouldn't say that,' he remonstrated.

'You mean, you don't mind?'

'Of course I don't mind. I don't mind what you've got.'

'Why?'

'Because I like you.'

'You like *me?*' she laughed, self-deprecatingly. 'A crock?'

'Stop saying that!' he scolded her. 'You're not a crock. You're very nice. I like you. Do you want me to prove it?' He took hold of her hand, which was as light as a feather.

'How?' she said archly, to his relief not pulling her hand away.

'By kissing you?'

God, he reflected wryly – he sounded like Jerry Devine in the play, who asks 'Mary', 'Let me kiss your hand, your little, tiny, white hand', much to the contempt of her father, who sneers: 'Are you takin' leave o' your senses, man?'

'You want to kiss *me?*'

'Yes. Can I?' God, her 'self-image' was so negative!

'If you want to,' she shrugged.

He leant sideways, keeping hold of her hand, and kissed her lightly on the cheek. 'There you are,' he said.

'Is that all?' she asked, glancing at him with a mischievous twinkle in her eyes.

His pulse started to race – she wanted him to kiss her properly! He put his arms around her wispy waist, pulled her close and kissed her on the lips. This time she responded by putting her arms around his neck and pressing herself against him. They kissed for a while, then she laid her head on his shoulder and he stroked her hair, as he had been dying to do all evening.

'What's wrong?' he asked, suddenly realising she was crying.

'Nothing. I'm sorry,' she sniffled, moving away, pulling a hanky from her sleeve, then dabbing her eyes and blowing her nose with it.

'Are you sure?'

'Yes,' she said brightly, tucking the hanky back in her sleeve. 'It's just me being silly.' She opened her handbag, took out a pill box and tried to open it, but couldn't, because her hands were trembling.

'Here, let me do it for you,' he offered, taking it and opening it. There were three pills inside. One of them was a black and green capsule, which looked positively lethal. 'What are they?' he asked.

'My uppers and downers,' she said drolly, taking them out, popping them into her mouth and swallowing them with a drink of orange juice one by one.

'You have to take them every day?'

'Every day, three times a day.'

'What do they do exactly?'

'They're supposed to stop me having fits.'

'And do they?'

'Not completely. They reduce them. The trouble is, they make me sleepy, too.'

'I see. What a drag. Are you sleepy now?'

'No,' she laughed, smacking his wrist playfully again. She

seemed to like smacking!

'So how did you get petit mal in the first place?'

'I had meningitis when I was a few months old. That's why I've got one leg shorter than the other.'

'Have you?' he pretended to be surprised.

'You must've noticed.'

'No,' he fibbed. 'Are you sure? Let me inspect!' He bent down and looked at her legs, on which she was wearing tights. They were rather nice legs, he thought, wanting to stroke them – but he had noticed she had a limp.

'You see,' she said, 'one is shorter than the other, isn't it?'

'I can see one is slightly *longer* than the other,' he joked, and to his relief she laughed. 'Anyway, it doesn't matter – mine are even longer,' he quipped, stretching his legs up in the air, and again, to his relief, she laughed.

'My legs are hairy, too, because of the drugs,' she said.

'Mine are even hairier – look,' he countered, pulling a trouser leg up, and she laughed again.

The people around them must have thought he was drunk, and he was a bit, but didn't care – he really liked her and was enjoying himself.

'So how did meningitis cause one leg to be shorter than the other?' he asked.

'I don't really know. Somehow it infected the hip bone and stopped it from developing properly.'

'I see.'

'At the moment it's all held together by a steel pin.'

He winced. 'You mean, you had to have an operation?'

'Yes.'

'When you were a baby?'

'No, about five years ago, when I started growing.' She was twenty now, he knew. 'You see, I am a bit of a crock, I'm afraid.'

'You mustn't keep saying that!' he told her off again, taking hold of her hand. 'Anyway, I don't care what's wrong with you. I like you.'

'Do you really?'

'Yes, I do.'

'Thank you,' she said, giving him a quick kiss on the lips.

'Would you like another drink?' he asked.

'No, thanks,' she shook her head.

'Do you want to go?' They had planned to go dancing in the Gresham Ballroom up the road – not that he really liked dancing.

'No, not yet. I want to know about you first. I've told you all about me.'

'I've already told you about me.'

'Not much. I want to know more.'

'Can I get myself another pint before the interrogation begins?'

'Go on, then,' she smiled and off he went to the bar.

'So, what do you want to know?' he asked, coming back with another pint of Guinness.

'You're twenty-six, are you?'

'Yes.'

'And you finished uni last year?'

'Yes.'

'So you started uni when you were twenty-one?'

'Yes.' He could see what she was getting at.

'So what did you do between leaving school and going to university?' It was the question he always dreaded!

'Oh, well,' he sighed, mimicking her. 'You have to know sooner or later, so I might as well tell you now, before we go any further.'

'Very funny,' she said. 'Go on – were you in prison?'

He spluttered with laughter as he drank, spilling some beer. 'In a sense, yes, actually,' he said.

'What do you mean? Tell me!' She sounded alarmed, to his amusement.

'I was in a seminary,' he confessed.

'You mean, you were studying for the priesthood?'

'Yes. You see – we all have our dark secrets.'

'I might've guessed,' she said, nodding.

'How?' He was on the defensive now.

'There's something about you.'

'What do you mean?' But he knew what she meant ...

'I don't know. There's something different about you.'

'Different? In what way?'

'Different from other men.'

'You've been out with a lot of men, have you?' he teased.

'A few,' she replied, archly.

'So how am I different?' He didn't really want to know!

'You're – I don't know, nicer somehow.'

'I see,' he laughed, adding half-seriously: 'I warn you, I might not be as nice as I seem though.'

'What was it like, the seminary?' she asked, ignoring the joke.

'I don't want to talk about that,' he said, serious now.

'Why not?' she asked.

'It depresses me. Maybe another time.' He might get another date out of it, he thought craftily!

'Anyway, it doesn't matter to me,' she said, to his relief not pursuing it.

'What do you mean?'

'I still like you.'

'I like you, too.'

'Do you?'

'Do you want me to prove it again?'

'Yes, please.'

He put both his arms around her, pulled her towards him and kissed her on the lips again. Then they sat silently for a while, arms around each other, her head on his shoulder, and listened to the music. There was no need to speak. They both knew. There would be many other times.

Suddenly, life was good – he had a good job, he liked the people he worked with, as well as the students, and he had a girlfriend. He was friendly with both of his colleagues – Roger, the Bohemian-looking teacher, and Melanie, the Socialist Worker. The three of them went for drinks together sometimes and talked about politics and literature, as well as the job, the students and life in general.

Roger was interesting, because he had an encyclopaedic knowledge of English literature, which he had studied at Oxford. He was also a good linguist, having travelled a lot and worked abroad in countries such as Yugoslavia and Poland, about which he told fascinating and amusing stories. He was a socialist, but his experiences of Eastern Europe had disillusioned him, so he tended to get into arguments with Melanie, who was more orthodox. Listening to him could be tiring, because he was so intellectual and well-informed – it was like being at a university lecture, as Melanie remarked to him in the pub once, when Roger had gone to the loo, having expatiated at length on the subject of his new book about the Earl of Rochester.

'Yes,' he agreed. 'Except that he's a lot more interesting than most university lectures I ever went to. Not that I went to many!'

Melanie concurred, laughing. He liked her more and more, because she was so fervent – almost fanatical – in her socialist beliefs. He was a socialist of sorts himself, though not like her in a very active way. He had become interested in Marxism through his Yugoslav girlfriend, Marina – even though she had jilted him. His interest had waned since, but been rekindled by Melanie, and he enjoyed discussing it with her, occasionally, like Roger, disagreeing with her.

He found her attractive, too, but kept his distance, because he had a girlfriend in Mary now and she had a boyfriend, who joined them for a drink occasionally. His name was Steve. He was a gnomish little fellow, with frizzy, ginger hair and a bushy, ginger beard. Sometimes he wondered why Melanie liked him – maybe because he not only looked a bit like Karl Marx and was Jewish like him, but was even more of a Marxist than Melanie herself, a fanatic in fact. He was a primary school teacher and intelligent, but seemed to have a hefty chip on his shoulder. He found his company uncomfortable, because he was so dogmatic, and one night, a bit drunk, had a heated argument with him.

'I'm sorry if I sounded a bit aggressive last night,' he apologised to Melanie at college the next day.

'Oh, don't worry, it wasn't your fault,' she said. 'That's Steve. He's always like that.'

'He seems terribly uptight about life. Why is that?'

'I think it goes back to his childhood and his relationship with his father. His father's Jewish and came here to escape from Nazi Germany, but has had a very hard time.'

'How do you mean?'

'Well, he's had to put up with a lot of anti-Jewish prejudice for one thing, but also he's poor, even though he's worked hard all his life.'

'What does he do?'

'He's a tailor.'

'Where does he live?'

'In Hackney.'

'Same as us.'

'Yes. So Steve hates the Nazis for forcing his father to come here, but also hates the system here for not giving his father a better life.'

'I see.'

'The trouble is, Steve hates his father, too.'

'Oh, why?' He was shocked.

'His father's very Jewish and he's rebelled against Judaism. He thinks it's a load of superstitious claptrap that's held his father back, made him weak, passive, a victim. They argue about it a lot. That's why Steve ran away from home when he was sixteen.'

'He never sees him?'

'Very occasionally. But they don't get on.'

'It's sad, I suppose.'

'Yes, especially as Steve's an only child.'

'How did you meet?'

'At a Socialist Workers' meeting.'

'Is there a meeting tonight?'

'Yes. Are you coming?'

'What's the topic?'

'Northern Ireland.'

'Oh, I'll definitely come then. I'll see you there.'

CHAPTER THREE

They soon started sleeping together, but didn't make love properly, because they were both afraid of her getting pregnant. In her case this was even more to be avoided than usual – because of her hip, it would have been dangerous for her and, because of her drugs, dangerous for the baby. He didn't trust condoms and, because of her drugs, she couldn't take the pill – not that she would do, anyway, being a good Catholic girl.

So their lovemaking was limited, but he didn't mind – he loved her and she loved him and there was no limit on love, as he told her. They promised to love each other for ever. Within a few weeks she had moved in with him and it wasn't long before, in the pub one evening, she asked him to marry her. However, he refused, just as he had refused Kalli.

'Why not?' she asked. 'Don't you love me?'

'I do love you,' he protested, 'but I don't believe in marriage. And I don't want a wedding ceremony – especially a Catholic one. I'm sorry.'

He was afraid his refusal to marry her – and his anti-Catholicism – would make her leave him, but it didn't. She was still a practising Catholic and went to mass every Sunday. He suspected she would like to convert him back to the faith, just like his mother. Little did she know what she was up against! She tried to persuade him to go to mass with her, but he adamantly refused – he would no more go to mass now than to a séance!

'Why not?' she asked.

'I don't believe in it any more. And I don't know how you can. It's a load of mumbo-jumbo.'

'You used to believe in it.'

'I used to believe in Father Christmas.'

'Don't you believe in anything any more?'

'I don't believe in fairytales. Heaven and Hell, for example.

Do you?'

'I believe in Heaven.'

'But not Hell?'

'I'm not sure about Hell.'

'That's very convenient,' he chuckled. 'Surely, if you believe in Heaven, you must believe in Hell, too? Otherwise, everyone has to go to Heaven, even sinners like me.'

'I don't know – maybe they don't go anywhere.'

'I should think that's what happens to everyone, but it's not what Catholicism teaches. Is it?'

'So you don't believe in life after death?'

'Of course not!'

'How do you know?'

'Because there's no *evidence* for it. Come on, it's just a fairytale, a fantasy! It may be a pleasant fantasy, but all the evidence shows that we die and decay and that's the end of us, as individuals at least.'

'I can't believe that. It'd make life meaningless.'

'Maybe life is meaningless.' He said it glibly, but it was a grim thought – so grim that sometimes he could hardly bear to contemplate it himself.

'In that case,' she said, 'life isn't worth living. We might as well kill ourselves and have done with it.'

'Maybe,' he agreed – sometimes he thought so himself – 'but just because life doesn't mean anything, in the sense that it doesn't lead to an afterlife, doesn't mean it's not worth living, does it? It may be nasty, brutish and short, but it does have its good moments, too.'

'Huh! Such as?'

'Well, sometimes it feels good just to be alive, doesn't it? At least, if you're healthy.' He realised that was a mistake, so carried on quickly. 'And then there are lots of things to enjoy, aren't there?'

'Like what?'

'Love. Romance. Sex. Friendship. Children. Eating. Drinking. Books. Music. Nature.'

'But it all ends.'

'Yes, unfortunately. All the more reason to enjoy it while it lasts.'

'What about God?'

'What about God?'

'Don't you believe in God?'

'Of course not.' He still felt guilty saying it – even after so many years. It just showed the power of brainwashing!

'So how did it all begin then?'

'Nobody knows.'

'It must've been God.'

'Mary, God's just an invention, a figment of people's imagination, precisely because we don't know.'

'You think it all happened just by chance?'

'Possibly. *I* don't know. Nobody really knows. It's impossible to know. It's a mystery. Anyone who pretends to know the answer is kidding himself. We just have to admit we don't know, we don't understand. We may do one day, through science or whatever, but for now we don't. We learn a little bit more all the time, but we still understand very little. Maybe in a few hundred or a few thousand years we'll understand. I mean, only a few hundred years ago people believed the sun went round the earth and the earth was flat. That was what the Church made you believe. You were burned at the stake if you didn't.' She had started him off on his hobby-horse now!

'Well, I believe in God,' she declared, as if he had said nothing.

'Prove it,' he challenged her.

It was a bit unfair, he thought – she couldn't argue on the same level as he, with his philosophical and theological training. But he couldn't resist arguing with her and, anyway, she might learn something from arguing with him. He might even learn something from her!

'I can't prove it,' she said. 'I just feel it.'

'There's no arguing with that,' he laughed.

'Don't you feel it?'

'Sometimes, I suppose,' he admitted. 'I mean, sometimes I wish there was a God. But feeling or wishing isn't enough to make me believe it, doesn't make it true.'

'It is for me.'

That was the difference between them, he reflected ruefully. It was the only serious difference. He both envied and despised her simple, childish faith. He didn't want to undermine it, but knew he would, just by being with her. Part of him would enjoy it, too – he had a subversive streak in his make up.

'Anyway, never mind,' she said.

'What do you mean? Never mind what?'

'I know you've suffered.'

'Have I? How?'

'I think you suffered at the seminary. That's why you won't talk about it.'

'Everyone suffers one way or another,' he shrugged, secretly wincing, because now she had touched on his sore spot. He really didn't like talking about it – the memories were too uncomfortable.

'Yes, but some of us suffer more than others.'

'Whatever *we've* suffered, it's nothing compared to what some people have to suffer,' he countered.

'How do you mean?' she demanded.

'Well, the world is full of suffering – poverty, hunger, war, disease, death … '

She was silent, seemed to have no answer.

'Anyway,' he carried on, 'a bit of suffering can be good for the soul.' God, he sounded like the priest he had once wanted to become!

'In what way,' she snorted.

'It can make you stronger.'

'That depends on what you have to suffer and if you're strong enough to start with.'

'I suppose so,' he conceded. Blimey, she was no pushover! 'Anyway, suffering here on earth saves you time in Purgatory, doesn't it?' he joked, deciding to try and make light of it.

'Huh,' she responded.

'Well, that's what Catholicism teaches, isn't it? Or don't you believe in Purgatory either?'

'As far as I'm concerned, this is Purgatory,' she retorted.

He was shocked at how bitter she sounded, but didn't show it.

'You mean, being here with me?' he joked.

'You know what I mean.'

'You might be right,' he laughed. 'Maybe we're being punished for things we did in a previous life.'

'It's not fair being punished, if you can't even remember what you did wrong.'

'Good point,' he agreed. 'But things are not so bad, are they?'

'Maybe not for you. You weren't prevented from getting qualifications and a decent job. You're physically perfect – you haven't got one leg shorter than the other. You didn't have to wear a calliper till you were fifteen, then have an operation to pin your hip together. Other kids didn't call you 'Hopalong Cassidy'. You don't have to take tablets every day of your life that make you dopey. You don't have fits two or three times a week, which means you can't do the job you want, can't drive a car, can't watch TV for more than ten minutes at a time. You don't understand.'

'I'm sorry,' he said, guiltily. 'I know you've had a rough time.'

'I'm still having a rough time.'

'Yes, but now you've got me.'

'Have I?'

'Yes!'

'Will you stay with me?'

'Yes. Of course.'

'For ever?'

'Yes, if you'll stay with *me.*'

'Oh, I'll stay with *you.*'

'So it's a deal then,' he grinned, offering to shake her hand..

'Don't be silly,' she said, giving him a peck on the cheek.

He put his arm around her and gave her a proper kiss back.

'I still don't understand, though,' she said.

'Don't understand what? The meaning of life?'

'Why you want to stay with me.'

'Because I love you.'

'But we're so different.'

'You mean, you believe in God and I'm an atheist?'

'No, don't be silly. That doesn't matter, does it? I mean, you're so clever, so intelligent, so well-educated, so physically perfect, and I'm so – '

'Don't say it! You've got to stop thinking like that! There's nothing wrong with you! You've got a lot going for you!'

'Like what?'

'You're intelligent, even if you're not very well-educated. You're pretty – at least, *I* think so. You're talented – you can sing. You can develop that. I'll help you. And most important of all, you're *you*!'

'Thank you, Fran. You're my knight in shining armour, aren't you?'

'If you want. Without the lance and charger, I'm afraid.'

'I love you!'

'Why? We're so different, aren't we?' he mimicked her.

'You make me feel happy. For the first time in my life.'

'Oh, now you're exaggerating! That's the Bailey's Bristol Cream that's making you happy.' He had persuaded her to drink something alcoholic for the first time ever.

'No, it's not. I've never really felt happy before. Not like I do now. Since I met *you*. I can't really believe it. It's like a lovely dream. I'm afraid I'll wake up and you'll be gone.'

'I'm not a dream, I assure you,' he said, giving her a hug. 'I'm real. I'm here with you. And I'm going to stay with you. I promise.'

'Oh, Fran, I do love you so much. You've no idea. I shouldn't tell you …' Suddenly, she started crying.

'Hey, come on, we're supposed to be happy,' he laughed, hugging her again.

'I *am* happy. I'm crying because I'm happy. It's stupid, I know.' She took her hankie from her sleeve, dabbed her eyes and blew her nose.

'It's not stupid! Come on, let's drink to the future.' He picked up his glass of Guinness and she her glass of Bailey's. 'To the future,' he said, clinking his glass against hers.

'Together,' she said.

'Together,' he agreed, taking a swig and giving her a frothy Guinness kiss.

She carried on working part-time in the Old People's Home, but he helped her to enrol on an evening O-Level English course at his college and started tutoring her. The work in the OPH was menial, but was the only job she could get with her condition and lack of qualifications, and then only because her mother worked there. She was well-qualified in the most important sense, however, in that she really did care about people, not just old people, but people in general, especially those in need, for she had a kind, caring nature.

She had tried to become a nurse, and was ideally suited for it by nature, but had been rejected because of her medical condition and lack of educational qualifications. He began to understand better her feelings of bitterness about 'the system', a bitterness that was the only warp in an otherwise lovely nature. Now, under his influence, she decided she wanted to be a teacher and he resolved to help her, no matter what the obstacles or how long it took.

He also decided to try and do something about her medical condition, so took her to see a new specialist for her epilepsy. The doctor told them there was no way of curing the condition, which was due to a lesion on the brain caused by meningitis, except possibly by an operation. They thought about this, but decided it was too risky. 'You might wake up a *complete* vegetable,' he joked. However, the doctor did prescribe her new drugs, which she could take less often and were less adverse in their side-effects, so she was less sleepy and could study better.

He also took her to see an orthopaedic specialist, who told them that the steel pin holding her hip together ought to come out. She had the operation soon afterwards and he went to visit her in hospital on the same day. When he walked into the ward and saw her, lying in bed with a drip in her arm, looking even more pale and fragile than usual, he felt a rush of pity for her.

The doctor had given her, at her own request, the pin they had taken out. He was shocked when he saw it – it was chrome, about nine inches long and came with a full set of screws. 'We can use it as a towel rail,' he joked, at which she forced a wan smile.

After she had recovered from the operation, her leg was even shorter than before. The specialist said a surgical shoe was essential to avoid deformation of her spine. After getting rid of her calliper at fifteen, she had refused to wear one. Now, reluctantly, she went to be fitted by the National Health 'cobbler'. The shoes they produced for her were the equivalent of National Health specs – functional but ugly. She broke down in tears when they got home and she tried them on. 'I can't wear these,' she sobbed.

'They're not that bad,' he tried to reassure her. 'You can wear long dresses. Nobody will notice.'

'They're awful!' she cried. 'Can't you see? And I don't want to have to wear long dresses all the time. I want to be normal. I just want to be normal, that's all.'

'I'll tell you what, then,' he said, putting his arm round her, 'we'll get some made privately, some decent ones.'

'It'd cost too much money,' she sobbed.

'Never mind about the money,' he said. 'We'll find the money somehow. Now stop crying. Here's a tissue. It's not the end of the world. At least you've got two legs, even if one is shorter than the other. Anyway, the exercises they've given you might make it stronger and longer. I'll pull it for you, if you like. I'm good at pulling people's legs.'

'Oh, Fran,' she laughed through her tears. 'I don't know what I'd do without you. I love you!'

'I love you, too. Now, what's next? Yes. We have to do something about that voice of yours. Get it trained. You might be famous one day. I'll be your manager if you like. I'll expect ten per cent though!'

He wanted her to develop her musical talent, so helped her to pay for singing lessons and bought her a guitar for her twenty-first birthday. She gradually became more confident about singing in public, despite her fear of having a fit, which sometimes happened, as long as he was there to rescue her. He hoped one day she might be able to sing professionally, since she did have an exceptional voice.

However, she never managed to overcome her nervousness about going on stage. Nor did she persevere with her guitar lessons, to his disappointment. He learnt a few chords on the new guitar himself, then it stayed in its case under the bed, gathering dust, a symbol of failure.

'For God's sake, woman, how can you do Pegeen? Pegeen is a girl of twenty! You'll be Widow Quin or nothing at all!' Seamus shouted. They – the 'Sugawn Players' – were reading for 'The Playboy of the Western World', which was to be their next production at the Sugawn Theatre. Maggy burst into tears and fled the room.

It was a drama – or melodrama – within a drama, because Maggy, who was married, was infatuated with Seamus, the director. Meanwhile, to his embarrassment, Seamus, who was gay, had taken a fancy to *him*! This made both Mary and Perry,

Seamus's 'boyfriend', jealous. So plenty of tension was generated at rehearsals, apart from the tensions of coping with the play.

'Why is he like that?' Maggy asked him in the bar later. 'Why does he hate me?'

'I don't think he hates you, Maggy,' he said. 'He's just not interested in you. I mean, as a woman. He's gay. That's all there is to it.'

'He likes you, you know.'

'Does he?' He blushed, pretending to be surprised. It was the last thing he wanted to hear!

'You must've noticed, Frank.'

'But he knows I'm not that way inclined.' Not any more, at least ...

'Of course you're not.'

'Anyway, he knows I'm with Mary.'

'Does Mary realise?'

'I think she senses something.'

'Has she said anything?'

'Not directly.'

'I hope he doesn't cause trouble between you. You're such a lovely couple. She's such a lovely girl. Are you going to marry her, Frank?'

'I don't know,' he laughed. 'Maybe one day. I don't really believe in marriage.'

'Why not?'

'I don't do very well in captivity.'

'Be serious, Frank! Why won't you marry her?'

'Has she put you up to this?' he laughed.

'No, but she does talk to me, Frank. She really wants to marry you. Why won't you? You'd make such a lovely couple!'

'We already are a couple,' he pointed out.

'I know you are, so why not get married and make it official? It'd make her so happy, Frank.'

'Marriage is just a trap as far as I'm concerned, Maggy.'

'Oh, yes, it can be a trap, all right, I suppose,' she sighed.

'You think so?'

'Oh, God, yes. I'm trapped. I don't know what to do.'

'You don't love your husband?'

'I never loved him, Frank. I love Seamus.'

'Why did you marry him, then?'

'I was pregnant.'

'Oh. Oh, I see.' He was shocked, but tried not to show it.

'Attitudes were different then, Frank.'

'Yes. Yes, I suppose so.'

'Besides, he's a brute. He hits me. And we have nothing in common. He's not interested in books or theatre or music or anything. I can't stand him. I have to get away.'

'Can't you just leave?'

'I've nowhere to go. If only Seamus was different. Why is he like that, Frank?'

'You mean, gay?'

'Yes.'

'God knows. I don't understand it. I don't understand how any man can fancy another man. It beats me.' He took a swig of Guinness, as if to emphasise it.

'You're so normal, Frank. And sensible. That's what I like about you.'

'I don't know about that!' he laughed, embarrassed, trying not to think about the past ...

'Oh, you are, you are. You should marry that girl though.'

'What are you two talking about, then?' Mary asked, suddenly coming into the bar from the rehearsal room and joining them.

'I was just telling him he should marry you,' Maggy said to her.

'He won't. I've asked him.'

'Frank, how could you refuse the girl?'

'I've told you, I don't do very well in captivity,' he quipped. 'Anyway, why should I marry an Irish peasant girl? I can do better than that.' Mary was playing a peasant girl in the production of 'The Playboy'.

'Hey, don't be cheeky!' Mary said, raising her hand as if to slap him.

'Give me a kiss, peasant girl!' he laughed, grabbing her wrist and pulling her towards him.

'Who do you think you are – the playboy of the western world?' she teased, pretending to pull away.

'No, the playboy of the East End!' he declared, pulling her close and kissing her.

'God, you'd make such a lovely couple walking down the aisle,' Peggy crooned.

'I think he secretly fancies Seamus, that's why he doesn't want to marry me,' Mary said, playfully pushing him away.

'Oh, God, have you noticed?' Maggy asked her.

'You'd have to be blind not to,' Mary said.

'I think you two are imagining things,' he said, scornfully.

'We're not!' they said in unison.

'You don't think he fancies me, really, do you?'

'It's obvious, Frank.'

'Oh, God, how embarrassing! What should I do?'

'You can go out with him, if you want,' Mary said. 'I don't mind.'

'Don't be funny,' he told her.

'He might give you the lead.'

'I don't want the lead, thank you. That would put Pat's nose out of joint, anyway!'

'I wish he fancied me,' Maggy sighed.

'Does he know how you feel about him, Maggy?' Mary asked her.

'He knows all right. I've shown him. But he pushes me away all the time.'

'Why do you like him?' Mary asked, in her innocent way.

'He's just so intelligent, so artistic, so creative …'

'But gay,' he added.

'Oh, Frank, don't say that. Maybe he'll change. Maybe I can change him. What do you think?'

'I don't think so, but you can try.'

'Will you help me?'

'What do you want me to do?'

'Don't encourage him to like you, will you?'

'You needn't worry about that, Maggy. On the other hand, maybe I could do with a change,' he joked, at Mary's expense.

'Watch yourself!' she said, giving him a playful clout.

Just then, Pat, the American from Chicago, who was playing the 'playboy', came in and joined them.

'Now Perry's just stormed out in a huff,' he told them.

'Oh, no! Why?'

'He seems to think Seamus doesn't like him any more.'

'He fancies Frank here,' Mary said.

'Hey, shut up!' he laughed.

'I think he has taken a shine to you, Frank,' said Pat.

'Oh, God, this is too embarrassing!' he declared. 'Do you really think so?'

'Yeah. Perry actually shouted, "Why don't you ask Frank to do it, then?" at him, before he stormed off the stage.'

'Oh, no!' he exclaimed, horrified. This was getting beyond a joke.

'I'll go and get Perry back,' Maggy offered, bustling out.

Jim, the landlord, who was playing a publican in his own pub, came in. 'Seamus wants Maggy back on the stage now,' he said.

'She's just gone to fetch Perry.'

'Jaysus!' Jim swore. 'This whole production's turning into a Whitehall farce!'

Gerry, the Dublin crane driver, who was playing a farmer, as well as making the set, came in, script in hand. 'Your man's going berserk in there,' he said. 'Where's Maggy? He wants her.'

'That's the whole trouble, he doesn't want her,' Jim cracked.

'What are you getting at?' Gerry asked.

'Apparently, it's Frank he wants,' Jim winked at him.

'Thank God it's not me!' said Gerry. 'Frank, if he wants you, go to him.'

'No thanks!' he laughed, uncomfortably.

Suddenly, the doors to the 'theatre' swung open and the leprechaun-like figure of Seamus appeared, eyes blazing: 'IF THAT FECKIN' WOMAN ISN'T ON THIS STAGE IN ONE MINUTE, SHE CAN HAND HER FECKIN EQUITY CARD IN FOR GOOD!' he bawled, then went back inside, letting the doors slam behind him.

'This is getting serious,' said Gerry.

'It's like a play within a play,' he observed to Pat. 'Shades of Hamlet?'

'Experimental theatre, it's called, I believe,' said Pat dryly, in his Chicago drawl.

'Black theatre!' he joked. 'How's the novel going?'

'It's going well. Trouble is, I don't have enough time to write.'

'Still working in the publisher's office?'

'Yeah. And I don't much feel like writing myself after reading other people's manuscripts all day.'

'I don't know how you do it.'

'What's it about?' Gerry asked.

'Well, it's about ancient Irish history, I suppose, but from the point of view of today. It's circular in form.'

'I won't ask any more. I know you writers don't like talking about work in progress,' Gerry remarked, drolly.

'You make him sound like James Joyce,' Frank chuckled.

'Jaysus, that fella could string a few words together, couldn't he?' Gerry declared.

'You could put it like that!' he laughed. 'Have you read any of his stuff?'

'I'm reading Ulysses now, as it happens.'

'Are you? What do you make of it?'

'I can tell it's bloody brilliant, even though I don't understand half of it.'

'Who does? When do you get to read? I mean, you work all day, don't you? And you've got a daughter.'

'I have, bless her, and I like to spend time with her when I get home. I read in the cab of the crane. Sure, it's a grand place to read. You're all on your own up there in the clouds. Nobody to disturb you.'

'It must be,' he laughed. 'You should write a novel up there. That'd be a first. A different viewpoint, anyway. A bird's eye view.'

'I might just do that,' Gerry said. 'Do you write yourself?'

'Yes, I'm trying to write a novel, actually.'

'What's it about, if I may ask?'

'It's just about a boy growing up.'

'Jaysus, we might all be famous one day!'

'Yes,' he laughed. 'We'll be known as the Sugawn Group!'

He was glad to have got the conversation away from Seamus' apparent fixation with him, but then Seamus burst into the bar again.

'Where's that feckin' woman?' he demanded.

'She went to get Perry,' Frank told him.

'Jaysus, I give up,' Seamus said, sitting down and putting his head in his hands. 'Somebody get me a gargle.'

'What'll you have?' Jim, the landlord, asked. 'A Black and Tan?' This was Seamus's favourite tipple.

'Make it a double Jameson's,' Seamus groaned, still holding

his head in his hands, as if in terminal despair. 'I feel like getting langers.'

'Ah, don't worry, Seamus,' Gerry laughed, patting him on the back. 'It'll be all right on the night!'

CHAPTER FOUR

'Which do you want first – the good news or the bad news?'

'The good news,' they all said. They were having one of their rare, informal meetings in the pub.

'I'm going to have a baby!' Janet announced.

'Congratulations!' they exclaimed in unison.

'Thank you,' said Janet. 'I'm going to take maternity leave from Easter, so one of you will have to take over. I thought you might like to do it democratically. Any suggestions?'

There was a silence, then Roger said: 'What about Frank? He seems to be good at organising.'

Frank reddened slightly, but remained silent.

'Melanie?' Janet asked.

'Yes, I can go along with that,' Melanie said.

'Frank?' Janet peered at him over her gold-rimmed specs.

'I don't mind,' he shrugged, trying to sound cool.

'That's settled, then,' said Janet. 'I'll brief you later, Frank.'

'So what's the bad news?' asked Roger.

'I went to a governors' meeting yesterday. They're talking about cuts.'

'You mean – we're in danger?' asked Melanie.

'Not immediate danger. I'm not supposed to tell you, because it's confidential, but I thought you ought to know.'

'Thank you,' said Roger and they all concurred.

'If they try to cut us, we'll fight!' Melanie declared, revolutionary instincts aroused.

'Hear, hear!' they all agreed.

'Oh, dear!' Roger sighed. 'It'd be such a shame if they closed us down. We've got such a good thing going here.'

'That's right,' they all agreed again.

'My advice to you all is to get a TEFL qualification, in case you do need to find another job,' said Janet.

'It's so silly!' Roger asserted. 'We've all got degrees in English. What better qualification is there to teach English?'

'I agree, but it's the way things are going,' Janct replied.

'I don't think I could face it! Not a course in TEFL-TATTLE!' Roger quipped and they all laughed, though somewhat nervously.

'Actually, I read linguistics at university, not English,' Janet observed. This was met with an embarrassed silence. 'Yes, it's usually a bit of a conversation stopper!' she laughed.

'Oh, dear!' Roger giggled, his hand over his mouth. 'I didn't mean ...'

'That's all right, Roger,' Janet said. 'I must admit, I didn't enjoy doing it. I wish I *had* read English!'

'What about you, Frank?' Roger asked him. 'You read English, didn't you?'

'English language and literature, actually,' he replied.

'What did English language consist of?' Melanie enquired.

'Anglo-Saxon, basically,' he said. 'I think that was because the professor at Manchester was a big Anglo-Saxon buff.'

'I wish I'd done some Anglo-Saxon,' Roger said. 'I'd love to be able to read Beowulf in the original.'

'Yes, well, that was good, I suppose,' Frank agreed. 'I must admit, I didn't enjoy it much at the time, but I'm glad I did it. A bit like Latin and Greek, I suppose.'

'Oh, did you study Greek?' Roger asked.

'Up to A-level,' he said.

'I envy you!' Roger exclaimed. 'I wish I'd done some Greek.'

'Yes,' he said, his pleasure clouded by a momentary memory of the priggish Father Percival, the priest who had taught them classics at the seminary. 'It does give you an extra insight into English, of course,' he added.

'You seem to have had a very classical education!' Melanie observed.

'Yes, I suppose so,' he laughed uncomfortably. 'We did no science at all!'

'What sort of school did you go to?' she asked.

This was a question that always made him uncomfortable. 'Oh, just an old-fashioned Catholic grammar school in Manchester,' he fibbed. In fact, it was only a half-fib – he had gone to Xaverian grammar school in Manchester for a year, before going to the junior seminary in the Lake District.

'So you did your degree in Manchester, too?' asked Melanie.

'Yes,' he said, knowing it was unusual to go to school and university in the same place and hoping they wouldn't ask for an explanation. 'I did my PGCE at Liverpool Uni though,' he added, to deflect further enquiry.

'Oh, dear!' Roger sighed. 'I haven't even got one of those!'

'To be honest, that was a bit of a waste of time,' he said. 'Anyway, you've got a degree in English from Oxford, Roger! I should think that just about qualifies you to teach English as a foreign language, doesn't it?'

'Apparently not any more, the way things are going!' Roger giggled, his hand over his mouth. 'Apparently, we all have to get ourselves a TEFL qualification.'

'I must admit, I don't like the idea myself,' Frank said.

'Well, it's that or be out of a job possibly,' Janet commented.

'Roger and out, you mean?' he couldn't resist wisecracking.

'Oh, dear, I hope not!' Roger chortled, hand over mouth, to his relief amused by the joke.

'Well, on that happy note I must leave you,' said Janet, standing up. 'I've got to go to another meeting at the main college. Remember, don't let on that you know anything. And think about what I've said. Have you got a class at main college, Melanie? I'll give you a lift if you like.'

'Oh, yes, that'd be lovely!' Melanie exclaimed – she taught A-level politics and history as well as EFL.

'Would you like another pint?' he asked Roger, when Janet and Melanie had gone.

'Just a half, thanks.' He was no boozer, this effete, Oxford-educated southerner!

'I say, I hope you didn't mind me proposing you,' Roger said, when he came back with the drinks.

'No, not at all,' he said. 'As long as I don't have to go to too many boring meetings. Have you made any progress with that Japanese girl, by the way?' Now that Janet – and especially Melanie, who was an ardent feminist as well as socialist – had gone, they were free to indulge in some politically incorrect 'men's talk'.

'Alas, no,' Roger sighed.

'What happened?'

'We had a good chat, but she told me she has a boyfriend.'

'Must be that bloke who teaches English lit. at the main college – Chris Harper.'

'Oh, dear!' Roger sighed again. 'How does she know him?'

'She goes to his A-level English literature class. I've seen her in the canteen with him. You really fancy her, do you?'

'Gosh, yes! She's very attractive, but very intelligent, too. She knows a lot about English literature.'

'Does she? How come?'

'She studied English literature at university in Japan.'

'Oh, I see.'

'She's actually read 'Ulysses', you know.'

'Has she?'

'Yes. I haven't even read it myself! Have you?'

'Well, yes, as it happens. I've got a special interest in Irish writers.'

'Of course, you're Irish, aren't you?'

'Yes, though I wasn't actually born and brought up in Ireland.'

'Where were you born and brought up?'

'Manchester. But my parents were Irish.'

'I see. Have you got a copy of Ulysses I could borrow, by any chance?'

'Yes, sure. I'll bring it in tomorrow.'

'Thanks. Maybe you could help me with some of the references.'

'Sure. I'm no expert though!'

'Do you know Ireland well?'

'Quite well, I suppose. We used to go every summer when we kids, but not to Dublin, to County Cavan, where my mother was born and brought up.'

'Oh, dear! My Irish geography's so poor! Where's that?' Roger giggled, his hand over his mouth.

'It's sort of in the middle, just south of the border.'

'I must visit Ireland some day.'

'Why are you interested in Ireland?'

'I'd like to see the places Yeats writes about.'

'Ah! You're keen on Yeats, are you?'

'Oh, yes! He's one of my favourite poets:

> "Light of evening, Lissadel,
> Great windows open to the south;
> Two girls in silk kimonos,
> Both beautiful, one a gazelle."

Lovely lines.'

'Yes, brilliant,' he agreed. 'You'll have to go to Ireland one day.'

'I hope so. How's Mary, by the way?'

'Oh, she's fine, thanks.'

'She's got a good heart, that girl. You're lucky.'

'Yes. The only trouble is, she wants me to marry her!'

'Well, why don't you?'

'I don't do very well in captivity.' He couldn't resist cracking the hoary old joke yet again.

'Oh, don't you?' Roger giggled. 'I'd marry her tomorrow!'

'Would you? Why?'

'Oh, life is rather lonely without someone, you know.'

'Yes, I suppose so. Isn't there anybody else you fancy, apart from the Japanese girl?'

'Not really. Can you recommend anyone?'

'Well, there is a Turkish girl in my class, but she's a bit on the plump side.'

'I don't mind! "Let me have women about me that are fat!" What's her name?'

'Fatimah, appropriately.' Roger's hand went back over his mouth. 'I'll introduce her if you like,' he offered, when Roger had finished giggling.

'Would you? That's very kind of you!' Roger exclaimed, with a twinkle in his eye.

'No problem,' he said, taking a quaff of his Guinness.

He was uncomfortable acting as a 'go-between' like this, but felt sorry for Roger. It could be beneficial for Fatimah too, he thought, if they hit it off – at least her English would benefit. The trouble was, he couldn't honestly imagine Fatimah, or any girl for that matter, liking Roger enough to have sex with him – not with those disastrous teeth, the dog's breath, the B.O. and the straggly grey hair! It was a pity, he thought, because if he got his teeth fixed and his hair cut, he wouldn't be a bad-looking bloke. This would be a good moment to mention it, he told himself – not for the first time but didn't dare.

'Do you think she might like me?' Roger asked. There was an almost childish innocence about him when it came to women.

'I don't see why not,' he fibbed.

'I never seem to have any luck with women,' he sighed. 'I wonder what I should do. What do you think? You seem to have no problem with them.'

He was amused to find himself in the position of advising anybody about women – he of all people, with his history. But he definitely ought to say something! 'Well, Roger, the first thing you should do is go to the dentist's, get those rotting fangs pulled out and some new ones put in, because they look hideous and your breath reeks like a dog's. On the way home, you should pop into the barber's for a haircut, because with your hair like that you look like some out-of-work, Old Testament prophet. And finally, when you get home, you should have a bath, because you stink like a skunk.' That was what he should say, if he was brutally honest, but of course he didn't.

'Well, I think all you need to do is smarten up your appearance a bit, perhaps,' he suggested, diffidently.

'Oh, I don't think appearances matter, do they?' Roger replied, dismissively.

'Well, I suppose they *shouldn't* matter,' he conceded, 'but they do to some people. To a lot of women, for example,' he added, pointedly.

'I don't really think women are so superficial, are they?' Roger asked.

'I don't know if it's superficial or not, but I think a lot of women do pay attention to appearances,' he argued, pointlessly he knew.

'Well, I'm not changing my appearance for anybody,' Roger proclaimed, somewhat haughtily.

In that case, stay lonely, Frank thought, exasperated by his attitude. God, he was so obtuse, so stubborn, so bloody blind! He felt rebuffed, but at least he had tried. 'Well, maybe you're right,' he said, finishing his Guinness and standing up. 'I've got to go. What about you?'

'Oh, yes, I'd better be off. I've got another class to teach.'

'Where's that?'

'Oh, a tin-pot little school in Carnaby Street,' said Roger, picking up his duffel-bag, standing up and slinging it over his shoulder.

They left the pub and said cheerio to each other. Roger strode off up St. Paul's Road towards the tube at Highbury Corner, while he took the opposite direction along Ball's Pond Road. As he walked, he couldn't help a wry smile at the oxymoronic thought of Roger and Carnaby Street. He felt sorry for him, because he knew he was lonely, but he had tried to help him. He had a brilliant mind, but he couldn't imagine any girl ever fancying him, with those teeth, that breath, the hair and the B.O. – especially the Japanese girl. She was young and attractive, rather sexy in fact. He almost fancied her himself! No, he mustn't think like that, he reprimanded himself – he had Mary. She might not be as sexy-looking or even as intelligent as the Japanese girl, but he loved her.

Did he? Sometimes he wondered if he didn't just feel sorry for her, feel more like a big brother or even father-figure than a lover. She certainly loved him – that he was sure of. That was reason enough to be faithful to her! Maybe he should agree to marry her. No, the very thought of a wedding ceremony, especially in a Catholic church, made him cringe. It had become something of an issue between them. He would do anything to please her, but not that!

'Hello, honeybunch! I've got some news for you,' he announced, giving her a hug and a kiss as usual when she came in.

'What?' she asked eagerly, taking off her mac.

'Let me make a cuppa first,' he said, going over to the kitchenette in the corner of the room.

'Is it good news or bad news?' she asked, coming up behind him and putting her arms around his waist.

'A bit of both, actually. Mostly good.'

'Tell me, Fran! Don't keep me in suspense!'

'Sit down. Just let me make the tea and I'll tell you.'

'You're wicked, Frank Walsh!' she said, giving him a playful push.

'Careful!' he remonstrated, passing her the cup of tea, taking his own and sitting down in the armchair by the window.

'Now, tell me!' she said, sitting on his lap.

'Janet's having a baby.'

'Is she? I wish I could have a baby!'

'Mmm, what, right now?' he teased, squeezing one of her breasts.

'Not right now, silly!' she said, smacking his wrist, then whispered in his ear: 'Tonight if you want.'

'You're very naughty!' he laughed, tickling her and making her wriggle and squeal. 'I don't think we could have a baby now.'

'Why not? Don't you want to have children?' She drew a fingertip over his face affectionately.

'Yes, I suppose, one day, but not now, not living here in a bed-sitter!'

'*They* do.' 'They' referred to the young couple who lived upstairs, an ambulance driver and his girlfriend.

'I didn't know Costas and David were having a baby,' he joked. They were the gay couple who lived in the room next door.

'Don't be silly – you know who I mean.'

'Yes – and look at the stress it causes them, living here in these conditions with a baby. They never stop rowing.'

'That's because he's playing around, not because they've got a baby.'

'Is it? You seem to know all the gossip!'

'I've heard her shouting at him.'

'You wouldn't really want to have a baby now, would you?'

'No, I suppose not. I want to complete my education first and get my qualifications. Anyway, I might never be able to have children.' She suddenly sounded dejected.

'Don't say that. You will! We'll sort that out when the time comes. Let's not worry about it now. I've got something else to tell you.'

'Go on!'

'Janet's leaving at Easter and they want me to take over.'

'Really? You've only been there a few months!'

'That's good news, isn't it?'

'It's wonderful! You'll be good at it, darling.'

'Do you think so?'

'Of course. You're good at organising. You're good at everything! Congratulations!' She took his face in her hands and gave him a kiss on the lips.

'Well, thanks for the vote of confidence! There's a bit of bad news, though, or potentially bad news.'

'What?' she asked, alarmed.

'Janet told us they're talking about cuts.'

'You mean – ?'

'It's possible. Let's not worry about it yet though. Let's concentrate on the good news.'

'I've got an idea – let's go for a drink to celebrate!'

'Can we afford to?'

'Oh, Fran, don't worry about money so much! I'll buy you a drink! Anyway, you'll be earning more money when you take over, won't you?'

'I don't know. She didn't say anything about that and I didn't ask her. I suppose so. I'm not bothered about the money, anyway.'

'I know, but money is important. You have a funny attitude to money! It's because you were in a seminary.'

He didn't like being reminded of that. 'I don't think so. I'm just not motivated by money. I know it's necessary, a necessary evil, but there are more important things.'

'I know, I agree with you. Let's not argue about it. Let's go out for a drink and celebrate. I want to ask you something, too.'

'Oh, what?'

'Wait till we're in the pub. Come on, let's go, ' she said jumping off his lap, grabbing his hand and pulling him up.

'Slainte,' he said, clinking his pint of Guinness against her glass of orange juice. 'So, go on, what do you want to ask me?'

'I want to ask you two things, actually.'

'It sounds serious. Let me have a drink first.' He took a sup of Guinness. 'Aah! That's good! Go on.'

'Can we go to Ireland for a holiday?'

'When?'

'In the summer. You don't have to visit your relations. We could hire a car and drive around.'

He hadn't been to Ireland since he had left the seminary, six years ago, because he was worried about being seen by his relations as a 'failed priest'. But what the hell, he thought now – he loved Ireland and he loved her, so he wasn't going to stay away from it for the rest of his life, just because he had made a ghastly mistake when he was twelve years old! 'Yes, why not?' he agreed, suddenly inspired by the idea. After all, she was right – he didn't have to visit his relations, anyway.

'Really?'

'Why are you so surprised?'

'I thought you didn't want to, you know, because …'

'It's a great idea!'

'Oh, Fran, I love you!' She put her arms round his neck and kissed him.

'Where do you want to go exactly?' he asked her.

'Where do *you* want to go?'

'I'd like to go to the West. I've always wanted to go there. You know, Connemara, Sligo ...'

'All right. We could visit my people in Meath on the way.'

'If you want.'

'We could visit your relations in Cavan, too, if you want.'

'I don't know about that,' he said, suddenly cool.

'Oh, Fran, just because you left the seminary doesn't mean you can never see them again. I'm sure they'd still love to see you.'

'They won't respect me in the same way though.'

'Will you at least think about it?'

'I'll think about it. What was the other thing you wanted to ask me?'

'Promise not to be angry?'

'Oh, dear! This does sound serious! I'd better have a drink to fortify myself.' He took a swig of Guinness. 'Go on.'

'I think you know what I want to ask you, don't you?'

'I've no idea. Go on. Don't keep me in suspense!'

'Can we get married?'

It was what he had been afraid of. 'You know what I think about that. Why do you keep asking? Why is it so important?' He couldn't help sounding impatient.

'It's not important for me. I know you love me and I love you and we're going to stay together for ever. It's for my mammy and daddy. They don't like us living together. I want to make them happy. I'm sure you feel the same about your parents.'

'My parents don't know I'm living with you. They don't know anything about my life. I don't want them to. That's why

I came here to London, to escape from them. I want to live my life the way I want.'

'I know, but Fran, I'm sure they still love you and care about you. Why don't you go and see them?'

He suddenly realised he hadn't seen his parents since leaving home for good nearly a year ago. 'Maybe I will, when I'm ready.'

'You should. After all, they *are* your parents. They brought you into the world and brought you up.'

'Only till I was twelve. They packed me off to a bloody seminary when I was twelve years old – still a child.'

'I thought you wanted to go.'

'Well, I did, but only because my mother wanted me to. Basically, I was brainwashed into it.'

'Why don't you tell me about it, Fran?'

'I don't want to talk about it,' he said, impatiently.

'Fran, what happened? Tell me about it. Was it really so bad?'

'Was it so bad?' he laughed ironically, alcohol loosening him up despite himself. 'To be separated from your parents and family when you're *twelve* years old? Cut off from all normal human relationships? Brought up and brainwashed by a bunch of weirdos in black frocks with no idea about education or child psychology?'

'They weren't all weirdos, were they?'

'Most of them were, one way or another.'

'How do you mean?'

'The way they used to abuse kids. That's what I mean.'

'In what way?'

'I really don't want to talk about it.'

'Tell me, Fran. I want to know. I want to understand.'

'Well, for example, they used to beat kids,' he said, taking another swig of Guinness. 'I think they enjoyed it, too, the sick sods. Got a kick out of it. Had no other emotional outlet, you see.'

'What did they beat kids with?'

'With straps, canes, rulers ... The Dean of Studies, for example – Father Egan, his name was – he had a special strap made of whalebone and leather. It had lead weights in it, too, believe it or not! It was more like a bloody cosh! He brought it with him from Ireland apparently – he was Irish, as it happens, but he was a real nutter, in the Christian Brothers mould. I think he's teaching in a school in Ireland now. I feel sorry for the poor buggers he teaches! He was only a little twerp of a fellow, but he was a real bully, a real psycho! Used to fly into a rage for the slightest thing, fling a book, a board duster, chalk, anything at you. He'd give you the strap for anything, too. Used to carry it around in his cassock pocket, like some sort of weapon. He was a sicko!' He must be getting drunk, but he didn't care, he told himself, taking another swig of Guinness.

'Did he ever give you the strap?'

'Yes, a few times. You automatically got the strap from him if you were on the Black List.'

'What was that?'

'It was a list of people who'd done badly in their studies that week. Everyone's marks were read out in public every Friday evening and if you'd done badly, which meant got two marks under five, your name was put on the Black List, which was actually typed out in black and put on the notice board. Some poor kids were on it every week without fail, which meant they got belted by that bastard every week without fail, regular as clockwork!'

'So why did he give you the strap? You were never on the Black List, were you?'

'No, luckily. In fact, I was always on the Honours List. That meant all your marks were above seven. That list was typed out in red and put on the notice board next to the Black List. They were very sophisticated in terms of educational psychology, the Ghosters, as we called them.'

'So why did he give you the strap then?'

'He didn't like me for some reason. Had a down on me from day one, even though I was bright. I remember on my very first day, the day I arrived, I knocked an ornamental brass dish over in the hall of the Fathers' House with my suitcase as I was going in. It fell on the floor, which was tiled. Made an awful clatter! He just happened to be walking up and down the veranda outside, saying his breviary, so he stopped and hissed, 'You eejit!' at me. Can you imagine? There I was, a twelve-year-old kid in short trousers, lugging a big, heavy suitcase up the steps, having just arrived in this strange place, and that's all he can say to me? This is a supposedly holy, pious priest saying his breviary, *praying*? Can you imagine the mentality? Well, he was a *mental* case, I suppose.'

'He didn't give you the strap then, did he?'

'No. He wasn't quite that nuts, I suppose. I was terrified though. He was terrifying to a twelve-year-old. He looked like something out of a horror film. Had a bald, skull-like head and deathly-white face, with really deep-set eyes. Used to go round in a black cloak. We used to call him 'Dracula', in fact.'

'So, what did he give you the strap for?'

'Oh, everything and anything. Just for pronouncing something wrong in French, for example, because he taught us French. Sadistic little swine, he was. He wasn't as bad as the Director though.' As soon as he said it, he was sorry – the alcohol was really loosening his tongue and his memory now – but it was too late. He knew she would pursue it.

'Who was he?'

'I don't really want to talk about him or any of this.'

'I want to know, Fran. Tell me, please.'

'Why do you want to know? Why are you so interested? It's all in the past. I want to forget about it. I want to pretend it never happened!'

'I only want to know because I love you, Fran. I'm interested in you. I want to know about you. I want to know everything about you! Why don't you want to talk about it? You shouldn't keep it locked up inside. You should get it off your chest! Please tell me! Who was he? What did he do? Tell me.' She stroked his cheek tenderly.

It was difficult to resist when she put it like that. He would tell her, he decided, but not everything. He couldn't tell her everything. He couldn't tell anybody *everything*. The very thought of it sent a ripple of revulsion through him.

'Well,' he said, 'if you really want to know, his name was Father Reid, but we called him 'Greg', because he looked like Gregory Peck – he was young, only about thirty, tall, dark and handsome. He was in charge of us. He was good-looking, but he was a bastard, a complete control-freak and a bully, too, like the Dean of Studies – but worse. He used to love belting kids. I remember once, he flogged a kid almost to death in the study hall in front of everyone. Just a new kid in short trousers, too – like me.'

'Why did he do that?'

'Oh, the kid, Cooper was his name, had been a bit cheeky or

disobedient or something, that's all. I remember him bellowing, 'I'll break you! I'll break your stubborn pride!' while he was belting him. The poor kid ended up on the floor, crying and begging for mercy, but he just carried on belting him. What a bastard! I think he actually enjoyed it, got a kick out of it. Sick bastard, he was. I was shocked. I was afraid he was going to kill him.'

'Couldn't somebody have stopped him?'

'We were all too scared of him. Remember, I was only twelve and I'd only been there a few weeks, like the kid he was flogging. I was really shocked. I kept thinking, 'Why doesn't one of the big boys go and stop him?', but none of them did. Even they were scared of him. He was a big bloke himself, over six foot. Anyway, he was a priest, and you didn't dare touch a priest. It would've been like a sacrilege, a mortal sin! It would've meant certain expulsion, too. He expelled the kid next day. He flogs the kid to within an inch of his life and on top of that expels him! Can you believe it? The poor kid must have been traumatised. I often wonder what became of him. Probably did him a favour expelling him, actually.'

'Did the Director ever give you the strap?'

'Yes, a few times.'

'What for?'

'Oh, breaking some petty rule or other. There were so many bloody rules, it was impossible not to break one sooner or later. For example, you weren't allowed to keep your hands in your trouser pockets – in case you touched yourself, I suppose. If one of the 'seniors' saw you, they would 'send you up' to Father Director and you'd get the strap. I think I got 'sent up' for that once. You could be sent up for breaking silence, breaking bounds, being cheeky to a senior, all sorts of silly things.' He was going to mention 'grouping', but decided not to. 'I remember once I got chucked out of English class, he saw me in the corridor, took me to his office and gave me six of the best, three on each hand, really hard, with one of those fucking coshes the Dean of Studies had given him. It really hurt, I can tell you. Afterwards, my hands were paralysed with pain. In fact, I thought my fingers were broken.'

'Did you cry?'

'Yeah, but only after I'd left the office. I tried to run away! I'd only been there a few weeks and I was feeling homesick.'

'Did you run away?'

'No. Sometimes I wish I had though! I only got as far as the gate at the end of the drive, then I turned back.'

'Why?'

'Well, it was freezing cold, I had no money – we weren't allowed to have money – and I was a hundred miles from home. I was hungry, too, and it was almost dinnertime. The food was crap, but it was better than nothing, I suppose.' He laughed sardonically and took a swig of Guinness. 'Anyway,' he continued, 'I thought I really wanted to be a priest, despite what had happened. I'd been well and truly brainwashed! Besides, I was too ashamed to go home. I was afraid of disappointing my family, especially my mother. I was afraid of being seen as a failure. I was well and truly trapped, you see, psychologically and physically.'

'What happened when you went back? Did you get into trouble?'

'No. I would've done, but fortunately nobody noticed me missing.' He didn't tell her what had happened later that night.

'I'm sorry, love,' she said.

'You're sorry? What about?'

'You've suffered.'

'Oh, everyone suffers one way or another,' he shrugged, unused to being pitied by her – usually it was the other way round. 'It's past. It's finished. That's why I don't really like talking about it.'

'Thank you for telling me about it.'

'That's all right.' He hadn't actually told her the worst bit. 'Have you ever been back there?'

'No way! That's the last place I want to go!'

'I'd like to see it.'

'No way! I never want to see the place again.'

'Why not?'

'Too many bad memories. I told you, I want to forget about it.'

'I think something else happened there, didn't it?'

'What do you mean?'

'I don't know. Did something else happen?'

'Why do you say that?' She was right, but he definitely didn't want to talk about it.

'I don't know. You just seem to hate the place so much – almost irrationally.'

'I do. It was like a bloody concentration camp, full of sadistic guards. It wasn't the physical aspect that was the worst, though.'

'What was?'

'The emotional deprivation. It was a world completely without love or affection. You never got a hug or a kiss from anyone. I think that was the worst aspect of the place, of that way of life. There was no *love*, not in the normal, human sense of the word.' It sounded corny, but it was true – although in his own case, ironically, not completely true ...

'Well, I love you,' she said, kissing him, but he recoiled. 'What's wrong?' she asked.

'Nothing. I'm sorry,' he said, giving her a hug and a kiss. God, what was wrong with him? She was giving him the affection he claimed he had been deprived of and he was rejecting it. That would really mean they – the Ghosters – had won!

'It's all right,' she said, stroking his face. 'I understand what you've suffered. Thanks for telling me. I understand you better now.'

'Do you?' he laughed, taking a another swig of Guinness.

'I think so. I understand why you're so anti-Catholic, anyway.'

'I'm not anti-Catholic just because of that. I think Catholicism, like all religion, is superstitious nonsense.'

'Why do people believe it, then?'

'Because they need it. It gives them a sense of meaning and purpose in life. And it helps them to cope with death, if they can believe there's a life after death.'

'You don't?'

'Of course not!'

'Why not?'

'There's no *evidence* for it! It's just a fantasy! It's a very pleasant fantasy, perhaps, but nothing more. All the evidence suggests that when you die, that's the end of you, as an individual. Your body rots. Or burns to ashes.' He was sorry to sound so cynical, especially as she was so sentimental, but it annoyed him that people believed the unbelievable and unverifiable. Then they went to war and killed each other over it! 'You don't really believe in Heaven and all that, do you?' he asked her.

'Yes.'

'Why? Where's the evidence?'

'There's no evidence. It's just a feeling.'

'There you are – 'it's just a feeling'!'

'Let's not talk about that, shall we?'

'Why not?' he laughed. 'It's quite interesting.'

'Yes, but we know we don't agree, don't we? I believe one thing and you believe another.'

'OK, what shall we talk about, then?'

'What about Seamus? Is he really gay?'

'Of course he is – everyone knows that. It's obvious.'

'Do you think he fancies you?'

'He seems to! It's bloody embarrassing!' It was more embarrassing than he wanted to admit.

'I can't think why!'

'Hey, watch it!'

'You don't fancy him, do you?'

'Now you're really being ridiculous! You don't think I'm gay, do you?'

'Well, maybe just a little bit.'

'Well, we're all supposed to be a bit bisexual. Can't we talk about something else?'

'Let's talk about the future, then.'

'What about the future?'

'Getting married?'

'Oh, no, not that again!' he laughed, standing up, glad of an excuse to escape both past and future. 'I'm going for another pint! Do you want another drink?'

CHAPTER FIVE

Despite all the tensions and tantrums, 'The Playboy' was a great success. As usual they had a celebration party after the last performance, in Seamus's house in Islington. It was good 'craic', with lots of food and drink, and songs and music from the Sugawn Folk and others, including Mary. Late in the proceedings, Maggy approached him unsteadily in the kitchen, a glass in her hand, obviously sloshed.

'Frank, you were great,' she slurred, swaying. She was still in her costume as Widow Quin.

'Thanks, Maggy. So were you!' he said, taking another slug of his Jameson's. 'There's definitely an Oscar in it for you!'

'Ah, go away with you, Frank!' she said, obviously as pleased as punch. 'Frank, can I ask you for your advice?'

'My advice?' he laughed. 'Why me?'

'Oh, Frank, you know, you're so … so …'

'Be careful now, Maggy!' he joked.

'So … s-s-sensible,' she slurred, swaying alarmingly.

'I don't know about that, Maggy,' he laughed, not sure whether to feel pleased.

'You are. A lot more sensible than this lot. Look at them – they're all drunk! I'm drunk! I know I'm drunk! You don't think I'm terrible, do you, Frank? Jesus, what would the parish priest think!' Maggy taught in a Catholic primary school.

'We *are* here to enjoy ourselves, aren't we, Maggy? Let our hair down and all that.'

'You're not drunk though, are you, Frank?'

'Not yet. I've had a few though. I'm on my way!'

'I've never seen you drunk.'

'I usually do it in private, you see.'

'I can't imagine you drunk. Maybe you just hold your drink better than the rest of us.'

'Maybe. Anyway, what do you want my advice about? You know my fees have gone up, don't you?'

'That's another thing I like about you, Frank – you've got such a dry sense of humour.' As she said it, she swayed forward and spilt some drink on his shirt.

'Not so dry now,' he quipped.

'Oh, God, I'm sorry, Frank,' she slurred, trying to wipe it off. 'Oh, God! People will think I'm trying to rape you or something!'

'Don't worry. What is it, actually?' he asked, laughing.

'It's whiskey. That's whiskey with an 'e', Irish whiskey.'

'That's a terrible waste, Maggy,' he said, shaking his head. 'So, anyway, what did you want my advice about? Whiskey?'

'Do you think I should leave my husband?' That sounded slightly more serious!

'If he's violent to you, yes, definitely.'

'He is. He's a brute.'

'Well, leave him. The trouble is, where do you go?' God, he hoped she didn't ask Mary and him to take her in!

'That's the trouble, Frank. I've nowhere to go. I'd like to come and live here with Seamus. What do you think?'

'I don't know, Maggy. Have you asked him?' Oh, God, he thought, the woman is completely crackers!

'Do you think I should? Maybe I should. Maybe I should ask him tonight. I know he's gay, but it doesn't matter. There doesn't have to be anything physical. I'm not looking for that. Sex is not really important. I know it's different for men though, isn't it?'

'Is it?'

'You should know, Frank. You're a man, aren't you?'

'I think so, Maggy,' he said, looking down at himself as if to check.

'You're normal, aren't you?'

'I certainly hope so,' he joked – though he still sometimes wondered.

'I mean, you're not gay, are you?'

'Er, I don't think so,' he laughed, blushing slightly despite himself.

'That's another thing I like about you, Frank,' she slurred. 'You seem so *normal*.'

'Sensible and normal! I'm not sure if I should be pleased about this!' God, if only she knew!

'Don't be offended, Frank! I admire you, you know that.'

'So why do you want to live with Seamus?'

'I just want to be close to him. I love him. Am I crazy, Frank?'

'No, but, well, you know he's – '

'I know. I'm crazy. He doesn't want me. He's gay. What do you think makes him like that, Frank?'

'Maybe he went to a seminary when he was twelve and was brought up by a bunch of psychos and perverts,' he was tempted to say, but didn't. 'God knows, Maggy. I don't understand it. It's just the way he is. He can't help it, I suppose, any more than any of us can help the way we are.' There but for the grace of God, he thought!

'You're so understanding, Frank.'

'As long as he doesn't make a pass at me!' he joked.

'Oh, Frank, I think he realises you're straight. He knows you're with Mary. He knows he's got no chance with you. I wish he liked me instead of you. I wish he'd let me come and live with him. We could be so good together. We've got such a lot in common. We both love the theatre and painting and music and poetry. Do you think he'd let me come and live here?'

'I really don't know, Maggy. Why don't you ask him?' he said, without thinking.

'Do you think I should? Maybe I should. Yes. I'll ask him now,' she declared, staggering off.

'Maggy, I'm not sure if it's a good idea,' he called after her, but before he could stop her, she had gone, back into the living-room, where he could hear Seamus singing his party-piece, 'By The Banks of My Own Lovely Lee'.

Just then, Pat, the American, came into the kitchen with Peggy, his girlfriend from the Aran Islands. They were both still in costume – Pat as the playboy and Peggy as Pegeen, a peasant girl from the Aran Islands – which was more or less how she usually dressed.

'Where's she off to?' Pat asked, in his Chicago drawl.

'To ask Seamus if she can come and live here with him,' he said.

'Christ! I hope not. She drives him up the wall. Doesn't she know he's gay, anyway?'

'Yes, but she doesn't care. She's infatuated with him.'

'It's sad. Where's Mary?'

'She's in there somewhere. I think they want her to sing. What's the next production going to be?'

'Seamus said Jim's written a play.'

'Oh, really? What's it called?'

''God Is Dead On The Balls Pond Road'.'

'Hm. Good title. What's it about?'

'I believe it's something to do with corruption in the building industry. He was in the building industry before, wasn't he?'

'Yes, I think so. He was a quantity surveyor or something – whatever that is. When do we start?'

'Not till after summer. Are you doing anything in summer?'

'Yes. We're going to Ireland.'

'That's great! You have been before, haven't you?'

'Oh, yeah, lots of times. We used to go every year when we were kids. But I haven't been for a few years. It was Mary's idea.'

'Where exactly are yous going?' Peggy asked, a lovely Aran lilt in her voice.

'We're going to hire a car and tour round. Probably the West. I've never been there. What about you?'

'We're going to Ireland, too,' said Peggy.

'Are you? Whereabouts?'

'You tell him,' she said to Pat.

'We're going to stay on a little island called Gola, just off the coast of Donegal.'

'Oh. In a hotel?'

'No. It's a desert island!'

'A desert island?'

'Yeah. All the inhabitants have left and gone to live on the mainland or emigrated. The houses are still there though. An American guy I know – he's a translator – has bought one of them as a holiday home and told me I could use it. It'll be interesting, because there's nothing there – no electricity, no shops, no pubs, no people apart from one chap, the local teacher, who's retired and has a holiday home there, too. Name of Sean McGinley. Apart from him, just sheep, rabbits and seagulls!'

'It sounds great. Very romantic! You must tell me all about it when you come back.'

'Sure. We'll meet up for a drink.'

'Why don't we try to meet up over there?' Peggy suggested. Before he could answer, Seamus came rushing into the kitchen, glass in hand, and hid behind them, exclaiming: 'Jaysus, somebody save me from that feckin' woman!'

'Which woman is that, Seamus?' he asked, as if he didn't know.

'Maggy! The feckin' woman won't leave me alone! She's askin' me if she can come an' live here with me! Why the feck doesn't she go home to her husband?'

'Apparently, he beats her up,' he observed, matter-of-factly.

'I'll beat her up myself, if she doesn't feckin' leave me alone,' Seamus retorted, obviously somewhat the worse for wear. 'I'm going into the garden for a slash. If she comes lookin' for me, don't tell her where I am. I'll lie low out there for a while.' He staggered towards the kitchen door and walked into it. 'Jaysus, I must be feckin' langers,' he expostulated, opening it and staggering out, whereupon they all burst out laughing.

'What are you lot laughing about?' Jim asked, coming into the kitchen – having just played a publican in his own pub.

'Seamus is hiding in the garden,' he informed him.

'Hiding from whom?'

'From Maggy.'

'Doesn't she realise he's gay?'

'She does, but she doesn't care. She's infatuated with him.'

'God, the woman's completely bats!' he remarked, shaking his head.

'I hear we're doing a play of yours next,' he said, to change the subject.

'Well, Seamus is reading it, anyhow. I think he likes it.'

'What's it about?'

'It's about the construction industry.'

'You were in that, weren't you?'

'Yes, I spent twenty years in it.'

'Why did you leave?'

'I got sick of the corruption. That's what the play's about, partly.'

'So why did you go into the pub business?'

'I wanted to try my hand at writing, do something creative. I thought it'd give me time to write.'

'And does it?'

'Only because the wife helps. She runs the pub in the afternoon. That's when I write. It was only after I moved into the Duke that I got the idea for the theatre and the music. It used to be a billiard room, you know.'

'It was a good idea. Is there a part for me in the new play?'

'There's a priest in it. I think it'd suit you.'

'Oh, no thanks!' he laughed, embarrassed. God, they must be able to smell the seminary off him ...

Gerry, the Dublin crane driver, wandered in, a pint of Guinness in his hand. 'What's this?' he asked, in his good-humoured way. 'A cast meeting?'

'We were just talking about the next production, actually,' said Pat.

'Do we know what it is?'

'It's called, 'God Is Dead On The Balls Pond Road',' Pat said. 'Do you know who that's by?'

'It sounds like something by Ibsen, but I don't think he was familiar with the Balls Pond Road, was he?' Gerry said, in his droll Dublin way, and they all laughed.

'I don't think he was Irish either,' he added, raising another laugh.

'It's by Jim,' said Peggy.

'So what's it about?' asked Gerry.

'It's about the construction industry, so you'll be OK for a part, Gerry,' he told him.

'Jaysus, I'll have to consult my agent first,' Gerry quipped and they all laughed again.

At that moment, Maggy burst into the kitchen. 'Has anyone seen Seamus?' she slurred, tottering, her shawl falling off her shoulders.

'Not in here,' they all chorused.

'I think he's trying to avoid me,' she slurred. 'He must be in here somewhere.'

'Have you tried upstairs, Maggy?' he suggested.

'He's not upstairs and he's not downstairs. He must be outside in the garden,' she declared, tottering towards the door.

'Quick, go and warn him him,' Peggy whispered to Pat, who slipped out.

'He's not out there, Maggy. Let's look upstairs,' Peggy told her, taking her by the arm and pulling her back.

'He's out there, I know he's out there,' Maggy slurred, resisting arrest and staggering towards the door, but they all blocked her way.

'Jaysus, he can't avoid her all night,' Gerry said under his breath. Maggy broke free from Peggy and pushed her way out into the garden. A few moments later, a leprechaun-like head with a goatee beard appeared around the door. 'Has she gone?' Seamus asked, squinting around.

'She's out there looking for you,' he said. 'You'd better come in.'

'Holy Mother of God, that woman'll drive me to drink,' Seamus said, staggering in, making for the drinks and pouring himself a large whiskey.

'You know you're crazy about her, Seamus,' Gerry teased him.

'I'm crazy all right!' he said, knocking back a slug of whiskey.

'Seamus! There you are, darlin'!' Maggy declared, stumbling back into the kitchen.

Seamus took one look at her and scampered off into the house like a frightened rabbit.

'Seamus, darlin'! Come here! I want to ask you something!' Peggy called out, staggering after him.

As soon as they were gone, they all burst out laughing again.

'This is better than Brian Rix,' Frank remarked.

'Ssh! Is that Mary singing?' Peggy asked.

They stopped laughing and listened to the familiar high, sweet, tremulous voice coming from the living room.

'Let's go inside. Come on, Frank,' Peggy said, pulling him by the arm towards the tiny, packed, living-room, where Mary was singing 'The Wild Rapparee', unaccompanied, to the hushed crowd. He stood at the back of the room and listened. As always, Mary was standing with her arms folded and her eyes closed while she sang. It was a good song and she sang it beautifully, if somewhat nervously. Looking around the room at the rapt audience, he couldn't help feeling a surge of pride, that all these clever, talented people were listening to her and she was *his*. His only worry was that she might have a 'fit', as she sometimes did, especially when she was nervous, but if she did, it wouldn't matter too much, he told himself – he'd look after her, as he always did and always would. He loved her!

'So, where did you go?' Pat asked, a few weeks later. He was wearing a waistcoat over a T-shirt and smoking a pipe.

'We drove all round the West – Clare, Galway, Connemara, Mayo, Sligo,' replied Frank. They were having a drink in the Sugawn after the summer holiday.

'What did you think?'

'It was great,' Mary said.

'Yes,' he agreed. 'It's beautiful. I really enjoyed it. I've never been to that part of Ireland before.'

In fact, he had more than 'enjoyed' it – going back to Ireland, for the first time in years, had been a deeply emotional experience for him. It had been like a return to his roots, to his spiritual homeland, to the land of his birth. He hadn't actually been born in Ireland, but he felt it was his 'birthplace' nevertheless. After all, it was the land of his ancestors and the place where he had spent the happiest times of his childhood – summer holidays on the farm where his mother had been born and brought up.

He remembered the first sight of the Irish coast from the deck of the car ferry, like a ribbon of emerald green on the horizon of the Irish Sea, with the misty Wicklow mountains in the background. He had felt an almost mystical thrill and, epiphany-like, realised that he loved Ireland, always had and always would, that Ireland was in his blood, in his bones, in his heart, in his very soul. It had been like the beginning – no, the resurrection – of a passionate love affair …

'So yous didn't get to the Arans?' Peggy asked. As always, she was dressed like the Aran Islander she was, in a long black dress, with a black shawl.

'No, we didn't have time,' he said. 'We'll have to save them for another time.' There would be other times, he had decided – he wanted to explore the whole of Ireland, especially the places with literary connections, such as the Aran Islands, Sligo, Dublin … 'Sorry we didn't manage to meet up. How was your island, anyway?'

'Interesting,' Pat said, in his laconic drawl, puffing on his pipe.

'How long did you stay on it?'

'Six weeks altogether.'

'Did you spend the whole time on the island?'

'Virtually. We came off once a week to pick up supplies.'

'How did you do that?'

'Hitched a ride on a fishing boat. The island is still used as a kind of base by local fishermen. Or with Sean McGinley, the retired teacher I told you about. He has his own boat. What's this it was called?' he asked Peggy.

'"An Feileacan",' she said. 'That's Gaelic for 'butterfly'. It's a Gaelic-speaking area, you see. Do you know any Gaelic?' Being an Aran Islander, she was a native Gaelic speaker.

'No. I must try to learn a bit,' he said, resolving to do so. In fact, he was going to study all things Irish, he had decided – history, language, literature, music …

'So what did you do on this island?' he enquired.

'Well, we did a lot of reading, didn't we?' Peggy said, with a little ironic laugh.

'That's true,' agreed Pat. 'There were some interesting books in the cottage. I read a novel called, 'Langrishe Go Down', by a fellow called Aidan Higgins. Have you heard of it?'

'Can't say I have,' he shook his head. 'Good?'

'Brilliant!' Pat proclaimed. 'You'll have to go there and read it!'

'I'd love to,' he said. 'Maybe next year.'

'We could go there for our honeymoon,' Mary suddenly piped up.

'Are yous two getting hitched then?' Peggy asked, eyes glinting. 'That's great news!'

'Hould your horses,' he laughed. 'Do I look like a condemned man?' This prompted Mary to give him a dig in the ribs.

'I'm working on him,' she said to Peggy.

'We're thinking of it, too,' Peggy said.

'Really?' he asked, surprised. 'Are you, Pat?'

'I think that's the royal 'we' she's using,' Pat drawled, taking a puff on his pipe.

'He's married to his writing,' Peggy said, 'but I'm working on him, too.'

'We have to preserve our artistic freedom as long as possible, don't we, Frank?' Pat observed dryly .

'Absolutely,' he agreed. 'Did you manage to do any writing while you were there?'

'Yes. I finished my novel.' It sounded like 'narvel'.

'Really? Well done!' He couldn't help feeling a prick of envy. 'What's it called?'

'It's called, "Fatherland".'

'What's it about?'

'You don't have to answer that,' Gerry, who arrived with a pint in his hand, interjected, 'but anything you do say …'

They all laughed and said hello, pleased to see him, jovial as ever. He was wearing a leather jacket, jeans and cowboy boots.

'It's about a man whose father disappears in Dublin,' Pat answered, 'so he travels all over Ireland searching for him. Physically and figuratively.'

'Sounds interesting! Have you got a publisher?' he asked.

'That's what I'm trying to do now. That's the hard part! I've sent it to several, including a few in Ireland.'

'Well, good luck. I'll look forward to reading it.'

'How's your magnum opus?'

'Oh, I'm still working on it,' he laughed.

'What about you, Gerry?' Peggy asked. 'Have you finished yours?'

'Jaysus, I haven't even started. I think I'm suffering from writer's block,' he joked, making them laugh again. 'To tell you the truth,' he added, seriously, 'after reading that fellow Joyce, I don't think I'd have the nerve.'

'He's a hard act to follow,' he agreed, 'but you should have a go.'

'I think I'll leave the writin' to yous educated fellows.'

'You don't have to be educated,' he told him. 'Sean O'Casey was a labourer, wasn't he?'

'That's right,' said Pat. 'Have a go, Gerry. Everyone's got something to say.'

'My bleedin' gaffer'd have something to say if he caught me scribblin' up there! I might though, now that you mention it. Sure, why not?'

'Good man yourself, Gerry,' Jim, the landlord, commended him, coming over and standing by the table.

'How's the script, Jim?' he enquired.

'It's nearly done. We'll be ready for a read-through next week.'

'Will you have a drink, Jim?' Gerry invited.

'I have one at the bar, thanks,' Jim declined.

'Trying to get in with the author, so you can get a good part, eh, Gerry?' Peggy teased.

'Sure, aren't I surrounded by bleedin' authors!' Gerry laughed.

'Well, would-be authors,' he laughed.

'Seamus, how are you?' Peggy said, as Seamus came over to join them.

'Jaysus, I'm langers already,' he announced, sitting down unsteadily with his pint of Guinness. He waved to the members of the group, who were tuning up on the stage.

'Where've you been?' he asked him.

'I went to a matinee of 'Waiting for Godot' at the Royal Court and had a few jars afterwards with a couple of the cast.'

'Not with Sam himself?' he asked.

'Ah, I told him I was too busy to see him,' Seamus riposted.

'Was it a good production?' he asked, seriously.

'Ah, it was brilliant. We'll have to do it.'

'I don't know if the Sugawn is ready for Beckett,' commented Pat, puffing on his pipe.

'The Sugawn is ready for good theatre, full stop. How's the script coming along, Jim?'

'Just tidying up the last act. Be ready for next Tuesday.'

'Are you going to do the priest, Frank?'

'I don't know,' he said, secretly squirming. This was so ironic – he had hoped never to wear a dog-collar again. 'What about Gerry?' he suggested. 'He'd make a good priest.'

'I can't, I'm an atheist,' said Gerry, and everyone laughed.

'So am I,' he declared. 'At least, I'm an agnostic, anyway.'

'What does that mean?' Gerry asked.

'It means you don't know what you are,' Pat said, to general laughter.

'Ah, go on, Frank, you do it,' Seamus said, ruffling his hair, a gesture he had taken to doing lately and which made him cringe.

'Yes, go on, Frank – you'd make a good priest,' Peggy urged.

God, it was funny – those were the exact words his sister, Molly, had said to him, when he told her he was thinking of leaving the seminary. He was in hospital, having just had an operation on his knee, and at the lowest point of his life, being in a state of intense physical pain as well as severe mental depression. In fact, he was so depressed he had tried to commit suicide by saving up the painkillers they gave out and swallowing them all at once one night ...

'He nearly was a priest once,' Mary suddenly piped up again.

For a moment, he could hardly believe his ears. That was supposed to be a secret between them, something he had never told anyone else and told her not to. He gave her an angry glance, hoping nobody had heard.

'Were you really, Frank?' Peggy asked.

'Nearly is the operative word,' he laughed, secretly furious with Mary for revealing his 'skeleton in the cupboard'.

'So did you go to a seminary?' Peggy pursued.

'That's right,' he admitted, taking a sup of Guinness.

'You didn't get ordained, did you?'

'No, I managed to escape before that,' he joked, still furious with Mary. He didn't like talking about it, didn't want to be asked questions about it, wanted to forget about it!

To his relief, at that moment the group struck up with 'Wild Rover', so the conversation stopped. He took another sup of Guinness and pretended to listen to the song, though he had heard it a hundred times before and inside he was seething with rage at Mary for revealing his 'secret'. He was so enraged he couldn't bring himself to speak to her or even look at her, recoiled when she tried to touch him.

After the first set of songs, he stood up, pretending he wanted to go to the loo, and slipped out of the pub. He needed to be alone for a while. It was a balmy September evening, with a technicolour sunset forming a spectacular backdrop to the otherwise drab side-streets and buildings, mostly blocks of council flats with a few factories mixed in. The sunset – in conjunction with the alcohol – would normally have lifted his spirits, but tonight he just felt depressed. She had *betrayed* him!

How could she have done that? He knew she probably hadn't intended to, had just let it slip out, but now he'd have to answer a hundred and one questions. How could she have been so stupid? He had never felt so angry with her before!

She kept talking about marriage in public, too. That annoyed him almost as much. Why did she do that, when she knew it annoyed him so much? What was wrong with her? He loved her, but he was starting to wonder if he could trust her. It was so depressing! Everything was going so well and suddenly she had spoilt it! He felt like not going back inside, like walking off and leaving her there, but he couldn't. He might as well try to enjoy the rest of the evening, he told himself, going back in. He'd have it out with her when they got home.

'Why the fuck did you say that?' he demanded angrily, when they got home, pouring himself a whiskey, even though he was already drunk. On the way home, he had given her the 'silent' treatment, refused to speak to her.

'I'm sorry,' she said, annoyingly. 'I didn't know it was private.'

'You did know! I told you it was private! I told you I don't like talking about it.'

'I'm sorry, love,' she said again, which annoyed him even more.

'And you as good as told them we were getting married.'

'I just said – '

'I've told you, I don't want to get married and I don't want to play a priest. But you keep talking about marriage in public! Why? Are you trying to embarrass me? Are you trying to trap me? Trying to blackmail me into it?'

'Oh, Fran, I'm sorry, don't be angry. I don't want to embarrass you or trap you. I love you. You don't know how much I love you.'

'Well, you've got a fucking funny way of showing it!'

'I'm sorry. I won't mention it again.'

'You'd better not.'

'Come to bed.' She had already undressed and got in – naked, he wasn't too drunk to notice.

'I don't want to go to fucking bed!'

'Why not?'

'I don't feel like it, that's why!'

'Are you still angry?'

'Of course I'm still fucking angry!'

'Because I said you were going to be a priest or we were going to get married?'

'Both, for Christ's sake! Both!'

'You shouldn't be ashamed because you were going to be a priest.'

'I'm not ashamed! I told you, I just don't want people to know! I don't want to talk about it! It's private! It's past! It was another me! Can't you understand that?'

'Maybe you should talk about it.'

'Why the hell should I talk about it if I don't want to?'

'I think it would be good for you to talk about it. I think you've got a hang-up about it. That's why you're so anti-Catholic.'

'It isn't! I'm anti-Catholic because I think Catholicism is a load of crap, like all religion. Can't you understand that?'

'Yes, but I think what happened in the seminary has got something to do with it.'

'What do you mean, 'what happened in the seminary'?'

'I don't know what happened exactly.'

'I've told you what happened!'

'You haven't told me everything though, have you? I know something happened that you don't want to talk about. Why don't you tell me, Fran?'

'I've told you, I don't want to talk about it!' he shouted. Christ, she was persistent! But she was perceptive, too. 'Don't you understand?'

'All right, I'm sorry. I won't mention it again.'

'And stop telling people we're getting married. It's not true.'

'All right. Now come to bed.'

'I don't want to go to fucking bed! I don't want to sleep with you!' He didn't often lose his temper like this, but when he did ...

'Please, Fran. I'm sorry. Come to bed. I won't say anything about either subject again. We can make love if you want.'

'I don't want to make fucking love! Don't you understand that? Don't you get the message?'

'You don't want to make love with me?'

'Not tonight, no.' He said it coldly and clinically.

'You don't want to sleep with me?'

'No, I don't.'

'Where are you going to sleep?'

'In the armchair. On the floor. It doesn't matter.'

'Fran, please – '

'Will you shut up, go to fucking sleep and leave me alone! I don't want to talk to you! I don't want to make love with you! I don't want to sleep with you! I don't even want to see you!'

'Goodnight, then,' she said, turning her back to him.

To his further irritation, she started crying. He jumped up, put some music on and poured himself another whiskey. Then he sat down in the armchair again and drank, trying to forget about the past, trying to forget she had betrayed him, trying to pretend she wasn't there, listening to her sobbing. Christ, she had well and truly ruined his evening! She had well and truly ruined everything! He took another large slug of whiskey. He wanted to drink himself into oblivion. It was the only way to forget, to escape from the ghosts of the past that always came back to haunt him, to forget that he had once been a happy, *innocent* boy, that he had wanted nothing more than to be a priest and serve God. But it had been taken away from him by that man. He didn't want to admit it to her or even himself, but he knew that deep down she was right. That bastard had somehow injected a germ of evil into his soul and poisoned him. That was why he had lost his faith, lost his vocation, lost his innocence, lost everything he had once loved and believed in. Christ, all he wanted to do was forget about him, forget about the past, but people kept reminding him! Even *her*! Why? Didn't she understand that by reminding him about it, she was dragging him back, pushing him away from her, pushing him back to another time, another place, another planet, a dark planet that was light years away from here and now, from her?

Obviously she didn't understand! How could she? It was a world away from her experience. He shouldn't be angry with her. He certainly shouldn't leave her. That would definitely mean *they*, the Ghosters, had won! No! Never! He mustn't let them take her away from him. She was good! She was real! She was true! She was the very antithesis of them. Suddenly, he felt sorry for her and sorry for being angry with her. He stood up, lurched over to the bed and collapsed onto it beside her.

'I'm sorry,' he whispered, throwing an arm round her.

'It's all right, darling,' she said, turning to him and putting her arms around him. 'I love you.'

'I love you, too,' he slurred, kissing her.

'Do you want to make love?' she whispered.

'Mmm,' he murmured, caressing her. 'Do you?'

'Yes, but I think we'd better leave it till the morning,' she said.

'All right, in the morning,' he murmured, gratefully, slipping into bed beside her and hugging her tightly …

CHAPTER SIX

'I've got some bad news, I'm afraid.'

'They want to close us down?' asked Melanie.

'Yes,' he answered glumly.

He had convened an emergency meeting in one of the classrooms after class. The principal had called him to his office in the main building earlier to tell him.

'The bastards!' Melanie exclaimed. It sounded funny in her cut-glass, middle-class, RP accent!

'Oh, dear,' Roger sighed. 'I knew it was too good to last. What are we going to do?'

'We'll fight it!' Melanie declared. 'We can't just let them close us down! Don't you agree, Frank?'

'Yeah, sure, but how?' This was all new to him, but he was inspired by Melanie's militancy.

'We can organise a petition, a demonstration, a march, even a sit-in. We can't just let them close us down without a fight.' Melanie was in her element!

'Absolutely,' he agreed.

'Do you agree, Roger?' she asked.

'Oh, dear, yes, I suppose so,' Roger sighed. He seemed shell-shocked.

'You haven't told the students, have you?' Melanie asked him.

'No. I only found out this morning. Should we tell them?'

'I think we have to. We have to involve them,' she said.

'We'll tell them tomorrow, then, shall we?' he suggested. 'What do you think, Roger?'

'Yes, of course. I don't hold out much hope, but we have to fight. What reasons did he give?'

'Oh, you know, the usual rubbish – cutbacks, rationalisation … '

'How I hate that word!' Roger declared.

'Under a Labour government, too,' Melanie commented, with

an ironic laugh.

'Yes,' Roger sighed. 'Seventies Britain – a land fit for heroes!'

'So, what exactly are we going to do?' he asked. 'We need to plan something, don't we?'

'I've got a suggestion,' Roger said.

'What's that, Roger?' he asked.

'Let's retire to the pub and discuss tactics.'

'That sounds like a good idea to me,' he laughed. 'Mel?'

'Yes, good idea,' she agreed, slinging her bag of 'Socialist Workers' over her shoulder.

'The revolution starts here!' he proclaimed, standing up. 'To the barricades, comrades!'

'Hello, honey,' he said to Mary, opening the door of the room for her when she arrived home from college. 'Cup of tea?'

'Yes, please, darling!' she said, giving him a customary peck on the cheek.

He went over to the cooker to make the tea, while she put her bag down, took off her coat and sat down.

'What's wrong?' she asked.

'What do you mean?' Trust her to notice!

'You're very quiet!'

'Am I?'

'Yes. What's up? Tell me!'

'I got some bad news today,' he admitted at last.

'What?' she asked, anxiously.

'Let me make the tea first,' he insisted.

'Fran, don't keep me in suspense! It's not about your parents, is it?'

'No. Wait a minute. Here's your tea.' He gave her a cup of tea and sat down in the armchair with one himself.

'Go on, then!' she ordered, taking a sip of her tea.

'They want to close us down.'

'You mean – completely?'

'Yes. Completely.'

'So you'll lose your job?'

'Yes. And the others, Roger and Melanie.'

'It could be worse. I thought someone had died.'

'It's bad enough.'

'Fight it.'

'That's what Melanie said.'

'Are you going to?'

'Of course. I don't think there's much hope though.'

'You have to try. You can't let them get away with it without a fight. So much for Harold Wilson and Labour.' She became uncharacteristically belligerent about anything she perceived as unjust, because of her own experience.

'I agree. We're going to fight. It's bad news though.'

'Yes, but it could be worse. Anyway, if you have to, you'll find another job.'

'Where?' She seemed relatively unfazed by the news, somewhat to his surprise.

'You could try at my college.' She was doing her O-levels at another college. 'You're good – you're well-qualified and experienced. They should be glad to have you.'

'Thanks. It might not be so easy though. I think I'll have to get a TEFL qualification. Do they do it at your place?'

'I'll find out for you. Don't worry about it. Whatever happens, we're together. We've got each other, haven't we?' She went over and sat on his lap, one arm around his neck.

'Yes. That doesn't pay the rent though,' he said, putting an arm round her slender waist.

'Don't worry about the rent! I'll pay the rent!'

'How?'

'I'll get some more hours if necessary.' She meant at the Old People's Home, where she worked part-time.

'But you need the time to study.'

'I could do a few more hours. Anyway, don't worry. It's not the end of the world, even if it does happen. We'll get through somehow. We'll survive, won't we?'

'Yes, I suppose so. It's a bit depressing though. We've got such a good thing going, everyone's happy – Roger, Melanie, me, the students – and they want to close us down!'

'Don't let them grind you down, Fran! That's what you're always saying to me! You have to fight it. I'll help you. How do Roger and Melanie feel?'

'Roger seems pretty depressed about it. Melanie's up in arms.

She's in her element, talking about organising a petition, a demo, even a sit-in.'

'She's right. It's better to be angry than depressed.'

'I know. It's hard not to feel a bit demoralised by it though.'

'You mustn't! We'll fight it together. Now, stop thinking about it. I want to ask you something.'

'What?'

'Are you going to visit your family next week?'

'Yes, I suppose so. Why?' he asked, suddenly tense.

'Can I come with you?'

'Why?' he asked, even more tense.

'I want to meet them, especially your mother and father. I've been living with you for nearly two years and I've never met them.'

'I don't think they want to meet you though.'

'Why not?'

'Precisely because you're living with me. In sin, as they see it.'

'So, why don't we get married?'

'Oh, no, not that again! You know what I think about that.' He might have known this was coming!

'Fran, please, just think about it. If we got married, I could go and see them with you. Maybe they'd even come here to see us.'

'They've never shown any interest in coming here.'

'Only because I'm here.'

'Even before you were here.'

'Did you ever invite them?'

'I shouldn't need to invite my own parents to come and see me, should I? Your parents have come here without being invited, haven't they?'

'Yes, but they're different.'

'My parents have actually passed through London on the way to America to see my sister and not come to see me. What do you make of that?'

'Fran, I'm sure they would like to see you and where you live, but you know how they feel.'

'Do I? How?'

'They feel that you've rejected them, turned your back on them. After all, you didn't contact them for more than a year after you left! They didn't even know where you were!'

'I've turned my back on them? They're the ones who sent me to a bloody seminary when I was twelve years old! Twelve years old! A child!'

'You said you wanted to go.'

'I thought I did. I did. But you know why, because I'd been brainwashed to want to. I don't want to go over all that again, Mary.'

'I know. I'm not asking you to. I know you don't like talking about it and it depresses you. I'm just saying, maybe it's time to forgive and forget or at least understand, meet half way.'

'I have forgiven, even if I haven't forgotten. I've been to see them, haven't I? They're the ones who won't reciprocate. I've already gone half-way, more than half-way. I went all the way to Manchester – I didn't insist on meeting them in Birmingham!' He was joking, but underneath he felt bitter about their intransigence.

'If I could just meet them, I'm sure they'd like me and I could help them to understand.'

'Where would you stay?'

'I could sleep on a sofa. I know they wouldn't let me sleep with you.'

'*Sleep* with me? My mother wouldn't even let you in the house!' he laughed sardonically.

'She would if we were married, wouldn't she?'

'I've told you, I don't want to get married. I don't believe in it. Anyway, I'm not sure she'd accept you, even if we were married.'

'Why not?'

'She's insanely jealous of any girl I associate with.'

'I'm sure she'd accept me if we were married. If we don't get married, it means I can never meet them.'

'That's their problem.'

'It's my problem too, Fran.'

'Why?'

'We're going to be together for ever, aren't we?'

'Yes. I hope so.'

'So, I want to be able to go everywhere you go. I don't want to be shut out of part of your life. Do you understand?'

'Yes, I suppose so.'

'Will you think about it?'

'What?'

'Getting married?'

'I'll think about it. Not now though. I'm tired.'

'I know you're tired now. I don't want you to think about it now. What are you going to do this evening?'

'It's my turn to cook, isn't it?'

'Yes, but I'll do it if you like.'

'No, I'll do it. I'd like to go for a walk first though. Do you fancy a walk?'

'I've got too much homework.'

'Do you mind if I go on my own?'

'I need some help.'

'What have you got to do?'

'An essay.'

'On what?'

'Julius Caesar.'

'Can I go for a walk and help you when I get back? I need some fresh air and exercise.'

'On one condition.'

'What's that?'

'Think about what I said.'

'What's that?'

'Getting married and visiting your parents.'

'OK.' God, she could be manipulative when she wanted to be! Talk about emotional blackmail! He knew she was right, and knew she loved him, but it didn't make him like the idea of marriage any more.

'Promise.'

'Promise. Can I go now?'

'Give me a kiss and a cuddle first.'

He did so, though he didn't feel very amorous, and she got off his lap. He stood up, took his jacket from the back of the door and put it on. She followed him to the door.

'See you later,' he said, opening the door, giving her a peck on the cheek and going out.

He crept downstairs and slipped out through the front door as covertly as he could, not wanting to meet any of the neighbours – especially 'Jolly Super', as he called her, it being her catchphrase. She lived in the ground-floor flat and was a hospital matron. She was another one with a posh voice, but she was also very bossy and very nosy. She seemed to think the house was one of her wards!

He hurried down the front steps and through the scruffy front garden into the street, where he paused to think about where to go, relieved at having escaped undetected – unless 'Jolly Super' was peeping through her net curtains, as was her habit. It was a sunny spring evening, with a balmy breeze blowing – on such an evening there was really only one place to go.

He walked down the main road towards the Marshes, rush hour traffic whizzing past, pumping out carbon monoxide. As soon as he could, he turned off the road and cut across Millfields Park towards the river, joining the towpath at Latham's timber sheds – great barns full of wood from the forests of the world, with cranes jutting out over the water, where barges full of logs were unloaded. He paused to gaze at the sheds for a few moments, awed by their size and the thought of the far-flung forests the timber had come from – the forests of Scandinavia, Russia, Malaysia ... Then he crossed the metal bridge over the river to the towpath on the other side and walked upstream.

The Marshes stretched away to his right like a green prairie. They were looking their splendid best in the evening sunshine: meadows of silvery-green grass, sprinkled with blue, white and yellow wildflowers, rippling silkily in the breeze; tall reeds dancing playfully to some inaudible music of their own; green riverbanks laced with creamy-white parsley; hawthorn and elderberry bushes dripping with sweet-scented, creamy blossom; poplars swaying languorously against the skyline; and in the broad, bright-blue sky itself, candy-floss clouds floating dreamily …

As he strolled along the towpath, he tried to work out why he felt so tense lately. Obviously, it was partly because his job was under threat, but also because Mary kept pressuring him to get married. Why did the idea of marriage scare him so much? He didn't believe in the necessity of a public ceremony or legal contract of any sort and certainly not in the idea of a wedding ceremony – especially in a Catholic church. Something else bugged him about it, though. Was it because he was afraid of being trapped again, as he had once felt trapped in the seminary? He still had nightmares about it! It was partly that, he thought. After all, he was only twenty-eight. He had only escaped from the seminary seven years ago – it was too early to lock himself up in an another institution! That was what she didn't understand. And, if anything ever went wrong between them, he wanted to be able to escape easily, without the hassle of divorce. The thought of that terrified him! Not that anything would go wrong, but ...

He paused to look at the river. The water looked filthy, but there were geese and ducks and other waterfowl, such as moorhens and coots, swanning about happily enough on it. Swans too! There must be fish in it, he supposed, since there were usually anglers on the banks – not that he had ever seen one catch anything. What a pointless pastime it was, he reflected, though he had once enjoyed it himself, as a teenager on holiday in Ireland. But that had just been an excuse to escape and be on his own for a few hours. God, the long, solitary hours he had spent by lonely loughs in County Cavan! What a misfit he had been! Maybe it was the same for the anglers here – they just wanted to escape from wives and kids and get a bit of peace and quiet and fresh air after working in offices, shops and factories all day. He couldn't blame them in a way, though he now found the idea of hooking a living creature through its lips and dragging it out of its natural element barbaric. He had only ever caught a fish once himself, a pike, which his aunty had gutted, scaled and cooked for dinner. He still felt guilty to this day about having been responsible for its death, though he had to admit it had tasted good and pike were pretty unappealing creatures – freshwater mini-sharks!

The water sloshing against the tyres hung over the side of the riverbank made a pleasantly rhythmic, gurgling noise. The breezes rustling the stalks of dry, yellow grass had a similarly lulling, soothing effect. This was one of the reasons he liked coming here so much. Why some of the grass was so yellow and dry, he couldn't understand, since it was only April. Well, April was the cruellest month, according to T. S. Eliot, though he had never been quite sure why he had said that. Maybe because April weather was so changeable? There were large clumps of nettles and dock, making a lush green contrast with the yellow. He remembered how as kids on holiday in Ireland they used dock leaves to rub on nettle stings.

Suddenly, a Red Admiral butterfly fluttered prettily by, while in the sky a hawk hovered aerodynamically with sinister but exquisite poise. A pair of swans glided regally past, dispersing the geese, ducks and other lesser fowl imperiously. What a great place this was! It was like having a slice of countryside, a nature reserve, right on your doorstep! It certainly made the area – otherwise rather drab – bearable to live in, as did the trees that lined the streets: horse chestnuts, silver birches, limes and cherry trees, all budding, the latter covered in frothy clouds of pink and white.

On this side of the river there were almost no buildings for as far as the eye could see, apart from pylons, so it was easy to imagine you were in the countryside. It was certainly hard to believe you were still in London, less than ten miles from Piccadilly Circus!

He crossed back to the other side of the river by the metal Horseshoe Bridge, as usual stopping on the bridge to gaze at the boats moored in the Marina and alongside the riverbanks, as well as those passing underneath – mostly small cruisers and gaily-painted narrow-boats, plus a few racing skiffs and canoes from the nearby rowing club. He crossed over the bridge and strolled past the café into Springfield Park, walking up to the top of the hill. There he paused for a while, enjoying the panoramic view of the river, the Marshes and the reservoirs spread out below. The park itself was delightful, with its impressive variety of trees and flowers – daffodils, primroses, hyacinths, tulips, rhododendrons, lilac – and its grassy slopes sweeping down to the river.

After a while, he ambled down to the river again and followed the towpath to the Robin Hood, a large pub overlooking the river. It had a patio with wooden tables and benches, where he liked to sit and sup a pint or two while gazing at the view over the Marshes. He hesitated about going in, because he had already been away for over an hour, but couldn't resist. He collected a pint of Guinness, a packet of crisps and sat at his favourite table outside.

The sun was sinking flamboyantly on the Marshes, but it was still warm. It was great to be able to sit outside, he reflected, taking a first sip of his Guinness and already feeling more relaxed. OK, his job was under threat and his girlfriend was pressuring him to do something he didn't want to do, but life wasn't bad. He would fight to keep his job – and the jobs of Roger and Melanie – but if the worst came to the worst, he'd find another one. As for Mary and marriage – he wasn't so sure. He didn't want to get married, wanted to preserve at least the illusion of freedom, but on the other hand he did love her and wanted to make her happy.

The trouble was, as she said, if he didn't marry her, he would never be able to introduce her to his parents. Under pressure from her, he had managed to achieve some sort of reconciliation with them, by going to visit them for the first time since he had come to London. He knew they were offended by the way he had gone off to live in London without contacting them, but they had seemed genuinely pleased to see him. The Return of the Prodigal Son? Maybe, but he still felt uncomfortable with them, as he did with all his family.

That was another consequence of having left home when he was twelve to go to the seminary – he had become disconnected from them, physically and emotionally. In fact, the priests at the seminary – the Ghosters – had actually made a point of brainwashing you to become 'detached' from family ties, from all normal human ties of affection – especially sexual ones of course. How wicked! How stupid! What crackpots they were!

Another consequence was that you became institutionalized, so that going back to live in a family, in a suburban semi, had been difficult. His family didn't really understand that. How could they? Part of his problem with his parents was that he still blamed them for letting him go to the seminary and throwing his life off its normal course. He knew they thought they were doing the right thing, and had no idea of how unhealthy, how sick, the place was, but he still blamed them, in part at least. Of course, they were victims, too, he realised, victims of their Irish Catholic conditioning.

That was another source of tension between them and him, the fact that he hadn't just left the seminary, but the Church as well. That was something he knew they could never accept and one of the reasons he had left home. Would he have lost his faith if he hadn't gone to the seminary? Probably yes – his two brothers weren't exactly passionate believers any more, as far as he could make out. They certainly didn't go to mass, yet they continued to live more or less happily at home. The trouble was, *he* was different, *he* was special, at least as far as his mother was concerned – he used to be her idol, the apple of her eye, her golden boy, because he was going to be a priest and now, in her eyes, he was a degenerate atheist. From golden boy to black sheep! It was sad, but there was nothing he could do about it – except try to show them a bit of filial affection by visiting them occasionally, as he was going to do next week.

Should he take Mary? After all, it was largely because of her prompting, good-hearted as she was, that he was going. No! It was impossible. The very thought of introducing her to his mother made him cringe. There was no way of knowing how his mother would react. She might refuse to let her into the house. There might be an embarrassing scene. And then he would never feel able to go back himself. It was Catch 22! There was only one solution and that was to get married, as Mary wanted. God, between them, they had him well and truly trapped! But even then there was no guarantee that his mother would accept her. He'd have to think about it though. After all, he really did love Mary and wanted to stay with her for the rest of his life.

He looked at his watch – it was nearly eight o' clock! He had been out for almost two hours. He was tempted to have a second pint, but decided he'd better go home. He had to help Mary with her essay, so he needed a more or less clear head. The Guinness had already started to make him feel tipsy, since he had had nothing to eat before going out. He knocked back the last bit, licked the froth off his moustache, stood up and set off back along the river towards Lea Bridge Road, home and her, reciting, 'Friends, Romans and countrymen ...' aloud as he went.

CHAPTER SEVEN

They petitioned, they marched and they protested, but the campaign failed and the EFL department was closed down. The students had to look for new classes and they had to look for new jobs. On the last day they had a party. They were all disappointed, because they had enjoyed working together and become good friends, but they promised to keep in touch. Roger especially was disappointed, although as usual he appeared upbeat.

'Have you found anything yet?' Frank asked him.

'I still have ten hours at this crummy little place in Carnaby Street, acksherly,' Roger said.

As always, Frank couldn't help a smile at the mention of 'Carnaby Street'.

'Yes, Carnaby Street!' Roger chortled, his hand over his mouth, seeing the funny side.

It was funny because Roger's dress-sense was about as far away from Carnaby Street as could be imagined – he always wore a tatty old T-shirt, baggy cord trousers and scruffy barefoot sandals. He looked like a tramp, with his straggly grey hair and battered duffel-bag slung over his shoulder – not to mention his B.O. and rotten teeth.

'Ten hours isn't enough, though, is it?' Frank asked, seriously.

'Oh, it's enough for the time being,' Roger assured him. 'I need time to finish my book off, anyway.'

'Which one is that?' he enquired, impressed by his productivity.

'Oh, it's about a chap called Owen Seaman. I don't suppose you've ever heard of him, have you?'

'Er, I'm afraid not,' he admitted, trying to appear as if he was rifling through an immense mental file of knowledge about obscure writers. *How typical of Roger to write about someone no one has never heard of!*

'Oh, it's all right,' Roger said. 'You don't need to feel ashamed in the least. You wouldn't have heard of him, unless you were a fan of the 1890s like me. You're not, are you?'

'Er, not especially …'

'No? No, of course not. Why should you be? I got into the 1890s at Oxford myself. Anyway, Owen Seaman was quite a big name in the 1890s, though nobody knows him now. He made his name as a parodist – you know, parodying the great names of the day, people like Yeats, Swinburne, Le Gallienne …'

'I see,' Frank interjected, impressed as always by Roger's enthusiasm and erudition, but not sure he wanted to know any more just then. To his relief, Melanie appeared.

'What about you, Mel?' he asked, turning to her. 'Found anything?'

'I've picked up a few hours at Tottenham College,' she said. 'Some EFL and A-level history. Have you managed to find anything?'

'Not really,' he said. 'I've enrolled for a TEFL course at the college where Mary's studying.'

'Where's that?' Melanie asked.

'Waltham College,' he said. 'Walthamstow?'

'Oh, yes,' Roger chipped in. 'William Morris's house is there. I went to see it only last week.'

'Was he in?' Frank couldn't resist joking.

'I hope not!' Roger giggled, hand over mouth. 'He's been dead for nearly a hundred years!'

'Oh, I see,' he laughed. 'Who was he exactly?'

'Oh, dear! He's another 1890s figure, I'm afraid,' said Roger. 'Not just a writer, also a designer. A great socialist, too. Somewhat forgotten and neglected, nowadays, alas. They've turned his house into a museum-cum-gallery. It makes a pleasant excursion, because what used to be his garden is now a rather pretty park. Lloyd Park, it's called.'

'I'll have to pay a visit,' he said, feeling ignorant, as so often, in front of Roger.

'Do you have to pay for this course?' asked Melanie.

'Yes, unfortunately. Two hundred quid.'

'Can you afford that?'

'Not really, but a TEFL diploma is necessary to get a decent job these days, I'm told.'

'Oh, dear,' Roger sighed. 'In that case, I've no chance!'

'Why don't you apply for this course?' he suggested.

'I couldn't afford it,' Roger said, 'but even if I could, I don't think I could do it. I think I'm a bit too old and set in my ways. Anyway, I don't believe you can teach anyone to teach. You can either do it or you can't. It's largely a matter of personality, isn't it?'

'I agree,' he said. 'But you've got to have a piece of paper to prove it these days, apparently, so I thought I'd better get one. The trouble is, for this course you've got to have some teaching, so they can observe you, and I haven't got anything yet.'

'Can't they give you some teaching?' asked Melanie.

'They say they've got no vacancies.'

'What are you going to do then?' she asked.

'I don't know. I don't fancy going back to a private school, but I might have to. I'll see.'

'Well, best of luck,' she said.

'It's so sad,' Roger sighed – he was given to sighing. 'They're so short-sighted! We've got such a good thing going here and they're closing it down.'

'Maybe we should open our own school,' he said, casually.

'What a good idea!' Roger exclaimed.

'Yes, that is a good idea,' Melanie agreed. 'It'd have to be a cooperative, of course.'

'Of course,' they agreed.

'Let's think about it, shall we?' Melanie said.

'Yes. We'll meet and talk about it, shall we?' Roger suggested and they arranged to do so.

'What are you doing in the summer, Frank?' Melanie asked.

'I'm teaching on a summer school.'

'Oh, really, where?'

'In Dublin.'

'Oh, how lovely! Where exactly?'

'At Trinity College. That's a university right in the centre of the city, apparently.'

'Ah, Oscar Wilde's alma mater!' Roger declared. *Trust him to know!*

'How did you find that?' Melanie asked.

'Quite a coincidence, actually. It's being organised by a chap I used to go to school with, called Charles. I met him by chance the other day. He saw me in a play in the Sugawn and recognised me, so we got together. It turns out he was staying with a friend of his just round the corner from me! Anyway, he's just come back from making a packet TEFLing in Kuwait, so we got together for a drink. Haven't seen him for nearly ten years! He's a Mancunian like me, but was a few years ahead of me at school. It turns out he's not only living round the corner from me, but also teaches EFL like me. Small world!'

'How amazing!' exclaimed Melanie .

'Dublin! I envy you!' exclaimed Roger.

'Yes, it should be good,' he said. He was really looking forward to it – he would have a few weeks in Ireland and make a bit of money at the same time. 'What about you, Roger?'

'Oh, I'll be teaching in Carnaby Street and finishing my book,' he said.

Melanie moved away to talk to some students, so he decided it was safe to ask Roger about the Turkish girl he had 'recommended'.

'Any luck with Fatimah?' .

'Alas, no,' Roger sighed. 'I invited her out, but she told me she lives with her uncle, who runs a kebab shop, and isn't allowed out on her own except to go to school. So I thought I'd better beat a hasty retreat. I had visions of an irate Turk chasing me with a kebab knife!' Fran remembered having exactly the same thought about Flora, the Greek-Cypriot girl he had fancied.

'And making kebabs of your bollocks,' he quipped, making Roger dissolve into a fit of the giggles, both hands over his mouth.

'Nobody else in your sights?' he asked, when Roger had recovered.

'Oh, there are plenty I fancy, but, alas, it doesn't seem to be reciprocal!'

'Oh. I'm sorry.' He really did feel sorry for Roger – he was hopeless with women. If only he'd do something about his appearance, especially his teeth! He was tempted to mention it again, but didn't dare. 'You must get lonely.'

'Yes, indeed, life is lonely sometimes,' Roger sighed. 'How's Mary, by the way?'

'Oh, she's OK, thanks. She's taking her English O-level today. I hope she passes.' She should do, he thought – he had spent enough time coaching her.

'I'm sure she will,' Roger nodded, reassuringly. 'You're very lucky there, aren't you?'

'How do you mean?'

'Mary. She's got such a good heart. You should cherish her.'

'I do,' he said, touched.

'Oh, I know you do,' he said. 'You look after her very well. I just wish I could find a girl like that.'

'I'm sure you'll find someone sooner or later.'

He wasn't so sure really – he couldn't actually imagine any girl wanting to kiss Roger, with those hideous teeth, not to mention the bad breath and BO.

'I'm starting to wonder!' he said. 'I wish I knew what I was doing wrong!'

This was yet another chance to tell him, he thought, but after the last rebuff, still didn't dare.

'God, Roger, don't ask me – I'm no expert on women!' he laughed. If only he knew how 'inexpert' he was!

'You seem to have a lot more success than me! At least you've got Mary.'

'Yes, I've struck lucky there, I know.'

'Very lucky,' he insisted, munching yet another sausage roll. He noticed Roger was getting a pronounced paunch, to add to his image problems.

'Yes. Well, I suppose we'd better circulate among the students a bit, hadn't we?' he said. 'This is your chance to chat a few of them up. There's Tina and Simona over there. Why don't you go and practise your Italian on them?'

'Mm, yes, you're right, I will,' he said, making a beeline for two young Italian girls.

'Catch you later,' he said, feeling guilty about inflicting Roger on them, and turned to chat to Woje and Grazna, the young Polish couple in his Proficiency class.

The summer turned out not too badly in the end – Mary passed her O-levels, the college where he had enrolled for the TEFL course gave him a job for September and he taught for six weeks on the summer school in Dublin.

He really enjoyed Dublin, because he had free accommodation in a student flat in Trinity College, the Oxford-style university in the centre of the city, and he only had to teach in the mornings. In the afternoons, he was paid to take students – mostly French, German, Spanish and Italian – out to interesting places in and around Dublin, places such as Howth Head, Joyce's martello tower at Sandycove, the Hill of Tara, Glendalough and Monasterboice. In the evenings, he took them out to listen to Irish music in pubs and concerts or to the theatre – for all of which he was paid!

It was great – he was in his favourite country, he had money in his pocket, so he could afford to go out every night, which he did, and he enjoyed both teaching and socialising with the students. There were some attractive women on the course too, but he was careful not to get too friendly with them, because he didn't want to be unfaithful to Mary.

Mary came to stay with him for the last week and after the summer school they went with Charles, the organiser, on a trip around the south-west of Ireland, in Charles's mini. He had become friendly with Charles, although he wasn't Irish, was four years older and they hadn't been friends at the seminary – in fact, Charles had once been 'First Auxiliary', or head prefect, so something of an authority figure.

They spent a lot of time reminiscing about the seminary – usually over a jar or two of Guinness – and he was pleased to find Charles was just as jaundiced as he about the place and some of the people, especially the Director. Charles was highly intelligent and a shrewd judge of character, so had some perceptive views of priests and students they had both known. All the same, he was shocked by what Frank told him about the Director, even though he didn't tell him everything.

'Actually, I did try to tell him once I thought his behaviour was improper,' Charles informed him. 'When I was First Auxiliary. Ah, what heady heights!' They were enjoying a pint of Guinness in a pub in Lisdoonvarna, having booked into a bed and breakfast, where Mary was still resting.

'Did you? What did he say?'

'Oh, he was indignant, predictably, told me he wasn't doing anything wrong, it was only what would be done in hospital and, anyway, it was none of my business.'

'That was just like him, to try and justify it on 'medical' grounds. So you didn't pursue it?'

'No. I wish I had now, after what you've told me. I'd no idea he went that far!'

'He should have been defrocked!' he laughed, trying to make a joke of it.

'He should have been bloody arrested and locked up for child abuse. Do you remember the way he flogged that kid, Cooper, in the study hall, in front of everyone?'

'I certainly do. He was in my class, Form One, only twelve years old like me. It was awful. I was terrified! I kept wishing one of the bigger kids would stop him. He seemed to go berserk, didn't he? What was it he kept shouting, while he flogged him with that bloody cosh – "I'll break you! I'll break your stubborn pride!" I really thought he was going to kill him!'

'I know. It was shocking. I wanted to stop him. I regret to this day I didn't. The poor little sod must've been traumatised for life. He left soon afterwards, didn't he?'

'The swine expelled him next day. Did him a favour, I suppose. Imagine being taken away from the bosom of your family at the age of twelve to a place like that, run by a bunch of transvestites, to be terrorised by that bastard! It was criminal.'

'It was. He should have been prosecuted.'

'It's too late now, of course.' He couldn't help feeling sad about it.

'I thought there was something fishy about the way he was supposed to have dropped dead so suddenly. Now I understand. He topped himself.'

'Yeah. Sad, even so.'

'He was a fucker. Fucking around with little boys.'

'Remember that strap he used to use?' Frank said, to steer the subject away slightly.

'That fucking strap!' Charles exclaimed. 'What was it made of – whalebone and leather?'

'That's right. It was weighted with lead, too, apparently. It was more like a cosh than a strap.'

'It was a fucking offensive weapon!' Charles declared. His language tended to become somewhat colourful after a few drinks, he had noticed. But so did his own!

'Yes,' he laughed. 'He got it from the Dean of Studies, didn't he? Apparently, he brought a whole armoury of them over from Ireland with him.'

'He was another fucking head-case!' Charles declared.

'Yeah. A real head-banger!' he agreed.

Charles laughed. 'That's a good expression! Where's it from?'

'Oh, I think it's Mancunian,' he laughed. Charles was a Mancunian like himself, which was something else they had in common, as well as their shared history.

'Is it? I haven't heard that one before. I'll have to put it in my vocabulary.'

''Lexis', you mean,' he said, making fun of TEFL jargon, as they enjoyed doing.

'Lexis,' Charles nodded solemnly. 'Do you remember the way he used to stand on a chair when he was teaching singing class, he was such a short-arse?'

'Yeah,' he laughed. 'A right little twerp, wasn't he? Used to enjoy terrorising us nippers though.'

'He was another bully, that's why.'

'Yes, I suppose so. Terrible temper. Remember the way he used to fling a liber at you if you got a note wrong?' The 'Liber Usualis' was the brick-like tome they used in singing class for Gregorian chant.

'I certainly do,' said Charles. 'I was the organist, remember. He used to throw one at me if I played a bum note!'

'He really was a nutter,' he laughed, shaking his head. It was funny looking back, but it hadn't been so funny then …

'Did you ever serve mass for him?' asked Charles.

'No, thank God!'

'He chucked the missal at me once. Hit me, too.'

'That must have hurt!' he laughed. 'Must have thought it was a missile, not a missal!'

'It's even heavier than a fucking liber, I can tell you! At the end of mass, when he was divesting, he used to fling his vestments on the floor if you weren't quick enough to take them. He was a complete madman. Do you know where he is now?'

'No. In a mental asylum?' he suggested.

'He's actually not very far from here. At Blackrock College.'

That was the order's school in Dun Laoghaire, just down the coast from Dublin.

'You're kidding!'

'I'm not.'

'How do you know?'

'Big Jake told me.'

'Big Jake' was the nickname of another chap who had been in the seminary with them, who Charles was still in contact with. It was funny, he reflected, how they reverted to juvenile nicknames when talking about the past. It made him feel slightly uncomfortable.

'That's incredible!' he said. 'Do you think he's still as barmy as ever?'

'I daresay,' Charles replied. 'People don't change, do they?'

'Christ, I feel sorry for the kids there, then.'

'Maybe we should go and duff *him* up.'

'Yes,' he laughed, adding seriously: 'What we really ought to do is take out legal proceedings against him. Prosecute him for child abuse. Maybe it's not too late in his case.'

'Maybe it's not,' Charles agreed. 'Maybe we should. I don't think we should let the bastard get away with it scot-free, do you?'

'No, I don't,' he replied. 'The trouble is, I don't want to go back, if you see what I mean. I want to move on, forget about the past. I try not to think about it and I never talk about it – except with someone like you, of course.'

'I know what you mean. I'm exactly the same. I never tell anyone. Haven't you told Mary?'

'Yes, but not everything. Don't tell her what I've just told you, will you?'

'No, of course not.'

'I don't really like talking about it, even with her. She's always trying to dig it out of me. She thinks I ought to talk about it, it's wrong to suppress it.'

'I don't think we suppress it, just because we don't want to talk about it all the time. We want to get on with our lives, look forward, not back.'

'Exactly. It's funny, in a way it all seems unreal to me now, like a dream – a rather bad dream – or even another life. It's only seven years since I left, but it feels like – like light years away.'

'I know. It's such a bizarre way of life, when you think about it. Why did you leave, by the way? The usual reason?'

'What's that?'

'Sex.'

'No, actually. At least, not consciously. I think I could live without sex, if I wanted to. If I had a good reason to.' Was he deluding himself, he wondered?

'So why?'

'I lost my faith, I suppose.' It pained him to admit it, even after all this time.

'You mean …?'

'The whole caboodle – God, Catholicism, the Church …'

'I see. So you don't go to mass any more?'

'No. Nor confession. Nor rosary, sermon and benediction,' he joked, making him laugh. 'What about you?'

'I still believe in God, if that's what you mean. I mean, I think there must be somebody or something up there that started it all off. I still go to mass, too, but more for the liturgy than anything, so I suppose I'm still a practising Catholic of sorts. I don't believe all the claptrap about indulgences and so on though. I don't go to confession any more either.'

'So why did *you* leave, exactly?'

'Well, partly because the Ghosters seemed to be stuck in the nineteenth century – they were a nineteenth-century invention, after all. But mainly because of women.'

'Women?'

'Yes, you know, those strange creatures that constitute half of the world's population?'

He laughed. 'You mean, you decided you couldn't live without them?'

'Absolutely. There were a few very fuckable ones on the course, weren't there?'

'Yes, there were, I suppose,' he agreed, slightly shocked by Charles's 'lexis'.

'Did you manage to get off with any of them?'

'No,' he shook his head. 'I was tempted, but I have got a girlfriend, you know.'

'A very nice one, too. I'm looking for one myself.'

'Are you? A girlfriend?'

'A wife.'

'You want to get married?'

'As soon as possible.'

'Why?'

'I want to start a family. Have a couple of kids. I am thirty-two, you know. Not getting any younger. Tempus fugit and all that. I want a business partner, too.'

'I see. Nobody on the course you fancied?'

'There was one, actually. She was in the lower level, so you might not remember her. Nadia. Polish-French girl. Unpronounceable Polish surname. Very Parisienne.'

'Oh, yeah, I remember her. Quite attractive. Not very good pronunciation.'

'Bloody awful! I'll have to give her some private lessons when I go back to Paris. Nudge, nudge.'

'You've arranged to see her, have you?'

'I certainly have. She lives in Paris, fortunately. I invited her to come with us on this trip, but she had to go back to work.'

'What does she do?'

'She's some sort of accountant. Not an accountant, exactly. Book-keeper – is that the English expression?'

'I suppose so. She sounds as if she might be a useful business partner, then.'

'Yes. I don't just want her as a business partner though. I want her to be the mother of my children, too. What about you?'

'What about me?'

'Are you going to get married?'

'I don't want to, but Mary does. She's trying to pressure me into it. It's a bit of a problem between us.'

'Why don't you want to get married?'

'Well, first, I don't want to get married in a Catholic church, which is what she wants, of course. And second, I just have this irrational fear of being trapped. It's got something to do with the seminary, I suppose. I think I hate the idea of being bound by vows or a legal contract of any kind. Not that I let the vows prevent me from leaving the seminary.'

'Didn't you get dispensed from your vows?'

'No. I couldn't wait. They didn't mean anything to me by then, anyway.'

'So you're still under vows of poverty, chastity and obedience?'

'Yes, I suppose so,' he laughed. 'I don't have much choice about the poverty. I think I can do without the chastity though. And I was never very good at obedience.'

'Yes, you were always a bit of a rebel, as I remember.'

'Yes, a fully paid-up member of the awkward squad,' he laughed. 'I do like to challenge the accepted order, I suppose. Provide a bit of opposition. No, obedience was never my strong point. Especially if I don't have any respect for those I'm supposed to obey.'

'I'm the same, believe me. Lucky we never had to go in the army, isn't it?'

'Yeah. I think the seminary was worse, mind you.'

'I'm sure it was. It was like being in a fucking concentration camp. At least squaddies get out to play once in a while.'

'Yeah. When you think about it, it's a bloody miracle any of us managed to emerge even half-normal.'

'I don't think we are normal, actually. But then again, who is normal?'

'How do you mean?'

'Well, I think we've all been mentally and emotionally scarred to some extent by the experience. Don't you?'

'I suppose so.' He didn't really want to pursue this line of enquiry. 'I like to think I'm reasonably sane and well-balanced, though.'

'Me too, but maybe we're the lucky ones.'

'Maybe,' he agreed, not sure if he was one of the lucky ones, in fact, wondering if he should reveal all of his dark secret to Charles. 'I'm just bloody glad I escaped when I was twenty-one, before too much damage had been done, while I had a bit of my youth left. I feel sorry for those who leave later, especially after they're ordained. It must be almost impossible for them.' He wanted to divert the conversation away from himself.

'Some of them just end up topping themselves, of course. Like Pat Murphy.' Pat Murphy was a young priest they had both known.

'Oh, Christ, he didn't, did he?' he gasped, shocked not just by the information, but Charles's flippant choice of expression. It was one of his habits, he had noticed, to toss out little conversational grenades like this. 'That's tragic! What did he do?'

'Apparently, he threw himself under an underground train. In London.'

'Oh, God, no!' he exclaimed, horrified.

It was just what he didn't want to hear. It was what Mark had done. He had felt like doing it himself for a while. Well, not throwing himself under a train – that was too gruesome – but throwing himself into a river or something. Disposing of himself, anyway. He wondered if he should tell Charles, but decided not to. The memory was too painful.

'Why on earth did he do that?' he asked, shutting the memory out.

'He couldn't cope. He was an alcoholic, of course. He became an alcoholic in Africa. Who wouldn't, stuck on your own in the middle of the fucking African bush. It'd drive anyone to drink.'

'Didn't he get into trouble with a woman?'

'Yeah, apparently he was screwing some black woman out there. Got her pregnant. That's why they brought him home and stuck him back with us. Good thinking! Treated him like shit. No fucking support for the poor bloke after he left, of course, or after they chucked him out. Or the woman and kid. No Christian charity there, the callous bastards!'

'That's terrible. Tragic. I didn't know that.' He shook his head sadly, thinking, '*There but for the grace of God ...*' 'Stories like that really do make you realise how lucky you are, don't they?' he said.

'There are probably lots of similar stories, if we only knew. I mean, screwed-up people, screwed-up lives.'

'I suppose so. I was pretty screwed-up myself for a while after I left. Maybe I still am!' He was only half-joking.

'What did you do after you left?'

'I was too depressed to do anything for a few months. I think I was in a state of shock. Then I did a series of stupid, menial jobs, such as milkman, van driver, encyclopaedia salesman – didn't sell a single one – even worked in Kellogg's cornflake factory, till I went to uni. I didn't want to go to uni, because I couldn't face the thought of writing essays and doing exams, but my parents pressured me into going. I don't know how I managed to get through it, to be honest, I was in such a state of depression. Somehow or other, I managed to pass my finals and get a half-decent degree as well. Bloody miracle! After my degree I did a PGCE at Liverpool Uni., then I went to London.'

'Why did you go to London?'

'I needed to get away from home, needed to be free. It's only after I went to London that I started to feel free, could forget about the past, could be myself. Could reinvent myself, if you like. Also, I'd decided I didn't want to try and teach English lit. to fourteen-year-olds, most of whom weren't really interested, for the rest of my life – three months' teaching practice in a grammar school in Liverpool was enough to tell me that – so I decided to teach EFL to adults, for which London is the place, of course.' It wasn't the whole truth, but …

'Did you have a job there?'

'No. I just put all my worldly possessions in a couple of bags, drove down in the old banger I used to have and started looking for a place to live and a job. Took me a week. I slept in the car a couple of nights – bloody cold and uncomfortable, I can tell you – and in hostels. Met a few funny characters in those places! I was starting to run out of money and thinking about giving up, when I found a room and a job on the same day.'

'The room's OK. Where did you find a job?'

'Oh, a 'hole-in-the-wall' private school in Soho. Shakespeare School of English, it was called. Run by this fat, pompous, public-school twit called William St. John-Fortescue. The school was a bit of a racket – a bit of a visa shop – but it was OK. Met my first girlfriend there. A couple of girlfriends, actually.'

'Tell me more!'

'The first one was called Marina. She was Yugoslav. From Belgrade. Only eighteen. About to go to medical school. Very bright. Attractive, too.'

'Did you screw her?'

'She was the first girl I ever actually slept with. Not that I told her that – she thought I was really experienced, being six years older than her. I did have a relationship with a girl next door in Manchester, but she wouldn't sleep with me – she was only sixteen, a schoolgirl, doing her O-levels. It was the first time for the Yugoslav girl, too. We were both technically virgins, I suppose.'

'What was she like?'

'In bed? Very passionate. But she wouldn't let me actually, you know, fuck her. She was terrified of getting pregnant.'

'Quite right, too.'

'Sure. The trouble is, she wouldn't even let me use a condom. Not that I'd ever used one before!'

'Did you have any?'

'I bought some. I was too embarrassed to buy them in a chemist's, of course, so I bought some from a machine in a gents' toilet. I even felt embarrassed doing that! Waited till the toilet was empty. Felt as if I was committing a mortal bloody sin! That's Catholicism for you!'

He realised the alcohol was loosening his tongue to the point of garrulousness and wondered if he would regret telling Charles all this in the morning, but carried on. 'Actually, she did agree to try and use a condom eventually, but – irony of ironies – when we tried to use one, I couldn't do it.'

'You mean, you couldn't get a hard-on?'

'I got a hard-on, but couldn't keep it up. It was so fucking frustrating, if you'll pardon the pun.'

'So what happened?'

'Oh, it didn't matter too much. Not to me, anyway. It wasn't just about sex. I mean, I really was in love with this girl. In fact, I almost married her.' He paused to take a swig of Guinness. Had he really loved her, he wondered, or had he been using her?

'Go on! I thought you didn't believe in marriage!'

'Well, I didn't, and I don't, but I agreed to marry her, because she wanted to stay in Britain, so it was partly a marriage of convenience. It wasn't just that though – I really *wanted* to marry her. We actually arranged the register office and everything.'

'So what happened?'

'She didn't turn up.'

'You're kidding!'

'I'm not,' he laughed bitterly. 'She scarpered off back to Yugoslavia instead.'

'Fuck me! You must've been devastated!'

'I was, I suppose. It took me quite a while to get over it.' Was he over it even now, he wondered?

'Why did she do a runner though?'

'I don't know. I think she just got cold feet about the whole idea.

She used to tell me she felt guilty about deserting her country – they're very patriotic. She reckons Yugoslavia is going to disintegrate completely when Tito dies, which is liable to happen any day, apparently.'

'I see. Pretty unforgivable thing to do though. Do you still have any contact?'

'No. I've never really forgiven her, to be honest. And no more marriages of convenience. No more marriage!'

'Who was the second one?'

'She was Greek. Very different. Her name was Kalli. She worked as a singer in Greek restaurants. I used to go and listen, get free wine and food. She was a belly-dancer, too, believe it or not! She told me she'd been an actress and a model in Greece, gave me a photo of herself as a model, which I've still got somewhere. She was very attractive. Very sexy. I really fancied her. Couldn't believe my luck when she asked me to go for a drink with her. Yes, *she* invited *me*. I wouldn't have had the nerve to ask her. She told me she wanted to ask me for a favour. Anyway, we ended up having a passionate relationship. She was a bit of a bombshell in bed, I must say. Taught me a thing or two, I can tell you!'

'So how did it end?'

'It turned out the favour she wanted was for me to marry her, so she could stay in Britain. She left Greece because of the political situation, you know, the Colonels and all that.'

'What did you say?'

'Well, of course, I couldn't bring myself to do it, especially after what had happened with the Yugoslav girl. I was afraid of the illegality, too. Also, I couldn't help suspecting she was using me.'

'So you refused?'

'Yes. I sort of regret it now. What do you think?'

'I don't blame you. I don't think I'd do it. Too dangerous. Where is she now?'

'I'm not sure. I don't know if she went back to Greece – I hope she's safe if she did – or if she's still around London, illegally. Anyway, I think it's put me off marriage of any kind for life.'

'Mary won't like that.'

'No, I know she won't.' At that moment Mary came into the pub.

'Speak of the devil!' Charles exclaimed.

'Are you two still yakking about that seminary?' she asked.

'No, we're talking about you, actually,' Charles riposted.

'Oh, yes? And what have you been saying behind my back?' she demanded, touchily. God, she was so sensitive, so insecure, he thought!

'I was just telling Frank that if I were he, I'd marry you tomorrow, darling,' Charles declared, grandly.

'You see,' she said, sitting down and giving him a playful dig in the ribs.

'Well, please invite me to the wedding,' he joked.

'You're so stubborn, aren't you?' she said.

'Don't worry, I'll work on him for you,' Charles told her. 'What can I get you to drink, my darling?'

'Orange and lemon with ice, please, Charles,' she said, playing up to him.

'It's my round, I'll get it,' he said, standing up, glad of the excuse to escape to the bar for a few minutes.

He was slightly irked with Charles for taking her side, though he knew he was only joking. Or was he? He could tell he liked her. She looked very pretty tonight, he noticed, glancing over at her talking and laughing animatedly with him – she was wearing a green velvet dress and a white ribbon in her long blonde hair, which she had obviously washed for the occasion. He wondered if she fancied Charles. They did seem to hit it off well together. And Charles wouldn't be a bad catch. Maybe he ought to marry her, before he lost her.

CHAPTER EIGHT

'I'm afraid I'll have to withdraw from the course – I can't find any teaching.'

It was early September. He had come back from Ireland and gone to the college to see the lecturer in charge of EFL, a bespectacled, middle-aged woman of ample proportions called Bertha – a name that somehow suited her.

'Oh, no, you can't do that!' she exclaimed, spraying bits of the roll she was chomping on all over him. 'We need well-qualified people like you. I'm sure we can find you some hours. Let me look at the timetable.' She scrabbled about among the heaps of papers, books and other detritus on her desk, pulled out a bulging loose-leaf file and opened it, spilling leaves on the floor.

'You need two different levels for observation purposes, don't you? I can give you eight hours elementary and eight hours proficiency,' she said, ripping another chunk out of the roll and swilling it back with coffee from a plastic cup on the desk. 'That's sixteen hours. Would that be sufficient?' she asked, masticating on the roll and spraying bits of it around the office as she spoke.

'That would be great, thanks,' he said, trying to keep out of range, which was difficult, because the office was little more than a cupboard, almost filled by the desk and a couple of filing cabinets, with heaps of books and papers on every available surface. She herself filled up most of what space was left. 'God, what a funny woman!' he thought, but at least it looked as if he had landed a job, which was a great relief.

'Do you think you'll be able to manage a proficiency class?' she enquired, swilling down another mouthful of the roll with coffee from the plastic cup, spilling some of it over her pneumatic bosom.

'Well, I have got an honours degree in English language and literature,' he said, smiling.

'Have you? Yes, it's on your CV, isn't it? Where is that?' She scrabbled about among the debris on the desk again, then in the drawers and eventually fished out a piece of crumpled paper. 'Here it is! Oh, you've got a Cert. Ed., too, I see. From Liverpool. How did you find that?'

'Well, you just go straight down the East Lancs Road from Manchester,' he was tempted to quip, but thought better of it – he might lose the job before he got it!

'It was quite useful, I suppose,' he fibbed – in fact, it had been a waste of time, pedagogically-speaking. 'Especially the three months' practical,' he added. That had been useful in a sense, because it had made him realise he didn't want to spend the next forty years of his life trying to teach English literature to unappreciative adolescents, especially adolescent boys.

'Where did you do that?' she asked, still munching.

'A boys' grammar school in Liverpool,' he told her, wondering why she was asking.

'Why didn't you go into secondary school teaching, then?' she asked, wreaking yet further destruction on the roll.

God, it was almost as if she suspected something, but of course, she couldn't, could she? 'Well, I just like the idea of teaching adults, people who are a bit more mature and motivated than kids,' he replied uncomfortably. It was only half-true, but he couldn't tell her – or anybody – the other reason.

'So what gave you the idea of going into TEFL?' she asked, stuffing the last of the roll into her mouth with both hands, taking another slurp of coffee from the plastic cup, spilling some again, and gobbling it up.

'Oh, I got the idea of doing EFL from an Iranian student I lived with at uni. He was an engineering student and asked me to help him with his English, so I did and I found it very rewarding.'

'And you've already done three years at Hackney College, is that right?'

'That's right. I was actually in charge of the department for most of that time.' He immediately realised it might have been a mistake to mention this – she might feel threatened.

'So why did you leave Hackney?'

'They closed the department down. Cuts.'

'That's disgraceful! Did you resist?'

'Oh, yes, but to no avail.'

'Well, their loss is our gain.'

'I hope so!'

'I'm sure it will be, dear. I'll draw up a timetable and a contract for you to sign.'

'When do I start then?' he asked, amused but touched by the 'dear'. Maybe the old bag wasn't as bad as she appeared!

'We're enrolling this week. Classes start on Monday. Can you pop back in tomorrow to collect the timetable, sign the contract and so on? I'll brief you a bit more then, too.'

'That's fine, thanks.' He stood up to go.

'Excuse me if I don't stand up.'

'That's all right, thanks. I'll see you tomorrow,' he said, opening the door and squeezing out, glad to make his escape – he had started to feel claustrophobic in the cluttered, cupboard-like office, especially since Bertha filled most of the space with her hippo-like bulk and had table manners to match.

'God, what a strange woman!' he thought, making his way back along the rather sterile, cream-painted corridor to the exit – but at least he had a job again! Walking down the broad front steps, he suddenly realised how demoralised he had been without one. He was a lecturer again! He could start earning money again! No more queuing up for the dole!

Reaching the front gates, he stopped and turned to look back at the college. It was an impressive, wide, red-brick building, with a mock-Greek, colonnaded entrance in the middle, from which a broad flight of steps ran down to lawns, where flowers slept in beds and weeping-willows wept. To either side of the lawns there were car parks, almost empty at this time of year.

It was certainly more impressive-looking than his previous college, and coming here with Mary, he had often thought how proud and pleased he would be to teach at such a place. Now he actually had a job here! It was incredible! Every cloud had a silver lining! Mary would be so pleased – it meant they could start saving to buy a house.

He decided to go to a pub for lunch and a drink to celebrate. There was a pub he had noticed, called 'The Bell', at the junction farther down the main road. He'd give that a try, he thought, setting off along the main road, past the town hall next door. This was an even bigger, more impressive building than the college, though somewhat Nazi-looking in architecture, built of white stone, with a green clock tower on top, and a large fountain and even more spacious lawns and flower beds in front.

Next to the town hall were the magistrates' courts, also somewhat fascist-looking, with their grey concrete walls, then a row of small shops – stationery, photography, post office, sandwich bar, even a sex shop – and finally the pub. This was a handsome, ornate, Edwardian-looking building on the corner of the junction, with a large bell hanging outside.

He went in through the swing doors into a large, comfortable-looking, oak-panelled lounge with wooden tables and red leatherette armchairs. He immediately felt at home – it reminded him of the pub they had lived in when he was a boy, just before he went to the seminary, which he had happy memories of. It was a good omen, he sensed, going up to the bar to order himself a pint of Guinness and sandwich – somehow he thought he was going to enjoy working at Waltham College!

'Oh, that's really good news!' Mary exclaimed, throwing her arms around his neck and kissing him.

'Yes,' he beamed, sitting in the armchair with her on his lap, her arms around his neck, his around her slender waist.

'I knew you'd get something!' she enthused.

'Did you? How?'

'It's obvious you're a good teacher. You're well-qualified, you've got experience and – well, it's obvious, just from the way you look, the way you speak, the way you are.'

'Well, thank you for the vote of confidence!'

'Is it full-time?'

'No, sixteen hours a week. It's enough. I don't want to be full-time.'

'I know. That's all right.'

'It's only a one-year contract, too, so I won't get paid during the holidays. I'll still have to do the summer-school.'

'I'm sure Charles will give you a job in Dublin again.'

'I hope so.'

'I'm sure he will. You did a good job for him this year. He'd better!'

'Thanks,' he laughed. 'What if the college doesn't renew my contract next year though?'

'They will, don't worry. Once they see how good you are. So, does it mean we can buy a house?'

'I suppose so.'

'Don't you want to?'

'Yes, of course I do. I don't want to live in a bed-sitter for the rest of my life!'

'Can we get married, too?'

'God, you know how to put the pressure on, don't you!'

'Can we, Fran? Please say yes! You don't have to believe in it or anything.'

'Why do you want to get married?'

'Oh, Fran, you know why!'

'No, I don't. Tell me!'

'It would make my mammy and daddy happy.'

'They're very nice people, but I'm not getting married just to make them happy.'

'Oh, Fran, you're so stubborn! It's not just to make them happy. It'd make me happy, too. You said you wanted to make me happy, didn't you?'

'Yes. God, talk about emotional blackmail!'

'What a horrible thing to say! All right, if you don't want to marry me.' She took her arms from around his neck and folded them, pouting.

'I'm sorry. Don't go all sulky on me now. I didn't say I didn't want to marry you, did I?' He pulled her towards him. 'Just tell me why getting married would make you happy. Aren't you happy as we are?' He realised this was a 'game' he might easily lose.

'Of course I'm happy. I love you. We love each other, don't we?'

'Exactly. So why do we need to get married?'

'Oh, Fran! I just want to have a special day, when I can wear a white dress, walk down the aisle, invite all our family and friends, have a party, let the whole world know we're together for ever. I've dreamed of it ever since I was a little girl. I know it may sound silly to you, but to me it would mean so much. It's probably the only special day I'll ever have. It's only one day. That's all I'm asking – *one* day.'

'Oh, all right, I suppose so,' he shrugged. 'Since you put it like that.'

He could hardly believe he had said it, but he didn't have the energy – or the heart – to resist her any more. She had gradually worn his defences down, not just with words, but with love and affection. And he really did want to make her happy. He was just not sure if he was qualified to.

'Oh, Fran, do you mean it? Are you serious? We can get married?' She stared at him in delighted amazement.

'If it makes you happy,' he shrugged.

'Oh, Fran, don't be like that! Try to sound happy!'

'I am happy! That's the point – I'm happy as I am!' He couldn't resist firing a last shot, pointless as it might be.

'I know. I am too. But you'll enjoy it. You will.'

'I don't know about that! When?'

'What about next summer? Say July. We can have a honeymoon in Ireland, then do the summer school in Dublin. What do you say?'

'All right,' he shrugged, giving in completely. 'Who are you going to invite?'

'Everyone! All our family and friends!'

'Including my parents?'

'Of course! You have to invite them! That's half the idea, to make them accept you and me together.'

'They won't come,' he said, a sudden sinking sensation in his stomach.

'What? They won't go to their own son's wedding? What parents wouldn't go to their own son's wedding? Of course they will, Fran! If you invite them. As long as it's in a Catholic church, of course.'

If she thought *he* was stubborn, she didn't know how stubborn his parents could be! Also, she was forgetting that his mother had once hoped to see her son ordained a priest, so a wedding was very much second best, a wife someone to resent, to be jealous of …

'Does it have to be in a Catholic church? Couldn't it just be in a register office?' He knew he was wasting his breath, but felt he had to put up some last-ditch resistance.

'Oh, Fran – I'm not getting married in a register office! I want to do it properly! I don't think my mammy and daddy would go to a register office, never mind yours.'

'I suppose not,' he admitted, caving in.

'You agree, then?'

'I suppose so – if it makes you happy.'

'I want you to be happy about it, too.'

'Well, you know how I feel.'

'Please, Fran! It's only one day! Try to be positive.'

'All right, all right, I'll try.'

'Good boy. Will you tell your parents?'

'What?'

'That we're getting married!'

'Oh, God, I don't know.'

'What don't you know?'

'How to tell them. You mean, phone them? Write to them?'

'No. I think we should visit them and tell them in person.'

'Both of us?'

'Yes. Tell them you're visiting them, but I'll come with you. They won't shut the door in my face, will they?'

'They might!' He had a horrible sense of foreboding.

'Fran, they're not monsters!'

'My mother's a wonderful woman in many ways, but she can be a bit of a dragon, I'm afraid.'

'Don't worry. I'll talk to her. It'll be all right, you'll see.'

'I hope so.' Unfortunately, what he could 'see' was trouble with a capital T, to quote the Horslips song.

'When can we go then?'

'I don't know. Maybe in a few weeks. After I've settled into my new job.'

'Are you going to tell them about that?'

'Do you think I should?'

'Of course! They're your parents! They'll be pleased for you.'

'I don't know about that. They don't seem to take much interest in me or my life.'

'Why do you say that?'

'Well, they've never come to see me here in London, have they?'

'I'm sure they'll come to your wedding. It'll be a way of reconciliation.'

'I just hope you're right.' Maybe she was. Maybe he was too prejudiced. After all, his worldview had been badly warped.

'Don't you trust me?'

'Yes, I do. I know you've got good instincts in these things.'

'Do you want to phone them now?'

'No. I'll wait till I get my contract tomorrow. I'll phone them tomorrow evening.'

'Promise?'

'Promise.'

'I love you, Frank Walsh,' she declared, flinging her arms around his neck again and giving him a kiss. 'Do you love me?'

'Of course I love you,' he said, giving her a squeeze.

He did love her, but he had a horrible feeling that somehow they had set a time-bomb ticking …

'Get that hoor out of my house!'

His mother, still in her nurse's uniform, had come home from work to find Mary and him chatting with his father in the kitchen. He could tell immediately she was a bit tipsy. She must have had a sherry or two with the station-master at the station again.

'Ahem, Nan, there's no need for that,' his father admonished her in his mild-mannered way.

'Get her OUT!' his mother shouted, slamming the kitchen door shut and storming unsteadily upstairs.

'I'll go and speak to her,' his father said, standing up, embarrassed – he hated any kind of 'scene'.

'No, I'll go,' Frank offered, standing up too, shocked and embarrassed himself, though he had been afraid of something like this.

He left Mary sitting at the kitchen table, looking an even whiter shade of pale than usual, went upstairs and knocked on his mother's bedroom door. There was no answer, so he opened it and went in. His mother was sitting in bed, in her petticoat, having taken off her uniform. He noticed an open sherry bottle on the dressing-table beside her.

'What's wrong, Mum?' he asked, choking.

'I don't want that hoor in my house!' she snarled. 'Get her out and don't bring her back!'

'She's not a 'hoor',' he said, calmly. 'You've no right to call her that.'

'I can call her what I like!' she yelled. 'She is a hoor! She's been sleeping with you, hasn't she?'

'That doesn't make her a hoor,' he protested, choking back anger.

'It does in my book!'

'I'm going to marry her.'

'Marry her if you want! What the divil do I care? You don't care about me or any of us any more!'

'I was going to ask you to come to the wedding.'

'Are you going to marry her in a Catholic church?'

'Of course. She *is* a Catholic.'

'But you're not! You don't go to mass, do you? You don't even believe in God any more! Sure, it'd be a mockery!' Unfortunately, this was all true.

'I'm going to marry her anyway,' he repeated, suppressing his anger.

'Marry *her*! A spastic as well as a hoor!'

'My God! *You're* not even a Christian, never mind a Catholic!' he shouted back at her, unable to contain his anger any longer, then rushed out of the room and downstairs to the kitchen, where Mary and his father were still sitting at the table in embarrassed silence.

'Come on, we'd better go,' he said to Mary, putting his jacket on.

'Ahem, I'm sorry, Fran,' his father said, standing up, mortified.

'It's all right, Dad,' he said, feeling sorry for him. 'I think it's better if we leave though. Come on, Mary, let's go.' Mary was still sitting at the table, looking dazed. Oh, God, he thought, I hope she's not going to have a fit! 'Mary, come on, let's go,' he told her, helping her up, taking her by the arm and leading her to the door.

'Bye,' he said, shaking hands with his father. 'Thanks for the tea.'

'I'm sorry,' his father said to Mary, shaking hands with her, but she seemed too stunned to reply.

'Bye,' he said again, ushering her out of the back door and into the car, getting in himself and driving away quickly.

'Well, that was a bit of a disaster,' he said, when they were safely back on the road to London.

She didn't say anything. She was staring straight ahead, still in a daze.

'I'm sorry, love,' he said. 'But it was your idea. I tried to warn you.'

'I know. Never mind,' she said at last, but he could tell she was badly wounded.

'Don't feel too insulted,' he said, giving her a peck on the cheek. 'She'd react like that to any girl I brought home. Except possibly the Blessed Virgin Mary.'

'I realise that now,' Mary sighed. 'I think she still wants you to be a priest.'

'That's right,' he agreed, glad she understood. 'She can never forgive me for leaving the seminary. Or worse, for leaving the Church.'

'It's understandable,' she said.

'What do you mean?' he laughed.

'I'd feel the same if you were my son. She's jealous. She loves you.'

'It's a strange way to show it,' he replied bitterly.

'We *are* still getting married, aren't we?' she asked, putting her hand on his thigh.

'Yes, of course,' he said. 'If you still want to.' He half-hoped she might have changed her mind after what had happened and he'd be off the hook.

'I want to. Do you?'

'Yes. On the terms agreed.'

After a lot of discussion, he had finally agreed to get married in church, with a nuptial mass, making it clear that, one, he was doing so only to please her and her parents, whom he had come to like and respect, and, two, he believed in neither the legal nor religious significance of marriage.

'You remember?' he asked, glancing sideways at her.

'Yes.'

'You realise they won't come now, don't you?'

'Neither of them?'

'My mother definitely won't come and my father won't if she doesn't, even if he wanted to.' He knew this was a crushing blow for her.

'What about the rest of your family?'

'Oh, they'll come. They're not so narrow-minded. Kevin'll come for the craic. What about *you*?'

'What about me?'

'Will you come?'

'Very funny,' she said, giving him a playful dig in the ribs with her elbow, so that he almost swerved out of lane.

'Hey, careful!' he laughed. 'Or we'll both be going to our funeral, not our wedding!'

They got married the following year, on a hot July afternoon, in St. Scholastica's, the local Catholic church. All their families and friends came, including Roger, Melanie, the crowd from the Sugawn Kitchen and one or two colleagues from his college – but not his parents. He had gone to Manchester again a few weeks before to make a last appeal, but to no avail.

'Sure, it'd be a mockery,' his mother said. 'You don't believe in Catholicism any more, do you?'

'What about you, Dad?' he turned to his father, ignoring her question.

'Ahem. I have to agree with your mother, Fran. I mean, you're getting married in a Catholic church, but you're not a practising Catholic any more, are you? You're not even a Christian any more. You don't even believe in God.'

'Sure, he's an atheist,' his mother said, scornfully.

'So, you're not coming because it's in a Catholic church?' he asked, wincing at the way she said 'atheist' – to her being an 'atheist' was worse than being a robber, rapist and murderer all in one!

'That's right,' his father said.

'But if I got married in a register office, you wouldn't come either, would you?' he argued, knowing it was futile.

'Well, that wouldn't be a proper marriage, would it?' his father said. 'Not in the eyes of God.'

'I see – I can't win then, can I?' he said, gutted, getting up and walking out of the house in disgust.

In spite of this display of intransigence, right up to the very moment of the ceremony he hoped they might relent and turn up, but they didn't. He was hurt and embarrassed – as was Mary – but they were both determined not to let it spoil the occasion, so told people his mother was ill – as in a way she was.

Just before the ceremony, they paid the parish priest his fee by signing a cheque on the altar, which he couldn't help feeling was somewhat ironic, especially as he suspected the money would go straight into the drinks kitty – both the parish priest, a wiry little Welshman, and the sacristan, seemed to be permanently tipsy. The sacristan had a half-bottle of whisky in his cassock pocket, from which he and the parish priest took surreptitious slugs throughout the ceremony. As a result, they conducted it like a pair of bumbling, music-hall comedians, provoking sniggers of amusement from the congregation.

He didn't mind, because it helped to relieve the strain of what was for him an ordeal. However, he tried to endure it with good grace, because he could see that Mary was happy. She looked radiant in her long, white bridal gown, but he was worried she might have a fit during the ceremony, which made it even more of a strain.

However, there was something much more worrying on his mind – the ceremony was a mockery, as his mother had commented, in more ways than one, because over the past few months an awful realisation had slowly but inexorably dawned on him: *he didn't love her!* He liked her, he felt sorry for her, he felt protective towards her, but he didn't *love* her. They were very different, emotionally, mentally, intellectually. Worst of all, he didn't find her sexually attractive any more. Here she was, looking radiantly happy, all because she was getting married to him, but he didn't love her, didn't fancy her and didn't even believe in marriage!

God, what a mess, he couldn't help thinking during the ceremony! Nor could he help remembering other ceremonies he had forced himself to go through without believing in them – the reception of the habit at the junior seminary and his first vows at the end of the novitiate, when he didn't even believe in God any more. Why did he keep getting into these situations? What was wrong with him?

He tried to put these painful, negative thoughts out of his mind by looking forward to the reception – a good nosh and a few pints would soon cheer him up! There was the honeymoon to look forward to as well – they were going to stay on Gola for a few weeks, the island off the coast of Donegal that Pat had told them about, before going to Dublin for the summer school.

'Here are the directions and so on,' said Pat, taking an envelope out of his inside suit pocket and handing it to him. 'Have a good time. Don't forget to give Sean my regards.'

He had had the ritual first waltz with Mary and sat down to have a drink with a few of the Sugawn crowd, watching the dancers and listening to the Sugawn Folk, who were supplying the music.

'Thanks,' he said. 'What are you doing this summer?'

'We're going to the Arans,' said Peggy. She was dressed all in black as usual, even though it was a wedding, not a funeral!

'Don't forget to read that book,' Pat added.

'What's it called again?' he asked.

''Langrishe Go Down' by Aidan Higgins. It's brilliant.'

'I'll look forward to it.'

'Tell me what you think.'

'I'll give you a full reader's report.'

'There are a few other good books in the cottage, but you'll be taking your own reading, I suppose?'

'Of course. I'm reading 'Strumpet City' by James Plunkett at the moment. It's about the Dublin strike of 1913. It's a cracking good read.'

'What about Mary?'

'I've given her a whole reading list! She's going to do A-level English next year, so …'

'You should read 'Philadelphia Here I Come'', said Seamus, butting in. 'We might do it for our next production.'

'Who's that by?'

'Brian Friel.'

'It's a lovely wedding, Frank,' said Maggy. 'Mary looks beautiful. Such a beautiful dress, too.'

'Thanks, Maggy,' he said. 'So when are you two going to get hitched?'

'Seamus, darling? When are we going to get hitched?' Maggy said to Seamus. She was a bit tiddly.

'Jaysus, woman,' Seamus retorted. 'I've told you before, I don't do very well in captivity.'

'I meant Pat and Peggy!' Frank said, laughing.

'I don't do very well in captivity either,' Pat drawled.

'Oh, you men!' Peggy expostulated. 'You'd think marriage was some form of punishment.'

'Maybe it is!' Gerry chipped in.

'Actually, we're seriously thinking of doing it next year, aren't we?' Peggy said, turning to Pat.

'Yes, you are, my dear, aren't you?' said Pat dryly, in his Chicago drawl, and everyone laughed.

'You could have a joint wedding with Seamus and Peggy,' Mary suggested.

'What a good idea!' Peggy exclaimed.

'Jaysus, will yous stop talking about marriage – it's morbid!' Seamus growled, getting up and going off.

'We *are* at a wedding!' Gerry called after him.

'Seriously, have you asked him to marry you?' he quizzed Maggy.

'I have,' she said.

'What did he say?'

'He said he would.'

'Really?'

'On one condition.'

'What's that?'

'I have to get divorced first.' They all laughed again.

'You mean from him?' Gerry joked. 'It might be the best way to do it – get the divorce out of the way first.' This got another laugh.

'Are you going to get divorced?' he asked her, seriously.

'I've already started proceedings,' she stated.

'Come and do the Walls of Limerick, woman,' Seamus ordered, suddenly re-appearing at the table, pulling Maggy to her feet and leading her onto the dance floor.

'Are they really going to get married?' Pat asked him on the side.

'Apparently,' he said.

'But I thought …'

'So did I.'

'Come on, Walls of Limerick,' Peggy interrupted, pulling Pat up.

'I'd better go and circulate a bit,' he said, not wanting to dance, standing up and going over to the bar, where not surprisingly he found his brother, Kevin, who was best man.

'A right farce this, isn't it?' Kevin commented, in his caustic Mancunian way.

'I suppose so,' he laughed, trying not to take offence. 'You're never going to get hitched yourself, then?'

'I'd sooner face a fucking firing squad!' Kevin quipped. He had obviously had a few pints already, not to mention whiskey chasers.

'It doesn't mean anything to me,' Frank said, 'but it makes her happy.'

'I just hope you don't live to regret it,' Kevin said, cryptically.

'What do you mean?' he asked, offended despite himself.

'Well, she's got you by the short and curlies now, hasn't she?' Kevin slurred, swaying slightly on the bar-stool. He was definitely well-oiled!

'Yes, I suppose so,' he laughed, 'but she knows it doesn't mean anything to me, I don't believe in it.'

'That won't stop her using it,' Kevin asserted.

'What do you mean?' he asked, annoyed now by Kevin's cynicism.

'If you have a bust-up.'

'Oh, I don't think so,' he said. 'I think I can trust her. We've talked it over and agreed it's only for show. Anyway, we're not going to have a bust-up. We're together for life, whatever happens, as far as I'm concerned. That's one part of it I do believe in.'

'What are you two gassing about?' Mary demanded, coming up to the bar in her wedding dress.

'Prices, love,' Kevin replied.

'What prices?' Mary asked, innocently.

'The price of love,' Kevin said, deadpan.

'Don't take any notice of him,' he told her, laughing it off. 'He's still sober. He'll lighten up when he's had a few more pints.'

'Are you going to have a dance with me tonight or not?' Mary asked Kevin, ignoring his remark.

'That'd be a waste of valuable drinking time, wouldn't it, love?' Kevin slurred, not budging from his perch on the barstool.

'I'll speak to you later, Kevin Walsh,' she pretended to scold him, unruffled by his apparent rudeness, knowing it was only the beer talking. 'Come on, Fran. It's the Siege of Ennis.'

'Fools step in,' he heard Kevin remark sarkily behind his back, as she led him off to the dance floor.

CHAPTER NINE

Gola is a tiny island off the coast of Donegal. It used to be inhabited by about thirty families, but by the time they arrived for their honeymoon, the natives had abandoned it for a 'better' life on the mainland or even farther afield, in Britain, America or Australia. The cottages in which they lived had been left in varying stages of poignant dereliction, except for two or three which had been bought as holiday homes.

The island was primitive, with no modern amenities – no electricity, running water, roads, shops or pubs, not even a church – but it was beautiful: a rugged outcrop of rock on the edge of the north Atlantic, covered by a patchwork quilt of brown bog and green fields, criss-crossed with tumbling dry-stone walls. The shoreline was an irregular ring of rocky indentations, sandy coves and stony strands, except on the western side, where there were rampart-like cliffs, against which the Atlantic ocean thundered relentlessly with a stereophonic, cinemascopic grandeur.

To reach the island they had to hitch a lift on a fishing boat out of the harbour at Bunbeg, a tiny fishing village on the wind- and rain-swept coast of Gweedore. This took about half an hour, across a choppy Atlantic sea channel and beneath a lowering, leaden sky, even though it was midsummer. When they alighted on the quayside with their luggage, feeling seasick, to their shock the fishermen asked for payment. However, neither the gloomy weather, nor seasickness, nor the apparent meanness of the fishermen were enough to stop them being immediately awed by the atmospheric, desolate, haunted beauty of the island.

Their cottage, one of a cluster near the crumbling main pier, was built of whitewashed stone, with a corrugated metal roof. It consisted of three rooms – a stone-floored living-room-cum-kitchen with a large, open fireplace and two bedrooms. It was in a mess, but the basic items of furniture, such as a table, chairs and bed, were still there, and once they had cleaned and tidied up, it was just about habitable. Indeed, once they got the turf fire going, it was quite cosy! He felt at home, because it reminded him of childhood summer holidays ...

They spent their time strolling around the island, which took only an hour; swimming and sunbathing, when the weather permitted; reading; collecting turf and driftwood for the fire on which, as well as a camping stove, they cooked; fetching water from the well and washing their clothes, which they did in the lake, a large pool of peat-stained water just behind one of the strands. The only other living beings, apart from Sean, the retired local schoolmaster, who occasionally came in his boat to spend a day or two in his holiday house, and local fishermen, who occasionally spent a few hours messing with their gear on the crumbling pier, were birds, fish, sheep, cows, rabbits and an ancient blind donkey called Bess, who had been left to live out her retirement in indolent, peaceful solitude.

For the first couple of weeks it was idyllic – the desolate beauty of the place, combined with the ozone in the sea air, as well as the incense-like smell of burning turf, were intoxicating. He felt as if he was on an almost mystical high, drugged by scenery, solitude, and the sheer romantic, timeless spirituality of the place. Ireland had always been a special place for him, a magical, mythical, fairytale, holy land across the sea, but now he felt as if he had been transported to an even more mysterious, beautiful, secret, sacred part of it.

Suddenly though, after a couple of weeks, the spell seemed to break and he felt himself slipping into a sense of anticlimax, isolation, oppressive confinement. He felt an insidious urge to get off the island, back to civilization, people, pubs, shops, even cars. At first he told himself it was a feeling that would pass, an inevitable reaction, like withdrawal symptoms, but day by day it got worse. Mary started to get on his nerves and they started to have silly rows, so that the atmosphere between them became strained. Absurdly, he started going out on his own, just to escape from her. Then, a couple of disturbing incidents happened ...

One night they were woken up by strange noises outside the bedroom window. It sounded as if a gang of men in hobnailed boots were tramping back and forth over the stony 'street'.

'What is it?' Mary whispered, clutching him nervously as they lay in bed.

'I don't know,' he whispered back, trying not to sound alarmed.

'Maybe it's those ghosts Sean was talking about,' she whispered. Only the other day, Sean had told them the island was haunted by the ghosts of drowned fishermen.

'Don't be silly,' he whispered back impatiently. 'There's no such thing as ghosts. There must be some rational explanation.'

'You don't know,' she whispered back fiercely. 'Oh, God, Fran, I'm scared.' The noises became louder and she clung to him tightly.

'For God's sake, Mary,' he whispered back angrily, 'don't be ridiculous. I'm telling you, there's no such things as ghosts.'

'Sean said he's seen them himself,' she insisted.

To his annoyance, she had fallen under the influence of Sean, a dogmatic, domineering, but charming old fellow, who had apparently been the terror of the local schoolchildren for thirty years.

'Sean says the island is full of rats, but we haven't seen any, have we?' Sean had apparently even written a novel in Gaelic about these mythical rats!

'I saw one,' she whispered.

'You imagined you did.'

'The trouble with you is you don't believe anything, unless you see it with your own eyes.'

'The trouble with you is you talk too much. Sssh! Listen!' The noise had stopped, but then started again, even more loudly.

'Fran! I'm scared!' She clung to him even more tightly. 'What is it?'

'*I* don't know!' he whispered. 'Don't start getting hysterical, for God's sake!'

He said it angrily, but was becoming more and more nervous himself – they were totally alone on the island, surrounded by darkness and sea. If there was someone – or something – hostile outside, they would have no chance. The clattering noises continued.

'Maybe it's IRA men,' he suggested, only half-joking. 'Maybe they've got a secret hideout or ammunition store on the island.'

'Fran! Do you think so?' She clung terrified to him.

'Well, it's an ideal place, isn't it, an uninhabited island? They could come and go by boat under cover of night.'

'I didn't hear an engine though. Did you?'

'They wouldn't use a boat with an engine, would they?' he replied, warming to his theme. 'They'd use a curragh or something.'

Curraghs were still in use locally – frighteningly fragile-looking craft for such perilous waters, which required considerable courage and skill to manage and even then, according to Sean, had accounted for many drownings over the years – Sean enjoyed talking about drowning and death in general, trying to frighten them as he had no doubt frightened generations of schoolkids.

'Maybe Sean himself has sent them to get us, for disagreeing with him about their tactics,' he added, again only half-joking.

They had got into an argument with Sean about the IRA that very day. Sean was a fanatical republican and nationalist, and expressed a vitriolic hatred of England and the English. He agreed with him about the aims of the IRA – a united Ireland – but disagreed with him heatedly about their methods. Sean, however, had tried to browbeat him into agreeing with him.

'Oh, Fran, you shouldn't have argued with him,' Mary remonstrated, still clinging to him in terror.

'Why not?' he whispered angrily. 'He's a fucking fascist! He thinks he owns this fucking island! He thinks he owns fucking Ireland! You may like him, but I don't.'

He didn't like him because, apart from anything else, he looked and sounded just like the Dean of Studies at the junior seminary, another 'Little Hitler' type. He half-regretted contradicting him now, though, especially as the noises had become even louder and closer. What if a gang of IRA men *had* come to shoot them in their beds?

'Fran, go and look!' Mary urged him.

'You must be joking!' he whispered. 'Ssh! Listen!'

The noises had suddenly stopped. They lay still, with bated breath and palpitating hearts, listening to the silence, staring at the small, ragged-curtained window through which some spectral moonlight filtered. Then, suddenly, somebody started pushing against the 'kitchen' door, as if trying to break in. His heart leapt into his mouth.

'Oh, God, Fran, they're trying to get in!' Mary whispered, starting to cry.

'Quiet, for Christ's sake!' he hissed, listening – it really did sound as if somebody was trying to force open the door. He was terrified himself now, but decided he wasn't going to die naked in bed – or let her – without a fight. He slipped out of bed, pulled on his trousers, put on his shoes and tiptoed towards the bedroom door.

'Fran, be careful!' she whispered, panic-stricken.

'Ssh!' He put his finger to his lips and tiptoed into the kitchen, where he picked up the nearest thing to a weapon he could see in the gloom, a broom or 'besom', as it was called in Ireland, made with heather. But that was too light, he decided, so exchanged it for a 'slane', a long-bladed spade used for cutting turf.

Gripping the wooden handle with both hands, heart pounding, he crept over to one of the front windows and peeped through, but couldn't see anything. He crept to the front door, unlocked it softly with the key, opened it slightly and peered out: from the side of the cottage several pairs of glimmering eyes stared back at him. Heart thudding now, he instinctively raised the slane to defend himself, but the eyes just continued to stare eerily back at him without moving. Then, peering more closely, he suddenly realised what they were – a flock of sheep! They had been rubbing themselves against the pebble-dashed wall. He stepped out, shouted at them and they ran off, bouncing bundles of shaggy wool, hooves clattering like hammers on the stony ground. He chased them well away from the cottage and returned, shaking his head and laughing out loud with relief.

As he approached the open door, though, he saw something that made him abruptly stop laughing – a ghostly figure wandering about in the darkness some distance away. For a moment, he thought it might be one of Sean's 'ghosts', then with a shock realised it was Mary, in her night-dress, having one of her 'fits'. He dropped the slane, ran after her, grabbed her by the arm and led her, jabbering incoherently, eyes staring wildly, back to the cottage.

The next day, they laughed about the sheep, but she didn't remember 'fitting', so he didn't mention it. However, he was secretly worried by it, in a way he had never been before – why, he wasn't quite sure. Then, a few days later, something else happened that made him realise exactly why.

It was while they were walking on the cliffs at the back of the island. He had left her to collect some heather, when suddenly he heard her scream out his name. He swung around, afraid she had fallen, but she was standing a few feet back from the edge, staring in horror at something below. He rushed over.

'Look,' she said, gripping his arm and pointing down to the rocks far below.

Nervously, acrophobic at the best of times, he leant over and looked down. Splayed out on the rocks, washed by Atlantic rollers, lay the inert body of Bess, the donkey. A shudder of horror went through him – she must have wondered blindly over the edge.

'Oh, Fran, the poor old thing!' said Mary. 'Is she dead?'

'It looks like it,' he said, a lump in his throat. 'There's nothing we can do, anyway.'

He stared down at the donkey's lifeless body with a mixture of sadness and relief – relief that it wasn't Mary or, for that matter, himself. He felt sorry for the poor old donkey, but it had occurred to him that if one of them had an accident – broke a leg for example – there would be nothing the other could do. They had no way of communicating with the mainland, unless Sean or some fishermen happened to be on the island, which was infrequent.

'I hope she didn't suffer,' Mary said.

'Yes,' he agreed, though it struck him as a forlorn hope. 'We haven't seen her for a couple of days, have we? She might have been lying there injured.'

'Oh, God, Fran, I hope not,' Mary said, tears welling up in her eyes.

'Well,' he said, shepherding her away, 'there's nothing we can do now. We'd better tell Sean, I suppose. Come on, let's go.'

The donkey's death hung over them both like a black cloud for the rest of the day. He found it oddly depressing, not just because he was fond of the donkey, but also because her death was a grisly reminder of mortality, the meaninglessness, fragility and brevity of life. If he was right and there was no God, no afterlife, he reflected grimly, his own life was no more significant than the donkey's and might end just as arbitrarily, just as ignominiously, at any moment. It made a mockery of life! That was why so many people – including Mary – couldn't accept the idea that there was no God. On the other hand, he told himself, it was a reminder to enjoy life as much as possible while you could – carpe diem!

'Shall we go over to the mainland for a day or two?' he suggested to her that evening, as they sat reading by the fire of turf and driftwood. Even in his own ears, though, this sounded like an admission of defeat.

'Do you want to?' she asked, irritatingly.

'I wouldn't mind a break, just for a day or two,' he shrugged, trying to sound nonchalant. 'We could stay in a B and B. What about you?'

'I'm all right here,' she replied, to his annoyance, and added even more annoyingly: 'I thought you wanted to stay on the island for six weeks?'

'I did,' he replied, struggling to suppress his annoyance. Ironically, it had been his idea to stay on the island for six weeks, while she hadn't been too keen. 'I just thought you might fancy a break. It doesn't matter.'

'If you want to – '

'It doesn't matter. Forget it,' he said sharply, returning to his book.

It wasn't the novel Pat had recommended, 'Langrishe Go Down', but a book about psychology, called, 'Of Love and Lust', by Theodor Reik, which he had found in the cottage. He was reading it with a morbid fascination, because it seemed to confirm and explain, with scalpel-like logic, what he had suspected for some time – that what he felt for Mary was not love, but pity. And this was supposed to be their honeymoon!

This realisation made him even more tense and taciturn than he had already become. They had more and more rows, mostly petty. A couple of days later, they had a big row about the crucifix over the bed. He had removed it, as he had wanted to on day one, when she wasn't looking, even though he knew it would trigger an argument.

'Why've you taken the crucifix down?' she demanded, when she noticed.

'Because,' he said sarcastically, 'I don't want to sleep beneath the effigy of a semi-naked man dying an agonising, barbaric death any more.'

'What's wrong with it?' she asked.

'It's bloody obscene!' he shouted angrily.

'It's not just any man,' she argued. 'It's Our Lord! I'm putting it back.'

'You put it back,' he retorted coldly, 'and sleep with 'Our Lord' if you want, but I don't want to.'

'Where are you going to sleep?'

'I'll sleep in here, on the settle-bed. You make your choice – you can sleep with 'Our Lord' or me from now on. Think about it. I'm going for a walk.'

With that, he grabbed his jacket from the hook on the back of the door, went out, deliberately shutting it hard behind him, and strode off towards the lake. It wasn't the first time he had left her on her own, but this time, after what had happened the other night and the death of the donkey, he felt even more guilty than usual.

He knew she hated being left on her own, mainly because she was afraid of having a fit. Also, he knew she had started the argument deliberately, because he didn't want to make love with her any more. And he knew he ought to go back and say he was sorry. But he didn't, because he was angry – angry with her, with himself, with life – and because he knew saying sorry wouldn't solve anything.

According to Theodor Reik, an essential feature of love was the desire to be one with the beloved, to be united with her. If that was the case, he didn't love her. Far from wanting to 'be one' with her, he was bored by her, irritated by her, and wanted to get away from her – ironic as that was, since there were only two of them on the island!

Why didn't he enjoy her company any more, he asked himself? One reason was that he couldn't have an 'intelligent' conversation, couldn't discuss books or ideas, with her, because she had read so little and knew so little. That was understandable, but worse, he had come to realise, she wasn't *really* interested in books or ideas. He had drawn up a reading list for her, brought several of the books with them and tried to persuade her to read them, but it was useless – she never picked up a 'serious' book of her own accord, never read more than a few pages of anything, never finished anything, seemed incapable of understanding properly anything she did read.

It had taken him all his time to persuade her to read and help her to understand her set books for O-level English lit. She had only scraped a pass because it was partly based on course work and he had half-written her essays for her. As a teacher, he felt guilty about 'cheating', but *she* had been cheated, he told himself, so deserved another chance.

Her excuse for not reading was that her drugs made it difficult for her to concentrate, even to focus on the print – though he had bought her some new glasses. He sympathized, but it didn't alter the fact that she didn't read, so he couldn't have an 'intelligent' conversation with her. He remembered something his mother had said: 'You're making a terrible mistake, Fran. It doesn't matter how much you like her or she likes you – she's not on the same intellectual level as you.' At the time he had disregarded the remark as irrelevant, made out of jealous spite. In fact, it had made him all the more determined to stay with Mary and try to 'develop' her. Now, however, he realised bitterly that it was true, they were not compatible.

Even more worrying than not being able to talk to her, though, was that he no longer wanted to make love with her. This was the ultimate irony, on what was supposed to be their honeymoon! He tried to overcome his feelings of aversion, but by now, after three weeks on the island, he could hardly bring himself to touch her.

Was there something wrong with him, he wondered, standing on the cliff tops, gazing out at the immense Atlantic ocean? Maybe the Ghosters really had screwed him up! Maybe they had managed to kill the capacity for love, love in the normal, human sense, being the screwed-up, crackpot celibates they were. They'd certainly tried! Maybe he wasn't normal. After all, Mary was a lovely, sweet girl, if limited. Why didn't he love her any more? Maybe he was – No! He couldn't bear that thought. He couldn't bear the thought that he was abnormal in any way. If he really thought that, he would fling himself off the cliff right now, he thought, staring down with a shudder of horror at the rocks far below, where the dead donkey's carcass was still being pushed and pulled by the broad, booming Atlantic rollers, as if just another piece of flotsam and jetsam.

After all, he told himself, turning away quickly and walking on towards the boggy, high north end of the island, he wasn't off sex. It was just that he didn't want to have sex with *her* any more. He knew he wasn't off sex, because he had started masturbating. What a sick joke, he reflected shamefully: *masturbating* on your honeymoon! He *must* be bloody abnormal!

Suddenly, to his surprise, he saw her walking towards him across the bog, in her pink anorak and jeans. She was limping, as always, and using the 'walking' stick he had made for her to help her over the rough terrain. She looked *stricken*, he thought, as they approached each other. His heart went out to her. He wanted to stop and throw his arms around her. If she stopped, he would, he decided. But she didn't stop, so nor did he. They walked right past each other without a word, with hardly even a glance.

They were the only two people on the island, were husband and wife, were supposed to be on their honeymoon, and they couldn't even stop to speak to each other! It would be comical if it weren't so tragic, he told himself, carrying on towards the cottage. He had never seen her looking so sad, so forlorn, so *abject*, and it was *his* fault. *He* had broken her like this. He ought to stop now, before it was too late, turn around, run back, scoop her up in his arms and tell her he was sorry. But he didn't. He opened the door of the cottage, went in and put some new turf on the dying fire.

'You don't love me any more, do you?' she said sadly, in bed one night later, after he had resisted her advances yet again.

They had made up after their row about the crucifix and 'Our Lord' was back in place on the wall above the bed. He had decided to give in, feeling guilty.

'Of course I do,' he replied, her words like a knife through his heart. 'I'm just tired, that's all.' In fact, life on the island – the fresh air and exercise – was tiring, so that by bedtime all he wanted to do was sink into slumber, but he knew that was only an excuse.

'You never want to make love these days,' she said, accusingly.

'Maybe I just don't feel like it these days,' he argued wearily. 'Maybe there's something in the air.'

'You don't love me,' she stated matter-of-factly, turning her back to him.

'Because I don't want to make love with you doesn't mean I don't love you,' he argued, but to his annoyance, she didn't say anything. 'Does it?' he demanded, turning to her.

'Let's sleep if you're tired,' she said, which was uncharacteristically logical of her.

'If that's the way you feel,' he retorted huffily, turning away from her.

There was silence again for a few seconds. 'That's right, put all the blame on me,' he said to the darkness.

'I just don't think there's any point discussing it now, if you're tired,' she said. 'Let's sleep.'

Christ, she could be so bloody logical when she wanted to be! He *was* tired and wanted to sleep, but couldn't. He lay awake, angrily turning over what she had said. How could she accuse him of not loving her, just because for a week or two he hadn't wanted to make love with her? Was making love so important? Couldn't it just be a phase he was going through? Mightn't it just be the effect of the island, of being thrown too closely together without any escape?

Anyway, what about all he had done and still did for her, the way he helped and supported her, looked after her? Wasn't that love? Not according to Theodor Reik! According to Theodor Reik, love was incompatible with pity, because love meant the pursuit of one's 'ego-ideal' and pre-supposed both admiration and envy of the love-object.

He couldn't exactly say he admired or envied her. He remembered how he had felt sorry for her, because of her limp, when he had first seen her. Was that all he felt for her amounted to – feeling sorry? How sad! How pathetic! It couldn't be, could it?

Fuck Reik, he kept trying to tell himself, but Reik's theory explained how he felt about her perfectly. He was with her only because he felt sorry for her. His mother had said it. She had even said it herself the other day. He had denied it angrily, tried to deny it to himself even now, but couldn't – what he felt for her was 'pity', not 'love'. That was why he didn't want to make love with her. That was why he now found her company unsatisfying, even insufferable.

What should he do? That was the question he kept asking himself, as he wandered around the island on his own. Should he leave her? He ought to, he supposed, but knew he couldn't. He couldn't do that to her. It would shatter her already fragile self-esteem. She needed him, depended on him. He couldn't imagine her surviving without him. She might even commit suicide if he left her. Christ, what a dilemma to have on your honeymoon! He was well and truly trapped.

Besides, *he* might not 'love' *her*, but there was one thing he was absolutely sure of and that was that *she* loved *him*. She loved him with her whole heart, body and soul. Didn't she? Or did she just *need* him?

He remembered a discussion he had had once with Mark Gibson, a fellow-lecturer at the college. He was a tough South African ex-paratrooper, built like a bull, but very bright. He scornfully dismissed the whole notion of 'love', equating it with 'need'. ''I love you' equals 'I need you', no more, no less,' he asserted, in his bullish way. 'Love between a man and a woman is nothing more than mutual need fulfilment. You lend me your crotch, I'll lend you mine.' It was a horribly hard-boiled, cynical viewpoint and he had tried to argue against it, but not very successfully, found it impossible to refute, still did. Even if it was true though, it made the idea of leaving her unthinkable.

He'd wait till they got back to London and see how things went, he decided. Meanwhile, he'd try to be nicer to her. He was trying, but being stuck on the island alone with her made him even more moody. He was desperate to escape now, but determined to stick it out for the full six weeks.

Then, one afternoon, just a few days before they were due to leave, something happened that gave him the break he needed, but also made the idea of leaving her even more unthinkable than ever.

It was a hot, sunny day, which was unusual for Donegal – the weather had been depressing, with grey skies, chilly winds and relentless rain for days on end – so they decided to go swimming. They made a picnic, went down to the beach and spent the afternoon sunbathing and swimming.

The beach was idyllic – they were alone, the sun blazed down from a brilliant blue sky, the sand was like talcum powder, and the sea, though ice-cold, glittered like diamonds. The view of the mainland across the sea was like a picture postcard: in the background stood the mountains of Donegal, including Errigal, the highest, volcanic in both appearance and, apparently, origin. The lower slopes of the mountains were like green velvet skirts dotted with whitewashed cottages, from which ribbons of turf smoke twirled lazily upwards, perfuming the air with what for him was the most evocative smell in the world. It was paradise, yet he wasn't happy and worse, because of him, neither was she.

'I'm going in for another dip,' he said, jumping up and going into the water – to escape from both her and his depressing thoughts.

He had been swimming around for a while, when he suddenly felt a stinging sensation all over his body. He carried on swimming, supposing it was just the effect of the salt water on his sunburnt skin, or a thick clump of seaweed he had brushed against. After a while though, the stinging sensation became positively painful and he started to feel funny, so he came out of the water. He was shivering, though the sun was fire-hot, and felt sick. He started to dry himself off, deciding that was enough swimming for the day.

'What's wrong?' Mary asked.

'I dunno,' he said, trembling. 'I feel funny.'

'You're all red,' she observed, standing up and examining him.

'Am I?' He looked at himself – there were big scarlet patches all over his body. 'It must be the salt. Or the seaweed. There seems to be a lot of seaweed.'

'I didn't notice any seaweed. You're red all over.'

'It must be sunburn then. I'd better get dressed.'

'That's not sunburn – you weren't sunburnt like that when you went in.'

'I was a bit. Don't make a fuss. Let me get dressed.'

'Why are you shivering? It's not cold!'

'The water's cold.'

'It's not that cold!'

'It's like ice. You haven't been in as long as me.'

'I was in long enough. Are you sure you're all right?'

'Yeah. Stop fussing. I'll be all right in a minute. Oh, God – I feel really funny.' He was trembling violently now and couldn't breathe properly, as well as feeling sick.

'Fran! What's wrong?' she asked, alarmed.

'I dunno. I can't stop shaking. And – I – can't – breathe.' He was gasping for breath between the words.

'Fran, those red marks on your body – you've been stung!'

'Stung?' he gasped. 'Stung by what?'

'Jellyfish. Sean warned us about them, didn't he?'

'Yeah, but he said they were harmless, didn't he? Oh, God, I feel terrible, Mary. I – can't – breathe.' He sank onto his hands and knees on the sand, trembling and gasping for air like a fish out of water.

'Fran!' she shouted in panic.

'Go – and – get – Sean,' he gasped, on his hands and knees.

'Is he on the island?'

'I don't know,' he gasped. 'Go and look, please.'

'I don't want to leave you, Fran!' she protested. He could hear a note of hysteria in her voice.

'Go and look! Please! Quick!' he gasped.

She threw on her dress and ran off, limping. After what seemed like ages, she came running back, panting. 'Fran, Sean's at the pier. He'll take you over to the hospital. Can you walk?'

She helped him up and, leaning on her, he staggered, gasping grotesquely, to the pier, where Sean was waiting in his boat, 'An Feileacan', engine running. He stumbled in, collapsed onto the wooden seat and without a word Sean cast off. He opened the throttle fully, so that the boat bucked wildly as it ploughed through the choppy waters, making him feel even sicker, but it still seemed to take for ever to get to the tiny harbour in Bunbeg.

There they helped him out of the boat, bundled him into the back of Sean's old 'Beetle', which was waiting on the quay, and they drove off. By now he could hardly breathe at all – he was gulping desperately for oxygen, but there seemed to be none in the atmosphere. It was as if he was in the coils of a giant snake, an anaconda perhaps, that was slowly squeezing the life out of him. The gap between each gulp of air became longer and longer and between each gulp he felt as if he was about to black out, but he struggled desperately not to, because he knew that if he did, he would probably never wake up.

The car seemed to take an eternity, along winding, twisting, country roads. He started to lose consciousness, to give up struggling for air, to succumb to the blackness. It was hopeless. They weren't going to make it. 'This is it, this is the end, I'm going to die, here in Donegal,' he thought …

Strangely enough, the thought of dying didn't scare him. There was something seductive about it. At least all his problems would be over! He didn't really want to die, but if he had to, he would. He was amazed at how calm, almost serene, he felt about it.

Maybe he should say an Act of Contrition, he suddenly thought, gasping desperately for oxygen, just in case? No way, he told himself! And he felt pleased with himself, because it meant he had managed to unload all that superstitious claptrap about Heaven and Hell. He had beaten the Ghosters on that score at least! He wasn't going to relapse now, even though he might be about to die ...

It was a funny way to go though. Not very dignified or heroic. Maybe death never was. If he didn't make it, it would probably be in the newspapers tomorrow. He imagined the headline:

HOLIDAY-MAKER STUNG TO DEATH BY JELLYFISH

He was always making fun of gruesome Irish newspaper headlines about death and disaster – car crashes, farm accidents, drownings and so on, because they seemed to be so full of them. Now it looked as if he was going to be a headline himself. How ironic!

It was no joke though. They weren't going to make it. He was going to die. In between futile gulps for air, the waves of blackness were becoming bigger and bigger, trying to sweep him away into oblivion. He clung to the car door handle, like a drowning man to a rock, gasping desperately, trying to stop himself slipping away.

Suddenly, the car stopped with a jerk and the door opened. Swooning, he let go of the handle and almost fell out, but somebody caught him. Then he felt himself being lifted onto a trolley and pushed along. He could dimly hear footsteps and voices. He felt as if he was floating away into space ...

They stopped moving. A blurred face was peering at him. It looked like a nun. He must be hallucinating! He could hear a cacophony of voices and a babble of words, including the word 'antihistamine'. He could hear Mary crying in panic, 'Please don't let him die! Please don't let him die!' Hurry up, for Christ's sake, he thought – I can't hang on much longer. Then he felt a jab in his thigh and the 'nun' clamped a mask over his face. 'Breathe this in!' she urged. 'It's oxygen.'

He gulped it in greedily – at last he could feel air in his lungs again and it was the most wonderful feeling in the world! He wasn't going to die after all! He felt like death though, because suddenly he felt freezing cold and started trembling violently again, even though it was such a warm day. 'Don't worry, you're just in shock,' the nurse said, piling blankets on top of him. Funnily enough, that was what Father Director used to do when he was sick in the infirmary at the junior seminary, he remembered, drifting off into a deep sleep ...

They kept him in overnight and the next day Sean took them back to the island for the last few days, though by now he had had more than enough of it. Physically he was all right, except for feeling sore around the chest and sides, as if he had been crushed. Sean told them the local fishermen said they had seen swarms of Portuguese-Men-of-War in the sea the day before and he must have swum into one of them.

Curious, he looked up 'Portuguese-Man-of-War' in the encyclopaedia in the cottage and to his horror read that they injected a poison into their victim which paralysed the respiratory muscles and could kill, so he was probably lucky to be alive. It was ironic – he owed his life to Sean, whom he didn't much like, and to Mary, whom he didn't love any more. Her panic-stricken pleas, 'Don't let him die! Don't let him die!' to the doctor and nurses would haunt him for ever. How could he possibly leave her now?

CHAPTER TEN

'Why do you need other women?'

'For experience.'

'You can get experience with me.'

'It's not the same.'

'Why not? What do you do with them that you can't do with me?'

'Lots of things.'

'Such as?'

'Lots of things.'

'Tell me. Tell me what you want me to do and I'll do it. I'll do whatever you want.'

'It's not simply a matter of doing things. They're all different.'

'How are they different? They're all women, aren't they? All women are the same, aren't they?'

'You don't understand. Of course all women are basically the same, physically. But they're different people.'

'You're not interested in them as people. You just want to fuck them! I know you! Why don't you fuck me instead?'

'If you're going to talk like that, I'll go.'

'Well, why don't you make love to me nowadays?'

'I do make love with you.'

'No, you don't.'

'Yes, I do.'

'Once in a blue moon.'

'It's not once in a blue moon. How often do you want me to make love with you?'

'Every night or every few nights, like normal couples.'

' "Normal couples"! What are they? How do you know what normal couples do? Anyway, I don't give a damn about normal couples! I'm me. I'm different. Maybe I just don't feel like making love every night or even every few nights.'

'Why not? *That's* the question!'

'Because I'm not a fucking machine, that's why not!'

'Now you're "talking like that".'

'I'm not "talking like that"! You seem to think I can switch on just like that, whenever you feel like it. Doesn't it occur to you that I might be tired after working all day?'

'Tired after fucking other women, you mean!'

'If that's what you want to think, all right. But I'm not staying here to listen to your accusations and insults any longer. I'm going out.' He grabbed his jacket from the back of the bedroom door and rushed out of the flat, shutting the front door behind him. He ran down the dingy, malodorous stairs of the council block of flats they had moved into, past the overflowing bin at the bottom of the chute and towards the estate exit.

'Go on! Go and fuck one of your French or Italian tarts!' he heard her shout after him from the balcony, to his embarrassment, as he hurried out of the estate.

The 'estate' was a grim collection of red-brick, barrack-like blocks of flats, each five storeys high, with balconies on which washing hung, like proud proletarian flags. Between the buildings, there was asphalt with cars, mostly old bangers or wrecks, parked, and not a tree or flower in sight. It was a depressing environment, from which he was relieved to escape – as well as from her.

As usual when he wanted to escape, he went to the Marshes and walked along the river, stopping at the Robin Hood for a pint. It was a sunny autumn evening, so he sat at one of the wooden tables on the patio to enjoy the view of river, marshes, railway viaduct and reservoir.

Mary's accusation of infidelity rankled him. It was true he had been going out with one of his students. Her name was Grazia, she was Italian, she was twenty-one and he had been smitten by her the moment she walked into his classroom the first time, wearing a slinky red dress, and white, knee-length boots. She wore pink-tinted specs and wasn't really pretty, but she had long, luxurious, curly, black hair and a sexy figure, with gorgeous breasts. Not only did she have a sexy figure, she had a sexy voice, too, and a sweet, childlike nature that aroused not just his lust, but also his protective instincts.

The irony was that she wouldn't let him touch her, apart

from putting an arm around her waist and giving her a peck on the cheek. Only the other day he had gone for lunch at the house where she was an au pair and she had cooked spaghetti for him. Afterwards, sitting on the sofa and slightly drunk on Mateus Rosé, he had tried to kiss her properly, but she had pushed him away.

'What's wrong?' he asked her. 'Why won't you let me kiss you?'

'You are marrieda,' she said, in her sexy Italian accent, to his annoyance.

'You shouldn't be with me then, should you?'

'I don't do anything wronga,' she protested. 'I don'ta toucha you.'

'I only want to kiss you,' he pleaded – in fact, he wanted to do a lot more ...

'If you wanna kissa somebody, you shoulda kissa your wife-a.'

'I told you, I don't love her any more.'

'It doesn't matter, you are marrieda to 'er,' she said, maddeningly.

'I like *you*,' he protested.

'I like you, but only as a frienda,' she insisted. 'I don'ta do anything to upseta your wife-a.'

He had been mad with frustration at the time, but now he was half-glad she had resisted his advances, because he could still tell himself he had not been unfaithful to Mary. That was why her accusation of infidelity had annoyed him so much!

But he was annoyed with Grazia too. He felt she had led him on. In fact, he was starting to suspect she was a bit of a cockteaser! No, that wasn't fair – she was really a sweet, sincere, innocent girl. That was partly why he liked her so much. In fact, he quite admired her for resisting him. Maybe she wasn't all that innocent though. She shouldn't have gone out with him at all if he was married, but she had accepted all his invitations readily. He wouldn't ask her out any more. There were one or two other girls he fancied, though not nearly as much. He'd take one of them out – maybe Rosalia, the French girl. She was pretty, if a bit plump, and she obviously liked him. Yes, he'd ask Rosalia out and make sure Grazia knew, make her jealous. That'd teach her a lesson!

God, he must be starting to get drunk, he thought, even though he had only had one pint! He really fancied another one, but told himself he ought to go home and help Mary with her A-level Merchant of Venice essay. He stood up and, with a huge effort of will, resisted going back inside for another pint. Instead, he set off downriver towards home, trying to remember as much as he could about The Merchant of Venice.

He just couldn't keep his mind off Grazia though. Only yesterday she had brought a frozen chicken in a plastic shopping bag to class. When he had invited her for a coffee after class, she had said she had to rush home to put it in the freezer. 'Fretta', was it she'd said? What did that mean, 'in a hurry'?

'Don't worry,' he had said to her, 'it won't fly away.' She had found his little joke very funny, giggled her head off. She had a sexy giggle! Not to mention a sexy wiggle! What had she been wearing? A corduroy dress with white boots. And those violet-tinted specs. She had told him she didn't like Italy because it was too violent. People made a career of stealing, she said. Cheating the system was the done thing. There were too many rich men. That was why she lived in Greece. She told him the Greeks despised Greek-Cypriots and vice versa. She had such gorgeous breasts! How he would love to get his hands on them! She wouldn't let him touch her though. She wanted him to, he suspected, but wouldn't because he was 'marrieda'. He wished he hadn't told her now. No. He had to admire her principles. Actually, he suspected she was a bit shy and innocent. Was she still a virgin, he wondered? He wouldn't be surprised. He liked the way she bit her lower lip, pulling a little bit of the moist red flesh. It was so erotic! She didn't realise it of course. Or maybe she did. Maybe she did it on purpose, knowing the effect it had. Maybe she wasn't as innocent as he thought.

Stop thinking about her, he told himself! Think about The Merchant of Venice. They had studied it for O-level at the junior seminary. They had even done a production of it. But he couldn't remember much about it, which was a bit alarming. Maybe he just wanted to delete it from his memory, like the all the other stuff that had happened there. What was that famous speech? "The quality of mercy is not strained …" Oh, God, she was so sexy! "It droppeth as the gentle rain from heaven …" So gorgeous! "Upon the place beneath …" Forget her! She's just a cockteaser anyway. No, Shakespeare didn't write that, did he? He probably did somewhere! What was the next bit? Damn, can't remember! *Oh, God, I wish I didn't fancy her so much!*

CHAPTER ELEVEN

'Put your ass in the air!'

He was lying face down on an examination couch at the hospital. Embarrassed but amused, he did as the doctor ordered. The doctor stuck a thermometer up his backside and fiddled about with his balls. It was embarrassing, but if it saved his marriage, it was worth it, he supposed. It was ironic – at first he had argued vehemently against the idea of having a child, especially in the hope of holding their marriage together – then suddenly one day he had changed his mind.

'If you don't want to have a baby, I'm leaving,' Mary had said. 'There's no reason for me to stay with you any longer. You don't love me.'

The last bit had hurt, but it was true. He had carried on reading his newspaper.

'You could at least do that, give me a baby to love. But you're so stubborn, so hard, so selfish, you won't even do that, will you?' she said, bursting into tears.

'All right,' he said, lowering his newspaper.

'What do you mean, 'all right'?' she asked, through her tears.

'Let's have a baby, then.'

'You will?' she asked, surprised.

'Yes. I want to have one.' The idea of being a father had suddenly appealed to him and maybe it would hold them together.

'Oh, Fran, thank you, I do love you!' she exclaimed, jumping onto his lap, flinging her arms around his neck and kissing him on the cheek.

'Hey, watch my paper!' he remonstrated, jokingly.

Afterwards, they had tried hard for several months, timing intercourse carefully, but without success, and every month, when her unwanted period arrived, she had gone into a depression. It was all the more ironic, because they had always been so careful to use contraceptives – condoms and caps, since because of her medication, she couldn't take the pill – needlessly as it had turned out.

She had been for tests and cleared, so now here he was, on all fours on a hospital couch, with his bare backside stuck in the air, in the 'Fertility' Clinic at Saint Bart's Hospital. After examining him in this position, the doctor made him stand on a stool while he performed several more intimate investigations. This brought back uncomfortable memories, but he tried to blank them out.

'You're certainly not short of sandwiches in the lunchbox department, are you?' the doctor commented drolly, in his Northern Irish accent. 'If you get my drift.'

Frank laughed, trying not to redden.

'So no problems with erection. How's penetration though?' the doctor asked. 'That's the crucial thing, you know, not size.'

'Sorry?' he asked, not 'getting' his 'drift' immediately.

'When you screw, does Jack the Lad here go all the way in or what?' the doctor rephrased the question in his inimitable way.

'Er – not all the way exactly,' he said, reddening despite himself. 'It's a bit tight. My wife's quite a lot smaller than me. That's why, I suppose.'

'Could be psychological, though, could it?'

'How do you mean?'

'Some women don't loosen up enough if they're a bit inhibited about the old rumpy-pumpy. If you get my drift?'

'Er, yes, I see.'

'Would you say that might apply in your case? Or, I should say, your wife's case, I suppose.' He chuckled, pleased with his drollery.

'Er, I suppose it could do, up to a point,' he replied, realising immediately that wasn't the most felicitous expression in the context. Mary was a bit tense about intercourse, though not so much lately, as she so badly wanted to get pregnant. In fact, she had become something of a nymphomaniac!

'Aha, 'up to a point',' the doctor pounced on the phrase, chuckling. 'You need to get your missus to loosen up more maybe. A bit more lubrication might help. Do you use anything?'

'Er, no ...'

'Well, you can get lubricant for the purpose. And I don't

mean bicycle oil either.'

'No, I hope not,' he laughed, blushing despite himself.

'Although a bit of bicycle oil might not be such a bad idea,' the doctor mused aloud. 'No, you can get stuff from the chemist's. KY Jelly's a good one. Johnson and Johnson Baby oil would do, but you might as well get the proper stuff. So that might be worth a try. It might help to get Jack the Lad here a bit further up the Khyber. If you get my drift.'

'Yes, I'll try it,' he laughed, trying not to blush.

'You'd better pop into the supermarket and get yourself a packet of frozen peas, too, while you're at it.'

'Frozen peas?'

'Aye. Bird's Eye will do. That sperm count's still way too low.'

'Is it?'

'I'm afraid so.'

'Why is that?'

'Probably because you've got a varicocele down there.'

The word hit him like a bombshell – that was exactly what *he* had said to him all those years ago at the junior seminary. 'A varicocele?' he repeated, pretending not to understand, though he understood all too well.

'Aye. It's like a varicose vein. Down here in the scrotum. Except it's an artery. It's caused by the blood not being pumped back up. It's like a faulty valve, basically. It's the price we pay for walking upright.'

'I see. So what are the frozen peas for?'

'Ah, yes, well. The net result of a varicocele down there in the engine room is that it's too hot for the little blighters. The sperm, I mean. They don't like it hot! It kills them off. That's why, unlike the female of the species, in the male the works all hang out – the scrotum is outside the body – to keep the area cool. That's the theory, anyhow.'

'I see.'

'So what you have to do is keep the old tackle as cold as possible before you perform conjugals. You can do that by applying the frozen peas or an ice-pack of any sort.'

'How long for?'

'About twenty minutes should be enough. You don't want to be too brass monkeys down there, do you? You'll need to start wearing boxer shorts, too. Let the air circulate in the nether regions a bit more. If you get my drift.'

'Yes.'

'You can throw the old clobber back on now. On your way out make an appointment for three months' time. You'd better leave a specimen before you go, as well. Do you think you can manage one?'

That meant a specimen of semen, which meant masturbating into a bottle. 'I'll try,' he said, struggling not to blush again.

'Here's a bottle,' the doctor said, handing him a small plastic container. 'I've got a supply of dirty magazines here, if necessary.'

'I don't think that'll be necessary, thanks,' he laughed, hurrying out.

'Just leave the specimen with the nurse,' the doctor called down the corridor after him, to his further mortification.

He hurried down the corridor, relieved to escape. It was embarrassing, but hilarious as well. And worth it. The next part – masturbating into a bottle in a hospital toilet – wasn't as easy as it sounded, as he knew from past experience, but shouldn't be too difficult. All he'd have to do was think of Grazia. No! Not *her*! Forget *her*! Think of Sophie!

He decided to go for a pint and some lunch first. He found a pub nearby, ordered a ploughman's and a pint of Guinness and sat down. Almost reverentially he took his first sip, imbibing the bittersweet black nectar through its crown of coffee-coloured cream with a gasp of pleasure. The aroma and taste carried him straight back to Dublin, the summer and Sophie ...

Sophie had been one of the students on the summer school in Dublin that summer. She was French, but lived in Geneva, and was married, but unhappily, with a six-year-old son, whom she had left with his father in Geneva. She was twenty-five and worked as a laboratory technician.

He had fallen for her, though she wasn't at first glance his type. She wore a brown leather jacket and jeans, which with her cropped hair made her look a bit tomboyish, almost butch. However, she had a gorgeous figure with beauteous breasts and perfect, almost milk-white skin. There was a small bump in her nose, but this lent a certain charm to her features. She also had slightly prominent teeth, but again, this lent a certain puckish charm to her mouth, especially when she smiled. She had a very sexy French accent, too!

Best of all, though, she had a great sense of humour. At least, she used to laugh at all his jokes, both in class and in the pub, which was always a good sign. Women liked being made to laugh – maybe more than being made love to or at least as a prelude to making love. He had learnt that much about them!

The first time he had managed to get close to her was on an excursion to Glendalough. When he got on the coach, there was an empty seat beside her, so he took it. Talking to her was a bit of a strain, because her English wasn't very good, but he found her French accent sexy. There was something sexy about the way she laughed, too – especially when she laughed at one of his own bon mots. She laughed easily, but there was nothing 'silly' about it – it sounded totally spontaneous and natural.

He had tried to suppress his feelings of attraction, because they were both married, albeit both unhappily. Not only was he married, his wife was with him in Ireland! She hadn't gone on the trip, because she wasn't feeling well, which he was secretly pleased about, since he wanted to chat up Sophie. But it was out of the question to start anything with her, he told himself, trying to keep his eyes off her breasts and on the equally spectacular scenery of the Wicklow mountains.

When they arrived in Glendalough, he resolved to detach himself from her, but couldn't bear to, so stayed beside her as they followed the guide around, chatting and explaining things to her himself, cracking little jokes. As they listened to the guide explaining how, over a thousand years ago, this had once been a holy place, a monastic settlement, where monks had spent their days praying and studying, fasting and flagellating themselves, he couldn't help feeling a bit guilty, knowing that what he wanted to do more than anything else was screw the sexy French girl beside him.

He was amused to hear that Saint Kevin, the monk who had founded the place, had experienced similar 'temptations of the flesh'. Apparently, he had spent most of his time in a cave at the end of one of the two lovely lakes – 'Glendalough' meant 'glen of the two lakes' – trying to suppress his attraction to Saint Clare, a nun who was holed up in another cave and who apparently had a crush on him. But who was to say they hadn't succumbed to their mutual infatuation and had the occasional roll in the hay or the heather?

He had tried hard to suppress his attraction to Sophie, but without success. How ironic, he reflected now, supping his pint in a pub in Smithfield, that such a holy place would for ever be associated in his mind with sex!

The following afternoon he had gone for a stroll along Grafton Street, browsing in book and record shops, as he liked to do. After a couple of hours he decided to go for a pint, so wandered into McDaid's pub. He'd be fairly safe from meeting anyone there, he surmised – after a morning's teaching and lunch in commons with the students and other teachers, he enjoyed being on his own for a few hours.

He entered the pub, went up to the bar and ordered a pint of Guinness. While the barman performed the usual elaborate ritual of pouring it, he glanced around – there was an almost church-like atmosphere about the place, with its stone floor, marble-topped, altar-like bar and tables, wooden benches and stained-glass windows. He didn't much like churches any more, but he liked this pub, because it was supposed to have been a favourite haunt of writers such as Joyce, Behan and Kavanagh, and he enjoyed the illusion of being in the company of their ghosts.

It was only when he turned back to the bar to check if his pint was ready that he noticed her – she was sitting with her back to him at a table just around the corner of the bar. He couldn't help feeling a current of excitement, though he had resolved to forget about her. Unfortunately, he also noticed, she was sitting with another student, a Frenchman in his mid-thirties called Dominic. 'So she's off with him,' he thought, disappointed despite himself.

It was probably just as well, he decided, paying for his pint – it meant no complications. It was funny though, because the Frenchman already had his girlfriend with him on the summer school. They must have split up, he supposed, or he was just having a bit on the side. 'Well, that's the fucking Frogs for you!' he said to himself. No, he mustn't think like that, he told himself –

it was racist. Besides, all was fair in love and war, wasn't it? If Dominic had beaten him to it, so be it. In a way, he should be glad, because it solved his problem for him.

He collected his pint and went over to say hello. He didn't want to queer Dominic's pitch, but it would seem impolite if he sat on his own. Anyway, he was out of the race, so there would be no harm, he decided.

'Hello! What a pleasant surprise!' he said, to Sophie rather than Dominic, approaching their table. 'Can I join you?' *What a cheeky bugger I am!*

'Oui, pleez,' they both said, to his relief.

'Would you like a drink?' he felt obliged to offer, before sitting down.

They both declined, pointing to their glasses, but after a little more pressure Sophie accepted a Coke. He fetched it, gave it to her and sat beside her. To be polite, he asked Dominic a few questions about himself, but hardly listened to the boring, broken-English replies – he was too busy eyeing up Sophie, who was wearing her brown leather jacket and tight blue jeans as usual and had tiny silver studs in her ears.

It was just like on the coach the day before – every now and again, his arm or leg brushed hers, sending through him a frisson of excitement. Every now and again, too, he couldn't resist glancing sidewards and downwards to catch a tantalising glimpse of the tops of her breasts above the check shirt she was wearing. And every now and again he caught an erotic whiff of her perfume – all of which, combined with the relaxing effect of the alcohol, meant he was soon intoxicated with desire again.

'So, you live in Geneva?' he turned to her, deciding he didn't want to know any more about the boring, bespectacled Dominic, who was a history teacher, thirty-three years old and spoke even less English than Sophie. It was mean to move in on her, but all was fair in love and war!

'Oui, yes,' she said, in her charming French accent.

'What's it like?'

'Pardon?'

'Geneva – what's it like? Is it a good place to live?'

'Eez good for viseet, but I don't like leeve zere. Do you want come? If you want come, I geeve you my address.'

'Oh, yes, please,' he said, excited, but not sure if she was just being friendly. 'Why don't you like living there, then?'

'Eez boring,' she said. 'Trop – too bourgeois. You know 'bourgeois'? 'ow you say in Eengleesh?'

'We use the French word. Why do you live there, then?' he laughed.

'My 'usband, 'e 'as eez work zere.'

'Oh, so you're married?' he asked. He already knew she was, but wanted to make sure Dominic knew, hoping it might just put him off.

'Oui. I did not tell you yesterday?'

'Did you? What does he do, then?'

''e eez art professeur.'

'So where is he now? Why isn't he with you?'

''e eez in 'oliday in Corse. 'e doesn't want come to Ireland. 'e doesn't want learn Eengleesh. 'e prefer go sailing wiz ees friends to Corse.'

'I see. You've got a son, too, haven't you?'

'Oui. 'e 'as six years.'

'What's his name again?'

''eez name ees Chrétien.'

'That's 'Christian' in English. Don't you miss him?'

'Who? My 'usband or my son?'

'Well, both!' he laughed and Dominic laughed, too.

'I meess my son, but not my 'usband. We usually go to different 'olidays. We are not so good togezer.'

'Oh, I'm sorry.' In fact, he was guiltily pleased to hear this.

'Il ne fait rien. I am 'appy to be 'ere.'

'Are you?'

'Bien sûr.'

'Good! I think you should stop speaking French though! You need to practise your English!'

'I know – I'm sorry,' she laughed.

Her laugh made him feel dizzy with desire for her, but he tried to suppress the feeling – she was married and he was married, unhappily or not. There was Dominic, too – he couldn't quite work out if they were 'together' or not. Anyway, he wasn't going to compete with Dominic or anyone else for her. It was better to let him have her, if he wanted, and forget about her, he told himself.

'Well, I'd better be off,' he said, after a bit more chit-chat, finishing his pint and standing up to go, deciding to leave the field to Dominic.

'We go, too,' she said. 'But first I geev you address of my studio. You want?' she asked.

'Sure. I'll give you my address in London, if you want, too.'

They exchanged addresses, though he didn't really want to. It was a ritual he often performed with students, but rarely followed up by visiting them or even writing to them. He certainly couldn't see himself going to Geneva to see a married woman, especially when he was married himself.

They left the pub and walked the short distance to Grafton Street together, where he said cheerio quickly and deliberately walked off in the opposite direction to them, away from Trinity's 'surly face', as Joyce called it. He strode briskly up Grafton Street, towards Saint Stephen's Green, determined to forget about her, but couldn't resist a quick glance back, just in time to see Dominic escorting her in gentlemanly fashion across the road.

Oh, God, he thought with a groan, hurrying through the throngs of shoppers and tourists towards St. Stephen's Green – she was so lovely! He fancied her so much it was painful! It was out of the question though, forget her, let Dominic have her, he told himself, going into the park – he needed to sit on his own for a while, surrounded by flowers and trees, to try and clear his mind before going back to Trinity and Mary.

Somehow, he had contrived not to see her again until a few days later, when there was another coach trip. This time it was to Tara and the Boyne Valley. Tara was the supposed site of the palace of the ancient High Kings of Ireland, while the Boyne Valley was the site of the famous battle in 1689 between King William of Orange and James the Second, or Protestants and Catholics, English and Irish. Unfortunately, in his view, the Catholic James the Second was defeated, so the Irish yet again failed to secure their freedom from England. There wasn't much to see in either place – just a few fields, a hillock or two and a rather piddly river – but both places would always be memorable to him for other reasons.

On the coach there, quite by chance – or was it? – she was sitting just across the aisle from him, next to George, the octogenarian German student. At least there was no competition there, he thought. However, the ubiquitous Dominic was sitting right behind her – not that it mattered, he told himself, since he wasn't interested in her any more. For a while, as the coach made its way out of the northern suburbs of Dublin, he tried to ignore her, but she kept leaning across the aisle to talk to him, and every time she did so, he felt his resistance crumbling further, until in the end he gave in and started chatting to her, cracking jokes to make her laugh that charming, sexy laugh.

As the coach made its way north, she leaned over closer and closer to him, so he became more and more aroused. She was wearing a tight, v-neck sweater that emphasized her breasts and, unusually, a skirt, so short he could see her gorgeous legs and thighs for the first time.

'Francees, can I ask you someseenk?' she asked, leaning over.

'Yes?' he said, leaning towards her, so their heads were only inches apart and he could smell her perfume.

'Can I come in your class?'

'Can you come in my class? Oh, God, yes, you can, Sophie! You certainly can *come* in my class! I'll make you *come*! On the desk! On the floor! Wherever you like! As often as you like! I want to make you *come* like you've never come before! I want to fuck you like you've never been fucked before!' That was what he felt like saying, but didn't. 'Er, yes, I suppose so,' he shrugged. 'Why?'

'Alice says me you are good professeur.' Alice was her flatmate.

He was flattered, as always, but would have preferred to hear her say: 'Because I fancy you like mad and I want you to fuck me silly.'

'Is that all?' he asked, joking.

'Pardon?'

'Is that the only reason?'

'I seenk your class is interessant, because you tell about Ireesh 'eestoire.'

'Oh, yes, I do. Doesn't Fiona?'

'Non. Eet's boring.'

'Oh, I'm sorry to hear that. Fiona's a good teacher, I believe.

Anyway, you're very welcome to come into my class if you want, but you'll have to ask Charles. He's in charge.'

'Merci. Sank you. I ask eem today.'

'OK. You havc to work hard in my class though, you know. If you don't, I'll have to punish you.' He couldn't resist a risqué little joke!

' 'ow you like to puneesh me?' she asked with a heart-breaking, willpower-busting flutter of her eyelashes.

'How would I like to punish you, Sophie? I'd like to put you over my knee, lift your skirt up, pull your knickers down, stick my cock between your legs, spank you, then fuck the arse off you!' No, better not say that, he thought. A bit *too* risky! 'Oh, I don't know,' he said instead. 'How would you like to be punished?' Oh, God, he thought – this was getting seriously risqué! He'd better stop it before he went too far.

'You can puneesh me 'ow you like,' she said, in a sexy undertone and with a mischievous glint in her eyes, fluttering her eyelashes again, her milky-white skin flushing slightly.

'I'll see what I can think of,' he laughed, and half to his relief, half annoyance, Joseph, the rotund, garrulous, middle-aged businessman from Barcelona, came waddling down the aisle yet again to jabber to someone, so they had to separate.

When they arrived at Tara, he made a point of avoiding her and, for the rest of the journey, sitting somewhere else, though it tortured him to see her talking to Dominic or any other man. It was fun flirting with an attractive, sexy French girl, especially one who seemed to like him, but it was getting too dangerous, he decided. It had to stop. He was married. He couldn't do that to Mary, no matter how unsatisfactory their relationship.

A few days later though, something happened that changed his attitude. In a staff meeting, Mary publicly accused him of 'not communicating'. He was too shocked to say anything to her there and then, but let her know how he felt afterwards. 'So you think I don't communicate, do you?' he said to her. 'Well, I'll show you what 'not communicating' means.'

For the rest of the summer school, he gave her the cold shoulder – didn't speak to her, even though they were living in the same room and sharing the same bed. He felt *betrayed*. It was almost as if she had been unfaithful to him, which was ironic, when he was struggling so hard to remain faithful to her. In a way, he told himself bitterly, what she had done *was* an act of infidelity. And the fact that she was only there because of him made it even worse!

The very next evening, he was sitting in the Van Gogh, 'blowing the froth' off a few pints of Guinness with Charles, the summer school organiser, when a group of students wandered in. 'Oh, fuck!' Charles swore under his breath, not pleased to see them, but he was pleased, because Sophie was among them, in her leather jacket and jeans. They came over and exchanged a few pleasantries, but to his dismay, because there was no music, they left to try the Stag's Head across the road instead.

'Fuck me, that was a close shave!' Charles muttered.

'Yeah,' he laughed, secretly disappointed, and they carried on chatting.

A few minutes later, Sophie suddenly reappeared, on her own.

'Qu'est-ce qu'il y a?' Charles asked her.

'I come back because ze uzzer pub eez too noisy and too crowded,' she said. 'I was feel, 'ow you say, 'claustrophobe'? Tonight I prefer just to talk. Eez eet all right if I stay wiz you?'

'Bien sûr!' Charles said, with false bonhomie. 'Come and sit down!' He made room for her on the seat between them. 'Can I get you a drink?'

She took off her jacket and put it on the seat, but insisted on getting a drink herself, so went over to the bar. She was wearing a check shirt with a small silk scarf around her neck.

'She's extremely fuckable, isn't she?' Charles remarked, observing her at the bar.

'Yes,' he laughed, trying to sound indifferent.

'That Dominic chap's chasing her like mad.'

'Is he?' he asked, pretending to be surprised. 'I thought he had his girlfriend with him.'

'Oh, I think he's knocked *her* on the head.'

Sophie came back with her drink, sat down between them and they started chatting. He could hardly suppress his excitement at being close to her again, so close that their thighs touched. The more he drank, the more loquacious and daring he became, pressing his thigh closer and closer to hers. He fancied her more than ever! Did she feel the same though?

If not, why had she come back to the pub? Maybe she just wanted some free English conversation practice. Maybe she didn't really like the crowd she was with. Maybe she fancied Charles. A sudden stab of jealousy went through him at the thought. It was possible! Not because Charles was better-looking than he – he was several years older, bespectacled and balding – but because he was in charge, had an aura of authority, and was a good talker, too, especially when fuelled by Guinness.

In fact, to his annoyance, Charles started chatting with her in French, which he spoke fluently, since he lived in Paris. With his own rusty, A-level French, he couldn't compete. The swine might steal her off me, right from under my nose, he thought resentfully – even though Charles' wife was also in Dublin with him! Oh, well, he told himself, if he did, it would serve him right – it was what he had done to Dominic, or tried to. All was fair in love and war!

Then something even worse happened – Mary walked in. He ignored her, because he was still angry with her, but it was his round, so he had to go and get her a drink. When he came back, to his further annoyance she had sat in his place, next to Sophie. He refused to talk to her, but couldn't talk properly to Sophie any more either. Instead, he had to sit and listen to Charles chatting Sophie up in French that he could hardly understand. Suddenly, his evening had been ruined! He lapsed into a sullen silence.

It was silly, he knew, but he couldn't help it. Sophie seemed to have cast a spell over him. She was lovely, both physically and personally. He was infatuated with her! It was hopeless though. He was making a fool of himself. She seemed to have lost interest in him and was chatting vivaciously in French with Charles. This was the price you paid for being a romantic, he thought. Sooner or later you got hurt. In this case, sooner rather than later! He should have learned his lesson by now, learned that love was a dangerous sport.

'Anybody fancy a nosh?' Charles suddenly suggested.

'If you're paying,' Mary said, impishly.

'My privilege, my darling,' Charles said to her. 'What about you, Frank?'

He hesitated – he could opt to go with them, in the hope that Sophie would too, or decline and stay in the pub, in which case the danger was that he'd be left on his own. He certainly didn't want to spend the rest of the evening with Mary though.

'I'm not hungry,' he said, deciding to burn his boats. It was true. 'Actually, I rather fancy another pint.' That was true too.

'Tu veux manger?' Charles turned to Sophie.

He waited tensely for her answer. If she said 'yes', he was done for!

'I prefer drink also,' she said, to his secret delight.

'Let us go then, you and I,' Charles said to Mary, standing up.

Mary stood up and off they went. Suddenly, the whole evening had turned around and he was alone with Sophie! For a moment, he didn't say anything, hardly able to believe his luck. He felt as nervous as a schoolboy on his first date, but this was his big chance – he had to grab it!

'Do you really want a drink?' he asked her.

'Yes, please,' she said, shyly, with a coquettish flutter of eyelashes.

'What would you like?'

'I don't know. What do you seenk?'

'A whiskey?' he joked.

'OK,' she agreed.

'Really?' he laughed.

'Oui.'

'OK.' He went to the bar. When he came back with the drinks, he sat next to her again, clinked glasses with her and proceeded to chat her up, making her laugh her sexy laugh. Maybe it was the alcohol, but suddenly he felt as if he had kissed the Blarney Stone, felt as silver-tongued as Oscar Wilde! Chatting to her just seemed so natural, so easy. There was none of the tension he usually felt when chatting up girls – except for the tension of desire, which increased every minute.

But the minutes flew by all too quickly and suddenly the bell for closing time clanged deafeningly, as if rung by some mad fireman. It was always a dismal sound, but tonight more than ever, because he still hadn't told her how he felt – it was still all in his mind! Somehow, he had to let her know. As always though, he was terrified of being rejected, of feeling foolish, of having the illusion shattered. It was an old problem, this cowardice, this timidity, and he despised himself for it. Was it yet another by-product of his brainwashing by the Ghosters, he wondered bitterly? That thought disgusted him so much that he determined not to leave her tonight without taking the plunge.

They left the pub and, still chatting merrily, strolled back through the narrow side-streets to Trinity, through the huge, wooden front gate – like the gate of a castle – along the cobbled path between the chained-off lawns and soot-black, granite halls of residence, across the cobbled Front Square with its campanile, past the chapel and dining hall, and into Botany Bay, a side square containing tennis courts, where she was living. Fortunately it was dark and deserted. They stood chatting outside her 'house' for a while, but after a few minutes the conversation faltered – perhaps the alcohol had started to wear off – and, for the first time in the evening, there was an uncomfortable silence.

This was it, he thought. It was now or never. Was he going to blow it, say goodnight and go? What a coward he would be if he did! Not just a coward, a *cripple*! This was his very last chance – if he blew it, he'd never forgive himself. He ought to invite himself in for a coffee. He still might not have the guts to go through with it though. If only she'd invite him in, make it easy for him! If she fancied him, she would, wouldn't she? All she had to say was, 'Do you want to come in for a coffee?' – those few, simple, trite words! Why didn't she say them? What was she waiting for? No, she was a woman, and a foreigner. It was up to him!

But she said nothing. The tension became unbearable. Apart from anything else, he was afraid Mary, or Charles, or both of them, might wander along any moment. That would be the end of it. Maybe she was feeling exactly the same. Maybe she was just as nervous. His own cowardice made him squirm. Oh, God, what a stupid situation! He was a twenty-nine-year-old man, but felt as nervous and gauche as a teenager! It was up to him to break the stalemate! Say something! Anything!

'What are you going to do now – go to bed?' he blurted out and immediately thought: *'What a fucking stupid question!'*

'No, I don't seenk,' she replied. 'I'm not enough tired to sleep.'

'No?' he said, resisting the temptation to correct her grammar.

'What are you going to do, then?'

'Probably I will read.'

'Really?' he was surprised, because it was after midnight.

'Oui. I mean, yes,' she giggled.

'What are you reading?' Christ, he thought, another stupid question! Were they going to have a literary discussion now, standing here in Botany Bay after midnight? Why didn't he just get to the point?

' "Ze Pearl", by John – I don't remember …'

'Steinbeck?'

'Oui.'

'Why are you reading that?'

'For my 'cours'.'

'Do you like it?'

'Eez good, yes. Mais, c'est difficile pour moi.'

'Yes, I suppose so,' he smiled.

'You know zees book?'

'I haven't read that one, actually, but I've read most of his stuff. "The Grapes of Wrath" – that's his most famous one. Do you know it?'

'Si. I seenk so. But I don't read.'

'No? It's very good. You should do some time.'

She smiled and there was another uncomfortable silence. He couldn't think of anything else to say, yet couldn't tear himself away. This was his very last chance! He summoned up all his courage.

'If you don't want to go to bed, shall we go in and have some coffee?' he suggested, holding his breath for her reply.

'Oui, OK,' she said, turning and walking towards the door.

For a moment, he just stood there, not quite able to believe it. Then, relieved, he followed her into the flat, trying to suppress his excitement – going in for a coffee didn't mean she would let him go to bed with her, but at least he'd know the score. Anyway, he was happy just to be able to stay with her for a bit longer.

'Alice sleep in zere,' she whispered, opening the main door into the entrance hall of the flat, pointing at the first door and putting a finger to her lips.

He nodded and followed her through into the living-room, where she put the light on. To his surprise, there was an unmade bed in the corner. 'My bed,' she said, embarrassed, putting her bag down and hurrying to make it.

'Don't worry,' he laughed, but she ignored him. 'Why are you sleeping in here?'

'Ze bedroom eez too …' – she hesitated, searching for the word – '… too near of ze street – so eez, 'ow you say ...?'

'Noisy.'

'Oui. So I remove to in 'ere.'

'I see. Is Alice in?' He pointed to the bedroom wall.

'Oui, I seenk so.'

'Asleep?'

'I seenk. She go to bed early.'

'You don't mind sleeping in here?' He found it titillating to hover around the subject of bed – it might be the nearest he got, he reflected wryly.

'Eez OK.'

He glanced around the room – it was the standard Trinity student living-room, spacious and well-furnished, with a settee and two armchairs, dining-table and chairs, built-in bookshelves, mostly empty now, a gas fire and a plain, grey carpet. The wallpaper was grubby, the furniture shabby, the carpet threadbare and lighting dim, but it was comfortable enough.

'What do you like?'

'What? Oh, some coffee, please, if you have any.'

'Do you want eat someseenk?'

'Er – what have you got?' He was too nervous to be hungry, even though he had had no dinner, but he thought accepting something to eat might help him to protract his stay – not that she seemed in any hurry to get rid of him.

'You like some toast?'

'Yes, OK. If you don't mind.'

'I make for you some toast,' she said, without any hesitation, going towards the kitchen door.

'What about you?' he asked, following her and standing in the kitchen doorway as she fiddled with the gas stove.

'I take nuseenk.'

'No? Why not?'

'I don't want.'

'Are you sure you don't mind?'

'Eez my pleasure.'

He smiled at the expression – it sounded so sexy in her French accent, especially the word 'pleasure', which came out as 'pleezur'. He wondered back into the living-room, picked up the copy of "The Pearl" lying on the table and sat down on the somewhat lumpy settee to look at it. She seemed to have read only the first couple of pages, since only they were annotated, and there was a bookmark after them. It gave him a frisson to touch the paper she had touched, to read the exact words she had read – though evidently with some difficulty, since so many of them were underlined and had a French translation pencilled in above.

After a few minutes, she brought in a plate of toast and a cup of coffee. He put the book back on the table and took the plate and cup from her, placing the plate nervously on the arm of the settee. 'I can't eat all that!' he laughed.

'You mustn't if you don't want.'

'You can't help me?'

'Sank you. I am not 'ungry.'

'Sit down, anyway,' he said, starting to eat.

She returned to the kitchen, switched off the light and shut the door. Then she came back and sat beside him on the settee, but a little away from him and on the edge.

'It's nice,' he said, more about being together than the toast.

'Sank you.'

He carried on eating, though he had no appetite, was too excited at being alone with her, in her room – her *bedroom* – so late at night. What to talk about – that was the question? All he really wanted to do was put his arms around her and ...

'Do you find the book very difficult?' he asked.

'Yes. I want get a French translation.'

'That'd be cheating!' he laughed.

She furrowed her brow.

''Cheating'? You don't know that word?' He tried to think of the French word, but couldn't. 'Not honest?' he suggested.

'Ah, oui,' she said, understanding. 'But I must. Eet eez too 'ard for me.'

'Don't worry,' he smiled. 'I won't tell on you.'

She shook her head uncomprehendingly. He tried in vain to think of the French equivalent, regretting the rustiness of his French. 'I won't tell your teacher,' he said, in the end.

'Sank you,' she smiled. When she smiled, the corners of her mouth went up in a pert way that sent a dart of desire through him.

'I used to do it myself, when I was learning French,' he confessed.

'You stoodied French at ze school?'

'Yes. For six years, believe it or not.' He had actually passed French A-level, but it didn't seem to be much help now!

'You speak quite well,' she said.

'How do you know?' he laughed.

'I leesten you.'

'When?'

She shrugged. 'Avant. 'ow you say?'

'Before.'

'Before,' she repeated.

'I never speak French though,' he said.

'You do – I leesten you.'

'Well, maybe sometimes. Not often though. Anyway, I'm supposed to be teaching you English, not learning French.'

'You can do both.'

'Yes, that's a good idea.' Any excuse to be with her! 'You can teach me French and I'll teach you English. What do you say?'

'I like zees idée.'

He was delighted – it meant she was interested. 'Mm, that was good, thanks,' he said, putting down his cup.

'You don't want fineesh?'

'No, thanks. I'm full.'

'Pardon?'

'I'm full. Full? Er – je suis plein.'

She shook her head.

'Je suis plein,' he repeated. 'J'ai finis de manger. J'ai assez. Je n'ai pas encore de faim …'

She burst out laughing, which embarrassed but also excited him.

'Why are you laughing? Is my French so terrible?' he grinned.

She shook her head, blushing herself. 'Pardon. Tu as dis – you 'ave sayed, 'Je suis plein'?'

'Yes. Can't you say that in French?'

'Non. Eez different.' Again she smiled that little smile that puckered the corners of her mouth, revealing her teeth just a little, which he found so charming.

'What do you say in French, then?' he asked, and she told him.

'So what does 'Je suis plein' mean?'

'Eet means, "I am drunk".'

'Oh, no!' he laughed. 'No, I'm not drunk!'

Except with you, he thought, and wondered how much longer he would be able to spin it out. She was still sitting on the edge of the settee, but gave no hint that she wanted him to go. Was she just being polite, he wondered? No, she seemed quite relaxed, quite happy for him to be there. It was silly to just carry on making small talk though, he told himself – it was time to make a move, say something. What if she rejected him though? The thought crushed him. He'd never fancied any girl so much. He was besotted by her! He couldn't bear the thought of leaving without at least kissing her ...

There was an awkward silence, but she gave him no sign that she wanted him to kiss her – she was still sitting on the edge of the settee in a rather awkward-looking position, elbows on her knees, half-turned towards him, saying nothing, playing with one of the rings on her fingers. Later he would realise that she was virtually imploring him to kiss her!

He couldn't bear the suspense any longer. Impulsively, he leant forward, reached out and took hold of her finger. It was the first time he had ever touched her. He had never even shaken hands with her before and now he was holding one of her fingers – it felt so light, so delicate, so feminine! His heart raced with both excitement and fear, fear that she would pull her hand away, but she didn't.

'Where did you get the ring?' he asked, his voice sticking in his throat. It was a plain, thin, silver band, rather cheap-looking.

She turned her gaze to him, making his head spin. 'Eet eez from my 'usband,' she said, sending another stab of jealousy through him.

'Is it – your wedding ring?' he asked, hoping she would say no.

'Si. But we are not in ze love any more.'

She suddenly sounded so 'triste', his heart went out to her. He wanted to put his arms around her and hug her, but didn't dare. Instead, he held her finger a few moments longer, hoping he was transmitting what he felt, hoping to receive it back. Then he gently let her finger go and touched the silver chain dangling from her neck, which she had also started fiddling with.

'And this?' he asked, his voice sticking in his throat again.

'From a friend. A girl friend.'

He let the chain rest weightlessly on the tips of his fingers for a few moments, then let it go. Their eyes met and suddenly he knew.

'Sit back,' he said softly, putting his arm around her shoulders.

She leant back, he pulled her gently towards him, their lips met and they kissed, eyes closed, tongues darting excitedly in and out of each other's mouths. While they kissed, he caressed her, gradually moving his hand to her breasts, which he had ogled with such desire for so long. He fondled them excitedly for a while, then started to undo the buttons of her shirt. Suddenly, though, she pulled away and, alarmed, he was about to apologise, thinking he'd gone too far.

'Shall we use ze bed?' she murmured, to his relief.

He nodded eagerly. She stood up, took his hand and led him over to it. A few moments later they had torn each other's clothes off and were on it, making mad, passionate love ...

Ah, that night had been the most fantastic sex he had ever had! It gave him a hard-on, just thinking about it now in the pub – which was the object of the exercise. Unable to wait any longer, he finished off his pint quickly, hurried into the toilets, took out the little plastic bottle and made himself come into it. It didn't take long. 'Oh, Sophie!' he gasped, over and over again, as he came, remembering how they'd gasped out each other's names ecstatically, over and over again, on that wonderful, orgiastic night.

When he had finished, he felt dizzy, so had to sit down for a few minutes on the toilet seat. He studied his semen in the little plastic bottle – 'spunk' as it was vulgarly called. It looked just like glue! So this was what it was all about, this teaspoonful of colourless, cloudy, gooey liquid, he reflected wryly – all that mental, emotional and physical energy, just to produce this! Wasn't nature strange! And to think there were maybe millions of sperm – his future sons and daughters – swimming about in there! Or at least so he hoped.

As always after masturbating though, he felt ashamed, even though it was medically necessary, was in a good cause, might even help to save his marriage. It just showed the power of conditioning! It was ironic – for years he had been told that masturbation was a *mortal* sin, for which you could go to HELL, and here he was being *ordered* to do it! He should've done it fantasising about Mary though, he supposed. It would be even more ironic if it showed he was 'fertile' and saved his marriage!

He slipped the bottle into his pocket, went back to the clinic and handed it in to the nurse.

'It looks like you've had a good time!' she joked.

He gave her an embarrassed smile and hurried away.

CHAPTER TWELVE

'Gerry's dead,' Mary said, putting the phone down.

'You what?'

'Gerry's dead. He was killed at work this morning.'

'Killed? What do you mean? How?'

'He fell off a ladder or something.'

'Oh, God! That's – ' There was no word to express it. They had become good friends with Gerry, the Dublin crane-driver, who was a fellow-member of the Sugawn Theatre Group. 'Are you sure?' he asked, stupidly.

'Yes. Peggy's just told me.'

'I can't believe it,' he said, shaking his head.

'Poor Norah,' Mary said.

'Yes. How is she?'

'She's hysterical.'

'I just can't believe this! Where is he now?'

'In the hospital.'

'You mean – in the mortuary?'

'I suppose so. I'm not sure. She didn't say.'

'He can't be dead! I was laughing and joking with him in the pub the other day. His daughter's making her First Holy Communion next week. He was really looking forward to it. It's just too – too senseless.'

'God must have a reason.'

'Fuck God and his reasons!' he exclaimed, suddenly annoyed by her apparent passivity. 'You don't really think, if there was a God, he'd let something like this happen, do you? Unless he's some sort of psychopath.'

'Just because you don't believe in God, Fran.'

'I *don't* bloody believe in God! Especially when I hear something like this! I mean, Gerry Mulligan? The nicest, most inoffensive bloke in the world? Never did any harm to anyone?

With a wife and seven-year-old daughter? He's dead, just because he fell off a ladder? It doesn't make any bloody sense at all! It's bloody tragic! It certainly puts our problem in perspective, doesn't it?'

'What do you mean?'

'Here we are, arguing because we can't have a baby, because you think I'm having an affair …'

'You *are* having an affair, with that Italian one, aren't you?'

'I've told you, I'm not having an affair with her! I'm just friendly with her.' Not that he wouldn't like to have an affair with Grazia, but she wouldn't co-operate. How ironic!

'You did have an affair with that French one in Dublin, didn't you?'

She was referring to Sophie. It was true. To his horror, Mary had actually knocked on the door while they were making love that first time, calling out, 'Fran? Are you in there?'

He had told Sophie to keep quiet, but Mary had kept knocking and asking if he was in there. In the end, Sophie had gone to the door and called back: ''e was 'ere. But 'e left one hour ago. 'e sayed 'e was go for walk. I am sorry – I am sleeping.' To his relief, Mary had then gone away and they had carried on making love.

'Where've you been?' Mary had demanded angrily, when he got back to his own flat at about five in the morning. 'We've had a search party out looking for you! We were going to call the police!'

But he had just ignored her and got into the other bed – he was still punishing her for criticizing him in public. In fact, he had kept up the 'silent' treatment for the rest of the summer school, he had felt so angry, so *betrayed*. Ah, revenge was sweet, oh so sweet! Especially served cold.

'If you're going to start all that again, I'm going out!' he shouted, jumping up, grabbing his jacket from the back of the door and doing so.

He was glad of the excuse. He had been helping her with an essay on Robert Lowell when the phone rang. He was already suffering from 'cabin fever' and the news about Gerry's death was so depressing he would have no chance of concentrating. As usual when he needed to escape, he went down to the Marshes for a walk along the river and dropped into the Robin Hood, where he bought himself a pint of London Pride.

He couldn't believe Gerry was dead. It was midwinter and the scene looked appropriately, depressingly dead, but in his mind's eye he imagined it in spring: the vegetation high, the horse chestnut, cherry, laburnum and hawthorn trees in full bloom, the scent of lilac in the air, the meadow opposite a riot of wildflowers, butterflies and bees … Oh God, Gerry was dead? It was unbelievable, illogical, incomprehensible! It made a mockery of life, of all their problems and hopes and desires and dreams. What on earth was the point if you could be snuffed out just like that? 'Like flies to wanton boys …'

All the more reason to enjoy life while you could, he told himself over his pint – carpe diem! What did it matter if they couldn't have a baby? What did it matter if their marriage wasn't happy? What did it matter if he didn't love her? Either of them could be snuffed out at any moment, by some silly, stupid accident! It was all just a joke, a sick joke! If there was a God, he was a comedian, a comedian who specialised in sick jokes. He was a bloody psychopath! Christ, life was *meaningless*, whether there was a God or not. It was a no-win situation!

Sex was the best antidote to death, he reflected. The trouble was, he just didn't enjoy sex with Mary any more. It had become a mechanical, stressful, monthly ritual, timed to try and conceive. And every month, when her period came, she went into a depression. It had become an ordeal, instead of a pleasure. Thank goodness for Sophie! She had saved him from going crackers. The memory of that wonderful summer at Trinity had kept him going. Ironically, it had kept his marriage to Mary going too. It was hanging by a thread, but it was still alive.

At Christmas Sophie had come to visit him in London and at Easter he had gone to see her in Geneva. The memories had helped to make life bearable – his problems with Mary, the humiliations of infertility, and now the death of Gerry. And what sweet memories they were! He remembered meeting her at the airport and laughing at her, because she arrived with sunglasses on her head, even though it was December; going for drinks in his favourite pubs; sightseeing around London; listening to Irish music; shopping in Oxford Street, where she had bought a big Paddington Bear for Christian, her son; going for a walk here on the Marshes in the snow; how she used to say, 'Tu boude?', if he was quiet, so that it had become a joke between them; having dinner by candlelight; having a bath together; and of course, best of all, making love.

It was only in London at Christmas that she had told him she had been 'stérilisée', as she put it. It was only then he had noticed the scars on her breasts – self-inflicted as it turned out. It was only then she had told him how, only a year before, she had lain in a coma for three days after taking an overdose, because she was so unhappy with her husband and with life in general.

At Easter, on the plane to see her in Geneva, he had read a pornographic paperback called, 'I, A Man', by Sverre Holm, translated from Danish. He wasn't in the habit of reading pornography, but had forgotten to pack a book and picked it up on impulse in the airport W.H. Smith. Somehow, the title suited his mood – he felt like a 'man-of-the-world', flying out to Geneva for a 'dirty' weekend with his 'mistress'. It was the sort of thing he had read about in novels, but never actually done before. He had expected the novel to be trash, but in fact it was quite well-written, or at least translated, and it had made him feel even more excited at the thought of meeting and making love with Sophie again.

He hardly recognised her when he saw her at the airport – she was wearing a poncho, tight white cords and white, knee-length boots. She looked glamorous, like some sort of celebrity, a model maybe, and he could hardly believe she was *his*. He noticed other men glancing enviously when she welcomed him with a kiss and couldn't help feeling smug.

From the airport, they had taken a bus to her flat. It was old-fashioned and dark, with wooden floors, cushions rather than chairs, and lots of plants, the watering of which was a daily ritual. They had breakfast in the tiny kitchen – coffee and croissants – and spent that first morning making love in her bed, which was just a mattress on the floor. Luckily, Christian was at school. She had a kitten called 'Picardy' that they played with on the bed, too, though it had sharp little claws and gave him several scratches. She – or her son – also had a pet rabbit, which she allowed to run free around the flat.

When Christian came home, he had given him the toy car he had brought as a present for him. He was a lovely boy and he had enjoyed playing with him – with the car, doing jigsaws or chasing him around the flat, pretending to be a lion. In fact, he had got on so well with Christian that Sophie had become jealous! It had made him want to be a father even more, made him feel depressed at the thought that he might never be able to.

When he told her he had once been going in for the priesthood, she had told him she had an uncle who was a 'curé' and somehow that made him feel closer to her. That evening she had made dinner – chicken and some special vegetable of Geneva – and invited two friends, Jean-Marc and Madeleine, to show him off, he supposed. After dinner they had all sat around on the cushions, listening to jazz on the cassette player and chatting. Unfortunately, they had talked in French and he couldn't keep up, so went silent. 'Tu boude?' she had asked, several times, with that pert, sexy smile of hers.

The next day she had shown him around Geneva. He found it lived up to its reputation as a rather smug, self-satisfied, affluent, dull place. It seemed very straight-laced too. Well, after all, it was Calvin's old stomping ground! He laughed to himself now, because she had told him off for trying to kiss her in public, explaining that it wasn't 'bon ton'.

She took him, Christian, Picardy and the rabbit to the lake. The sun shone, the lake sparkled, the geyser spurted, the mountains in the background gleamed white with snow and it was all as pretty as a postcard. They went for a boat ride on the lake. Christian and he played with the toy car, the kitten and the rabbit in a sandpit by the lakeside. They took photos. They looked like a happy family and he wished they were!

The next day they went for a trip to the mountains. It was the first time he had seen the Alps or people skiing. She told him she was getting divorced and showed him the document detailing the property split. It was a sad document, but she didn't seem sad about it. He wished he was free to ask her to marry him. She was reading 'Death of a Salesman' for her 'cours', so he helped her with it. One morning she gave him a scare when she told him she might be pregnant, because she was feeling sick, but it turned out to be just her IUD.

All in all, it had been a great week. There had only been a couple of bad moments. One night she wouldn't make love, because

Christian was awake. 'Tu boude?' she had mocked him, because he had gone silent. Another time she had told him off for leaving the bathroom floor wet and again when he knocked over and broke a lamp-stand. Otherwise, it had been idyllic.

Which made what she had said to him on the morning of his departure all the more of a shock. They had spent most of the morning making love and got up late to have breakfast. At the end of breakfast, they still had some spare time before going to the airport. 'What do you want to do?' she asked.

'Let's go back to bed and make love,' he suggested, only half-joking.

He would never forget her reply: 'Yes,' she said, 'but eet will be ze last time.'

'What do you mean?' he laughed, thinking she was joking too.

'Zees will be ze last time.'

'You mean – till we meet again?'

'Non, eet weel be ze last time for ever.'

'You mean – you don't want to see me again? You want to end it?' He couldn't believe it!

'Yes, I sink eet eez finished.'

'Are you serious?'

'Oui, I am serious.'

'Why?' he demanded, starting to feel angry.

'Rien. I sink ze feeling 'as finished.'

Now he really was angry! To think he had been going to ask her to marry him! 'I see,' he said coldly, standing up. 'We'd better go then. If it's finished, let's go now and get it over with.'

They had driven to the airport in virtual silence, because he could hardly bring himself to speak to her. He was 'bouding' in a big way! And that was how it had ended. He realised now she was a rather shallow, superficial, flighty character, but he had no regrets. It was all grist to the mill.

'I don't believe in God any more,' Norah, Gerry's wife said, in her strong Dublin accent, when they visited her a few days after the funeral. 'He wouldn't have taken my husband away from me and her father from *her*. He was such a good husband and father. He never said a bad word to me. And he was crazy about

Siobhan. He was looking forward to her First Holy Communion so much! I'll never forget the day he died. 'Your daddy's late, he must be working till six,' I said to her, never thinking, when he didn't arrive home at the usual time. I can't bring myself to throw away his clothes yet. His jacket was split up the back – I'll show it to you later. I think it was where he tried to save himself, fallin' off the ladder. He was still conscious in the ambulance. All he had was a black eye. Apparently he was callin' out his daughter's name in the ambulance. Not mine, his daughter's. He was crazy about her. He loved me too, o' course. He was the best husband any woman could wish for. When I got the phone message from the hospital, they told me he only had concussion and a twisted back. In actual fact, both his legs was broken from knee to ankle. An' his skull fractured too. He landed on his feet, but hit his head on something on the way down. Anyhow, he had massive brain damage. They told me he'd be a vegetable if he survived the operation. I signed the form anyway. I wanted him back, even if he was a cabbage. The last time I saw him alive was on the trolley, when they were wheelin' him into the theatre. His eyes was rollin' an' he was still callin' out his daughter's name. I'll never forget that sight. Or the doctor's words.' She was crying now. '"Mrs. Mulligan," he said, "your husband's in a very bad way. We can't promise anything. Shall we get the priest?" "The priest?" I said. "It's the usual thing in these cases," he said. I knew then. He only survived the operation for five minutes. They put him in the chapel of ease. They didn't want to let me see him. "I'm not leaving here till I've seen my husband," I said. "It's out of the question, it's not allowed," they said. "We couldn't let you see him after what they've done to him." I insisted though and in the end they gave in. "On one condition," he said. "I cover his face. I couldn't let you see his face." So I never saw his face again. I only saw his hands. That was the last I saw of him. Oh, yes, I went to the building site. I demanded to see the spot where it happened, but they refused. Why was he climbing down any ladder without a hat on, I wanted to know? It'll all come out at the inquest, I suppose. I can't believe he's in St. Patrick's cemetery now. He liked cemeteries, because they're peaceful and quiet. He liked St. Patrick's. He didn't like the old part, mind you, but they put him in there. I should've had him cremated as he wished. I'll have to have him moved from there. He wouldn't be happy in there. The inquest is in two months. But I don't care about the money. It won't bring him back. He was such a good husband to me and father to her. I met him when I was sixteen. We were married when I was eighteen. Married for twenty-five years, we were.'

She broke down sobbing. Mary went over and put an arm around her. It was an aspect of Mary's character that he admired. It was just one of the reasons he wanted to make their marriage work. She really was a gem.

The following day he went to the hospital to get the result of his fertility test. He sat on one of the tubular steel chairs in the hospital waiting room and glanced around. There were some posters on the walls, which were painted in an insipid turquoise colour: a Constable and an Alitalia poster. There was also a rather tatty notice saying, 'SPECIMENS THIS WAY PLEASE'. There was a fire extinguisher, a weighing scales, a height measurer and some examination cubicles. It was depressing.

In the middle of the tiled floor, there was a coffee table with some magazines on it, mostly women's mags. One of them was a 'Woman's Realm', with a picture of a mother and quins on the front cover. Not very appropriate for an infertility clinic, he reflected wryly. The only other patient was a man in a wheelchair. He really didn't want to get into conversation about sperm counts with him, so picked up the magazine and pretended to read, hoping he wouldn't have to wait too long. To his relief a nurse called him in after a few minutes. This was it.

To his surprise, there were two other doctors as well as Mr. Hendry, the consultant, sitting behind the desk, all in white coats. Mr. Hendry stood up, shook hands with him and introduced the other doctors as a trainee and a visiting American infertility specialist. Then he invited him to sit down on the chair in front of the desk. The nurse sat on another chair to the side. It was almost as if he was on trial!

'The results of your tests are as follows,' the consultant said, taking some papers out of a green file. 'The sperm count is still rather low – seventeen million per millilitre. We really need twenty million. My American colleague here would probably say forty million. Is that right?' The American doctor nodded. 'So it sounds bad, but it's not a disaster. The problem is, you have a varicocele down there. There are no other problems evident. I wonder if you'd mind us taking a look?'

The nurse ushered him into a cubicle, told him to take his trousers and underpants down and stand. Fortunately, she was neither young nor attractive, so there was no danger of having an erection. Perhaps that was why she had been chosen for the job, he thought uncharitably. He was far too tense to have an erection, anyway.

The three doctors came in. The consultant crouched down in front of him and fiddled with his balls. 'Take a look,' he invited the other two, standing up. 'You won't see a better example of a varicocele than that.' The other two doctors crouched down and examined him. He had to struggle not to blush, not to remember ...

'All right, you can get dressed again,' the consultant said, patting him on the arm, when they had all had a good gawp. Then the doctors all went back into the consulting room, while he got dressed and followed them.

'A varicocele is caused by the blood not being pumped back up from down there,' the consultant explained. 'It's a fault with the valve. It's the price we pay for walking upright. We weren't designed to, you see. Is intercourse OK?'

'Yes,' he said, still struggling not to blush.

'Erection, penetration, all OK?'

'Yes, I think so,' he said, reddening despite himself.

'Has your wife had all the tests?'

'Yes.'

'Where? Here?'

'Yes.'

'She's ovulating OK? Her tubes are OK?'

'Apparently, yes.'

'I see.' The consultant turned to consult with his colleagues.

'So, does this mean I can never have children?' he asked, slightly miffed at being ignored.

'Not necessarily,' the consultant faced him again. 'There are things we can do. One of the things we can do is perform an operation.'

'An operation?' The very word scared him. That was the last thing he wanted!

'Oh, it's only a minor op. We make a small incision, about two inches, in the groin and tie off the artery to stop the blood getting down there.'

'I see. Would it require a general anaesthetic?'

'I don't think you'd like it with a local,' he smiled, as if it was amusing.

He was niggled by his manner, but decided to ignore it. 'And would I have to stay in hospital?'

'Only for about three days. You're a lecturer, aren't you? We could do it in August, if that'd suit you. You'll be on holiday then, won't you?'

Yes, but I don't want to spend it in hospital having a bloody operation. I want to spend it in Dublin, having a good time.

'Do you want to go ahead?'

'Er – what are the chances of success?'

'I'd say about seventy per cent, which is not bad. Wouldn't you?' He turned to the American doctor.

'Sure,' the American quack said. He wasn't very talkative, unusually for an American perhaps.

Seventy per cent? Was that all? He only had a seventy per cent chance of being normal and having children? What a depressing thought! 'Can I think about it?' he asked.

'Of course,' the consultant said, suavely. 'I know it's not a decision to take lightly. Go home and discuss it with your wife. I'll tell you what, we'll book you in, anyway, and you can always cancel if you decide against. How's that?' He stood up and offered his hand, obviously eager to see his next patient.

'Yes, all right, thanks,' he shrugged, standing up and self-consciously shaking hands with all three of them.

'The nurse will book you in at reception,' the consultant said, ushering him to the door and opening it for him.

'Thank you,' he said, going out.

'Nurse, varicocele for ligation,' he heard the consultant say to the nurse behind him, as he did so.

So that's what I am, he thought – *a varicocele for ligation! 'We can perform an operation.' Well, no thanks! Sod that for a game of soldiers!*

'Well?' Mary demanded, as soon as he entered the front door.

'It's not good news,' he said, giving her a perfunctory peck on the cheek and going into the living-room.

'What did they say?' she asked, following him.

'Make me a cup of tea,' he said, dropping onto the settee.

She went to the kitchen to do so. He was just stalling. He had already had a couple of pints of Young's Special on the way home, to help him absorb the impact of what the doctor had told him and to delay facing her, but he couldn't delay it much longer. He felt angry – angry with himself, with the doctor, with her, even though he knew that was irrational.

'They said I've got a low sperm count,' he told her, when she brought the tea.

'What does that mean?'

'It means there aren't enough sperm,' he said, sarcastically.

It was humiliating, to think they couldn't have children because of *him*. He felt like a failure and that wasn't a feeling he was used to. In a way, the tables had turned, the balance of power between them shifted.

'Does it mean we can't have children?'

'Basically, yes,' he said, bluntly.

'Can't they do anything?'

'Yes. They said I could have an operation.'

'What kind of operation?'

He hesitated, not really wanting to talk about it, but forced himself to. 'They make a two-inch incision in the groin and tie off the artery that's causing the problem.'

'Would you have to have a general anaesthetic?'

'I wouldn't have it with a *local* anaesthetic, would I?' he said sarcastically, despite himself.

'So you'd have to stay in hospital?' she asked, ignoring his sarcasm.

'For about three days, according to the quack.'

'Are you going to have it, then?'

'Have an operation? Just because I can't have kids? You must be joking!'

'Why not, Fran?'

Her matter-of-fact tone really narked him. 'Because I don't want a bloody operation! I don't want doctors sticking their knives into me! Anyway, he said it would only have a seventy per cent chance of success. If I can't have children normally and naturally, I won't have them at all. It's not that important. I'm not sure I want to bring children into this lousy world anyway.' That last bit was probably the Young's Special talking, he realised.

'I want to have children, Fran. I want to have your children.'

'Well, it looks as if I haven't got any children to give you, doesn't it?' He couldn't stop himself sounding angry now.

'Why are you being so negative?'

'Because it *is* negative! I'm infertile or 'subfertile', as they euphemistically call it. That's fucking negative, isn't it?'

'Why don't you have the operation? It might work.'

'Oh, it's easy for you to say, "Why don't you have the operation?", just like that. It's not you going under the knife, is it?'

'I've had operations. I'd do it if I had to.'

'I've had an operation before too and I don't want to have another one, unless it's absolutely necessary, thank you! I don't trust these bloody doctors!'

'It *is* necessary though, if we want to have a baby.'

'You're the one who wants to have a baby, not me! I don't care whether we have a baby or not!'

'You'd do it for one of your French or Italian tarts though, wouldn't you,' she said, bitterly.

'I haven't got any French or Italian tarts!' he shouted back. Ironically, it was true – Sophie had dumped him and Grazia still wouldn't play ball. There was a German girl he had gone out with, but Mary didn't know about that yet.

'Yes, you have!' she shouted back. 'You went to Geneva to fuck that French one, I know! And you're fucking that Italian one here. Why don't you fuck me! What's wrong with me?'

'If you're going to start that, I'm going out,' he said, jumping up and rushing out, slamming the front door. However, she opened it and followed him out onto the balcony.

'That's right, go and fuck her instead of me!' she shouted down the stairs after him, to his embarrassment, because neighbours were coming up – not that there was anything unusual about such scenes on the council estate where they now lived. 'Go on! Go and fuck her! I won't be here when you get back!' she shouted after him from the balcony, as he hurried out of the estate.

More angry than embarrassed now, he stopped, turned around and shouted back up to her: 'Go on, fuck off, then! I don't care!'

Then he turned and walked away.

CHAPTER THIRTEEN

God, how had it come to this, he thought, over a pint of London Pride in the Robin Hood? Swearing at each other in public! '*I won't be here when you get back!*' She hadn't meant that, had she? That really would be serious! It was so ironic – he really didn't have anyone to go and fuck, even if he wanted to, which he didn't. Well, he wanted to fuck Grazia, but she still wouldn't let him. He was really fed up with that girl. He was starting to think she was just a cockteaser. She was so damned stubborn! He still fancied her though. It was torture, going out with her and not being able to even kiss her. God, she'd looked so lovely the other night, when they went for a drink – she was wearing a long tartan skirt, maroon velvet shirt, black tie and slinky black boots, with a maroon velvet shoulder bag. There was a charming shyness about her, almost a gaucheness. He especially loved the way she said 'scherzo'. Women! He was torn between fascination and disdain for them.
Why did Mary have to make such a fuss about having a baby? 'Your French and Italian tarts'! The bitterness! 'Hell hath no fury ...' If only she knew! She didn't know about Katja. Or did she? She seemed to have a built-in radar. Maybe she was saving her up. If only Katja was here now! The ironic thing was, he had felt a massive sense of relief when she'd left ...

Katja had come to London to see him for three days. Like Sophie, he'd met her on the summer school in Dublin, and they'd had a fling, but it was really her friend he fancied, Steffi – blonde, svelte, sweet, sexy Steffi. They were both medical students. However, Katja seemed to fancy him, whereas Steffi didn't, so he got off with Katja. He didn't really fancy her, but thought it would be interesting to go to bed with her, because she was German and a medical student. She was a bit on the plump side, but good in bed. She seemed to have no inhibitions and was insatiable, wanted to screw all the time! Tired him out, actually!

She was intelligent though. He'd taken her to Dillons to buy a textbook. What was it called – 'Cell Cytology' or something? They'd gone to the British Museum. And to the theatre, to see 'Accidental Death of an Anarchist' by Dario Fo, which he'd enjoyed. They'd gone to the cinema too, to see 'Stardust Memories' by Woody Allen. It wasn't as funny as 'Sleeper', but OK. She'd taken him to a Russian restaurant, because she was half Russian, which he hadn't realised – hence the name, 'Katja'. What had they had – 'borscht'? 'Borscht' meant 'soup', she'd told him. That was the starters. The main course was 'chicken tsarevna', which meant chicken of the tsar's daughter or something. Or was it trout and almonds? There'd been musicians wandering about, playing Russian music. He had to pay them, but didn't mind, because they sounded good and he was in a good mood. In other words, he was drunk! Then they'd gone home and made love.

He'd done all the usual tourist things with her: Leicester Square, Soho, Piccadilly Circus, Tower Bridge, Whitehall, Westminster, Buck. Pal., St. Paul's, Oxford Street, even Harrods – not that she was really interested in shopping. She was more interested in museums, art galleries and bookshops. She was intelligent you see. Mind you, she liked pubs too. He'd taken her to the Victoria on Holloway Road to hear some Irish music. Segui were playing. She'd really enjoyed that. She'd enjoyed the Cockney Pride pub in Piccadilly, too – there was a really good pianist playing music hall songs on the 'joanna'.

It was there, he remembered, that she'd asked him a really funny question: 'Was London damaged during the war?' He'd told her about the blitz. She had no idea! She said she never got any anti-German feeling in London. She told him her father had been in a Russian prison camp till 49 and loved whisky, so he'd helped her buy a bottle of whisky in Harrods for him.

They'd had lots of deep discussions about marriage, sex, freedom, life, death, religion, philosophy, happiness, books, art, truth. He'd taken her to Biddy Mulligan's, where to his delight 'From Clare to Here' by the Fureys was on the jukebox as they went in. He told her about Irish music, history and Northern Ireland. Being intelligent, she was interested, you see.

Afterwards, on the bus going home, to his embarrassment, they'd been accosted by a drunken Scot: 'I'm Sco'ish! Wha' arre you?

Irrish? Arre ye prroud of your countrrymen, what those bastarrds do'? My motherr was borrn in Irreland and killed in Irreland. Is yourr girrlfrriend laughing at me? I'll kill herr! I'll take you on, too.' What a fucking idiot! Straight out of central casting! Luckily the West Indian conductor had chucked him off. 'C'mon. Off my bus. I don't know what he said to you, but I want you off my bus. You've already broken the law ten times. All I want is a nice peaceful ride.' '*My'* bus! He'd liked that bit. It'd all been a bit embarrassing though. Anyway, he'd had a good time with her, but was relieved when she went. He'd felt really guilty! He gave her a Bob Dylan cassette as a parting gift at the station when she left. She invited him to Berlin, but he knew he'd never go ...

How he wished she was here now though! He could do with someone to talk to, instead of talking to himself. He was so desperate for human company, he would even have been glad to talk to the mad woman who had accosted him on the way here. She had just came up to him and said, 'I hate Hackney. Look at the streets. They're so drab.' Then walked off. Funny.

The area was a bit rough, he supposed. Poor. Or 'socially deprived' to use the fashionable jargon. That was just a euphemism, wasn't it? But he liked the area. It was down to earth. The people certainly looked poor, but then he was poor himself! He couldn't afford to live anywhere better. He didn't particularly want to. He had been reading about Marxism and liked what he read, especially the anti-property part. It would be better if there was no private property, he thought. Although that might only be because of his background, he realised. Or maybe not. Not all ex-Ghosters thought the same, he was willing to bet. Some of them were probably into materialism in a big way. Maybe as a reaction against all the deprivation and 'poverty' claptrap. Charles was very much the capitalist, for example. Pretty right-wing. Still liked him though.

He got his kicks from sex rather than possessions, he supposed. From women anyway. Was that just a reaction to all the emotional deprivation of the seminary? Who knew? What did it matter? He'd be dead one day! Death did have dominion. Don't get morbid, he told himself! That was a great line from 'Lolita': 'For a long time after her death, her thoughts floated through mine.' 'As soon as he saw her, the engines of desire switched on with a quiet hum.' That was his own. Or was it? Sometimes you forgot whether you had read it or written it! It was certainly true of Grazia, anyway. He didn't think he could ever be a revolutionary in the Marxist sense, like Che Guevara, for example. He couldn't kill anyone. He could die for a cause, perhaps, but not kill. He couldn't even kill a chicken, never mind a human being! He had refused to do it once at the senior seminary and that pompous prat, Paul Hopkins, who was 'Master of Manual Labour', had reported him to the Superior for disobedience! He did have the good grace to come and apologise to him afterwards though. He wasn't a bad bloke really. What was he doing now, he wondered? He'd told the Superior he objected on grounds of conscience and the Superior was quite understanding about it, to his surprise. He should be a vegetarian, he supposed. It was hypocritical to eat meat if he didn't approve of killing animals. Maybe he would turn vegetarian one day.

Christ, he'd been so lonely at the senior seminary! He was living in a community, but felt so isolated. That was because he'd mentally left long before he actually left. He was on a totally different wavelength. It'd taken him so long to summon up the courage to actually leave. Thank God he had done though! It'd been like a living death.

He fancied another pint, but didn't have enough money for one. He was 'as skint as a rat', as he'd heard some character say in a pub the other day. Funny expression! It wasn't a funny predicament though. He'd had three pints already. That was enough. He'd just have to make this one last a bit longer. He didn't really want to get totally blotto. Well, he did, but …

He'd have to go home and face the music sooner or later. He might do some writing. He needed to get on with his novel. He had thought he could liberate himself sexually by writing about sex, but it seemed to be the other way round – he needed to liberate himself sexually so he could write about sex. That was a fantastic review of a Brian Moore novel he'd read this morning: 'Solid with authenticity; dialogue caught with beautiful exactness; physical precision expertly established; personalities and moods skilfully made visible in dress and mannerism. Interiors, always a speciality of Moore's, knowledgeably crammed with revelatory minutiae; exteriors equally good; narrative moves with effortless familiarity; details very crisply focussed.' Imagine having that written about you! Brian Moore was a brilliant writer. He must get hold of the book, what was it called, 'The Mangan Inheritance'? He liked that quote from something Dickens wrote to Forster, too. 'The wayward and unsettled feeling which is part, I suppose, of the tenure on which one holds an imaginative life ...' Was Dickens alive at the same time as Forster? He must have been. 'He gave more than he took, but received more than he was given.' Who said that? Maybe it was himself. It sounded clever, but he wasn't sure what it meant. He'd come across the word 'heuristic' today. That was a good test of vocabulary! He had to admit it had caught him out. He didn't like being caught out. That was good though – it would teach him a bit of humility. He didn't know much really, even though he was thirty-one years old.

What was he going to do about Mary? He had to try and save their relationship. But how? He needed to eliminate the element of pity for one thing. That was what had poisoned it. It was like a hidden germ. He hadn't realised it for a long time, but he felt sorry for her. He needed, she needed, they needed, to make it more equal. The trouble was, it wasn't equal. She hated the thought of being pitied of course. Quite rightly. It was difficult though. She was so vulnerable. Whereas he was so much stronger. Not that he didn't have his own insecurities. It was all relative, wasn't it? She hadn't liked it when he'd used the word 'delicate' about her once, blew her top! She'd really been hurt by life. He had to try not to hurt her any more.

Maybe he should have the operation. He really didn't fancy it though. It scared him, the thought of being anaesthetized, then sliced open ... It might not even work either. That would be just too devastating. Anyway, even if they managed to have a baby, it might not make things better. It might make them worse! Then the child would suffer as well. Christ, it was difficult to know what to do! He felt so confused, wished he had someone to talk to about it.

She was so unhappy. *He* was so unhappy! He hadn't realised till today how unhappy he was. It was a bit like before he'd left the seminary – he didn't realise until a long time afterwards just how unhappy he'd become there. Not until he'd tasted life outside. How good life was too! He might be down now, but really it was nothing like how he'd been then. He'd been suicidally depressed for a long time after he left. But he certainly wasn't going to kill himself because his marriage had broken down or he couldn't have children!

It was depressing to think he might never be able to have children though. That was one of the reasons he'd left the seminary, so he could be normal, have a normal life – become a 'father' in a different sense! Maybe he should try the op. It was so annoying! Why couldn't he just be *normal*? Most other men didn't have to have an operation just to have a baby! What was wrong with him? Why him? 'Why Us?' – that was the title of one of the books they'd given him at the fertility clinic.

What he really needed was a good fuck. *Go home and fuck your wife, you stupid sod!* He just didn't feel like it though. He just didn't fancy her any more. Those packets of frozen peas were real passion killers! She might not even be there when he got home. *Oh, God, I hope she doesn't leave!* It was that bloody sister of hers, Mona – she was a real trouble-maker. She was the one who was encouraging her to leave him. As if he were some sort of monster! She was a rabid feminist, that was why. He wished she'd keep her oar out. He couldn't blame Mary for looking for support from her though. Maybe her sister was right. Maybe Mary should leave him. Maybe they should call it a day. Maybe he had behaved badly. Maybe his behaviour was intolerable. Maybe he'd look back on all this one day and realise he'd been having some sort of mental aberration.

'Coltish' – that was the word he'd been looking for to describe Grazia. God, how he fancied that girl! He'd gone to visit her at the house where she was an au pair last week. Talk about 'bella vita', as she called it! It was a huge detached house in Woodford. There was a *grand piano*, covered with family photos, in the sitting-room! He'd always remember that room – it had a huge chintzy sofa and armchairs, plush wall-to-wall white carpet, massive marble fireplace, gilt-framed paintings all over the walls, oak wainscoting, chandeliers ...

He'd tried to kiss her on the sofa, but she wouldn't let him. 'Why not?' he asked. 'You are marrieda,' she kept saying primly, in that sexy Italian accent of hers. She always said that and it drove him mad! She'd sat there on the sofa, in that sexy, low-cut dress, with her slinky boots on, the tops of her beautiful breasts showing tantalisingly. It was like putting a dish of luscious fruit in front of a man dying of hunger and saying 'noli tangere!' God, how he'd wanted to undo those buttons on the front of her dress! He'd almost felt like raping her! He could almost understand why some men committed rape. In the end, he remembered, he'd got a bit cheeky, which was not like him. He'd been a bit drunk of course. He'd avoid her in future. Give her the cold shoulder. It was just too much like torture. Anyway, he really wanted to try and make it work with Mary ...

'Life is good, life is bad,
Life is happy, life is sad;
Between the two, we fall and fly,
But ours is not to reason why.'

Who wrote that? Was it his own? The thought of death really made life pointless. Yet we went on! Why? The logical thing would be to kill yourself, but we were too scared. That reminded him of something he'd seen parked next to a coffin in the undertaker's shop the other day – a pram! A rather interesting juxtaposition. Oh, God, he was getting morbid. *Stop!* Think about something else! That Indian bus conductor the other day, for example. 'St. John's church, please,' a passenger had said, asking for a ticket. 'Will you pray for me when you get there?' the conductor replied, giving her one. It'd made him smile. Well, you had to laugh or you'd cry! What about that grafito in the college toilet: 'Take Andrew's and watch the world fall out of your bottom.'

God, he felt so depressed! He didn't really know why either. He had no reason to be depressed. Yes, he did. He was infertile and his marriage was on the rocks. That was enough reason, wasn't it? He was probably too romantic about women, tended to idealise them. It was the Blessed Virgin Mary syndrome. What was it Mark Gibson had said the other day: 'Real women piss, shit, sweat and bleed'? He was a cynical bastard! He sort of liked him though, because he was so intelligent. And there was no bullshit about him.

Students said funny things sometimes. They'd been practising the past continuous the other day and he asked Florence, a French girl, 'So, what were you doing at nine o'clock last night, Florence?' 'I was in bed with my boyfriend,' she replied. Of course, everyone had burst out cheering and laughing. He couldn't help feeling jealous of her boyfriend – she was rather attractive. A bit young and immature though. He preferred

Grazia, but he seemed to have reached a dead end there. He might as well forget about her.

'COME 'ERE, YOU PERISHER!' some bloke suddenly shouted at his dog. People said such funny things. Like that Irish bloke arguing with a black bloke in the Victoria: 'Be careful, you fuzzy-headed oul' wanker!' It was racist, of course, but he couldn't help being amused by it. That was a good one of Gerry's: 'Silence is for slaves and saints – like suffering.' He was only a crane-driver, but he came out with things like that. Who said it first? He must have been the best-read crane-driver in Britain. It was hard to believe he was dead. It was so sad. It was just so fucking meaningless! 'Just because you find it meaningless,' Mary had said. 'Yes, I find it meaningless!' he'd replied. 'I have a right to know the meaning if there is one, haven't I? I'm a customer!' She was a typical bloody servile Irish Catholic: 'Ah, sure, it's God's will. God has His reasons.' Bollocks and bullshit!

Christ, it was cold here on the patio now, even though it was almost spring! The sky was heartbreak blue. Wood pigeons were gurgling. What a lovely sound! There were crows cawing too. That wasn't such a lovely sound. In fact, the air was loud with birdsong. Gulls were gliding around the ice-rink of the sky. On the ground, around the tables, pigeons were scavenging for food as usual. There was a smell of wood smoke in the air. It was a smell he loved. It reminded him of the smell of turf smoke in Ireland. Suddenly on the river appeared a tug towing three huge lighters. 'Lighters' was what they were called, he supposed, judging by the name on the tug: 'Thames and General Lighterage Ltd.' There was a name to conjure with!

The grass on the Marshes had a silvery-green sheen. That was because it was covered with gossamer. Dead leaves scuttled about. The river itself was a murky green colour. Winter was a bit depressing really. Roll on spring! That Spanish girl in his evening class was a bit mad. She was an air hostess for Iberia. Believed in reincarnation. Thought she was Mary Magdalene. 'You don't believe in the soul?' she'd asked him. 'So you think human beings are just digestive and reproductive systems?' It was a good way to put it, but a bit of an oversimplification of course. 'No, Ruth, we have minds, emotions, imaginations, memories as well,' he'd retorted.

A cat was stalking the pigeon. Go away, you horrible creature! He didn't like cats much. He'd seen a cat catch a pigeon on the estate the other day. The pigeon was on the other side of a low wall, so couldn't see the cat. The cat crept up on it really slowly and then pounced. There was a flutter of wings and that was it – the cat trotted off with the pigeon in its mouth. Nature red in tooth and claw. He felt guilty, because he could have saved the pigeon. It was just so horribly fascinating to watch. Poor old pigeon!

Never mind pigeons – what about us? He'd lost two friends this year – Gerry and Tony. Poor old Tony! He was one of the Sugawn crowd. He'd died of cancer in the summer, only fifty-something. It was a beautiful morning on the day of the funeral – sunny and warm. The front door was open when they arrived. He'd never seen so many wreaths! Tony's mother was there – a bent old woman of eighty-seven, with a walking-stick. 'Sad news, isn't it?' she said to him and Mary. How terrible, to lose your fifty-year-old son! All Theresa, Tony's wife, had seemed worried about was the state of the house. And the son and daughter-in-law lying in bed till midday, then getting up and washing their hair. 'I know it seems as if I'm just bitching,' she said.

They made a funny couple, Theresa being Irish and Tony so English. He was an exceedingly pleasant bloke. It was Theresa's second marriage. She told them the first sign of something wrong was tiredness. Apparently, Tony would come home from work and just stretch out on the sofa. She also told them Tony had said there was to be no mourning.

'He built this path,' Fergal, his stepson told them in the garden. 'He built the shed, too. He was very good to us. I was twelve, Connor was eighteen, when he married Mam. He saw us through our growing-up. I was only four when our dad died. My only memory of him is giving me a present of a cowboy outfit. I remember his face all right. Everyone said he was a great fellow. He just collapsed at work. He was diabetic, but nobody knew. My mother's family wanted to take over us boys. There was a big feud about it. They're very snobbish. My mother's got a huge inferiority complex. Anyway, she put us in a Jesuit boarding school and came to London. We hated the boarding school, so we left and followed her to London. Tony was in a terrible state at the end. He was in hospital for six weeks. They removed his stomach and his spleen. He was haemorrhaging all over the place – out of his nose, out of his mouth. They had to cut his pyjamas off, because they were soaked in blood. He refused painkillers. He was very brave. He was all right at first, but he went downhill rapidly.'

He could sympathise with Fergal about the boarding school! Poor old Tony. He'd been cremated. It was the first cremation he'd ever been to. He'd helped to carry the coffin into the crematorium. It was a pretty place – lawns, gardens, even a dove cote. The chapel had wood-panelled walls. Black marble altar with a brass crucifix on it. Very simple. A bit too simple perhaps, even austere. The priest had pressed a button, the purple velvet curtains opened, the coffin disappeared and the curtains closed. The final curtain!

He'd shaken hands with the priest on the way out. It was hard to believe that meanwhile Tony was burning like a pile of leaves. The sun was like a furnace by then. Theresa put on a good buffet back at the house. He couldn't forget what the silver-haired old lady, Tony's mother, had said: 'It should've been me, not dear, sweet Tony.' It was enough to make you weep. How on earth could there be a God?

Stop! Stop right there! You're getting morbid! You always do when you get a bit drunk. Morbid and maudlin. It'll only end in tears. Time to go home. Time to go home and face the music. Maybe I can make it up to her. Have to try. She's too good to lose. She doesn't deserve all this shit. I don't deserve her. She's too good for me. Maybe she can forgive me. I'll go and ask her for forgiveness. I'll throw myself on her mercy. I'll promise to be good. I'll promise to be as good as I know I can be. Oh, God, I can't bear the thought of losing her! I'm coming home, Mary. I'm coming home. I'm sorry. Please forgive me ...

CHAPTER FOURTEEN

When he arrived home though, she had gone. He was doubly shocked, because he didn't think she would do it. She'd probably gone to her parents' house, he supposed, but she might be out wandering the streets on her own. She could have a fit. Or be attacked. Or even try to kill herself.

He went out and searched the estate and surrounding streets, but there was no sign of her, so went back home. He could phone her parents to find out if she was there, but was too embarrassed. He put a Van Morrison album on, poured himself a whiskey and sat down. Why should he worry about her, he thought, after a few hefty slugs of Jameson's? *She* was the one who had left! Let *her* take the consequences!

He knew this was only the whiskey talking, because he did care about her, even if he didn't love her, but what could he do? He took another slug of whiskey and gazed around the room. Everything suddenly seemed to have taken on a poignant air of desolation, especially the little artificial Christmas tree they had put up together only that afternoon. It brought tears to his eyes. The only escape from guilt and grief was to drink himself into oblivion, which he did ...

The next day, after he had cleaned up the mess he had made when he had vomited, and had a bath, he phoned her parents. The phone was answered by Majella, Mary's younger sister, who was a bit of a tearaway. He was sure their mother was there, but was too embarrassed to talk to him. Majella told him Mary had gone to spend Christmas with her elder sister, Mona, who lived in Constanz. 'To be honest,' Majella said, in her candid way, 'I wouldn't fancy spending a whole Christmas alone with Mona myself.'

Neither would I, he thought, after he put the phone down, but it might be better than spending it alone, which was what was staring him in the face. It was bad news in more ways than one though. Mona was a fanatical feminist and career woman – a social worker – who would definitely encourage Mary to leave him.

So, he thought ruefully, this was his punishment, the price he had to pay, for his fling with Katja. The ironic thing was, he hadn't really wanted her to come to London. Well, he had, and the sex was good, but he had been massively relieved when she left. He didn't really fancy her any more. He certainly wasn't in love with her. He was in love with Mary. Or at least, he loved Mary. The trouble was, he didn't *fancy* her any more!

Was it all his fault? He knew he sounded like a bastard, but he wasn't really. He had tried to make it work. He still wanted to try. He just didn't want to have sex with her any more. Why not? What was wrong with him? Maybe the Ghosters had screwed him up after all. That bastard in particular. Maybe he was – oh, Christ, no! He'd rather kill himself than think that!

He only wanted other women because he didn't want sex with her any more. And because – no, he didn't even want to think about that. What he really wanted was an 'open' marriage, he supposed. Other couples did it. At least Jean-Paul Sartre and Simone de Beauvoir did! Why couldn't she? Because she was basically a narrow-minded, strait-laced, puritanical, conservative little Catholic convent girl, that was why. Christ, Catholicism had such a lot to answer for!

Had he made a terrible mistake, marrying her? He didn't want to think so, if only because it would prove his mother right. His mother had never accepted her. She was another narrow-minded Catholic. She had never even come to their wedding! That was a crime against humanity, if ever there was one. Neither had his father. He used to think his father was a bit more broad-minded, but he couldn't very well have come on his own, he supposed.

Anyway, now he was on his own for Christmas. That would be fun! He could go and visit his parents in Manchester, but he didn't want to – it would be too strained. He didn't want them to know what had happened. In a way, he didn't mind too much. He had mixed feelings about Christmas – he certainly didn't care for all the religiosity. He didn't really care for all the forced merriment either, though he knew that was probably another hangover from the seminary. On the other hand, he didn't want to spend Christmas on his own ...

In the end though, that was what he did. He treated it as a challenge, a kind of self-inflicted endurance test. As well as a penance perhaps. It wasn't too difficult, really. After all, he reminded himself, there were lots of lonely and homeless people who had to do it every year.

He tried to pretend Christmas Day was just an ordinary day, like any other. He spent the morning writing and in the afternoon went for a walk on the Marshes. He couldn't go for a drink because all the pubs were closed, as usual on Christmas day. He spent the evening reading, listening to music and watching television. He had the usual frozen convenience food for dinner, but treated himself to a glass or two of wine, followed by a few bottles of Guinness and some Jameson's. He drank himself into a stupor, but not before he had shed a few tears of self-pity ...

The days between Christmas and New Year were worse. He felt more and more lonely every day, but it was an interesting challenge, to see how long he could survive on his own, without talking to anyone and without getting drunk every day. He treated it as a test of character, spent most of the time writing, reading, listening to music and watching television.

There was a series of programmes on called 'Ireland: A History' by Robert Kee, which he found fascinating, since he was into all things Irish. There was another one called 'An Everyday Miracle', which was about the embryo in the womb. It was both marvellous and moving. In fact, it almost moved him to tears, maybe because he couldn't help thinking that he would never have an embryo of his own. He watched another programme, about weekend breaks in Dublin, including a segment about Trinity College, which brought back pleasant memories, but memories tinged with sadness.

He sank deeper and deeper into depression, felt as if he had been bereaved. Well, he thought, when your wife left you, it was a kind of bereavement. Maybe it was even worse!

He sometimes sat in St. John's churchyard. St. John's was a large, gloomy-looking church in the middle of hustling, bustling Clapton, surrounded by Victorian tombs and mausoleums. The tombs suggested that the area had once been genteel, but now it was rather rough. The church struck him as incongruous in every way – architecturally, socially, aesthetically, politically. It was also a Protestant church, but he had become very broad-minded about which church he did or didn't go to, since he considered all churches to be monuments to superstition.

Funnily enough, he found it soothing to be surrounded by the dead. The peace and quiet were part of it, of course, but there was also a feeling of, not 'schadenfreude' exactly, but something similar. On the one hand, he sometimes thought: 'Well, my predicament's pretty bad, but it's not as bad as yours!' On the other hand, he reminded himself, at least all their problems were over.

There was one part of the churchyard he particularly liked, the Walled Garden, which had a high redbrick wall separating it from the shops and offices next door. On a sunny day, even in midwinter, the wall seemed to collect whatever warmth there was and reflect it back, so that you could enjoy not just an illusion of peace, but also spring. He sometimes sat there for hours, reading and thinking, or rather, trying not to think, about what had happened.

There were usually a few winos sitting around too, swigging from cans and bottles. Sometimes they tried to talk to him, but he didn't want to talk to them – he felt sorry for them, but even more sorry for himself. 'Hello, sorh,' one of them – almost inevitably Irish – always said, when he saw him, but he always just nodded. It was embarrassing, as if he was one of them! He didn't want to join them or befriend them, even though he felt a certain sense of common humanity with them. After all, we were all lost souls, in one way or another, weren't we? There but for the grace of God …

So here he was, down among the dead men and deadbeats, he reflected wryly one afternoon. There was a low, bright sun in an azure sky. A gull wheeled aerobatically around the church tower. He could hear wood pigeons gurgling in the bare trees. He could smell wood smoke, which as always reminded him nostalgically of turf smoke in Ireland. The moss in the cracks between the flagstones looked like green velvet. A jet passed overhead, leaving behind a ribbon of gold. Honeysuckle draped over the redbrick wall. There were plants called 'Cat mint' and 'Swamp Cypress' – he only knew because the names were on them. The plane trees were bare, except for bobbles on the branches. What was the proper name for them, he wondered?

The bench he was sitting on was dedicated to the memory of some old dear called Betty Plummer, who had died five years ago. There was something poignant about that. It had been made in Gloucestershire, he noticed, so it had travelled all the way from Gloucestershire to London! He had never been to Gloucestershire, but he liked the sound of the name. It conjured up bucolic images of cricket on the village green, warm beer, Hovis, hay wains, Cider with Rosie … Part of the ground was designed as a draughts board and there was a sign that said: 'PLEASE SEE ATTENDANT FOR DRAUGHTS MEN'.

All these observations distracted him for a few moments, but he couldn't stop thinking about her for long. She was still with Mona, her social-worker sister, in Constanz. He had just received a letter from her, telling him she was leaving him and why. It was full of pompous, social-worker speak like 'discrepancy in ideas', 'the background to my decision', 'chronic unfaithfulness'. The last one made it sound like some incurable disease! Maybe it was. It all sounded so bloody self-righteous, but he knew it wasn't Mary talking. He couldn't blame her though, looking for support from her sister. He knew she had been badly hurt. It was just that her sister was such a screwed-up, man-hating harridan, it made him angry to think she was influencing her.

He felt like writing a sarcastic letter back, but there was no time – she was coming back tomorrow. So he had phoned that morning and spoken to Mona – Mary herself wouldn't speak to him, to his annoyance. He had asked Mona to explain why exactly Mary wanted to leave him.

'She's just not happy,' Mona said, in that self-righteous social-worker voice that annoyed him so much.

'What's she not happy about?' he asked, somewhat disingenuously.

'She's not happy about the marriage.'

'Why isn't she happy about *the* marriage?'

He felt enraged, but bit his tongue. What the fuck did a screwed-up spinster like Mona know about marriage, especially their marriage? She knew everything, by then, he supposed, morosely. That felt like a betrayal in itself – Mary had no doubt told her all the intimate details. Was he being irrational, thinking like that, he wondered?

'You seem to have such different ideas, don't you?' Mona said, in her maddening, school-marmish voice.

'I see. Well, thank you, Mona, and Happy New Year to you, too,' he had said sarcastically, putting the receiver down – he had had to or he might have said something much worse, such as: 'What do you know about my ideas, you fucking interfering bitch!'

An old woman in a blue woolly hat, black, man's overcoat and woolly mittens shuffled in, carrying a brown paper shopping bag, and sat on the bench beside him. He wanted to move, because she stank like a dead fish, but he didn't want to offend her, so he stayed where he was while she emptied some crumbs out of her shopping bag onto the ground for the birds.

She sat and waited patiently, but not a single bird took the bait, which made him feel even more sorry for her. Eventually though, a cheeky sparrow swooped down and started pecking at the crumbs. Then a whole aviary of sparrows, pigeons and blackbirds descended and began gobbling up the bread greedily. Even the lone seagull touched down and joined the feast. He was so delighted for the bag-lady that he forgot about his own problem for a few moments …

He wondered if he should go to the airport the next day to meet Mary. He wanted to, as a peace gesture, but the trouble was, he didn't know exactly where or when she was arriving. He'd have to phone her again, but didn't want to speak to her witch of a sister. Anyway, maybe it would be a futile gesture, he told himself.

He wondered if he was subconsciously testing their relationship by straining it to the limit like this. Or if he was subconsciously angry with her – and women in general – for not living up to his idealised image of them. He knew he was subconsciously afraid of women. Could it be subconscious if he knew it? Anyway, he feared there was a misogynistic streak in him and believed it was largely a result of being brainwashed by *them* – that bunch of black-frocked, cross-dressing, screwed-up celibates!

It made him angry, whenever he thought about it, but all the more determined to beat it. The trouble was, all the women he had known so far had disappointed him in one way or another: Sally, the girl next door, Marina, the Yugoslav girl, Kalli, the Greek girl and now Mary, the Irish girl. But maybe it was his own fault, for having too romantic an image of them.

Maybe it would be better not to meet her tomorrow, just let her go. She might be better off without him anyway – there was a cold, callous, even cruel, side to his character, he knew, which was probably another by-product of the seminary. It was a cold place, both physically and emotionally! Maybe 'hard' would be a better word. *She* was as soft as putty. On the other hand, he had started to suspect that she was actually quite hard at the centre, whereas he was hard on the outside, but soft-centred. 'Makes us sound like chocolates!' he chuckled to himself.

He had had to laugh last night – the landlady of the Sugawn had said to an obstreperous, drunken old man: 'I wouldn't put a milk bottle out on a night like this, but I will you, if you don't behave.' He wished he hadn't gone now. It was embarrassing, everyone asking: 'Where's Mary?' They were so used to seeing them together. He had had to tell a lie – well, a half-truth – and said she had gone to Switzerland for a short holiday with her sister. They probably suspected there was something amiss though. Damn, he thought – if she did leave, it would screw things up for him there!

On the way home the night before there had been a slanging match on the 38 bus, between a drunken Irishman – of the ignorant variety – and the sharp-tongued, sharp-witted West Indian conductress. The drunken paddy swore at her, because she insisted he bought a ticket, and told her to go back home where she belonged. 'We ain't goin' back, I tell you!' she bellowed back at him. 'Dat's good, comin' from you! You's a foreigner yourself! How long you bin here? You want to come home with me? I'll give you something to cheer you up, know what I mean? Has you finished yet?' That shut the ignoramus up, because everyone laughed.

It always made him angry when he heard one of his own behaving like that. 'Shut up, you stupid, pig-ignorant, drunk, thick, fucking mick!' he had felt like telling the Irishman. 'Don't you realise she's got as much right to be here as you? Didn't you watch 'Ireland: A History' by Robert Kee on telly last night and take notes? No, you didn't, because you were in the pub swilling pints of Guinness, you thick, fucking gobshite, you. Didn't you watch

'An Everyday Miracle' and don't you realise that she was once an embryo in her mother's womb, she's human, just like you?'

He couldn't quite work out why he didn't fancy Mary any more. She was quite attractive, in her mousy way. He still loved her, but he just didn't *fancy* her. Was it because he still subconsciously associated sex with sin? My God, was Catholicism really that insidious? Maybe he should try to get some counselling. Maybe they should both get some counselling. He didn't like the idea, but if it helped to save their relationship, it might be worth it. He would suggest it to her. If he ever saw her again ...

Christ, it was so lonely! He hadn't spoken to another human being for two weeks! He had been so lonely the other night he had gone to a Socialist Workers' Party meeting, half-hoping he might bump into Melanie, but she wasn't there. He had half-hoped he might even meet some other woman, but all the women looked so damned unattractive, with their short hair and dungarees, like prisoners of bloody war or something. Melanie, who was very attractive as well as intelligent, must be the exception to the rule, he realised.

It had alleviated his loneliness a little though, just to be surrounded by people, especially people he basically agreed with. The trouble was, they all looked rather ugly, or at least scruffy, in their anoraks and donkey jackets and duffel coats, with their badges on. Some of them look positively punkish. One fellow looked like the spitting image of Trotsky. He knew he shouldn't, but he found their shabby appearance depressing. It was enough to stop him joining, even though he agreed with most of what they said. But then, he was not a joiner, anyway. He was a loner.

One of the things he liked about them – about Marxism – was their internationalism. Workers of the world unite! He was all for that. It was their only hope. Otherwise, sooner or later, we'll blow ourselves to pieces, he thought. The funny thing was, after the meeting, there was an England international on and a couple of them were cheering the English team like mad, 'Come on, lads!' and so on. Well, it was against Germany, so maybe you couldn't blame them.

Maybe he should have blown his top with Mary's sister on the phone. She was so bloody self-righteous! 'Discrepancy in ideas'! She was right about that though. Mary believed in marriage –

meaning monogamy – whereas he didn't. He needed other women. He needed other women, because he didn't want to have sex with her any more. And because – no, don't even think it. How could he tell Mary that though? Or her interfering sister?

Anyway, life was too damn short to limit yourself to one person and one only! He wanted to have experiences. He had tried to tell her that before they got married, but she hadn't taken any notice. She just wanted to get married. Why? Because she loved him.

He loved her too. He missed her like hell! At home he was reminded of her all the time. That was why he had to get out, even if only to sit here among the dead and the deadbeats. That morning he had been reminded of her while watering the 'Bizzy Lizzy' someone had given them as a Christmas present. What a pity their marriage couldn't be kept alive so easily!

The thought that she really might not come back terrified him. He had to keep active, to avoid sinking into depression. He had to try not to think about her, but of course he thought about her all the time. She was a victim, he knew, and he felt guilty, felt sorry for her. But maybe he was just as much a victim, so felt sorry for himself too. He knew self-pity was fatal though. He told himself it wasn't the end of the world, it happened all the time. It could even be for the best. Sometimes that thought gave him a feeling of freedom, almost elation. It didn't last for long though. He soon went down again. It was a real roller-coaster! But it was his own fault. He had got on it, so he had to stay on it.

He loved her like his own flesh and blood, like a daughter! That was the trouble – like a daughter, not a wife. If only they could have children. It would hold them together. Maybe that was why she had left him really, not because he was unfaithful, but because they couldn't have children.

He'd phone her again and offer to meet her at the airport, he decided. He couldn't let it end like this. He'd offer to have the bloody operation! He'd even agree not to have any extra-marital relationships. He just wanted her to come home and they could work it out. All he had to do was get past that sister of hers. He really wanted her back. She would come back if he met her, surely? He really couldn't stand much more of this loneliness. He was going out just for the sake of going out. It was pathetic!

The other night he was so lonely, he had gone to Chat's Palace, a working-class social club. He just needed to be with people. There was a panto on, called 'Robbin the Rich'. He liked the title, so went in and watched it for a while. It was meant for children, but was quite amusing and he enjoyed it. Robin Hood was his favourite childhood character and he was all for robbing the rich to feed the poor. There shouldn't be any rich and poor! There certainly shouldn't be any poor. He was a socialist by nature, he supposed. He enjoyed the atmosphere of normality, too – the place was full of kids with their mums and dads, cheering and booing. But he couldn't help wondering sadly if he'd ever go to a panto with his own kids.

Afterwards, he'd had a few pints of Old Peculiar in the bar, which was full of people chattering and laughing, some of them black girls in lincoln-green tights from the panto, which he found amusing but refreshing. It was all very jolly and convivial, which both cheered him up and depressed him at the same time. That was the trouble with such gatherings, when you were on your own. There were a few attractive women around, but of course he didn't get talking to them or anyone, so ended up going home on his own as usual. He bought some chips on the way, finished reading 'Billy Liar', listened to some music, had a few whiskeys and staggered to bed drunk. It was the only way to forget ...

The other day he had had a really bad attack of 'cabin fever', so went to the library. He went into the reference room, to read a few papers and magazines, but couldn't stand the atmosphere – it seemed to be full of sad and lonely people like himself – so he went into the lending room instead, to have a browse. He picked up a book called, 'Sexual Psychology', opened it at random and the very first sentence his eyes fell on was: 'One common cause of conflict in married couples is the desire for or occurrence of extramarital sex.' He borrowed it, along with Ellman's biography of Joyce and Joan Baez's 'Diamonds and Rust'. That was one advantage of being on your own, he reflected ruefully – you got to read a lot of books, listen to a lot of records and do a lot of writing!

That evening, he still couldn't decide whether to phone her again or not. He knew he ought to, but the thought of being rebuked by that harridan sister of hers put him off. After dinner he found himself watching 'To Serve Them All My Days', about an idealistic young teacher in a public school. It reminded him of Mary, because it was one of her favourite programmes and, he suspected, she identified him with the main character. Watching 'himself' on television, he suddenly knew what he ought to do and picked up the phone. To his relief, Mary answered.

'Hello,' she said, coldly.

'Hello,' he said. 'How are you?'

'Not too bad, under the circumstances,' she said, sarcastically, which was most unlike her.

There was an awkward silence.

'Have you got something to tell me?' she asked – this was her witch of a sister speaking, he knew.

'I just wondered if you'd like me to meet you at the airport tomorrow,' he said, trying to keep calm.

'Oh, there's no need for that,' she said, breezily. He could tell she was acting. 'Why do you want to meet me?'

'I just thought you'd want me to, that's all,' he said. He knew it wasn't what she wanted to hear. She wanted to hear him say, 'I'm sorry. I love you. I want you back. Please come back.' This was his way of saying it though!

'I don't want you to,' she said, firmly.

'Why not?' he asked, shocked by her coldness.

'You're always saying I'm not independent enough. Well, I'll show you how independent I am.'

This dart hurt, especially as it had the barb of truth. 'Are you coming home?' he asked, ignoring it.

'I told you, Fran, I'm leaving you.'

'Do you mind telling me why?' he asked, refusing to accept it.

'You know why, Fran. Three into two won't go. I just can't stand it any more. I can't take any more.'

'I see. Are you sure you don't want me to meet you, anyway?'

'Yes, thanks. I'm sure.'

'But why not? Tell me,' he insisted, stubbornly.

'I don't want to discuss it now. Just don't meet me. I'm not coming home.' Then suddenly she hung up.

That really added insult to injury! He felt like phoning her back and blasting her, but didn't. He was too shocked by the change in her personality. He had really thought he might be able to persuade her to come home. He was starting to realise that he had really lost her and knew it was his own fault. A wave of despair went over him.

He jumped up and took his usual escape route to the pub. He went to the Britannia, which was an Irish pub, despite the name. It was Friday night, so there was an Irish singer on, wearing a bandana, red check shirt and green wellies, playing country and Irish on the guitar and mouth organ. It was embarrassingly bad, but the place was full of people, most well-oiled, and the atmosphere was convivial, so he stayed. He drank five pints of Guinness, then staggered back home, got the whiskey bottle out and put on Van Morrison's 'Astral Weeks', one of his favourite albums.

It wasn't long before he broke down in tears and started talking to the furniture: 'Why me? Why do I have to be infertile? I'm sorry, Mary, come back, please, I love you. I'll do anything you want. I'll have the operation. I LOVE YOU MARY!'

When 'Cypress Avenue', the last track on side one and his favourite track, finished, he stood up and staggered over to the stereo to turn the record over. The living room seemed to be swaying like a trawler in a gale, but he managed to turn the record over without dropping it or dropping the needle on it. As he did so, his eye caught a felt-tip pen on the mantle-piece. He picked it up and scrawled drunkenly on the wall above in large red letters: I LOVE YOU, MARY!

Then he staggered back to the settee, collapsed onto it, poured himself another glass of whiskey and drank himself into a stupor to the rhythms of 'Madame George' and 'Ballerina'. He didn't hear the last track, 'Slim Slow Slider', because by then he was well beneath the waves.

The next day was Saturday. In the afternoon he went to the launderette and did his shopping as usual. When he arrived home, to his surprise Mary and her father were there. Mary was packing a suitcase and her father was helping her. He was a bus inspector and was still wearing his uniform, including a peaked cap.

'So, an inspector calls,' he couldn't resist joking.

'Hello, Frank,' Mary's father said sheepishly, in his soft Irish brogue.

'Would you like a whiskey?' he offered, deliberately ignoring Mary and going into the kitchen.

Her father declined, as he knew he would, because he was a pioneer. He was a decent old codger, but a teetotaller.

'Are you sure?' he asked, teasingly.

'You know me, Frank,' he said. He was as embarrassed as he was himself.

'Would you like a cup of tea? Something to eat?' he asked.

'No, thanks. Nothing. Honestly. I'd tell you if I did.'

'What's she doing?'

'She says she's leaving you.'

'Really?' He pretended to be surprised. 'Why?'

'I don't know. She's *your* wife. Ask *her*.'

'What're you doing?' he called into the bedroom, where she was busy packing clothes into a suitcase. He resisted the temptation to make a crack about going on holiday.

'I'm leaving you,' she said.

'You're leaving me? Why?'

'You know why, Fran.'

'No, I don't. Tell me.' Of course, he did. Because he couldn't give her a baby. Because he had other women. Or so she thought. Well, he did have one or two ...

'I don't want to talk to you, Fran.' He could tell she was nearly crying.

'You see, she doesn't want to talk to me,' he said to her old man.

'It's between the two of yous – it's not for me to intervene,' he said, timidly. He felt sorry for him, piggy in the middle.

'How's the family?' Frank asked him.

'All fine, thanks,' he said, doing his best to be civil.

'That's my radio,' he said to Mary, seeing her pack the clock radio into the suitcase.

'It's mine,' she said. 'You gave it to me as a Christmas present, if you remember.'

'I paid for it,' he objected. He was being petty, he knew, but he was starting to feel annoyed by her attitude.

'You gave it to me, so I'm taking it,' she said, closing the suitcase.

'Go on, take it then,' he said, dismissively. It was too petty to argue about! He resisted adding sarcastically, 'I hope you enjoy listening to it'.

'Write to me at my parents' house,' she said, going out of the front door. 'Come on, daddy, let's go.'

'What makes you think I want to write to you?' he called after her, but she either didn't hear or chose to ignore him.

'So long, all the best, Frank,' her old man said, following her out with the suitcase.

He went out onto the balcony to watch her go and saw her glance back up as she walked out of the estate. He hoped she might change her mind and turn back, but she turned the corner and disappeared. He waited on the balcony for a while, staring at the exit in disbelief, hoping she might re-appear, but she didn't ...

In a daze, he went back inside, shut the front door and sank onto the settee. He couldn't quite believe she had actually left. He never thought she would have the guts. It was that sister of hers, Mona – *she* had put her up to it!

He suddenly felt lonely. He was on his own again. She was all he had and now she had gone, really gone, packed her bags and gone. He was all on his own in the big, wide world again, in this big, lonely city. He had a few friends of sorts, but nobody close to him, nobody who really cared about him, nobody who loved him. Gerry had been his closest friend and he was dead. *Fuck it!* There was only one thing to do – go and get drunk. Or 'langers', as Seamus would say.

He went to the Ship, another Irish pub just around the corner. There was a group called the Jamboree Country Sounds playing country and western and the place was packed with people, mostly Irish. The music was maudlin, but it suited his mood.

He bought a pint of Guinness and had to sit next to three colleens – they were all dolled up to the nines, no doubt to go dancing later at the Gresham on Holloway Road or some other ballroom. He studiously avoided catching their eyes. He wanted to be with people, but to be alone.

The girls were quite attractive, but he felt absolutely no interest in sex, which was a kind of liberation in itself. It was partly sex that had got him into this situation in the first place, he reflected morosely! *Well, it's sex that gets us all into this situation, isn't it?* Very funny. Anyway, the three dolly birds were puffing away like trains. That was enough to put him off, even if he had felt like chatting them up. It'd be like kissing an ashtray!

He looked around. In fact, most of the pub was smoking. Sometimes he thought the Irish were a nation of alcohol and nicotine addicts. There was something manic about it, as if they were making up for lost time, which maybe they were. Maybe it was just compensation for centuries of both political and religious oppression. He liked a few pints and a cigarette or cigar or two, but they couldn't seem to go two minutes without puffing. It was pathetic!

There must be some link between smoking and sexual repression, he thought. Smoking was a substitute for sex. They were probably as repressed as hell. His mother was the same, smoked like a trooper. It was a substitute for something, anyway.

He shouldn't be so critical, he told himself. After all, he was Irish himself. He was feeling cynical though. All those people enjoying themselves and he was there on his own. On his *fucking* own! Shit! Oh, well! All the more reason to hurry up and get drunk to forget ...

By closing time he had had five pints, but was still not drunk, so went home to finish the job off with whiskey. He knew he would wake up with a humdinger of a hangover in the morning and had to go back to work on Monday, but he needed to obliterate the pain. He listened to 'Blood On The Tracks' while he drank himself into oblivion on the settee. There were some great lines in Dylan, he thought, as he listened more and more drunkenly. Yeah, he too was going outa' his mind with pain. Pain that was like a what? Like a dagger to his heart. Oh, yeah. Except that his pain didn't stop and start. It was there all the time. And yeah, he'd thrown it all away ...

The next morning he woke up late with a horrible hangover. He noticed she wasn't beside him and wondered if it was a just a bad dream. But it was true. She wasn't there. She'd gone. She'd left him. He was alone.

He lay in bed, staring at the wallpaper for a while, trying not to think, which hurt both his heart and his head. Then he slowly got up. His head felt as if it was in a vice. He did everything mechanically, still trying not to think, which seemed to make his headache worse.

However, he couldn't avoid the thought of going back to work the next day. The thought was depressing, as always after a holiday, so he tried to put it out of his mind, but he needed to do a bit of preparation, so he did. Usually the pill was sweetened by the thought of seeing some pretty, young, foreign faces, but now that prospect left him utterly cold. He had gone right off sex. Sex was a nuisance! It screwed everything up. What had Kingsley Amis said – 'It's like being chained to an idiot'? He was right, the cynical, reactionary old bastard!

In the afternoon he went for a walk on the Marshes. The air was damp and cold and there was a Dickensian mist hanging over everything, especially the river. The water in the river looked evil – black, cold, dirty, stagnant. The trees were bare, the vegetation brown, yellow and scrubby-looking. It was all quite dismal, which suited his mood. Even the café was closed for some reason. A few gulls swooped about, squawking. Otherwise the only sign of life was one or two people walking their dogs.

Suddenly, as he made his way upstream along the riverbank, he saw a familiar shape looming out of the mist on the other side, striding along the towpath towards him. It looked like Roger! He paused and peered through the mist. Yes, it *was* Roger! He had his scruffy old duffel-bag over his shoulder and only he would wear a T-shirt and sandals in this weather.

Quickly, he stepped back and hid behind one of the arches of the railway viaduct, hoping he hadn't seen him. There wasn't much chance of that, because it was so misty and he was as blind as a bat, anyway. He waited until he was well past, then carried on walking rapidly in the opposite direction.

He must be going to visit him, he supposed, as he sometimes did on a Sunday afternoon. He was writing a book on William Morris, so he had probably visited Morris's house, which was now a museum, in Walthamstow, then gone striding down the High Street, Coppermill Lane and across the Marshes towards Clapton to visit him. Or he may have been in Epping Forest, to do some research on Edward Thomas, who he had been telling him about recently and who had apparently lived there for a while.

He felt guilty for avoiding him, because he knew he was lonely, but he didn't want to see or talk to anyone. He felt too depressed. He just couldn't face him, couldn't take his seemingly inexhaustible zest for life. The last time he had come to see him, when he had told him he might split up with Mary, Roger had said something that still stuck in his mind – and his heart – like a poison dart: 'But why? You have a home here.' He had said that because, of course, he was so lonely himself, with no wife, no girlfriend, no proper home.

Ironically, he was no better off himself now. Would he ever go for a walk along the river with Mary again? He felt guilty about her, too, though he didn't think he should. It was all too much of a strain – teaching, tutoring her, trying to write ... Maybe he should just pack up in London and go to France or Italy or Spain. Start again. Meet a Mediterranean woman. He could meet plenty of them *here* though!

It wasn't all his fault, was it? Something had gone out of their relationship. It made him sad to admit it. He had loved her once. She still loved him. Christ, it was so cruel, on both sides! He did miss the simple companionship. Maybe he should try to bring her back. How? Write a letter? A letter of surrender, capitulation, defeat. That letter she had written from Switzerland! Phrases like 'chronic infidelity'. That came from that bloody social worker sister of hers. She would never come up with a phrase like that on her own!

Anyway, what about her wedding vows, 'for better or for worse'. Didn't infidelity come under 'worse'? No, that was self-justifying sophistry! Christ, he wished she was here! Loneliness was so insidious, just like the cold and damp. It got into your bones. It got into your soul. On the other hand, if she was here, they would probably just argue over who made the dinner. At least he wouldn't be lonely though.

He had forgotten what it felt like to be lonely, he was so used to being with her. It was a bit scary, to think he was here all on his own in this huge city, where nobody really knew or cared about him. It was just like the feeling he had had when he first came, so in a way this was full circle. He'd better head home, he decided, before he got completely depressed and flung himself in the river. Not that he'd want to commit suicide in this river though – the water looked positively poisonous.

When he got home, he made himself some dinner – chicken and vegetable casserole from a packet. While 'cooking', he read a bit more of 'Fear of Flying', which had a horrible relevance to his own situation. He drank a glass of wine with his meal and watched telly – it was the only way to keep melancholy and morbid thoughts – and indeed tears – at bay.

Luckily there were some good programmes on, including a dramatisation of 'The History Man' based on the novel by Malcolm Bradbury. He felt like getting drunk, but allowed himself one can of Guinness only. It would be fatal to have a hangover tomorrow. It was hard enough, going back after three weeks' holiday, without a hangover to contend with as well!

It was going to be even more difficult this time, trying to appear cheerful and enthusiastic, knowing his wife had left him, knowing he had to come home to an empty flat again. And it was all so unnecessary, just a misunderstanding really. What a waste! But it was better not to think about it, he told himself. He'd just watch TV till he was tired enough to go to bed and then hope against hope that he could get at least a few hours' sleep.

In the end, the first day back at work wasn't too bad – he carried it off with his usual professional aplomb. The evening before was always worse than the actual event – the Sunday evening blues! Knowing what had happened hung over his head like a dark cloud all morning, but somehow he managed to get through his class. Well, you have to be professional, he told himself.

As always, he enjoyed meeting the students, but made a point of avoiding Bertha, his immediate boss or 'Section Leader', as she was now officially called, or 'Squadron Leader', as he sometimes joked with colleagues – among other, less polite names. He avoided her because he didn't want to be bear-hugged and sprayed with fragments of half-masticated sandwich at the same time, but more importantly because she was so *bossy*. She liked telling you what to do and when, where and how to do it, especially if you were a man, whereas he liked to be left alone to get on with his job in his own way. He was good at his job, he considered, and didn't need anybody to tell him how to do it!

After his evening class, he went for a drink in the student union bar with a few of his students as usual. He knew that as long as he was with people, he would be able to keep the blues at bay.

Besides, there were one or two girls he fancied, including Grazia, who looked as attractive as ever.

But he had given up on Grazia, so he studiously ignored her and turned his attention to Serena, another Italian girl who had just joined the class. She was twenty, petite, pretty, vivacious, charming and as bright as a button. She was very well-dressed, too, in a cream woollen suit with a silk scarf around her neck, so she looked sophisticated yet casual. Very stylish, very Italian.

She was buzzing with nervous energy – chatting, laughing, tapping the table with her fingers and the chair leg with her toe. Every now and again she tossed her hair back from her face with a suave flick of her hand – hair as glossy and sleek as a model's in a shampoo commercial, complexion as pink and clear as a baby's, hand adorned with pretty little rings. He felt himself becoming infatuated with her already and couldn't help wondering what it would be like to be on the receiving end of all that energy in bed.

At one point during the ebb and flow of conversation, she put her wrist under his nose and asked him what he thought of her perfume. It was like holding a glass of whiskey under an alcoholic's nose! 'Mm, not bad,' he said, head swimming with desire. God, he fancied her! And he thought he had lost interest in sex ...

The trouble was, there was an English student sniffing around her as well. He was young, tall, well-built, fair-haired and fresh-faced – annoyingly good-looking in fact. He had found out from him that his name was Terry, he was doing an evening class in A-level geography and he worked in a travel agent's. Part of him resented him encroaching on his 'territory', another part couldn't blame him for fancying her. She was very fanciable! He decided to let the 'interloper' have some time with her, not thinking he would be serious competition, and turned his attention to Sylvia from El Salvador.

Sylvia, who was short, chubby and dark, told him how she had come to Britain to escape from the civil war in El Salvador, where her father, who was a journalist, was a political prisoner, her brother had already been killed and her mother was in hiding. It was a grim story, which he didn't really want to hear, but it had a horrible fascination and put his own problems – serious enough as they were – into perspective.

Somehow they started talking about bombs and terrorism, though he didn't really want to – it was too depressing at the best of times. Serena chipped in to tell him that she had been in the Bologna bus station one hour before the bomb went off that had killed eighty people recently. He had a sudden horrible vision of her desirable body blasted to bits by a bomb ...

'Well, I'm glad they didn't get you,' he said, trying to put the image out of his mind, at the same time trying not to replace it with an image of her naked body in bed.

'Yes, otherwise we wouldn't have the pleasure of your company, would we?' Terry said dryly, but obviously thinking along the same lines as he.

'Thank you,' she blushed.

'They must be real bastards, the people who do something like that,' he said, a bit put out to see her falling for Terry's flattery. 'Of course, there are plenty of them around here, too,' he added, provocatively.

He had decided he didn't like this jumped-up, smooth-faced and smooth-tongued, young, southern-English twit with his Cockney accent muscling in on one of his 'girls', so he was leading him on to say something anti-Irish, so he could shoot him down in front of her. It was naughty of him, he knew, but all was fair in love and war.

'You mean the IRA?' Terry asked, taking the bait.

'That's right,' he said. He had him in his sights!

'Yeah, they are stupid bastards, aren't they?' Terry said.

'Why do you say that?' he asked, finger on the trigger.

'They should put their bombs in Buckingham Palace and places like that, not pubs in Birmingham,' Terry retorted, pouring cold water on his powder somewhat.

'I see,' he laughed, thrown off-target. 'Yes, well, maybe. I still don't approve of indiscriminately killing innocent people though.'

'Unless they happen to be members of the royal family,' Terry riposted. 'But then, they're not innocent, are they? Are they even people?'

'I get the impression you're not very keen on the royal family,' he laughed, disarmed. Maybe this bloke wasn't so bad after all!

'Let's say I'm not very keen on a gang of robber barons, shall we?' Terry replied.

He had to laugh again. 'I do agree with the IRA's aims, but not their methods,' he said.

'What exactly do they want?' Serena asked.

'They want to get Northern Ireland back from the British,' Terry told her.

'So Northern Ireland belongs to Britain?' she asked.

'Only because they stole it from the Irish,' Terry said. He actually seemed to know a bit about it!

'You're not Irish, are you, by any chance?' Frank asked him.

'Well, my parents were born in County Cork, so what does that make me?'

'Where were *you* born?' Serena asked Terry.

'I was born in London, in Walthamstow to be precise.'

'So you're English, are you?' she said.

'Ah! What did the Duke of Wellington say? 'Just because you were born in a stable, it doesn't mean you're a horse.''

'That's right,' he laughed. 'So you consider yourself Irish, do you?'

'I may not have an Irish accent, but let's face it, I am Irish, whether I like it or not,' said Terry.

'Good for you,' he said, shaking his hand. 'Me too. Some people of Irish descent don't like to recognise it, though.'

'I can't understand anybody wanting to deny their heritage.'

'Me neither. So are you into Irish music, then?'

'Not unless Pink Floyd are Irish! I'd like to get into it though. I just don't know where to go.'

'I'd like to hear some Irish music,' Serena said, in her sexy Italian accent.

'Do you know where we can hear some?' Terry asked.

'I do indeed. Would you like to hear some this Saturday?'

'That'd be great.'

They arranged to meet at the Victoria on Holloway Road, where a group called Crannog were playing, and invited a few of the others. He could tell Terry was besotted with Serena and she seemed to like Terry. He didn't mind letting Terry have her now – he seemed like a man after his own heart.

He deliberately didn't invite Grazia, because he just couldn't stand being near her, yet not being allowed to touch her. It was mean, but he felt a bit mean towards her – after all, *she* was the one who had refused *his* advances!

Anyway, he reminded himself, he was still married, even though his wife had left him, even though he didn't really believe in marriage. His marriage was on the rocks, but he was still hoping that somehow he might be able to salvage it. He had thought of a way of doing that – he'd tell her he'd have the operation. Then maybe she'd come back to him and they could try again.

CHAPTER FIFTEEN

A few days later, on Wednesday evening, Mary and her father turned up again, this time with a van and a pile of cardboard boxes. 'We've come to collect the rest of her things,' he said, sheepishly.

'I see,' he said nonchalantly, letting them in.

Mary walked straight past him to the bedroom, without speaking.

'Sorry about this,' her father said. 'Have to do these unpleasant jobs now and again.'

'That's all right, go ahead,' he said, feeling sorry for him. 'Would you like a cup of tea?'

'That'd be nice.'

'Does Mary want one?'

'I'll ask her.'

It was unreal – he felt as if he was acting in a play, as if it didn't really matter that his wife was leaving him, taking half of his life away from him. He seemed to have switched off, to be disconnected. Was that just a self-defence mechanism, he wondered? They probably thought he didn't care, but deep down he felt sick in his very soul. And he knew it would all come out later …

Mary declined the cup of tea, so he made one for her father and gave it to him in the bedroom with a plate of digestives, which he knew he liked. Then he went into the living room, put some music on – the Fureys – and sat down to read. He deliberately left the living-room door open so he could keep an eye on what they were doing, but also so they could hear the music – he wanted to remind her of what she was leaving, futile though he knew it was.

However, he couldn't concentrate on either 'Fear of Flying' or the music, because he could hear them moving about and murmuring next door. After half-an-hour or so, Mary came into the living-room with a box. He noticed she was wearing a green corduroy pinafore dress, which looked rather fetching on her, and felt a spasm of pain in his chest.

'Is it all right if I take my records?' she asked.

'They're yours,' he shrugged, resisting the temptation to say something sarcastic – they were mostly MOR or CnW: Jim Reeves, Nana Mouskouri, Big Tom and such like. In fact, he had secretly come to like them, but he used to make fun of them to her and tried to 'educate' her to listen to 'better' music, such as the Fureys, Bob Dylan and Van Morrison.

'Can I take this?' she asked, showing him 'Ride On', a Christy Moore album he had bought for her.

'It's yours,' he said, as if he didn't care, though he would be sorry to lose it. *He* listened to it more than she did! It was one of his favourite albums. On the back he had written, 'To my darling, Mary, Happy Birthday, with all my love, Fran.'

'I'm taking this, too,' she said, showing him a Mary O'Hara album somebody had given them.

'Just take whatever you think is yours,' he said, pretending indifference, keeping his head in his book. It seemed too petty to argue about records! But he kept an eye on her while she sorted through their record collection, just in case she tried to pinch a Bob Dylan, Van Morrison or Moving Hearts.

When they had finished, they took the boxes one by one downstairs to the small van they had hired. He didn't offer to help, because he didn't want to be involved – didn't want to help his own wife to leave him! Before they departed, he disappeared into the bathroom, turned the radio on, locked the door and had a bath, even though he didn't need one. He didn't want any ceremonial goodbyes, didn't want them to think his life wasn't going to go on as normal, just because she was leaving him!

'So long, then,' he heard the old man say through the bathroom door, as he left. Somehow it seemed a funny expression in the circumstances.

'Bye,' he called back, affably.

'Shall I close the front door?' the old man asked.

'Yes, please. If you don't mind,' he said, with just the faintest hint of irony.

A few minutes later, still lying in the bath, he heard their van rev up and drive off. Mary didn't even say goodbye him! He couldn't believe how hard she seemed to have become. It was that harridan sister of hers! Lying in his bubble bath, listening to the radio, he still couldn't quite believe what had happened, still felt as if he was acting in a play, as if it wasn't real, as if it was just a bad dream.

Later he went to the pub. There was an SWP meeting on, but he didn't go – he was too pre-occupied with his own problems to worry about the problems of the world. He was self-centred, he supposed, but who wasn't? Well, maybe Mother Teresa wasn't.

The pub was depressing – scruffy and with only a few equally scruffy-looking old codgers in. It *was* a poor, working-class area, he reminded himself. Still, the Guinness was good and the jukebox was playing some good records, such as 'Walking on the Moon' by the Police – for some reason that cheered him up slightly, perhaps because walking on the moon was the exact opposite of how he felt.

When he got back to his flat, the fact that she had gone and taken all her things hit him fully for the first time. There were spaces and gaps where her things used to be. The flat felt like a mausoleum. Her ghost hovered everywhere.

He knew he shouldn't, because he had to go to work the next day, but he put Into the Music on, poured himself a whiskey and knocked back a slug. He couldn't bear the thought of going to bed alone again or even going into the bedroom. He knew he would regret it in the morning, but the only way he would be able to sleep tonight was by drinking himself unconscious.

'Please make a point of coming to see me once a week at least,' Bertha, the Head of Department, said to him the next morning, catching him in the office as he collected his register.

'Yes, Bertha, I'll try,' he said, biting his tongue and fleeing the room as quickly as possible.

He had absolutely no intention of going to see her once a week, like a little boy – he couldn't stand the woman, because she was so bossy and overbearing, not to mention fat. He usually contrived to avoid her – as did most of his colleagues – but she had obviously noticed and this morning lain in wait for him. Why couldn't she just leave him alone to get on with the job in his own way?

It was a bad start to the morning, but once in class he switched onto automatic pilot and got through it, despite his hangover and his depression. Something else that helped him to get through was the thought of seeing Serena in the bar later, after his evening class ...

As it happened, he bumped into her in the corridor before class. At first, he didn't recognise her, because she was wearing a combat jacket and fatigues. He found such military clothes ugly in terms of both fashion and ethics, but he didn't care – she still looked gorgeous!

'Coming to the bar afterwards?' he asked, excited at the thought.

'I'm sorry – I can't tonight,' she said.

'Oh, why not?' he asked, crushed, but trying to sound casual.

'I 'ave to babysita,' she explained. 'I 'ave to go 'ome quickly. They wanna go outa.'

'Oh, I see. Well, next time,' he said, dashing off.

Damn them and their fucking babies, he thought! Why couldn't they stay at home and look after the brats themselves? He felt irrationally angry, as if he had been rejected. It wasn't that he expected or even wanted to get off with her – she was with Terry now – it was just that he enjoyed looking at her and listening to her, simply *being* with her. He did sometimes fantasise about make love with her, too, though. That wasn't being unfaithful, was it? Not that he had a wife to be unfaithful to any more.

After class, he went to the bar for a drink with the students anyway, but didn't really enjoy it, because neither Grazia nor Serena were there. He had given up on Grazia, but felt so depressed he would have liked to have her around just to chat to. There were a couple of new students, a Danish girl and a Dutch girl, both au pairs. The Dutch girl, Truus, was both blonde and beautiful. He couldn't resist chatting her up, but she told him she had a boyfriend. Sometimes the fates were against you and there was nothing you could do – you just couldn't win!

There was one ray of light – Mark Gibson, his South African colleague, came in for a drink and, like himself no doubt, to chat up the girls. Mark was short but built like a bull. He seemed to have the sexual appetite of a prize bull as well, because he was always sniffing around the women. He was always talking about them too – either about what he had already done to them or was going to do to them ...

Mark told him he had heard they might all be getting permanent contracts – most of them were still part-time, on temporary contracts, with no holiday pay, sick pay or pension. It was good news, but it didn't excite him as it should, though he didn't let Mark see that. Luckily, Mark was more interested in talking about Truus, the Dutch girl, how 'fuckable' she was and how many different ways he would like to 'fuck' her. He asked Frank about her and said he was going over to chat her up.

'You're wasting your time,' Frank told him. 'She's got a boyfriend in Holland.'

'I'm sure his dick's not that big he can fuck her from there,' Mark retorted, getting up to go over to her. 'Wish me luck!'

Frank laughed emptily. He watched Mark working on Truus with a mixture of jealousy and admiration, because she seemed to like him. He finished his pint and left early, feeling lonelier than ever. On the way home, he bought some fish and chips as usual, since there was nobody to make dinner for him any more. *Sometimes you just don't appreciate what you've got till it's gone!*

The front door bell rang. He went to open it and was shocked – Mary was standing there, with *both* her parents.

Her parents were in their Sunday best, her father in his suede car coat, with his deerstalker hat on, her mother in her fake fur coat. Mary was standing behind them, in a duffel coat, but she looked pretty. He had forgotten how pretty she was!

'Hello, Frank,' her father said pleasantly, puffing on his pipe.

'Hello,' he said, wondering why they were here.

'Well, aren't you going to invite us in?' her father asked.

'Don't worry – we haven't come to shout at you or talk about it,' Mary's mother chimed in. 'We just want to see you.' What a lovely woman she was, he thought, relieved!

'I'm sorry, come in,' he said, ushering them into the living-room, still wondering why exactly they had come. 'Would you like a cup of tea?'

'A cup of tea for me,' her father said, 'and a glass of sherry for Vera, if you've got one.'

'What would you like?' he asked Mary, who hadn't spoken to him yet.

'Nothing,' she said, frostily.

'There's no need to be like that, chuck,' her mother reproved her. The term of endearment went through him – reminded him of the pet names he used to have for her himself, but which he would never be able to use again.

'Make her a cup of tea,' her father said, to defuse the atmosphere. 'All right if I smoke?'

'Sure,' he said, going into the kitchen.

'Shall I help you?' Vera asked.

'No, it's all right, thanks,' he said. 'You sit down and relax.'

He went into the kitchen and put the kettle on. He wanted to be on his own for a few minutes, to collect his thoughts. He couldn't understand why they had come like this, without any warning. They couldn't have come just to make small talk! There must be some ulterior motive. But they were not like that. They were the most open, honest, straightforward and sincere people you could hope to meet.

He still had to be on his guard though. Sadly, he didn't trust Mary any more. She used to be an open book, like her parents, but under the influence of her sister, there seemed to be a streak of cunning in her character now that had never been there before. Or had it?

He served them tea, sherry and biscuits and they made small talk. At least, her parents and he did – Mary chatted happily with her parents, but maintained an icy silence with him. They told him all the family news, how Imelda, Mary's sister, and her husband had bought a house in Donegal and intended to move there, how they were having a party for Mary's brother Malachy's twenty-first soon and how they were both retiring from their jobs in a few weeks – Vera from the old people's home, Tom from the buses.

'What are you going to do?' he asked.

'We're going to go back home,' Vera said.

'Back to Ireland, you mean?'

'Aye. We're going to do some globe-trotting first though,' Tom said, in his droll way, puffing on his pipe.

He laughed, not sure if he was joking or not. He was amazed at how friendly they were, as if nothing had happened, as if everything was hunky-dory. Were they trying to soften him up, he wondered? He noticed how Mary chatted and laughed with her parents as if she hadn't a care in the world, but would barely look at him. Was she just putting on an act, he wondered? He couldn't help noticing with a pang again how pretty she looked in her pinafore dress, with a green velvet ribbon in her hair. It was all a strain for him and he was relieved when they decided it was time to go.

As they were leaving, to his amazement Vera invited him out for a meal. She was a bit tipsy on sherry, he noticed. He declined as tactfully as he could, saying he didn't think it would be a good idea in the circumstances. At the door she gave him a kiss. 'Well, goodbye, darling. We all still love you,' she said, 'and we're sorry this had to happen.' He was so touched he almost felt like crying. What a gem of a woman she was!

'Cheerio, Frank, keep in touch,' Tom said, offering his hand, which he shook, by now fighting to keep back the tears.

Mary walked out onto the balcony without saying anything.

'Are you not saying goodbye to him, pet?' her father called after her.

'Just tell your mother and father the truth when you write to them,' she turned and said to him, coldly.

Her mother had asked him if his parents knew what had happened, and he had said no, but he was going to write to tell them. In fact, he wasn't sure if he would. Why should he? They hadn't come to his wedding and his mother had never accepted Mary. They had never recognised their marriage, never even come to visit them. So why should he tell them, now that his marriage was over?

'The truth is many-sided, Mary,' he said, choking.

'Trust you to say something clever, Fran,' she retorted.

'You think it's simple, do you?' he asked, resisting the impulse to add a sarcastic barb, because he was angry now, as well as sad.

'You know what the truth is. Just tell them the truth,' she insisted, self-righteously.

'Yes, I will – I'll tell them the truth as I see it,' he replied, angrily.

'Oh, I know you will,' she riposted cattily. 'You'll twist it and turn it to suit yourself. You're good at that.'

'That's enough, now,' her father intervened, still puffing on his pipe. 'This isn't the time or place. Come on, let's go. I'd better get your mother home before she's done for being drunk and disorderly.' He ushered Mary and her mother, who was swaying about and giggling tipsily, down the stairs.

He watched them from the balcony as they walked out of the estate, Vera still swaying, Mary limping as always. He felt a stab of affection for her, though he was angry with her for being so uncivil. Before they disappeared, her parents turned and waved to him, so he waved back. Mary, however, didn't even give him a backward glance.

He went back inside, closed the door and sat down in a daze on the settee, shocked at how hard she had become. This was not the girl he had fallen in love with! He still loved her, but he might never see her again, he suddenly realised, and the tears finally came to his eyes.

He couldn't stay here in the flat on his own for the rest of the evening, he thought, blinking back the tears. It was like sitting in a mausoleum! He had to get out. He'd go out and have a few pints, he decided, standing up and putting his jacket on. He shouldn't, he told himself, because it was Sunday evening, and he had to go to work in the morning, but if he stayed here, he'd go bonkers.

'Oh, this is Francis Walsh come to say hello, is it?' Bertha asked sarcastically, munching on a biscuit.

Did the fat cow never stop grazing, he wondered? He had slipped into the office early to try and avoid her, as usual, but to his dismay, there she was, as large as life – no larger, a lot larger – wearing, of all things, a *cloak*. He bit his tongue, said good morning, grabbed his register and fled, before she could say anything else to annoy him or spray him with half-masticated biscuit crumbs.

Had she been lying in wait on purpose to catch him out, he wondered, hurrying off down the corridor to his class? If so, she was even more officious than he thought! As for the cloak – did she think it would hide the fact that she looked like a barrage balloon?

'Is Bertha round?' Mark Gibson asked, bumping into him in the corridor.

'She is of somewhat rotund proportions,' he quipped in reply and

Mark chuckled – he detested Bertha as much as he did, if not more.

'She's not usually around at this time, is she?' Mark asked.

'No,' he said. 'I think she's lying in wait for me, actually – she thinks I don't see enough of her.'

'There's too much of her to see as it is,' Mark said, and it was his turn to chuckle. 'Why can't the stupid cow leave people alone to get on with the job?' Mark added.

'My sentiments precisely. By the way, she's wearing a cloak.'

'A cloak? What's that about?'

'I suppose she thinks it'll disguise her bulk.'

'She'd need a marquee for that,' Mark said. 'Well, I'm not going in there now. I don't think I could face a be-cloaked Bertha first thing on Monday morning. I'll collect my register later.'

'It might be a good idea,' he said, hurrying into his class.

They were all there, sitting waiting for him, expectant. He really didn't feel like teaching this morning. But it was his job. *You have to be professional!*

'Good morning!' he declared, cheerily. 'Everyone had a good weekend?'

Better than mine anyway, I hope, he thought morosely, hoping they didn't ask him about it. 'Me? Oh, well, my wife left me, but apart from that, very nice, thanks.' It was a mistake to ask, he supposed, but it was his habit. On the other hand, he suspected there was a small part of him that wanted to tell them, to tell somebody, anybody, so that he could talk about it.

It was a Cambridge Proficiency class, which meant they were quite advanced – roughly equivalent to English O-level. There were about sixteen of them, of various nationalities: Greek, French, Italian, Spanish, Swedish, Austrian, Polish, Hungarian, Yugoslav, Turkish, Israeli, Indian, Iranian, Nigerian, Mauritian, Malaysian ... A real United Nations of a class! Most of them were girls, several of them au pairs. They were a congenial group and one or two of the girls were very 'fanciable', but he was in no mood for that.

They were also a bright and lively bunch, even on a Monday morning, and a few of them spoke eagerly about their weekend activities, such as going to the cinema and visiting museums or art galleries. Then came the question he had been afraid of.

'What about you?' asked Annette, the Swedish girl. He

suspected that she fancied him and he would have fancied her, if she hadn't been quite so plump, because she was both pretty and personable. And if he hadn't felt so depressed.

'Me? Nothing special,' he said. 'Went for a drink with a few friends on Saturday night, that's all.' Could they tell he was fibbing, he wondered, starting to blush? He wasn't a good liar! 'Well,' he said, quickly, 'shall we make a start? What are we going to do this morning?' He flicked through the course book. 'Oh, 'Inversion'. That sounds like fun! Anyone got any idea what 'inversion' might mean? And no, before you ask, it's got nothing to do with sex!' He couldn't resist making the joke, feeble as it was, but it did make them laugh – which was all part of the art of teaching, as far as he was concerned.

So they made a start on the grammar of inversion. He wrote as an example on the board, 'Hardly had I left the house, when I remembered I'd left my briefcase inside', asked them what was unusual about the syntax and from then on he was on 'automatic pilot'. Unfortunately, however, later in the lesson, he found himself 'flying by the seat of his pants', because he hadn't prepared it properly and there were a few tricky points. Somehow, though, he managed to get through without blowing his cover. Sometimes he felt like a complete fraud!

After the lesson, he occasionally went to the staff common room for a coffee and chat with colleagues, just to be sociable. Today, though, he slipped away quickly as usual, taking care to avoid Bertha. He didn't even stop to chat to any of the students. He just wanted to go home and be alone, even though he knew that would make him feel even more depressed.

That was how it was for the next few weeks – he went to work, went home to his empty flat, felt lonely, got depressed, went to the pub, got drunk, got more depressed, went for long, lonely walks and got even more depressed. He knew he had brought it on himself, but he still couldn't help feeling sorry for himself.

He was willing to talk to Mary, to discuss things, to make concessions, make promises, even go for the operation, try to make a new start, but she wouldn't even talk to him. Sometimes it made him feel angry and he thought, 'To hell with her,' but most of the time he just missed her. He knew that was partly selfish, because he was lonely, but as Mark Gibson said, there was no such thing as an altruistic action and everyone was basically selfish ...

Mark had come into the bar one evening, accoutred all in denim as usual, and told him he had just come back from an extended camping holiday in South Africa, where he had lived in a tent for a month. It was very believable, because he looked as brown as a nut. He was still as hard as a nut, too! He didn't really like him, but he enjoyed his sardonic humour and incisive, iconoclastic intelligence.

'Glad to be back?' he asked, ironically.

'Nothing a bottle of Scotch can't cure,' Mark replied, in his hard-boiled way. He was already a bit drunk, he realised. 'Any beautiful women in your class? I mean, *stunningly* beautiful women. There's nothing in mine.' Mark was even more obsessed with sex than he!

'There are a few fanciable ones,' he said, but he wasn't really in the mood for a 'laddish' conversation, lonely and frustrated though he was. 'Blondine over there, for example.' He nodded towards a willowy girl in a white jump-suit, with a pretty face and long black hair.

'Let me at her,' Mark said, pretending to pant with lust. 'I need a good screw. Christ, she's gorgeous! Nice tits! Is she French?'

'Yeah. She is attractive all right. A bit of a bimbo though.'

'Who the fuck cares? I don't want to discuss Wittgenstein with her! I want her for her body!'

He laughed, but wondered whether he was really joking or not. You could never quite be sure with Mark. Nobody could be so completely cynical and unsentimental, could they?

'Are there no women in South Africa, then?' he asked.

'Not screwable – it's a great country, but the women are shit. That's why I came here in the first place.'

'I thought you left because of the political situation.'

'Oh, that stinks, too. It's obscene.'

'You were in the South African army, weren't you?'

'Yah. Parachute regiment. I actually volunteered for the paras, believe it or not. I was a lot leaner and fitter then. Fucking mistake though. I was shit-scared the first time I jumped! I got out as soon as I could. I got used to jumping – I just couldn't stand waiting around while some arsehole made his mind up. Couldn't stand the parades either. Or the officers. They were sadistic cunts. Enjoyed making you fall in the mud. I was never actually in combat. I've never actually killed anybody. After I left, I got politically involved in Lesotho and Soweto. Got picked up by the police and beaten up. My head swelled up like a pumpkin. I gave £300 to the MPLA. I'm a bit less idealistic now though.'

'So what happened then?'

'That's when I decided I had to get out of South Africa. I went to the Middle East. Became a Buddhist. Spent a year meditating in the desert. I like Buddhism because it's a godless religion. I learnt to distance myself, stand back, stand outside. It comes in useful. In traffic jams for example.'

'So after the Middle East what did you do?' he asked, still not sure if he was joking.

'I came to England.'

'And started teaching EFL?'

'Actually, I got involved in drug-pushing first.'

'God, you've had a chequered past!'

'Yah. I got out of that because I couldn't stand the hassle any longer. Then I tried writing. I've written some awful poetry. I wrote articles for magazines. Items of topical interest. Had to do a bit of research. I had one acceptance, but four rejections. Pornography is where the money is. I can't write pornography though. I can do it, but I can't write it.'

'So you started teaching EFL?'

'Yah. It's a load of shit though, isn't it? I've got to get out of it. Teach something with a bit of content. I've applied to do a degree in psychology at the Poly.'

'Really? Does Bertha know?'

'No. Don't tell her.'

'Don't worry – I don't tell her anything. She's a stupid cow, isn't she?'

'She's a fucking bully, too. She wants me to teach on Tuesday evenings as well as Mondays and Thursdays! "What do you do on Tuesday evenings, Mark?" she asked me. "I'm busy," I replied. "But you don't teach," she said. "But I'm busy," I replied. "I have got a life outside EFL," I told her. Anyway, it's only £2 an hour. The fucking cleaners get that.'

'So you refused?'

'You bet your bottom dollar I refused.'

'Good for you.'

'If I could, I'd put a noose round that woman's neck.'

'I'm not sure I'd go that far, but I know what you mean. It'd have to be a strong rope to take that weight!'

'Yah. Be easier just to poison her. I've got some rat poison at home, as it happens.'

'So what's your class like?' he asked, laughing.

'Oh, they're fine, except there are no fit women. I don't have any problem with the students. It's funny though – I felt quite jumpy before teaching tonight.'

'That's because it was your first class for a while.'

'In fact, I always feel a bit jumpy before teaching. Just like parachuting. Don't you?'

'Sometimes I feel a bit nervous, yeah. Especially if I haven't prepared properly.' Like this morning, he thought to himself. 'Well, it is a performance art, isn't it? A bit like going on stage.'

'Yah. Anyway, that's enough of this garbage. That Blondine's a fucking cracker, isn't she? Do you think she might fall for my charms?' He had been glancing lasciviously at her while talking to him.

'Well, she is wearing a jump suit, so you might be all right,' he joked. 'Ask her to drop in on you.'

'I'm going to chat her up,' Mark declared, standing up unsteadily. He seemed surprisingly tentative for someone with such a macho, hard-nut persona.

'Good luck,' he said, as Mark made a beeline for her.

The ironic thing was, Mark got off with her, and kept telling him over the next few weeks how fantastic she was in bed. He wasn't exactly jealous, because he didn't fancy Blondine at all – in fact he was pleased he had brought them together – but he couldn't help feeling slightly envious and all the more depressed about his own situation.

Writing was his main consolation – sometimes he thought it was better than sex. It wasn't enough though. He did a lot of reading too. But sometimes his flat felt like a tomb and his bed like a coffin. Sometimes he thought he'd go mad with loneliness and frustration. There were even moments when he felt like rushing out and pouncing on the first woman he saw. He really could almost understand how some men were driven to rape. Sexual frustration could drive you crazy. He felt craziness invading his system like a virus – even though he liked to think of himself as so balanced, so civilized, so mature, so intelligent, so sensible, so well-adjusted, so responsible. Sometimes he wondered if he was losing his mind. Perhaps this was how it started ...

One Saturday night on the way home from the pub – alone as usual – he was accosted by a woman staggering along the pavement. She was young, in her twenties, he guessed, and looked quite well-dressed in a smart red suit. As she got closer, he could see that she looked quite attractive too, in a sluttish sort of way, with long though dishevelled platinum-blonde hair and thin, heavily made-up features. But she had obviously had one too many.

'Are you the law?' she slurred, putting a hand on his chest to stop him. 'You're C.I.D., aren't you? You know how I know? You've got big feet! Will you take me home? I'm drunk. I know I shouldn't be, but I am.' She swayed backwards, so he grabbed her by the arm.

'I'm not the law,' he said, amused, but also alarmed.

He didn't really want to be responsible for a drunk woman, but he didn't mind playing the Good Samaritan occasionally. That was one bit of Christianity he could still buy into. He realised that he wasn't being entirely altruistic though, because holding the woman's arm sent through him a tiny electric shock of sexual excitement. After all, he was a bit drunk himself and hadn't touched a woman for months now. He let go of her, shocked in more ways than one.

'Will you take me home, anyway?' she slurred, swaying. 'I know I can trust you. I can tell by looking at you. You won't harm me. I won't harm you either. I'm not a pro. I'm not on the game. I've never been on the game. I'm not offering you a bunk-up or anything. Mind you, if you wanted one, you could have one. Do you want one?'

'No, thanks, it's all right,' he laughed, embarrassed, but for a moment tempted, so desperate was he just for some physical closeness. 'I'll take you home if you want, though.'

'Thank you,' she slurred. 'I knew you were a gent. I knew I could trust you. I just want to get home to my kids.'

The mention of kids suddenly filled him with a mixture of horror and pity. She had probably left them on their own to go out drinking and they were waiting for her, frightened and alone, the poor little blighters. Then a strange, painful thought flashed through his Guinness-sozzled mind: *I wish I had kids waiting for me. A wife and kids ...*

'Let's go, then,' he said. 'What's your name? Where do you live?' He had decided to be businesslike about this now.

'My name's Rita. I live on the estate over there.'

'That's where I live. Come on, let's go.'

'Just light a fag for me first, will you?' she said, fumbling one out of her handbag, but dropping it on the pavement.

He bent down to pick it up, handed it to her and lit it for her. He just wanted to go now – he was afraid the real police might happen by and he would get into some sort of trouble. He ushered her safely across the main road and into the estate.

'Thank you, you're free now, you can go,' she slurred, gave him a kiss on the cheek and tottered off before he could say anything.

He watched her disappear, relieved, but also disappointed. Why was he disappointed, he wondered? It wasn't as if he would take advantage of her for a quick, easy 'bunk-up', as she quaintly put it, tempted as he had been for a moment. Apart from anything else, he would be afraid of catching something.

Letting himself into his cold, dark, empty flat, he suddenly realised why he felt so disappointed – he was alone again! For a few minutes he had forgotten about it. It was pathetic, he knew, but that was how desperate he was for female company. He was like some starving wretch pathetically grateful for a scrap of food found on the street. Christ, it wasn't only pathetic, it was humiliating! There was only one escape, one way to blot it all out.

He switched on the gas fire – not to gas himself, but because it was cold. He wasn't quite that desperate yet. He lit the fire, switched on the stereo and put Astral Weeks on. Then he poured himself a large whiskey, sat down and took a large slug.

CHAPTER SIXTEEN

God, even the dog seemed to have a purpose, he thought morosely, as a mangy-looking stray dog hurried past him, head down. It was Sunday evening and he had gone out for a walk. He didn't have anywhere to go or anyone to go with – he just had to get out of the flat for a while or he would go crazy with 'cabin fever'.

London was such an interesting city, it was amazing what you came across, just wandering around. He had walked through Finsbury Park all the way up Seven Sisters Road and Holloway Road towards Highgate Village. As he was passing Whittington Hospital, what did he see but a plaque on the wall, saying that the step of Andrew Marvell's cottage lay four feet below the ground!

He couldn't help thinking of Marvell's poem, 'To His Coy Mistress', especially the first few lines:

'Had we but World enough, and Time,
This coyness Lady were no crime.
We would sit down, and think which way
To walk, and pass our long Loves Day.'

The words cheered him up for a moment, but then he also remembered the lines:

'But at my back I always hear
Time's winged Chariot hurrying near:
And yonder all before us lye
Desarts of vast Eternity.'

These reminders of his lack of 'mistress' and his mortality didn't help to improve his mood, so he put the poem out of his mind and carried on up the steep hill towards Highgate Village. About half way up the hill there was a high, iron bridge, which according to a notice was called 'Suicide Bridge'. He hurried on.

A little later, he passed a Catholic church – and not just any old Catholic church, but a 'Passionist' Fathers' church! He knew he shouldn't, because it would stir unpleasant memories, but a morbid curiosity impelled him to go inside.

It was Sunday evening and there was a mass going on. He stood at the back of the church and observed the ritual with amazement, not having been to mass for years. It was amazing that places like this still existed, he reflected, that you could step off the streets of twentieth-century London into this bizarre, arcane, medieval world of magic, superstition and melodrama. As it happened, the priest, druid-like in his chasuble, had reached the climactic part of the mass, the consecration, so he had to self-consciously bow his head with pretended reverence, as the priest murmured the words of 'consecration' over the host, then the chalice of wine, genuflected, raised them aloft, and genuflected again, all to the jingling of a bell rung by the server, who was attired in a white cotta and black cassock, while the congregation bowed their heads reverently.

It seemed incredible to him that all these people had left their televisions to come here on a Sunday evening, that they really believed something supernatural was happening in front of them, that they really believed the priest had the power to change bread and wine into the body and blood of Jesus Christ, that God was made present on the altar before them. That was what Catholics believed, wasn't it? Yet they all looked so sane, so normal, so ordinary! To see them in the street, you'd never suspect they had such barmy, bizarre beliefs!

To him it all seemed like black magic and mumbo-jumbo now. Lurking at the back of the church, he felt as uncomfortable as if he had accidentally intruded upon a séance or voodoo ceremony. He wanted to slip out, but felt compelled to stay a bit longer, because in spite of his disbelief, he felt strangely at home. He reminded himself that not only had he once believed in all this himself, he had actually wanted to be a priest. The thought now made him secretly cringe with embarrassment.

As if to rub it in, one of the priests, a 'Passionist Father', suddenly started hovering close to him at the back of the church. He glanced at him with a mixture of revulsion and fascination. He was wearing the black habit of the order, with the black and white badge of a bleeding 'Sacred Heart'. The thought that he had dressed like that himself once made him shrivel inside with shame, so he slipped out of the church and hurried away, half-afraid the figure in the black frock might follow him and try to drag him back, to recant his atheism and confess his sins.

Through gaps in the buildings, he could see the sunset, a spectacular scarlet gash across the western horizon. Somehow, it put his petty little problems in perspective! He walked north, trying not to think about the past, or the present, or the future, trying not to think about anything. He ended up in the Archway Tavern, where there was some good Guinness and good Irish music, in the form of Dingle Spike, to help take his mind off things for a while.

At college the next day there was some bad news. Bertha called a special meeting to tell them that the Education Authority wanted to prevent the introduction of Associate Lectureships by saying that part-time lecturers like himself must be limited to ten hours a week, which was not enough to qualify. They wanted them to sign a new contract if they worked more than ten hours, abrogating their right to the new status. 'Bastards!' he thought to himself.

'It's disgusting! It's outrageous! I wouldn't sign a document like that! Would you?' expostulated Bertha, ample bosom heaving with indignation, specs dangling over it on a silver chain.

He couldn't abide the woman, but he had to give it to her – she was on their side on this one, thank goodness. She was a dragon and a battleaxe, but that also made her a formidable enemy or ally.

'Actually, I would *think* about it, to be frank,' one of his colleagues said, in answer to her question, to his disgust.

'I think we should get the union onto this,' he said, adding pointedly: 'I mean, it's a matter of principle, isn't it?'

'Hear, hear!' the others said.

'After all, who are these jumped-up jacks-in-office in the town hall?' he commented scathingly and they laughed.

'Fucking Nazis, just like the architecture,' Mark Gibson said, in his cynical South African twang, provoking more laughter. The town hall happened to be next door and wouldn't have looked out of place in Hitler's Munich. Or Stalingrad.

They discussed the matter further and voted to make it a union issue. Having proposed it, he was delegated to notify the union. He felt angry, because the new post of 'Associate Lecturer' would bring about a dramatic improvement in their conditions – they would be entitled to all the rights of a full-time lecturer, such as holiday pay, sick pay, pension, security of tenure and so on. Also, he wouldn't have to work six weeks of his summer holiday on the summer school in Dublin – much as he enjoyed it.

The others saw him as a bit of a militant, which he wasn't really. He saw himself as more of a subversive – if he disagreed with something, his usual strategies were passive resistance, civil disobedience and non-cooperation. However, he felt so angry about this that he was more than happy to put his head above the parapet. At the same time, he had to admit to himself that, outrageous as the news was, some of his anger was an overflow from his personal life. His personal life might be in a mess, but he wasn't going to let the bastards in the town hall screw up his professional life as well!

When he went into the bar after his evening class, Serena gave him a friendly wave. His heart leapt, because she looked gorgeous, but immediately sank, because Terry was with her, feeding her cream crackers. 'God, he's crackers about her,' he reflected wryly. He was crackers about her himself, but had resolved to leave her alone. He liked Terry too much to step on his toes. Anyway, she was obviously crackers about Terry as well!

Grazia was in the bar, too, but he was staying away from her for different reasons. He couldn't stand the way she seemed to lead him on, but then wouldn't let him touch her. It was like a form of torture! Besides, she was wearing baggy black trousers, which looked ridiculous on her. He sat and talked with a few of the other students instead. Rosalia, the French girl, seemed to like him, so he chatted her up, even though he didn't fancy her, because she was a bit too tubby for his taste. It was mean, but he just wanted to make Grazia jealous.

As the winter weeks slipped by, he slipped deeper and deeper into depression. It was a vicious circle – the more depressed he felt, the less he wanted to see people. But the less contact he had with people, the more lonely and depressed he became. He knew it, but seemed to be too paralysed to do anything about it.

He stopped going to the Sugawn, because he was too embarrassed to go without Mary, to tell them she had left him. They must think he had emigrated! Then one night, on his way home from a pub, where he been drinking on his own as usual, he bumped into Pat and Peggy. They looked like a real pair of bohemians – Pat, tall and cadaverous, in a long, black overcoat and Peggy, tiny by comparison, in her long, black, Aran peasant-woman's dress, complete with shawl.

'Hi! Long time, no see,' said Pat, in his Chicago drawl.

'Yes, I know,' he said, trying to think of some plausible reason, but unable to.

'What have you been up to?' Pat asked.

'Oh, I've been at the Victoria on Holloway Road – they've got some good music there,' he said. 'What about you? Have you been at the Sugawn?'

'Yeah. We've been doing a read-through.'

'Oh, what is it?'

' 'Shadow of a Gunman'.'

'Ah, O'Casey. Good. What part are you going to play?'

'I think Seamus wants me for Donal Davoren. There's an IRA man going, if you want it.'

'Not again, thanks!' he laughed. 'I've handed in my revolver!'

'You should come down for the reading next week, anyway.'

'I'll think about it.'

The last thing he wanted to do was take part in a play, though he knew it would probably be good for him, take him out of himself. He was already playing in his own private tragicomedy! He was about to say cheerio, when Peggy asked him the question he had been dreading.

'Where's Mary, by the way, Frank?'

'Mary? She's – er – ' He tried to think of a fib, but couldn't, decided there was no point, anyway. 'Actually, we've, er, we've split up.'

'Split up?' Peggy asked, incredulously.

'Yes.' It was funny – he felt as if he was confessing to some monstrous, unnatural crime. Well, it did seem unnatural ...

'You haven't, have you?' she gasped, open-mouthed. You could tell she was an actress!

'Yeah,' he said, bowing his head, as if he had murdered her. Maybe in a way he had.

'Really?' Pat asked, eyebrows raised.

'Yes,' he said, like a condemned man.

'You're not having us on, are you, Frank?' Peggy asked.

I knew it would be like this. They can't believe it. They've never seen us apart. There is something unnatural about it.

'No, it's true,' he confirmed, squirming inwardly.

'Well, that is a surprise!' Peggy exclaimed.

'Yes, I suppose so.'

'Why?' she asked.

'We had a row.'

'Can't you make it up?'

'I don't know. We'll see. Anyway, how are you?'

'I'm pregnant.'

Oh, God – talk about twisting the knife in the wound!

'Are you? Congratulations! When's it due?' He tried to sound interested, but all he wanted to do was get away.

'June.'

'So are you doing a part in the play?'

'Seamus wants me to do Minnie Powell, but I don't see how. Sure, I'll be five months gone!'

'Doesn't Minnie Powell get pregnant?' he joked.

'No,' Peggy laughed. 'Not in post-Victorian Ireland!'

'We could rewrite the script,' he suggested and they both laughed.

'How's the writing going?' Pat asked.

'Oh, as usual – slowly,' he said. 'How about you?' He didn't really want to talk about it. He just wanted to go home and get blotto.

'It's hard to find the time, but I'm making progress.'

'Good. Well, I suppose we'd better go home.'

They said goodnight and he carried on along Balls Pond Road, hoping he didn't meet anyone else. It was funny – the lonelier he was, the more alone he wanted to be! He felt like a criminal, an exile, a misfit, an outcast. He remembered the last time he had felt like this. It was when he had left the seminary.

He couldn't hide from Roger though. He kept phoning, but he had stopped answering the phone, because he didn't want to talk to anyone. One Sunday afternoon, Roger knocked on the front door, but he didn't answer – he was too depressed to talk to him. He couldn't take his seemingly inexhaustible zest for life, no matter how erudite or interesting he was. Besides, he had always felt sorry for him, because of his inability to find a girlfriend, and now he was in the same boat! The irony was just too much to bear.

He spied him from the bedroom window, as usual dressed in anorak, cords and sandals, with his duffel bag over his shoulder, long, straggly, grey hair fluttering in the wind, florid face even more flushed than usual, no doubt from the exertion of having tramped across the Marshes. He carried on knocking in his persistent way, to his annoyance, but he just couldn't bring himself to open the door.

Eventually, with a mixture of relief and guilt, he watched him give up and go away, but not before he had dropped a copy of Private Eye through the letterbox. That was typical of Roger – he always had something interesting or amusing to offer – but it made him feel even more guilty.

The following Sunday afternoon there was another knock on the front door. Who the hell was that, he wondered, going to spy from the bedroom window? It couldn't be Roger again, could it? But amazingly it was, dressed exactly the same. Even more amazingly, there was a girl with him!

She looked Japanese and was rather attractive. It couldn't be …? Yes, it was, the Japanese girl Roger had been chasing when they worked together at the other college. She couldn't be with him now, could she? He couldn't believe it! The thought made him feel even less like talking to him, but he couldn't ignore him again. Anyway, he was curious, as well as excited by the girl, so he opened the door.

'Hello! Meet Yoko,' Roger declared proudly.

'Hello. Not Yoko Ono, I suppose?' he couldn't resist joking.

'Oh, no, not that Yoko!' Roger giggled, his hand over his mouth.

'I see. Ono Yoko, not Yoko Ono?'

'Oh, dear, this could get terribly confusing!' Roger giggled even harder.

'Hello,' he said, shaking hands with the Japanese girl, the contact sending a current of guilty pleasure through him. 'Come in.'

He ushered them into the living-room and offered them a drink. Roger had a sherry as usual, followed by a cup of tea, but Yoko would have only water. She told him that she came from

Tokyo and Roger had met her again by chance in his evening class at Chalk Farm Adult Education Institute, where he now did some teaching.

She also told him that she was a graduate in English from Tokyo University. So she was intelligent as well as attractive, he thought, noticing that she had sexy legs, because she was wearing a short, black skirt, as well as a black pullover.

'Oh, yes, she's actually read Ulysses, which is more than I can say for myself,' Roger declared, obviously eager to impress upon him how clever she was.

'Have you?' he asked her, appearing suitably impressed. Roger had told him this before, but he hadn't been sure whether to believe it or not.

'Oh, yes, we had to read it, but I didn't understand all of it,' she said modestly. 'It's velly difficult.'

'Well, yes, even for a native-English reader,' he said. 'I don't understand all of it myself!'

They talked about Joyce and Irish, English and, indeed, European literature, for a while. At least Roger talked about European literature, eruditely as always – he himself didn't know much about it. She was obviously with Roger because of his mind rather than his looks, he thought, glancing at Roger's long, grey hair, carious teeth and bulging paunch as they chatted, and wondered if he had been to bed with her ...

If he had, he was a jammy bastard, he thought jealously, because she was gorgeous! It made him feel even more bitter and twisted about his own situation. After a while, Roger inevitably asked him the question he had been dreading.

'Where is Mary, by the way?'

'She's living in a hall of residence,' he said, evasively.

'Because it's so far to travel, you mean?'

'Well, no,' he said, deciding there was no point trying to hide what had happened. 'We've decided to go our separate ways. At least, she has,' he added, with a tinge of sarcasm.

'Oh, I see,' Roger said. 'I had no idea. I'm sorry to hear that. Why did she leave? Or maybe you don't want to talk about it.'

'It's OK,' he shrugged, suddenly rather glad to be able to talk to someone about it. 'I suppose mainly because I want to be free to have other relationships.'

'I see. And have you had other relationships?'

'I've had one or two,' he admitted, sheepishly. 'She seems to think I've had loads though.'

'I don't think Mary could accept that,' Roger said.

'She can't,' he agreed.

'She is really devoted to you.'

'Yes, I know.' That word 'devoted' made him feel so guilty! 'That's part of the problem,' he added.

'It's two different ideas of freedom, isn't it?' Roger said.

'Yes, I suppose so,' he said. 'I wouldn't mind being monogamous, but there is another problem.'

'Which is? I'm sorry – I don't wish to pry. Don't say anything if you'd rather not.'

'No, it's all right. I don't mind. The other problem is that she wants to have a baby, but we can't.'

'I see. Is that because of her or you?'

'It's because of me, apparently. I've had tests and they say I'm infertile – or rather 'subfertile', as they call it.'

'I see. Do they know why?'

'Well, they think they do. They say they can do an operation to rectify it, but I don't fancy it.'

'I understand,' he nodded sympathetically, munching yet another digestive.

He felt embarrassed talking about it, especially in front of Yoko, so he changed the subject by asking her more about herself. She told him that she preferred Britain to Japan and would like to live here permanently, somewhat to his surprise.

'You'll have to find an Englishman to marry, then,' he joked. 'Or have you already found one?'

'Oh, dear, we've only just met properly!' Roger chortled, his hand over his mouth, but he could tell he was pleased at the suggestion.

'Sorry if I'm jumping the gun,' he said to Yoko, who of course didn't understand the expression, so Roger explained it to her and she laughed coyly.

God, she's lovely, he thought, looking at her as they carried on chatting. *Roger's a lucky sod! I wouldn't mind marrying her myself. Except that I've already got a wife. Or at least I did have ...*

He was pleased to see Roger with a girlfriend at last – especially such an attractive one – but it made him feel even more depressed about his own situation. Making cheerful conversation was a strain – much as he liked Roger and easy on the eye as his girlfriend was – so he was relieved when they finally left.

Afterwards though, a sudden wave of loneliness swept over him. He knew that if he stayed in, he would sink into a depression, so he forced himself to get up and go out.

He took a bus to Highbury Corner and walked up Holloway Road. He tended to gravitate towards Holloway Road whenever he was at a loss, probably because it was where he had first arrived in London, so it had a nostalgic, symbolic appeal to him. He remembered parking his little Austin A40 van, with all his worldly possessions inside, in a side street, and taking his first-ever tube ride from Holloway Road station into the centre. He remembered how excited he had felt when he first stepped out of the underground station at Piccadilly Circus, because it was his first time in the big city, where he had dreamed for so long of coming.

Why had he come here to London, he reflected, as he ambled up Holloway Road? Because he had wanted to escape from the past. He had wanted to find a new life, to forge a new identity. He had wanted to be free. He had wanted to have experiences. He had wanted to meet people – especially women – and do things, all the things he had once thought he would never be able to do.

The other attraction of Holloway Road was that it had a lot of Irish pubs. He would walk all the way up to the Archway Tavern, to have a couple of pints and listen to Dingle Spike, but on the way he would stop for one in the Victoria and another in the Cock – although tonight he might give the Cock a miss, since he used to go there on Sunday nights with Mary to listen to Irish showbands and it reminded him too much of her.

Another thing he liked about Holloway Road was the spectacular sunsets. There was another one this evening, like a giant electric fire all along the western horizon to his left. At each side-street he stopped to gaze at it in awe – there was nothing like a good sunset to put you in your place and your problems in perspective!

He suddenly felt hungry, so he stopped for dinner at the Paradise Café. This was a transport caff, run by an excitable old Italian couple and full of young Irish navvies. They must have finished the lunchtime session in the pub, because they were obviously well-oiled, and were stoking up for the evening session. He felt at home among the Irish accents, but also felt sorry for their owners – they were obviously wifeless and a long way from home and family. But then, so was he!

He listened amused to snippets of their conversation: 'The landlord offered me £300 to leave.' 'Oh, I wouldn't moind that!' 'Entertaining Mister Sloane'? That was Beryl Reid, wasn't it? And Harry Andrews.' 'Bit of a homosexual, Harry Andrews, isn't he?'

Funnily enough, he found himself next to the same trio in the Holloway a couple of hours later, but by then they were getting irascible. 'Bin friends twenty year, me n Felim. Always fallin' out. But we're together again at the end o' the day.' 'Edumacation. That's the thing. You have to work four times as hard without it.' 'You're talking shite! You don't know what you're talking about!' 'Am I not allowed to say anything?' 'What do you want to say?' 'Feck off. I'll say no more.' And so it went on. They sounded as if they would end up fighting before the night was through!

He bumped into Tom Kerrigan, who had taught in Dublin with him, in the Victoria and told him Mary had left. 'What, again?' he said. 'What do you mean?' he asked, surprised. 'Well, relations were a bit strained in Dublin, weren't they?' said Tom. He was a sarky bastard! There was no use looking for sympathy from *him*.

It was nearly midnight when he got home, well-oiled like the three Musketeers he had overheard earlier. He knew he shouldn't, because he had to teach the next day, but he felt too depressed to go to bed. So he put on Astral Weeks and poured himself a large whiskey.

On the way into college for his evening class, he met Eleni, a Greek girl, and stopped to chat to her. She was friendly and not bad-looking, but he didn't fancy her. There were only two girls he fancied – Serena and Grazia – and neither of them were available. Just his luck!

He felt so depressed, so dead inside, that he was hardly capable of teaching, but somehow he got through the lesson. *You have to be professional!* Afterwards, Grazia came to the bar, as usual, but he deliberately ignored her. Instead, he chatted up Blondine, Lou and Nadège, three French au pairs. They were all 'gorgeous chicks', as Mark would say, but he wasn't interested in them, because they were bimbos. Something was bugging him and he couldn't quite work out what. Then he realised – Serena wasn't there. She hadn't been in class either!

He must be in love with her, he thought, but it was pointless – she was obviously in love with Terry and Terry was crackers about her. He suddenly felt fiercely jealous and wondered if he had made a mistake in letting Terry have her. She might not have been in class, but she certainly had class! Maybe it wasn't too late to claim her back from him? No, he couldn't do that – Terry was a good bloke, he liked him, they had become friends. He did have some principles! Let him have her, forget about her, he told himself. Then she walked into the bar.

God, she looked gorgeous! Drop-dead gorgeous! She was wearing her cream trouser suit with a long, glittery scarf around her neck. He couldn't let him have her! He wanted her! He was going to have her! He had met her first! She came to join him at his table. There was only one snag – Terry was with her. And he offered to buy him a pint of Abbot. He couldn't take her away from him now!

To his annoyance, Grazia had been trying to catch his attention all evening, but he had deliberately ignored her. Then, as they were leaving, she put a hand on his arm and stopped him. A current of excitement shot through him, despite himself. What did she want, he wondered? Maybe she wanted to go home and make mad, passionate love with him at last …

'Can you do me favour?' she whispered, in that sexy Italian voice of hers, exciting him even more.

'Sure, what?' he said. *'Plees, take-a me 'ome-a with you and fucka me silly,'* he hoped she might say, but what she actually said was: 'Can you lenda me some money?'

'Sure. How much do you need?' he said, trying not to sound too disappointed.

'Twenty poundsa?'

'I've only got five on me,' he said, taking his last fiver out of his back pocket and handing it to her.

'Grazie. I give it backa nexta weeka.'

'That's OK. What's happened?'

'People are so strange-a. I lenda my money to Beni, but she don'ta give it backa.'

'Oh, I see. Well, you live and learn,' he pronounced, sagely. 'So now you're broke, are you?'

'What means 'broke-a'?' she frowned.

He explained, suddenly feeling sorry for her, regretting having ignored her earlier. He wanted to put his arm around her, take her home with him, look after her, and yes, fuck her. If only she would let him! But it was hopeless – she wouldn't let him even touch her. So reluctantly he said goodnight and set off walking towards the station, feeling more frustrated and lonely than ever.

To make matters worse, he saw Terry and Serena in each other's arms at the bus stop as he passed, which sent a pang of jealousy through him. He said goodnight to them quickly, without stopping, pretending to be in a hurry to catch the last train home.

In fact, he was in no hurry to go home at all. Standing on the windswept, empty, bleak, desolate platform at Walthamstow Central, the thought of going home alone to his cold, empty flat had never felt more depressing. He almost felt like throwing himself under the train when it arrived, rather than getting on it.

The next day, Friday, he went to the bank to take some money out as usual. He also wanted to change the joint account he had with Mary back to a single one in his name. After all, he told himself, it was mostly his money. He had always supported her financially, as well as otherwise. However, the clerk told him that her signature would be needed to change it and he couldn't even withdraw any money from it, because the bank had been 'instructed by your wife's solicitor to put the account on notice, in order to protect both parties'.

'Oh, so she's got a solicitor now, has she?' he thought, shocked and angry. He was so angry that he demanded to see the manager, demanded to be able to withdraw his own hard-earned money from his bank account. However, the manager, in his grey pinstriped suit, said he couldn't do anything. 'After all, you can't saw a sofa in half, can you?' he smiled patronisingly, enraging him even more. But he could tell he was up against a bureaucratic brick wall, so gave up and went out, to get drunk and plot his retaliation. If she wanted war, she could have war!

Later, sitting on his own in the pub, having drunk five pints of Guinness, he noticed a girl who reminded him of Marina, his Yugoslav girlfriend, who had jilted him on their wedding day. This girl looked the same, with her pageboy hairstyle, baby-like complexion and humorous smile. She was wearing a pink sweater and long, peasant-style skirt, just like Marina, and on her bare feet a pair of schoolgirl sandals. The sandals especially sent over him such a wave of romantic nostalgia that he started fantasising about trying to get in touch with Marina again, about going to Yugoslavia to search for her, because after all she had been the first big love of his life.

The next morning, however, when he woke up with a crushing hangover, he realised how drunk he must have been, how mad the idea was. After all, it was nearly *ten* years now since she had left. She might be married with children! Besides, *she* had left *him*, walked out, stood him up, run away, deserted him, on the very day they were supposed to get married. He could never forgive her for that. God, how desperate he must be, he realised, to be thinking about her at all! And what a fool he had been to lose Mary! Maybe he should agree to have the operation and ask her, *beg* her, to come back.

CHAPTER SEVENTEEN

By the next day though, he had changed his mind. He wouldn't have the operation – he didn't want some quack sticking a knife into his belly and doing God knows what damage! Why should he? *She* was the one who had left *him*! Besides, she now had a solicitor on the case and was stopping him from getting to his own money. To hell with her!

But as the midwinter weeks crawled by, he felt more and more depressed. This was the worst term of the year at the best of times – it was a long, thirteen-week stretch without any half-term break, the days were short, the skies were slate-grey, and the weather was cold and damp. To make matters worse, he caught a filthy cold.

At college, he felt he was starting to lose his grip, at least on his evening class. There was a gaggle of French girls – Blondine, Pascale, Florence, Nadège, Lou and a new girl, Catherine – who just wouldn't stop chattering throughout the lesson. He had tried separating them, but it hadn't worked, so after class one evening, he took them aside.

'Why do you keep talking, when I'm trying to teach?' he asked them, trying to sound reasonable.

'Per'aps becoz ze class is so boring,' Nadège said, in her execrable French accent.

This was just about the last thing a teacher wanted to hear. It was like a punch in the solar plexus. Teachers were so vulnerable, he thought, because they were on show every time they went into the classroom. Not just your knowledge or expertise, but your personality was on trial. She might as well have told him he was a boring person. He felt insulted, but also furious. He wanted to riposte, 'You are boring, too. You are a stupid, boring, empty-headed, bird-brained bimbo.' It was true, even though she was also annoyingly attractive. But of course he couldn't say that to her.

'It may be boring for you,' he smiled sarcastically, 'but it's not boring for all the students. You are the only ones who talk and disrupt the lesson. It's very bad manners, you know. Very inconsiderate.'

They apologised, promised to stop chattering and trooped off, suitably chastened. He felt a sense of triumph, but at the same time more depressed than ever, because in his heart of hearts he knew they were at least partly right – because of his state of mind, he wasn't teaching very well. He had always prided himself on his professionalism and popularity as a teacher and now, for the first time ever, his professional pride had been dented.

His mood was made worse when Serena didn't appear in the bar afterwards. It was doubly pathetic of him, he told himself, because first he shouldn't be so obsessed with her and second he knew she was in love with Terry. Instead, he found himself talking to Costas, because he seemed lonely and he felt sorry for him. However, conversation was difficult, because his English was weak, the bar was crowded and there was a Swedish heavy-metal group called 'Vettan' on.

Costas was a new student, Greek, twenty-three years old, painfully thin, dressed in a green combat jacket and jeans, with a wispy, gingery beard and a hunted look about him. He told him that he was from Athens, where he had studied hotel management and catering, that his father worked as a farm labourer and taxi driver and that his brother was a theology student. He said that he didn't like Athens, because it had no parks and was both crowded and polluted. He told him that he lived in the YMCA opposite and that it was OK, but the food was terrible. He also told him that his father sent him money, which made Frank feel even sorrier for him.

Talking about Athens reminded him of Kalli. An image of her singing in the Acropolis, looking and sounding like Shirley Bassey, flashed into his mind and he felt a painful pang of nostalgia for her. He wondered where she was and what she was doing – probably singing in a restaurant somewhere at this very moment. Had he made a mistake in refusing to marry her? God, he really must be desperate, fantasising about old girlfriends! He knew you couldn't and shouldn't go back to the past ...

Grazia came into the bar. She looked sexy, in a long, figure-hugging, red dress and knee-length boots, but he ignored her and carried on masochistically pretending to listen to Costas, who was now chewing his ear off about American bases in Greece and the threat of nuclear war. However, Grazia sat next to him and handed him a small plastic bag. It was a present from Paris, where she had been for the weekend. He opened it and inside was a tin of Dutch cigars. She knew he liked cigars.

'Grazie! Thanks very much,' he said, touched.

He ought to give her a kiss, but couldn't bring himself to. If he did, he would catch a whiff of her perfume and start succumbing to her charms again. As it was, he had almost cured himself of his infatuation with her.

'You didn't tell me you were going to Paris for the weekend,' he said, accusingly.

'You donna aska me,' she replied, in her sexy Italian voice.

She was smiling, but there was a note of accusation in her voice too, which sent a stab of guilt through him – she had obviously noticed that he had been ignoring her for the past few weeks. It made her gift of the cigars all the more touching.

'And who did you go with?' he asked, winking.

'I goa witha Beni,' she blushed. Beni was her female friend, also Italian, the one who had failed to return the money.

'Oh, yes, we believe you!' he joked.

Actually, he didn't feel like joking with her. He really was put out that she hadn't told him she was going nor had invited him to go with her. The thought of a weekend in Paris with her made him almost swoon and he realised that he still fancied her like mad.

'I'm going to Paris myself at Easter,' he said, smugly. Charles, the old seminary friend who ran the summer school in Dublin and who lived in Paris, had invited him.

'Will you go weeth your wife-a?' she asked, to his annoyance. Was this her way of fighting back?

'Oh, I don't think so,' he laughed. 'I want to enjoy myself!' *Actually, I'd like to go with you ...*

Ian, another colleague, and Mark came into the bar and joined them, so she moved away. Ian asked him about Mary and he told him that they had split up.

'I'm sorry to hear that,' he said. 'Never mind, we're all in the same boat round this table. If that's not a mixed metaphor!'

'How do you mean?' he asked.

'Well, you've been married before, haven't you?' he said to Mark.

'I've got the scars to prove it, too,' Mark said.

'Let's see them then,' he laughed.

'Oh, they're mental scars, don't worry,' said Mark.

They talked about marriage and divorce for a while, but he didn't relish the conversation. In fact, he was sorry he had revealed his situation to them and wondered why he had. He could have just said, 'Oh, she's fine, thanks.' He wanted to talk to someone, but as soon as he did, he regretted it! Why couldn't he come to terms with the fact that she had left him? Why was he so embarrassed about it? Maybe because he hadn't completely given up hope that she would come back to him. 'Got any plans for the weekend?' he asked, to divert the conversation.

'We're going to the RSPCA to buy dogs,' Ian said.

'Are you?' he asked, surprised.

'Yah. A dog beats a wife any time,' Mark said, in his acerbic way.

They seemed to have become quite pally with each other and, absurdly, he felt a tiny prick of jealousy. They chatted about dogs for a while, then moved away to chat up 'his' French girls. They were welcome to them!

Grazia, seeing him free for a moment, came back to talk to him, but he immediately put his guard up. She seemed to be flirting with him again, but he was determined not to succumb to her charms. She was a cockteaser, he told himself, whether she knew it or not. She told him she wanted to go to Israel at Easter and asked him for advice about how to travel.

'Why do you want to go to Israel?' he asked. 'You're not Jewish, are you?'

'No. I justa wanna see eet,' she shrugged.

'But why Israel especially? There are hundreds of countries in the world!'

'I 'ave a frienda there,' she admitted.

'Oh? Male or female?'

''e ees a man.'

'Aha! A secret boyfriend!'

''e's nota my boyfrienda! I 'aven't got a boyfrienda. 'e ees just a frienda. 'e has invited me.'

Why is she telling me this, he wondered? If he hadn't known how naïve she was, he would have thought she was deliberately trying to make him jealous. He told her he didn't know much about Israel or travelling there and that she should go to a travel agent's. He immediately felt guilty about being so cool with her, but she really was such a cockteaser – whether she knew it or not.

'Tu as vu qui vient d'arriver?' he heard Nicole, one of the French girls, say, and saw Saeid coming into the bar.

Saeid was a refugee from Iran. He was a Baha'i and had fled Iran after the revolution, because the Baha'is, being the 'Jews' of Iran, were being persecuted by the Ayatollahs. He was apparently from a wealthy family, but they had been dispossessed of all their property before fleeing. He found him interesting and amiable, but to those empty-headed, immature French girls he was a figure of fun, because of his effusive manner and because he was short and fat.

'Francis, hello!' Saeid greeted him, like a long-lost brother, proffering a chubby, hirsute hand, a big black and gold signet ring on one plump finger.

'Good evening, Saeid,' he said, shaking hands with him.

'Francis, I am so happy to see you!' Saeid declared, beaming. 'I want to invite you to party.'

'What party?'

'Naw Ruz party.'

'What's that?'

'Naw Ruz is Baha'i New Year.'

Saeid explained further and he agreed to go. It was in a couple of weeks in High Barnet. He wasn't really keen, especially as there would be no beer, but he was curious. Besides, he had nowhere else to go!

Later, as he was about to leave, Grazia came and sat beside him again. He wished she wouldn't, because the sight of her breasts and the smell of her perfume turned him on, despite himself.

'Can you give-a me favour?' she whispered sexily in his ear.

'I'll try,' he said, hoping she might say: 'Take-a me 'ome-a weeth you and fucka me senseless.' But he knew she probably just wanted to borrow money again.

In fact, she told him she had been arrested for evading her fare on the tube and needed a character reference for the court. He was shocked, but readily agreed. He couldn't help feeling that he was being used though. Soon afterwards, dejected, he said goodnight and left.

To make his mood worse, he saw Serena with Terry at the bus stop in front of the college again, Terry with his arm around her. She was wearing her cream trouser suit and looked gorgeous as usual.

'Hello! Were you in the college bar?' he asked.

'We looked in, but it was too noisy, so we went to the Bell,' Serena said.

'I see! Our company not good enough for you, eh?' he said, only half-joking, and added quickly in case they took it amiss: 'So what are you doing at Easter?' Not that he really wanted to know.

'We're thinking of going to the Lake District,' Terry said.

As always, that particular collocation of words – 'Lake' and 'District' – set off in him a combustible mixture of emotions. 'Oh, you mean together?' he asked, looking at Serena, hoping to hear her say: 'No, of course not! What do you think I am? Anyway, I'd prefer to go somewhere with *you*! It's *you* I like really, not Terry. Will you take me somewhere?'

'Si,' she said, twisting the knife in the wound.

'Well, that's good,' he said cheerily, wishing he hadn't asked. 'It's a place I know well.'

'Oh? How come?' asked Terry.

'I went to school there, as it happens.'

'Really? I thought you were from Manchester?'

'It's a long story. I'll tell you another time.' He wouldn't though – he hated talking about the past.

'Got any tips then?' Terry asked.

To his relief, before he could reply, their bus came and they started to get on.

'Sure,' he said. 'We'll talk about it in the bar next week. Good night!'

They get on the bus together and he strode off towards the station, trying not to think about the past, or the present, or the future ...

He had never felt so lonely in his life, he thought, then corrected himself – he had felt worse after leaving the seminary. In a way, it was worse now though – he had a wife, but had lost her, he was surrounded by women, but couldn't get off with any of them, he was surrounded by millions of people here in London, but he might as well have been on the moon!

On Saturday evenings he sometimes walked to a new pub he had discovered, called the White Horse, on Liverpool Road. It took about an hour, but it was good exercise and whetted his thirst. There was an Irish group on called the 'Connolly Folk', named after the Irish rebel and trade union leader, James Connolly – a character he found both interesting and inspiring. As the group's name suggested, they played a lot of rebel songs, which he enjoyed, being a bit of a rebel himself, as well as other stuff. They were very good, with two guitarists, a fiddler and a great singer. And it was free!

When he got home, he would open the Bushmills, put some Van Morrison or Bob Dylan on, smoke one of Grazia's cigars and drink himself into a stupor. It was the only way to kill the loneliness and sexual frustration. He usually woke up on the settee in the early hours of the morning, feeling dreadful, and crawled off to bed.

Sometimes he went to the King's Head theatre pub at the Angel. It was full of slightly pretentious, middle-class, leftish, liberal, well-educated, arty people, but he liked the atmosphere. Maybe that was because he was not so unlike them. You actually heard people talking about books and plays – as well as football and sex. They had good music on too, usually something jazzy or bluesy. And, of course, they had some interesting plays on in the theatre. Even the graffiti in the toilets were quasi-literary. One he particularly liked was: 'Death is the greatest kick of all. That's why it's kept till the end.' Sick but ...

It was strange – when you felt like this, the slightest thing could set you off. One evening he saw a couple snogging in a car in a pub car park and suddenly felt a jealous rage against them, against Mary, against Grazia, against Serena, against everyone and everything. He started to wonder if he was losing his marbles! He could understand how people could be driven over the edge and commit terrible crimes, such as rape. He sometimes felt like raping someone himself – Grazia, for example.

Grazia was driving him mad. He couldn't get away from her. She kept foisting herself on him. What a cockteaser she was! It was a horrible thought, but he was feeling horrible. He couldn't get Serena out of his mind either. He knew it was crazy, because she was with Terry, but he was infatuated with her. She was so intelligent, as well as attractive. If anything he fancied her even more than Grazia, who was gorgeous, but no intellectual. He had to stop himself having fantasies about going to bed with both of them. At the same time! It was sick, but he felt sick, sick in soul.

On Saturday mornings he went to the supermarket and launderette. Afterwards, if it was warm enough, he would sit for a while in the walled garden of St. John's church, where there were usually a few winos or other down-and-outs hanging out, swigging from bottles. He felt a strange empathy with them. Maybe that was because he felt, just as with the clientele in the King's Head, that he wasn't so different from them. It wasn't entirely inconceivable that he could end up among them one day, alcoholic and homeless. There but for the grace of God he went already! Was that why he avoided talking to them?

One day, a toothless old crone in a woolly hat and filthy overcoat came up to him. 'Hello, angel,' she croaked. 'Chilly, today, ennit? Still winter, ennit? What beautiful 'air you got! What an 'andsome man! You live rahnd 'ere? You wouldn't 'ave a couple o' coppers for a cup o' char, would you?' He smiled and gave her a ten-pence piece. 'You wouldn't 'ave a five to go with it, would yer, dahlin? They charge fifteen, now.' 'Sure,' he nodded, giving her another ten.

Part of him was grateful to interact with another human being, but really he just wanted to be left alone to feel sorry for himself. It was a selfish attitude, he supposed, but he didn't have time for anybody now. He just didn't feel like socialising. He had avoided Roger again last Sunday. Roger had dropped a letter, as well as the usual copy of Private Eye, through the door. He felt all the more guilty when he read the letter, because it was so sympathetic about his situation.

How ironic the situation was! How the tables had turned! For years he had been feeling sorry for Roger, because he had no girlfriend. Now Roger had a girlfriend – a rather sexy one too – and Roger was feeling sorry for *him*! It was humiliating! He would have to write a letter back or phone him and make some sort of excuse for not seeing him.

In the afternoon he read a newspaper and fell asleep on the settee. When he woke up, it was eight o'clock. He felt too depressed to go out on his own, so cooked himself some dinner from a packet and watched TV. There were two good films on – 'Sons and Lovers', which was one of his favourite books, and a war film called 'Operation Daybreak', about the Czech resistance movement in the Second World War, which he found engrossing – not least because he fancied one of the women resistance fighters. He also had a few beers and whiskies and smoked one of Grazia's cigars, while trying not to imagine making love with her.

He went to bed at one o'clock, but couldn't sleep, because he felt too cold, lonely and frustrated. He started fantasising about Grazia, though he knew he shouldn't. He imagined she was in bed with him and they were making love. He unbuttoned her dress, undid her bra and fondled her breasts, while she played with his cock. Then he took off her knickers and fucked her from front and back. Finally, he imagined she was sucking him off and he made himself come.

Afterwards, as always, he felt relieved but guilty – and lonelier than ever. He still couldn't sleep properly – he kept dozing off, but waking up again. He put another blanket on the bed, but still felt cold. Well, it was still winter – his very own personal winter of discontent.

The following week Charles comes over from Paris, so he went for a drink with him. He told him about Mary and, somewhat to his surprise, he was very understanding.

'I don't want to play uncle,' he said, 'but if the sex part goes all right, everything else will. I can't imagine Mary going with anyone else. She likes you. I mean, really likes you. She won't share you. Women won't. Women are different from men. They have this thing about loyalty. I'd never do it to Nadia, simply because it'd hurt her too much. She doesn't believe fidelity is possible though. The mistake you've made is you've let Mary know. If I did it, I'd do it secretly.'

After Charles left on Sunday, he was 'alone again', as the song said. He spent most of the day reading and writing to distract himself. He was reading a novel called 'Monk Dawson', by Piers Paul Read, which had a morbid fascination for him, because it was about an ex-monk. By six, though, he had a bad attack of 'cabin fever', so went out. He took the tube to Highbury Corner and walked up Holloway Road, stopping at the Paradise café for some dinner. As always, he was amused by the hilariously bad-tempered old Italian waitress.

'I tell you, we ain't got no chicken soupa!' she shouted at an Irish navvy, who had complained. 'That's what I say you! That's why I give you mushrooma! 'Ere, you wanna this boileda bacon or no? What? You no wanna chipsa? You say chipsa! You tryin' be funny tonighta?'

After dining, he strolled up Holloway Road to the Favourite, but was dismayed to find it empty – he had been hoping to hear some traditional music as balm for his troubled soul. He bought a pint of Guinness anyway and sat on his own, gazing disconsolately at the décor: grimy windows with grubby lace curtains, brown, smoke-stained ceiling, chipped wood-panelled walls, blocked-up fireplace with a cracked vase of plastic flowers on the mantelpiece and flyblown mirror above. There was the inevitable cigarette machine, gold-painted, rusting, antique radiators and plastic lampshades. On the tiny stage there was nothing but a battered upright piano and a stack of tubular steel chairs. The tables and chairs in the bar were fixed canteen-style to the floor, which was covered by shabby, red lino.

God, he thought, without the music and the craic, it was a depressing dump! There were photos of famous musicians and musical trophies around, but these only accentuated the desolation of the place. Evidently he was too late for the afternoon session and too early for the evening one, but he wasn't going to hang around. He finished his pint and tried to slip out without being noticed by the landlady, but in vain.

'Good night, love,' she called after him, in a Galway accent, making him feel guilty for leaving, since he was her only customer.

He went to the Victoria, where there was music and people, but nobody he knew. He really wanted some company, so phoned a couple of friends, but predictably neither of them could join him for a drink. He wished he hadn't bothered, because it made him feel even more lonely.

However, the music was good, so he decided to stay and bought a pint. He noticed two Spanish girls and was tempted to chat them up, but couldn't be bothered. What was the point, he thought? They weren't particularly attractive anyway. *Talk about cutting off your nose*! So he ended up standing and drinking at the bar on his own for two hours. He went home half-drunk and was tempted to finish the job off, but resisted. He had to teach in the morning and knew that there was nothing worse than trying to teach with a hangover. It was hard enough with a clear head!

He saw Bertha several times the next day, but avoided her. It was a bit difficult, because she was wearing a tent-like, funereal, black dress, which made her look even more like a barrage balloon. It was like a game of cat and mouse! He couldn't stand the woman at the best of times, but he really didn't want to speak to her today. He was in such a bad mood that if she told him to do something he didn't want to do, he might say something he would regret, such as, 'Fuck off, Bertha, you big, fat, bossy, interfering, domineering busybody!'

The French girls in his evening class drove him mad with their incessant chattering, but he managed not to lose his temper with them. Afterwards, Serena was in the bar, looking as gorgeous as ever. There was a concert by the Furey Brothers the next evening, which he was tempted to invite her to, but didn't. There was no point – she was with Terry. In the end, he was glad he didn't, because Terry came in later – good-looking bastard that he was – and she was all over him. Good luck to him, he thought, squirming with jealousy.

The next day the weather was cold and foggy, which didn't help his mood. On the way home from work, he went into the Clarence for a pint. He was still debating with himself whether to go to the concert or not – he didn't fancy going on his own. He was tempted to phone Serena and invite her, but didn't. He ended up drinking several pints, getting drunk, missing the concert and feeling more miserable than ever. What had he done to deserve this? Hadn't he been punished enough?

Suddenly, 'What Becomes of the Broken-Hearted' by Colin Blunstone came on the jukebox and, to his embarrassment, tears welled up in his eyes. He left the pub quickly and staggered home. He was too drunk and depressed to cook. Anyway, he wasn't hungry. He put the Fureys on the stereo, got the bottle of Bushmills out, slumped onto the settee and poured himself a large glass.

The next day he was sorry! He had to teach a Business English class, which was mind-numbingly boring at the best of times, but with a hangover was a real test of endurance. On top of everything, the numbers were down to six, which was worrying. He could only suppose the students were as bored as he was himself. He was afraid Bertha would find out and start asking questions. He didn't want to give her any ammunition! He had to do something to make it more interesting for all concerned, he resolved.

At the end of the class, he wanted to rush off, but got involved in a discussion about theology with Jason, who was a Jehovah's Witness. He suspected Jason wanted to convert him. He didn't tell him that he had once been a fully paid-up member of a religious cult with even stranger beliefs than his, namely the 'Holy Ghost Fathers'. Yes, even the name was more ridiculous than theirs!

'Are you a Christian?' Jason asked him, in the course of the conversation.

'Well, I'm a Catholic, actually. Or at least, I was brought up as a Catholic.'

'I don't wish to offend you,' Jason said, 'but is Catholicism Christianity?'

He laughed and said he half-agreed with him, though he was offended too. He could see where Jason was 'coming from'. He had obviously been thoroughly brainwashed and came across as a bigot, albeit a pleasant, well-mannered bigot. It dismayed him, because he was only seventeen. It reminded him uncomfortably of how he must have been himself when he was seventeen. He had been a 'novice' in the 'Holy Ghost Fathers', for God's sake! At least Jason wasn't wearing a black frock ...

Of course, there was no point discussing religion with a Jehovah's Witness. It was like banging your head on a brick wall and flogging a dead horse both at the same time. They believed they knew all the answers. It was all in the Bible! For example, Jason told him, it was foretold in the Bible that the world would end with a nuclear war.

'Where does it say that in the Bible?' he enquired.

'Have you read the Bible?' Jason asked.

'I have read the Bible, believe it or not,' he replied, amused at being patronised by a seventeen-year-old.

'You have to read the Bible with a theme though,' Jason asserted. *God, they always have an answer*!

'Of course, if you read the Bible with a 'theme', you'll find whatever you're looking for,' he replied, knowing it was futile. 'Anyway,' he added quickly, afraid he was going to start quoting him chapter and verse, 'why does God want to destroy the world, if He created it in the first place and He loves it?'

'It's God's way of punishing human beings.'

'Why does God need to punish human beings?'

'God's punishments are necessary as an example to others. To stop them being bad.'

'So if you're bad, and you die, what happens? Do you go to Hell?'

'God gives you a second chance after death, but if you're still wicked, you're annihilated.'

'I see.' That word 'annihilated' – he said it with such relish!

He already had a headache and this was making it worse. *It really is like banging your head on a brick wall!* He decided to escape, before Jason informed him that he was predestined for Hell.

'Well, it's all very interesting, but I've got to go and teach another class,' he said, picking up his briefcase.

'Can I give you some literature about it?' Jason asked, taking some papers out of his bag.

'No, thanks,' he said, making for the door. 'We'll talk again next time, if you like. Got to go. Be good!'

The French girls in his evening class were quiet, thank goodness. In the bar afterwards, Grazia gave him a sandwich from Selfridges, where she had found a job on the sandwich counter. He was touched. She told him that she was going to a rock-jazz concert on Saturday. 'Who with?' he asked, jealous despite himself.

'Nobody,' she said. It was his cue to invite himself and he was tempted, but resisted the temptation. It would be just too frustrating! She always led him on like this, but he had learnt his lesson. He was cutting off his nose to spite his face, but that was better than sitting next to her without being able to touch her for a whole evening. That really would be torture!

However, he knew he would regret it when the weekend came and he did, because he had no one to go out with as usual. To make matters worse, on Saturday night, for some reason, he dreamt about Sophie, dreamt he was making love with her. When he woke up on Sunday morning and realised it had only been a dream, he was gutted – which was ironic, because he wouldn't go back to Sophie if she begged him. As far as he was concerned, she had betrayed him. She had used him, played with him, had a good time with him, then tossed him aside when she was bored with him. Now he realised she was a bit of a tramp and felt ashamed of himself for having fallen for her – much as he had enjoyed fucking her.

On Sunday afternoon, Roger turned up again. He didn't feel like seeing him, but let him in. He couldn't avoid him again! He was with Yoko, his new Japanese girlfriend. God, she was gorgeous – slim, slinky and sexy! He couldn't quite understand what she saw in Roger, with his long grey hair, carious teeth, bad breath, big paunch and scruffy clothes.

She loved him – if she loved him – for his mind, he supposed. He couldn't imagine how she slept with him or had sex with him. How on earth could she kiss him, with those rotting fangs and bad breath? Good luck to him though. He was glad he had found somebody, even though he couldn't help also feeling a twinge of jealousy. He wouldn't mind sleeping with her himself! She had a lovely, svelte figure. Apparently, she was into tai chi, so that was probably partly why. She always wore black, he noticed – today she was in a short black skirt and black sweater that emphasised her small but pert breasts provocatively. Roger, meanwhile, was in his usual sandals, cords and T-shirt, with his duffel-bag stuffed full of books, papers, mags and a plastic mac. He could smell his BO even from across the living room.

'I don't want to poke my nose in, but have you heard from Mary?' Roger asked, when Yoko excused herself to go to the loo.

'There's been no contact,' he said.

'Actually, I met Mary last week.'

'Really?' He was shocked.

'Yes. She phoned me up and invited me to visit her in her hall of residence in Trent Park. Lovely place, isn't it?'

'Yes, it is.'

He could just imagine Roger stomping across it in his sandals, with his duffel-bag slung over his shoulder!

'Did you know there was a German prisoner of war camp there during the war?' Roger proffered.

Trust Roger to have dug up an interesting fact like that! 'Really?'

'Yes. It was just for German officers though, apparently.'

'Oh, really?' He would have been interested under different circumstances. 'Why did Mary want to see you?'

'Oh, I think she wanted to talk to somebody who knows you. Actually, I think she wanted to communicate with you through me, though she didn't actually say so.'

'So what did she have to say for herself?' he asked, trying not to sound too interested.

'Well, her last words to me were that if he was ill or anything, "my heart isn't completely cold", to quote her verbatim.'

'I see,' he said, touched, but at the same time piqued. Why couldn't she tell him that herself? Why did she have to go through Roger?

'It suggests she might be willing to try and make up, doesn't it?'

'I suppose so.'

'What do *you* want to do?'

'I don't really know, to be honest.'

'She looks pretty lonely. She doesn't seem to be enjoying herself. She doesn't like the break. Now's the time to make a move.'

'I think it's up to her to make a move, isn't it? She's the one who left me.'

'I see. Perhaps. I gather it all hinges on a conflict of ideas of freedom, especially sexual freedom.'

'Yes, partly.'

'She says you want to be free to have other relationships, I gather.'

'Yes, I suppose so.' He didn't really feel like discussing it, felt embarrassed. 'But she can't accept that.'

'Most women would be the same, though, wouldn't they?' He started to get the feeling that Roger was on her side rather than his.

'How would *you* know?' he felt like asking him, but didn't, just shrugged, 'I don't know.' *I don't care either! I'm not interested in 'most women'!*

'The trouble is, you know, she does love you, to use a rather old-fashioned word. She wants to give her all.'

'I see.' He really didn't feel like discussing it further.

'I'm sorry if I'm poking my nose in,' Roger said, getting the message. 'Maybe you don't want to talk about it.'

'No, it's not that,' he said. 'I just don't think there's any point. As you say, we have two different ideas of freedom. And ne'er the twain shall meet.'

To his relief, Yoko came back into the room at that point, so he had an excuse to change the subject. He asked her if and when she intended to go back to Japan, while trying not to look at her too lasciviously.

'I hope never,' she said.

'Never?'

'Oh, dear! Yoko hates Japan,' Roger chortled, his hand over his mouth.

'Really? Why?' he asked, relieved to have neatly changed the subject.

'It's too noisy and too legimented,' Yoko said.

'I see.'

'Also, there are no pensions,' she added.

'Oh, dear! That wouldn't make any difference to me,' Roger chortled again, his hand over his mouth. 'I haven't got a pension!'

'Well, me neither,' he said, 'not till I'm 'fractionalised' next year.'

'Oh, dear, that sounds painful,' Roger laughed and asked him to explain, which he happily did – anything to avoid talking about Mary.

They carried on talking about 'fractionalisation', pensions, Brazil and 'Christmas with Count Stenbock', Roger's latest book. He was too depressed and pre-occupied to be really interested, but pretended to listen with interest as Roger expatiated eruditely on Count Stenbock, an eccentric Nineties poet.

When they eventually left, he was relieved, but immediately felt lonely again. He went to Chat's Palace, where there was a Women's Voice benefit, with a punk band on. It wasn't really his kind of music, but he liked to think he was doing his bit politically. Anyway, at least he could have a few pints and feel that he wasn't entirely alone in the universe for a couple of hours.

CHAPTER EIGHTEEN

'I wanna see you,' Serena said, sitting beside him.

She was wearing a tight red sweater, tight blue jeans and knee-length boots. A wave of almost unbearable desire swept over him.

'At your service,' he said cheerfully, trying not to ogle her sublime breasts.

'We wanna go to Irelanda at Easter.'

'I thought you were going to the Lake District?'

'We changed our minda. Terry wants to discover his rootsa.'

'I see.' He was relieved they weren't going to the Lake District, because it meant he wouldn't have to talk about it. It always brought back unpleasant memories. He was pleased to hear they were going to Ireland, because it was his favourite place in the world. However, he couldn't help feeling a spasm of jealousy to think she was going with Terry, not him.

'Can you tell us where are the best places and best way to go?' she asked.

'I'd be delighted!' he said.

At that moment, to his annoyance, Terry came into the bar and joined them, having just finished his A-level geography class. He had been hoping to have her to himself for a few more minutes! To his further annoyance, Terry gave her an affectionate peck on the cheek. However, he bought him a pint of Abbot, so he was mollified and proceeded happily to tell them about Ireland.

While he was doing so, he noticed that Grazia was listening in. She looked rather fetching in a floral shirt, suede waistcoat, baggy trousers and bootees. He suspected she was jealous of Serena, so he couldn't resist rubbing it in a bit by being extra friendly to her. If he made her jealous enough, he thought craftily, she might just give in to him.

He talked to Ian and Mark as well, just to rub it in even more. They had been to the RSPCA to buy dogs at the weekend, though he didn't understand why blokes like them wanted a dog. Were the dogs substitutes for women, he wondered? If so, it was pretty pathetic! But who was he to talk? He didn't have a woman either!

When she got chance, Grazia asked him about his weekend and he told her he had had a great one. He knew she wanted him to ask her about her jazz-rock concert, but he didn't. It was mean and he was cutting off his nose to spite his face, he realised, but he had given her lots of chances to gain his affection and she had always rebuffed his advances. He really didn't like being rejected and she had rejected him once too often. She might not consciously be a cockteaser, but that's what she was. Not with *him* any more though! She'd have to do or say something very dramatic to get his attention now, such as: 'Please, Francisa, take-a me 'ome-a witha you tonighta and fucka me gooda!'

However, she hadn't read the script, so he ended up going home on his own as usual.

Sitting in the walled garden of St. John's church one Saturday, he noticed the crocuses, daffodils and primroses were out and the cherry trees were budding. The sun even made an occasional, shy appearance. He suddenly felt cheered up – it was spring at last!

He went to the laundry and library, did his shopping, then went home and made lunch. After lunch he snoozed on the settee. When he woke up, he washed up and cooked himself some dinner: boiled potatoes, cauliflower, finny haddock. Then he went out, still in a surprisingly good mood

It didn't last long though. He tried the Three Wheatsheaves first, but the band was bad and the place was dead. Then he tried the King's Head, but it was so jam-packed he couldn't even get in. He ended up in a disco pub of all places, hoping vaguely he might meet a girl, but of course he didn't, so as usual he went home feeling depressed and hit the whiskey bottle.

On Sunday afternoon, to recover from his hangover, he went down to the Marshes for a walk by the river. The fresh air, reeking with the rank whiff of river water and vegetation, was like a dose of smelling salts. The flora and fauna, especially the wildfowl – swans, ducks, moorhens, coots, herons – provided a therapeutic sense of reconnection with nature. While the narrow-boats chugging up and down awoke pleasant reveries of escape to a slower, more peaceful and serene world, far from the madding crowd ...

Later in the evening he went for a meal in an Indian restaurant in Stoke Newington, then to the Weaver's, where there was some decent Irish music. After a couple of hours on the Marshes, a good meal and a pint of Guinness, he felt considerably more at ease with the world, yet something was bugging him. It took him a while to realise what it was – the French girls in his evening class. They had become a seriously disruptive influence and he had to do something about them, but because of his own vulnerability at the moment he was afraid to.

In class the following week, they were worse than ever, so he ordered them to move places. At first he was afraid they would refuse, but he carried it off with a show of masterfulness. Afterwards, in the bar, he told them they were 'méchantes'. Nadège thought it was all a great joke. 'Francees est fâché!' she declared to her chatterbox mates and they all giggled. He laughed himself, but the strain was getting to him. To everyone's surprise, he left the bar early and went home.

On the bus home, he was the only passenger. The conductor must have been feeling lonely, because he started telling him about his problems: 'I spent two grand in six months on Southern Comfort. Six or seven bottles a day I was getting through. You get immune to it in the end. Don't drink now. Doesn't bother me. I been up since 4.30, 'cos my missus is ill. 'Ad to phone the doc. Influenza, ennit? There's a bug goin' rahnd, yer see ...'

He was glad to get off the bus. The last thing he wanted to do was listen to other people's problems. He had enough of his own! He could do with some Southern Comfort himself, he thought, but Jameson's would do. He had started drinking every night, even when he was teaching the next day, even though he knew that was a slippery slope.

The following Saturday, he felt so lonely that he decided to go to Saeid's 'Naw Ruz' party after all. He met him at his flat, where he was still getting ready. He was wearing a white suit with white shoes and a tie with a tiepin and matching cufflinks. He brushed and combed his hair and sprayed cologne on his face. 'Let's go, my friend,' he said, when he had finished pomping himself up.

They went in Saeid's car to the vicarage, to collect the vicar and his secretary, Mrs. Rutherford. He felt a morbid curiosity, because he had never met a vicar close up before. They went into the church to find him distributing prayer-books. He was bespectacled, with thick white hair parted down the middle, and was wearing a black cassock. 'God, how ridiculous he looks!' he thought, remembering with a cringe that he had once dressed the same.

The church was dim and dusty and obviously High Anglican, because there were lots of statues and icons around. It could almost have been a Catholic church, the only thing missing being a tabernacle. It gave him the creeps, so that he was glad to get back outside into the spring sunshine.

They went in Mrs. Rutherford's Morris Minor to the party, which was in a school hall in High Barnet. At the entrance there was a table with seven objects all beginning with 's' in Farsee, Saeid's language – objects such as an apple, blade of grass, coins, pepper, even a bowl of goldfish. There was also a picture of the prophet's son in a glass case. In the hall, where decorations had been put up, there were crisps and chocolate biscuits on the tables.

There were lots of prayers and speeches and performances by a violinist and two Indian girl dancers. Afterwards, food was served, including a delicious Persian aubergine stew with rice. This was followed by a disco. It was all very pleasant, the people were charming and there were lots of well-dressed, attractive-looking women. However, the women only accentuated his loneliness and there was no alcohol to take the edge off it. He suspected Saeid would like to convert him to the faith, but there was no chance at all if he couldn't have a drink! He was tempted to slip out to the nearest pub for a pint on the sly, but resisted.

He felt obliged to make conversation with 'the reverend' as Saeid amusingly called him, since he was sitting next to him, but it was hard work – the reverend seemed singularly uninterested in him. However, he held a certain grotesque fascination for him, so he asked him if he was 'high' or 'low'.

'Oh, I try not to categorize myself, but I suppose I'm 'high',' the reverend said, in his very RP voice.

'How long have you been in your parish?'

'Fifteen years – but I've just been offered another parish in Scunthorpe.'

'Scunthorpe?'

'Yes. I have written to the bishop to ask him what I've done wrong!'

He laughed, but this was about the only spark of humour the reverend betrayed. It was an uphill struggle to get any more out of him, so after a few more questions, he discreetly moved away. However, he was then buttonholed by Saeid, who expounded the Baha'i religion to him. It sounded quite attractive as religions went – pacifist, non-political and internationalist. But, as with most religions, he just couldn't swallow all the supernatural claptrap that went with it.

Afterwards they went back to the vicarage for coffee. They sat in ancient leather armchairs in front of a wainscoted fireplace in a small, cluttered living-room, with blue walls and wooden shelves full of enormous, leather-bound tomes. Two cats jumped up and down, Sam, a Siamese, and Susie, a black stray. There was a battered old piano, an ancient radio and equally ancient loudspeaker. In the fireplace there was a coke scuttle. An old clock ticked loudly on the mantelpiece. He felt claustrophobic, could hardly wait to get out.

Saeid explained how Baha'is were being persecuted, even killed, by the Islamic fanatics in Iran, which was why he was here. His parents and some of the rest of his family were still there, but they had lost everything. He maintained that the Iranian revolution had been 'engineered' by America. Frank found this bizarre, but not entirely incredible – he knew how calculating, cunning and callous any ruling class could be. That was why they were the ruling class!

Afterwards, he went back to Saeid's flat with him and they ended up chatting till five in the morning. They talked about love and marriage and he found himself telling him about Mary, even though he hardly knew him – maybe because he hardly knew him. He liked him though and he seemed to be intelligent behind the ingenuous exterior. Saeid said he wished he had a wife or girlfriend and was obviously lonely. He suggested they go and see Mary and offered to drive him there the next day, Sunday. He accepted, so stayed at the flat, sleeping on the sofa.

They got up at one, had toast and tea on a Persian newspaper on the floor, phoned Mary to tell her they were coming and drove in Saeid's car to her hall of residence. This was located in Trent Park, on the semi-rural northern outskirts of London, and difficult to find. When they finally did find it, it was difficult to get in – there was a high, green, metal fence around it and a checkpoint with a security guard who looked like a South American general. It looked more like a prison than a student hostel!

Eventually though, the generalissimo allowed them in and they found Mary's room. It was the usual student's study-bedroom – small, with fitted furniture, but clean, comfortable and modern. She had a tape of 'The Jazz Singer' by Neil Diamond on in the background, which he remembered buying for her and wondered if it was deliberate, to remind him of happier times ...

He hadn't seen her for several weeks and was surprised by how wan but pretty she looked in a green, pinafore dress with a green velvet ribbon in her long, straw-coloured hair. He immediately felt a familiar wave of affection for her and wanted to give her a hug, but she didn't even allow a peck on the cheek. He also noticed the built-up 'surgical' shoe she was wearing to disguise her short leg and a familiar stab of pity went through him. He tried to suppress the feeling though, knowing it wasn't supposed to be healthy – at least not according to Theodor Reik. He hoped she didn't have a 'fit' while he was there.

He introduced Saeid, who immediately excused himself so they could talk. 'When shall I come back?' he asked, tactfully.

'Give us half-an-hour, please,' he said.

He made small talk with Mary for a while, then she asked him, 'Why do you need so many women, Fran?'

'I don't,' he said, defensively. 'I may like chatting them up, but that's all.'

'You did more than chat up that Sophie, didn't you?' *That* Sophie!

'How do you know?'

'You were with her that night in Trinity, weren't you?'

'You don't know that.'

'Tell me then.'

'Why should I? That's my business. Anyway, what's the point of dragging that up now?'

'Because I think you have a problem.'

'Oh, yes? What's that then?' He didn't like the accusatory tone of this.

'You know what I mean.'

'No, I don't,' he said, though he did. 'Tell me.'

'You're a sex-maniac.'

'Oh, yes?' he laughed. 'Why should that be, then?' It was the wrong question, he knew.

'It's all because of that seminary you went to.'

'Really?'

'Yes. You were so suppressed for so long that now you're trying to make up for it by having sex with as many women as possible.'

'It's a good theory,' he said, sarcastically.

'You don't agree?'

'No.'

'Why not?'

'Well, most men are promiscuous by nature, so that doesn't make me different.'

'Yes, but most men control it.'

'Do they?'

'Also, I think you feel you have to prove you're not homosexual by going with as many women as possible.'

'That's bloody ridiculous! It's just amateur psychology. It's so simplistic! I'm not homosexual! What makes you think I'm homosexual?'

The quotation, 'Methinks he doth protest too much', flashed through his mind.

'I don't know,' she said. 'It's just something about you, Fran. I think something happened at that seminary.'

'What do you mean, 'something happened'?'

'I don't know. Did you have a homosexual relationship with somebody there?'

'Of course I bloody didn't!' This was only half-true.

'*Something* happened then.'

Something happened all right, but he didn't want to talk about it, not to her, not to anyone. 'It was a bloody abnormal, unnatural situation all right, but nothing happened!' he insisted.

'So why are you so interested in other women then?'

'I like variety,' he shrugged. 'I like meeting people of all sorts – including women. That's one reason I enjoy my job.'

'You don't have to have affairs with them though.'

'Who said I do? That's mostly your imagination, because you're jealous. I may flirt with them. You're jealous if you see me talking to another woman.'

'If I'm jealous, it's because I love you, Fran.'

This took the wind out of his sails – he had been gearing up for an argument. 'I love you, too,' he said spontaneously.

'So what do you want to do?' she asked.

'I want you to come back.'

'I can't come back just like that, Fran, not after all that's happened.'

'Why not?'

'Well, for one thing, I can't just leave this place. I've got to keep it till the end of the year. And if I did come back, there would have to be certain conditions.'

'Go on.' He didn't like being talked to like this, but it was worth it if she came back to him, he supposed.

'Well, first of all, you have to promise not to have other women. I know you want to, Fran, but I can't accept it. Most women couldn't.'

'All right.'

'You promise?'

'Yes. Anything else?'

'Yes. What about children?'

'What about children?'

'I want to have children, Fran. I want to be a mother. Will you have the operation?'

'Yes, if it's so important to you.' He said it almost without thinking and immediately wondered if he would regret it. 'Is that all?'

'No. There's one other thing?'

'What's that?'

'I want you to take me to the Lake District.'

'The Lake District? Why?' he asked, though he knew.

'I want to see the school you went to.'

'I have to think about that.'

He hadn't been back since he had left, sixteen years before. He had never wanted to go back, wanted to put it behind him, forget about it, edit it out of his memory, pretend it had never happened. Suddenly though, he realised he was far enough away from it to go back, going back might even be somehow 'cathartic'.

'OK,' he shrugged, though he knew he might regret this, too.

Saeid came back and they went out for a meal and a drink. Mary was more like her old, sweet self and he realised how much he missed her. A big black cloud seemed to have cleared from the sky. When they got back to the hall, Saeid and he were not allowed in, because visitors were not allowed after half-eleven. It really was like a bloody prison! He had been vaguely hoping he might be able to have a few minutes with Mary in her room, maybe even a kiss and a cuddle. However, she did at least let him give her a hug and a kiss goodnight, so that was progress of sorts.

'You're favourite girl won't be coming in tonight – she's babysitting,' Terry said, in his droll way, joining him in the college bar.

He was disappointed, but not too much, because there was a new girl in the class that he fancied. She was German and her name was Babsi. The name suited her, because she was a bit of a baby – only sixteen – slightly chubby, with a baby-like complexion and short fair hair. She was wearing a football shirt with navy-blue cords tucked into suede desert boots. She also had a silver cross on a chain around her neck, which intrigued him. She reminded him of Marina, except for the clothes.

He bought her a pint of Guinness and proceeded to chat her up. Grazia was there, in a sexy, low-cut black dress, and he knew this would make her jealous, so he enjoyed it all the more. He had tried to give her a simple kiss on the cheek the other day and she hadn't let him, so it was sweet revenge. He had decided that she had some incurable hang-up about sex. She had as good as told him so herself. He would like to have cured her, but she wouldn't even let him try, so what could he do? Did she expect him to go out with her without being allowed to touch her? What was wrong with her? How many chances did she want?

Babsi told him how her father had been reluctant to let her come to England on her own. His instinct had been right, he thought, with men like himself around! No, he was only joking, of course, he wouldn't do her any harm. In fact, he felt rather protective towards her, more like a father than potential lover. Or was he kidding himself?

She told him she liked classical music and Bach was her favourite composer. This disappointed him slightly, since he wasn't really into classical music himself. She said she had a West Indian 'friend' in Gloucester Road who could get her free tickets to classical concerts, but she couldn't go because she didn't have any smart dresses or shoes!

'Do you like Irish music?' he asked her, sensing his opening.

'I don't know it,' she said. It was funny how sexy a German accent could sound!

'Why don't you come to an Irish concert with me and find out?' he suggested, seizing his chance, and to his delight she eagerly accepted.

He made a date with her for Saturday and went home feeling happier than he had felt for months. He had something to look forward to at weekend! He might even manage to go to bed with her! Suddenly life seemed worth living again. It was funny to think such a simple thing as sex could make so much difference.

Not that he necessarily wanted to have sex with her. She was very young. It would be enough just to have some pleasant and attractive female company. Besides, he had promised Mary to be faithful, so he had better try if he really wanted to get back with her and make it work. Why should he be lonely meanwhile though? He'd had enough of loneliness!

On the following Saturday he took Babsi to the Victoria on Holloway Road to listen to Segui and she loved it. She loved Guinness, too, so he was doubly delighted. He didn't attempt to touch her though. He made a date to go to the cinema with her on Wednesday, hoping he would be able to at least get an arm around her there, if not a leg over.

They went to see 'The Elephant Man', but incredibly there were no two seats together. He was devastated! In the end, the usherette let Babsi sit on her little fold-down seat at the end of a row and brought an easy-chair for him to sit on beside her. It was better than standing or even sitting on the floor, but it was no good at all for snogging. Sometimes you just couldn't win!

The film was moving, if somewhat sentimental. He was amused, not by the film, but by Babsi, who childishly pulled her pullover up over her eyes whenever the 'elephant man' himself appeared on the screen. He couldn't help feeling excited by this too, because he had noticed that she had big breasts and suddenly he had an almost irresistible urge to touch them. He was tempted to try and put an arm around her, hoping at least to have a cuddle, but it was just too damned awkward.

In the pub afterwards they chatted about the film and other things. He asked her what her father did and she told him he was an Evangelical-Lutheran bishop! She said she believed in Christianity, but not 'everything' in the gospels and not in going to church – except to play the guitar at confirmation classes. He told her how he had almost become a priest, but was now an atheist, and she said that was all right, because the priest at her church was a self-confessed atheist too, which made him chuckle!

She told him how she had been terrible at maths at school, scoring one out of fifteen in her last exam, how she had left school early and worked as a residential social worker in a children's home, how the kid she looked after here wouldn't talk to her at first, how she went jogging on Hackney Marshes, and how she wanted to be a sports teacher in the future – but felt the world didn't have much future …

He told her he was writing a novel.

'Vot is it about?' she asked, obviously impressed.

It was funny how it always impressed women if you told them you were a writer, even if you hadn't been published! 'It's about a boy growing up,' he told her. 'I think what you call in German a 'bildungsroman'.' Now she was even more impressed!

'Aha, so it's about 'little Franz', is it?' she asked, cutely.

'Partly,' he said, impressed himself.

'Perhaps I vill appear in it,' she said.

'Perhaps,' he laughed.

'You must let me read a few pages.'

'Perhaps,' he repeated, teasing her.

'Von day, when it's a bestseller in Germany, I can say, "He vos my teacher!"'

'You never know!' he laughed, flattered by the thought.

Afterwards he saw her home, hoping to give her a kiss at the garden gate. He suspected she would like him to, but something held him back. He couldn't work out whether it was because she was so young and innocent or because of Mary at the back of his mind. In the end, she rather charmingly said, 'Thank you for your company', and went in, leaving him to go home feeling confused. He had enjoyed meeting her, but couldn't quite make his mind up whether he fancied her or not, whether she fancied him or just saw him as some sort of father-figure, whether he wanted to see her again or not.

'That woman is fucking impossible! I gave her a right bollocking. I felt like giving her a knee in the goolies. Do you know what she's asked me to do?'

Mark, his South African colleague, was talking about Bertha, but he wasn't really listening. He was thinking about Babsi, because she hadn't come to college. Had he upset her? Besides, there was a very loud heavy-metal band called 'Parachute' on, so he could hardly even hear himself think.

All 'his' girls were in the bar – Serena, Grazia, Rosalia and the funny little Greek girl, Eleni. She had told him that she was having trouble with the Home Office, because her visa had run out and she couldn't extend it.

'Will you marry me, darling?' she asked. This was a running joke between them.

'Yes, but the price has gone up to £200,' he joked, but he wasn't really in the mood for repartee with her – he was worried about Babsi and, anyway, it reminded him uncomfortably of Kalli. He wasn't even completely sure that Eleni was only joking.

To his relief, Babsi came into the bar at that very moment and squeezed herself in beside him. She was wearing a green cape over her usual sloppy-joe pullover, cords and desert boots.

'You look like Zorro,' he quipped, but had to explain the reference. 'Anyway, you're late for class! Where've you been?'

'I have to – how you say – babysit?'

'Ah, you've been sitting on the baby,' he joked and they all laughed.

It was the kind of lame joke you could get away with as an EFL teacher, so you could delude yourself you were Oscar Wilde, especially when you were slightly drunk, as he was by now, having downed two pints of Abbot on an empty stomach.

'What do you talk about with Eleni?' Babsi asked him, in her innocent way.

'I've just agreed to marry her,' he said, putting his arm around the aforementioned Eleni.

'You are going to marry to Eleni?' Babsi asked. She actually believed him! And was actually jealous!

'Yes, for a fee of £200,' he said, making them all laugh again.

'I thought you vere serious,' Babsi said, laughing too.

'You know me, I'm never serious,' he said to her.

'I go to get drink,' she said, taking her purse out and standing up.

'Don't forget you owe me a pint of Guinness,' he said to her.

'Ah, now you are serious,' she smiled at him.

'Absolutely. That's a serious matter. Have you got enough money?'

'I think so,' she said and went to the bar.

'So, you get your pint of Guinness,' she said, coming back and giving it to him.

'Thank you,' he said, raising the glass. 'Cheers.'

'Can I ask you something?' she said later, in the interval, when it was quieter.

'You can ask, but I might not answer,' he laughed, sensing what was coming.

'Are you married?'

'What do you think?' he asked, dodging the question.

'You do not look like someone who is married.'

'Don't I? Why not?'

'I don't know. You seem as if you are free.'

'Well, I am free,' he said – which was half true.

'Perhaps you will marry me.'

'Perhaps,' he laughed, taking it as a joke.

Thinking about it later, though, he suspected she had actually been serious, and was both touched and flattered. But, of course, it was out of the question. She was too young – only a schoolgirl really – and anyway, he was already married! He really did want to try and save his marriage.

The next day, he tried to contact Mary several times to invite her out for a drink. He wanted to tell her he would take her to the Lake District and have the operation, do whatever she wanted, if she would come back. But there was no answer.

Feeling lonely, he was tempted to call Babsi, but didn't – he had decided to try and break from her. He ended up going on his own to the Bull and Gate in Kentish Town, where Crannog were playing. However, there was hardly any atmosphere, because there were only three other people in the large concert room, three girls. He felt conspicuous, sitting on his own, and kicked himself for not inviting Babsi.

'Why don't you come and join us?' the three girls suggested, so he did.

It turned out they lived above the pub and were environmental health officers, whose jobs involved inspecting restaurants, slaughter houses and sewers. They were friendly, but none of them was particularly attractive, so he went home feeling more frustrated than ever and got out the whiskey bottle.

On the following Tuesday, which was the last day of March, he realised from his diary that it was exactly three months since Mary had left him. He phoned her, but again there was no answer. He couldn't help suspecting she was trying to avoid him! He spent the evening trying to fend off the blues by listening to Ravi Shankar, writing and watching TV.

The next day he tried to phone her four times from four different phone boxes, but it was always engaged. She was definitely trying to avoid him! But why? He went to the Archway Tavern, feeling dejected. As he went in, the landlord was chucking out a West Indian man. The West Indian was obviously a bit drunk, but he had seen more inebriated paddies in there, so suspected the motive was racist. Disgusted, he made a point of helping the West Indian get a taxi and decided to boycott the place, at least for the night.

On Thursday he didn't go to the bar after his evening class. He felt too fed up to be sociable and also didn't want to see Babsi. He really wanted to break it off before it went any further, to try and save both her and himself from being hurt. It was weird though – drinking on his own in another pub, he felt not only lonely, but guilty, too. God, I'm a sad case, he thought!

Just to rub salt in the wound, who should he bump into the next day, walking down the market on his way home from college, but Serena. 'You weren't in the bar last nighta, you naughty boy!' she told him off. For some reason he found this such a turn-on that he could hardly bear to look at her, never mind talk to her. She not only looked gorgeous, but had oodles of personality, too! He fancied her more every time he saw her. How he wished he hadn't let Terry have her!

'What are you doing?' he asked her, having made some lame excuse about last night.

'Some shoppinga,' she replied. 'I just boughta these trousers. They are 'orribile, I know, but they only costed one pounda.'

He look down at them. They were made of blue nylon and would have looked cheap and nasty on most women, but not on her. 'Maybe, but they look good on you,' he said, smoothly.

'You'll make my face like my pullover!' she replied, blushing.

He looked at her pullover and laughed, because it was bright red, as well as tight. It accentuated the shape of her gorgeous breasts beautifully. He started blushing himself, because he realised he had been looking a bit longer than strictly necessary.

'Well, ciao, nice to see you. Gotta go,' he said, hurrying off, though he didn't really have to go.

He walked on down the market feeling more fed up than ever, but not too fed up to be amused by some of the market traders' patter. 'Form a queue, you'll all get served,' one of them, without a single customer in sight, declaimed to the empty space.

Further along there was an old crone loudly denouncing the 'Romish' church and the papacy. She was obviously bonkers, but he stopped to listen to her rantings for a few moments, with a funny mixture of reactions. On the one hand, he agreed that the Catholic church was a sinister, superstitious, secretive society, as she claimed. On the other hand, he had once been a fully-paid-up member, almost an apparatchik, so he couldn't help feeling insulted, despite his cynicism. Old allegiances really did die hard!

He walked on to the end of the market – supposedly the longest street market in Europe – and then down Coppermill Lane, with its rows of Victorian terraced houses, to the Marshes. He could have gone home by train, but walking was good for him mentally and physically, especially when he felt like this. The Marshes were especially therapeutic, because he needed solitude and the soothing effects of water, wildflowers, wildfowl, reeds ...

As always, passing the water works, he stopped to enjoy the view of the reservoir, with its tree-clad island in the middle. It reminded him of the lakes of both County Cavan and Cumberland. The island was a heronry and you often saw herons flapping to and fro or perching statuesquely on their long spindly legs on the bank, spear-like beaks poised to catch a fish. There were no herons apparent today, but there were flocks of geese and ducks, as well as what looked like cormorants, which reminded him of Gola, the little island off the coast of Donegal where Mary and he had spent their honeymoon.

He tried not to dwell on such memories though and walked on to the river. This was the river Lea, which was a tributary of the Thames. It wasn't much of a river, in fact looked more like a canal, with its murky water and narrow-boats and barges plying up and down, but it was better than nothing. There were more unspoilt stretches where you could imagine it as it must have been a hundred years or more ago, idyllically pastoral, surrounded by reed beds and meadows. He also liked to imagine Vikings sailing up it in their longboats, since according to local history books they had done so, though that was a thousand years or more ago.

He walked downriver to the bridge at Lea Bridge Road, where he had a pint of Young's at the Prince of Wales, pausing en route to watch logs being unloaded from a lighter at Latham's timber sheds. Then he walked back upriver, stopping for a pint of Fuller's at the Anchor and Hope. As he drank, he gazed out through the tremulous poplars over the Marshes – the river, reed beds, playing fields, railway viaduct and water works. The tower blocks, church spires and factory roofs of Walthamstow and Leyton were far away on the horizon, so it was easy to lose yourself in the illusion of being somewhere else, another world, another time, another place …

The following day, Saturday, he phoned Mary again, but still couldn't get through. In desperation, he phoned Babsi – he couldn't face the thought of another Saturday evening on his own. However, her landlady told him she had gone shopping to Oxford Street. He was surprised by this, because he didn't think she was interested in 'shopping'. Desperate for company, he tried again at seven and Babsi answered, but said she was too tired to go out. He tried to persuade her, but it was no good.

'I vould not be funny to be viz,' she said. 'I feel sleepy. The trouble is, I haf no one to sleep viz. I like somebody sleeping next to me.'

'I'll come and sleep with you,' he said cheekily, and the thought suddenly excited him.

'I do not zink my landlady vould allow it,' she said.

'In that case, you can come here and sleep with me,' he said, even more cheekily.

'I do not zink it is good idea,' she said, primly.

'Oh vell, in that case, you can fuck off and sleep on your own,' he felt like saying, suddenly infuriated by her attitude, but he didn't. Instead, he just said sarcastically, 'In that case, sweet dreams,' and put the phone down.

He immediately felt sorry, because she was a nice girl, but he was fed up – fed up with her, with Mary, with everybody and everything. So as usual he went out and got drunk on his own, came home and got more drunk, then crawled off to bed on his own and relieved himself fantasising about Serena.

CHAPTER NINETEEN

It was Sunday afternoon. He was sitting in his study, writing, when there was a knock at the door. He rushed to open it, thinking it might be Mary, but it wasn't – it was Roger, on his own.

'Where's Yoko?' he asked, inviting him in.

'Oh, she was feeling a bit tired, so she stayed at home. Acksherly, I've got some news to tell you.'

'She hasn't left you, has she?' he asked, alarmed.

'Oh, no, quite the reverse!' he laughed, his hand over his mouth. 'We got married yesterday!'

'You got married?'

'Yes. That's why I'm here. I thought you should be the first to know.'

'Well, congratulations! Where did you do the dastardly deed?' *And why wasn't I invited?*

'Oh, just at the local register office, you know. Yoko didn't want any fuss, so that's why we kept it very quiet and didn't invite anyone.'

'Quiet? It sounds positively cloak and dagger!' he joked, though he felt miffed.

'Oh, no, it wasn't that secret,' Roger chortled, his hand over his mouth.

'What about witnesses?'

'Oh, that was no problem, we just dragged some poor chap in off the street,' he giggled. He seemed to think this was hilarious!

'Well, congratulations!' he said again, shaking his hand.

He was pleased, of course, but still felt slightly miffed that he hadn't been invited. He felt a twinge of envy, too, because now the tables were completely turned – Roger was married and he wasn't. He even felt slightly jealous, because Yoko was rather sexy.

'Have you heard from Mary, by the way?' he asked.

'Not since I saw you last,' Roger said. 'Have you?'

'I've been trying to get in touch, but can't get through.'

'She is under pressure with exams, isn't she?'

'I suppose so. I get the feeling she's trying to avoid me though.'

'I don't think so. I think she does want to get back with you. She loves you, you know.' He nodded solemnly.

'She has a strange way of showing it.' This sounded bitter, he realised, but he was feeling bitter.

'I don't want to pry, but have you decided anything?'

'Well, I've decided to have this operation.'

'What about the 'freedom' question?'

'I'm prepared to be monogamous.'

'I think that's all she wants. She does genuinely love you. I know that.' Roger nodded his head solemnly again.

'She also wants me to take her to the Lake District.'

'The Lake District? Why?'

'To see my old school. That's where I went to school.'

'Did you? Which school was that?'

'Oh, just a minor Catholic public school,' he fibbed.

He didn't tell him that it was a seminary, that he had once wanted to be a priest. That was something he didn't like to tell anybody, something he was able to talk about only with fellow ex-inmates like Charles. He had told Mary, of course.

'Why exactly does she want to visit your old school?'

'I suppose she thinks it will help her to understand me better,' he laughed.

'I see. So what was it like?'

'Well, let's say the regime was rather – rigorous,' he said, choosing his words carefully. What an understatement! It had been more like a blooming concentration camp!

'Was it all male?'

'Oh, yes! All male! The teachers were all priests.' *Not to mention sadists! Not to mention ... No, don't go there!*

'So there were no girls or women?'

Roger seemed fascinated. People usually were! Which was why he didn't like talking about it.

'No. I didn't meet any girls till I was eighteen!' Actually, he hadn't really met any girls till he was twenty-one, after he had left the senior seminary, but he didn't tell Roger that. 'Mary thinks that's why I'm so interested in women now.' *Why did I say that?*

'Oh, I don't think there's anything unusual about red-blooded males like ourselves being interested in women,' Roger giggled, his hand over his mouth again.

'No, I suppose not,' he laughed too, glad to lighten the conversation. These were waters he didn't really want to go too deeply into, with Roger or anyone.

'Anyway,' he added, just to steer the conversation further away, 'it'll be good to have a look around the Lake District as well. I'll take her to Grasmere, of course. If I can get hold of her, that is.'

They went on to chat about Wordsworth, Coleridge and co. and, somehow, Tchaikovsky. Roger told him that Tchaikovsky hadn't died of cholera, as was commonly believed, but killed himself because of a homosexual relationship with the nephew of Count Stenbock, who was the subject of his latest book. It was all very interesting, but he wasn't really in the mood, and was relieved when Roger left. He took him to the bus stop and Roger happily agreed to ask Mary to get in touch with him.

Roger was going home to his sexy Japanese wife, he reflected ironically, as he walked back, while he had no one to go home to. It used to be the other way round! Suddenly, he just couldn't face going back to his empty flat, so decided to go for a walk.

He went down to the Marshes as usual and walked up the river. He stopped for a pint of London Pride at the aptly named Anchor and Hope, even though it was Sunday and he had to work the next day. However, one pint led to another and he ended up going home drunk. He tried to watch 'Hedda Gabbler' on TV, but fell asleep, so crawled off to bed. But he couldn't sleep, because he couldn't stop thinking about her.

'Hello. Is that Mary?'

'Yes.'

'At last. I've been trying to get through to you for ages. How are you?'

'I'm as well as can be expected under the circumstances, I suppose,' she said, sarcastically.

'Where've you been?' he asked, ignoring the sarcasm.

'I've been at the hall. Why?'

'I've been trying to contact you.'

'I've been busy studying. I've got exams soon.'

'I see,' he said. What was the point of arguing with her?

'Where are you?' she asked.

'I'm in Paris.'

'Paris?'

'Yes, Paris.' He couldn't help feeling rather pleased to spring this surprise on her – it might make her realise he still had a life, despite her departure. It might even make her sorry she hadn't answered the phone before, since if she had she could have been with him.

'Why are you in Paris?' she asked and he could hear a tiny note of resentment, as well as suspicion, in her voice. Good!

'I'm having a dirty weekend,' he quipped and immediately regretted it.

'Who are you with?' she demanded.

'I'm not with anybody, silly,' he said. 'Well, I'm with Charles. He asked me to take some summer school brochures over, so I'm having a little break. You could've come, but I couldn't get hold of you.' He couldn't resist rubbing it in a bit. 'How are your parents?' he asked, as a sop.

'They're fine. What about the Lake District? Are we still going?'

'If you still want to.'

'When?' she asked, curt.

'Next week. I get back from Paris on Tuesday, so we could go on Wednesday.'

'Good. Call me at this number when you get back from Paris. Bye.'

'Bye,' he said, though she had already put the phone down.

God, she sounds so hostile! Maybe I shouldn't have made that crack about a 'dirty weekend'. Maybe I shouldn't have come to Paris. No! What the hell! It's not every day you get the chance to go to Paris!

'How is she?' Charles asked.

'Still very hostile,' he said. 'Even though I've agreed to take her to the Lake District next week.'

They were in Charles's flat, sipping post-prandial whiskey, smoking cigars and chatting, while listening to Liszt on the stereo. Charles's flat was on the top floor of a 'bâtiment' in the very centre of Paris. Funnily enough, it was next door to a convent and from the window, as well as the Eiffel Tower, you could see nuns gliding meditatively, as if on castors, around their garden, just as they had once done themselves …

'"Hell hath no fury",' Charles commented, blowing out some cigar smoke.

'I know. She seems almost implacable.'

'Don't worry. She'll come round. So you're going to visit the alma mater, eh?'

'Yes. I've got grave reservations about it though. I've never been back. Have you?'

'No. Never really fancied it before. Thought it would bring back too many morbid memories. Wouldn't mind going back now though. Enough water has flowed under the bridge, I suppose. Christ, it's what, twenty years now?'

'For me, sixteen. The thought still gives me the heeby-jeebies though.' *That's an understatement!*

'It'll be all right. At least the Ghosters aren't there any more.'

'I wouldn't go anywhere near it if they were!'

'What exactly is it now?'

'Some sort of field study centre, I believe.'

'Ideal location for that sort of thing, when you think about it.'

'Absolutely. Magnificent location – right on the edge of the Lake District, surrounded by all that scenery. Pity they didn't let us make proper use of it all, wasn't it?'

'Well, the stupid bastards had no imagination, did they?'

'It was more like a bloody prison than anything else, when you think about it.'

'A borstal!'

'Imagine, we spent six years of our bloody lives there!'

'You don't remember Doc Murray, do you?'

'No. He was before my time.'

'He was a fucking psychopath!'

'He can't have been worse than Greg.'

'He was a psychopath, too. The way he flogged that kid, Cooper, in the study hall that time. With that leaded, whalebone belt.'

'Yeah. Only twelve years old, still in short trousers. Poor kid. Wonder what he's doing now?'

'Must have been traumatized for life.'

'I wouldn't be surprised. We were traumatized just witnessing it.'

'You must have been absolutely terrified.'

'We were. I remember just sitting there in the study hall, shocked, thinking, *'Why doesn't someone stop him?'*'

'I'll never forgive myself for not getting up and beating the shit out of him. I suppose he had us all intimidated, even us seniors. He was a classic bully, of course.'

'Yes. And the really sick thing is that while he was flogging defenceless little kids black and blue, at the same time he was doing you know what.'

'Yes. I must say, I'm shocked by what you've told me. I mean, I knew he used to bath kids. As I told you, I even went and told him I thought it was 'inappropriate' behaviour once, when I was First Auxiliary.'

'Yeah, you said. What was his reaction again?'

'He freaked out, of course. Bawled me out of his office, then gave one of his blood-and-thunder conferences in the study hall. You must remember them.'

'Yeah, I do. He was good at those, wasn't he? Ranting and raving. Roaring and bellowing. Classic sign of a guilty conscience, I suppose.'

'I must admit I was shocked when you told me he had topped himself. I really thought he'd had a heart attack.'

'He didn't have a heart attack. He was only in his thirties and there was no history of heart trouble or anything else. He might have been mentally sick, but physically he was perfectly fit. He topped himself.'

'How do you know that though?'

'Oh, it all came out later. I thought everyone knew.'

'I didn't! I'm still shocked! How did he do it? Took a bottle of pills?'

'Probably. He had enough of them in his bedroom, didn't he?'

'It was like a bloody apothecary's!'

'That's right,' he laughed. 'I must admit, I feel a bit guilty about it though.'

'What, because he topped himself? You don't need to feel guilty. He was a sick bastard.'

'Yes, well ... ' He was shocked at Charles's vehemence.

'He should've been locked up.'

'You think so?'

'Absolutely. He may have ruined people's lives. That kid Cooper for example. He might have gone on to do even worse. No, I've no sympathy for him at all.'

'Well, I'm just glad he didn't mess me up too much.'

'What was it he said you had?'

'A varicocele. That's a varicose vein. In the scrotum.'

'How the fuck did he know about that? Not that he should've been looking at your scrotum in the first place.'

'No, I suppose not,' he laughed. 'I think he fancied himself as a bit of a doctor. He had loads of medical textbooks in his room, if you remember.'

'It's the bit about the Germolene that gets me.'

'I know. Looking back now, it's hilarious!'

'And how long did all this go on for?'

'About two years.'

'Two years!' Charles shook his head.

'Yeah. Till I was fourteen. Then he just dropped me like a hot potato. I remember at the time feeling really perplexed. And rejected. For ages I kept wondering what I'd done wrong, why he didn't like me any more.'

'It's a bloody miracle you didn't turn out gay.'

'Actually, I did go through a sort of homosexual phase while I was there. With Mark Brown.'

'Yeah, you told me. That was fairly normal in the circumstances though.'

'You know I met him afterwards?'

'Did you? Where?'

'In a pub in Holborn. Just after I first went to London. He was teaching EFL in a private school like me. The funny thing is, I was with my girlfriend – the Yugoslav girl I told you about – and he was with his boyfriend. One of his students. A Greek-Cypriot boy.'

'Go on – what happened?'

'Nothing much that night. We talked a bit, but we couldn't talk much, because he was with someone and so was I and I was going to the theatre. He was a bit drunk anyway. But I met him a few times afterwards.'

'You didn't have an affair with him, did you?'

'No! I'm not gay, amazingly. The trouble is, he wanted to. He said he was still in love with me.'

'That must have been very difficult.'

'I found it very embarrassing. It caused trouble between me and my girlfriend, as well as between him and his boyfriend. In the end, I had to stop seeing him, because my girlfriend thought I fancied him. She was jealous.'

'So you stopped seeing him. How did he take that?'

'He didn't. He killed himself.'

'You're joking?' Charles said, shocked.

'No. At least, I think he killed himself. Threw himself under an underground train. He was drunk, so he might have just fallen, but I think it was deliberate. He had an alcohol problem, in fact.'

'Christ! All because of that place. That fucker!'

'In a way, yes.'

'Did you go to the funeral?'

'You won't believe this, but it was on the very day I was supposed to marry this Yugoslav girl.'

'So did you go?'

'She didn't want me to, but the wedding was in the afternoon and the funeral was in the morning, so I had to go, didn't I? I mean, the guy was dead partly because of me, I suppose.'

'I don't think you can say that. Anyway, what happened?'

'I went to the funeral. Catholic church in south London. Met his parents. Felt sorry for them. They asked me if anything had happened at school. They said he'd never been the same since he left.'

'Did you tell them?'

'No. I wanted to, but I chickened out. I just couldn't do it. I thought it would just be too much for them. It was bad enough for them burying their son who had committed suicide and knowing he was gay, without finding out what had happened at school.'

'What did happen, exactly?'

'Well, Greg found out about me and Mark, went berserk and tried to expel me.'

'What do you mean, 'tried to expel you'?'

'Told me I couldn't receive the habit. Wasn't even going to let me do my bloody A-levels at first.'

'You must've been devastated.'

'I was suicidal! Then I found out from Mark that Greg was doing with him exactly what he used to do with me. The bastard was jealous! Can you believe it?'

'I can't. The plot thickens. So what did you do?'

'That was when I confronted him. Told him I'd reveal all, if he didn't let me receive the habit. Told him if he expelled me – this was right before A-levels – I'd shop him to the Superior, to the Provincial, even to the Pope if necessary.'

'What did he say?'

'He went into one of his apoplectic rages, of course, shouting and ranting at me. Tried to intimidate me, like the big, blustering bully he was. Of course, by then I was seventeen and taller than him, so he couldn't. I wasn't going to back down, because I was fighting for my life. I even thought he was going to hit me at one point. I had to run out of the office.'

'Fuck me!'

'Next morning he was found dead in bed. He'd taken an overdose. The heart-attack story was just for appearances.'

'It all adds up.'

'Yeah. It's tragic, in a way, isn't it? I mean, he was quite an impressive character in his own way, wasn't he?'

'I suppose so. He was a good historian. Bloody good-looking too – tall, dark and handsome. Cut quite a dash in that black frock-coat, didn't he? I think all the girls in the shops in Grange fancied him like mad.'

'Ironic, isn't it? If only they'd known.'

'If only. I must say, I'm staggered. I'd no idea it was as bad as this. Have you told anyone else?'

'No, you're the first.'

'What about Mary? Told her?'

'No. I'm not sure if I want to. That's why I don't really want to go back to the place. It'll just stir up too many disturbing memories.'

'It might exorcise them. Anyway, carry on, what happened after the funeral?'

'I got to the register office just in time, but she'd gone.'

'Gone?'

'Yeah. She'd flown the coop. Literally. My witness told me she'd gone to the airport to catch a flight back to Yugoslavia.'

'What did you do?'

'I raced off to the airport and got there just in time to see her plane taking off.'

'You must've been devastated. Again.'

'I was. Lost a girlfriend and a 'boyfriend' all in one day! Must be some kind of record! I can laugh about it now, I suppose, but I was gutted.'

'Did you ever hear from her again?'

'No. I can understand her getting cold feet about the wedding, though it was her idea, but no communication – I've never forgiven her for that.'

'Well, I can see why you don't fancy going back!'

'Yeah. The ironic thing is, Greg was right! I *have* got a varicocele! That's why I've got to have this bloody operation.'

'It'll be all right, don't worry. Come on, let's blow this pop stand and go for a toddle. I'll show you a few of the sights. We can have a beer somewhere too.'

He was glad to go out. After talking about the past so much, he needed some air. They left Charles' apartment and strolled along the Champs Elysée towards the Arc de Triomphe, stopping in bars for the occasional beer en route.

As with all foreign places, he felt a certain sense of unreality, strolling along the Champs Elysée. This in turn made the past seem even more unreal. In fact, he started to wonder if he had imagined it all, if it was just some bizarre, bad dream. Of course, he knew it wasn't – at least no more so than the present.

He was excited to be in Paris, with its mystique, its romantic and literary associations, but all the time, at the back of his mind, hovered the image of Mary and the thought of their trip to the Lake District next week. What ghosts would it disturb? Would it exorcise them or bring them back to haunt him?

CHAPTER TWENTY

'This is it,' he said to Mary, pulling up in front of the main gate.

It was just as he remembered it – two square, grey, stone pillars and, behind the grey-stone, crenellated wall, a sign that now said:

FYLDE FIELD STUDY CENTRE

'That used to have the name of the school on it,' he told her. There used to be a Latin motto too, 'Euntes ergo omnes', but he didn't bother to tell her. She wouldn't understand.

'What was the name?' she asked.

'St. Mary's Missionary College, but we used to just call it Castlehead. That was the original name of the house. It used to be engraved on these pillars. Come on, let's get out and have a look.'

They did so, though she seemed reluctant. The name was still there on the pillars: 'CASTLE' on one, 'HEAD' on the other. Seeing it suddenly sent a tremor of apprehension through him.

'What's that?' Mary asked.

'That's the lodge,' he told her, turning to look at it.

It was a small, quaint-looking house, even smaller than he remembered it, with pointed roofs and tall chimneys, built of the same grey stone as everything else in the area. There was a little wooden sign on it that said, 'GRANGE LODGE'. A feeling of 'déjà vu' swept over him. Of course, he realised, he had been here before, but it now seemed as if in a previous incarnation.

'Who lives there?' Mary asked .

'I don't know who lives there now, but it used to be the caretaker. Till the bastards sacked him.'

'Why did they sack him?'

'Because he had a teenage daughter and they thought she might lead us astray. Can you imagine the mentality?'

'They sacked him just because of that?'

'Yes. And his wife, who was a cleaner. Can you believe it?'

'Did they give them some redundancy money?'

'You must be joking!' he laughed.

'That wasn't fair, was it?'

'Of course not! It was bloody disgusting. So much for Christian charity! These days they'd be up in front of an industrial tribunal. Quite right too.' It still made him angry even now to think about it, but he had to control his feelings, he told himself – lots of things were going to disturb him today. 'Come on, let's drive in.'

'Are we allowed to?'

'Well, we haven't come all this way just to look at the lodge, have we? Come on.'

It was exasperating – she was the one who had brought him here, against his will, and now she was afraid to go in! It was typical of her timidity, but he had to try not to show any annoyance – their 'reconciliation' was still only a day old. They had driven up to Grange-over-Sands only the day before …

When they had arrived, they had to look for accommodation, which caused a minor tiff. She wanted to stay in the Crown Hotel, at the top of the steep main street, but he said it was too expensive and insisted on a B & B, which they found easily enough and which had proved fine.

After checking in, they had gone out for an evening stroll, followed by a drink and dinner. It gave him an almost 'illicit' thrill to stroll around the town and along the prom with the freedom of an adult – the last time he had done so had been in a 'crocodile' of boys, in groups of three, juniors at the front, seniors at the back, all in their blue caps, blue blazers and grey flannel trousers.

Last night they had slept together for the first time in three months, but hadn't made love. He wanted to, but she said she wasn't 'ready'. He was hoping she would be more amenable tonight, which was another reason to avoid any friction today.

They got back in the car and drove slowly through the open gates, then along a long, narrow, straight drive, on either side of which there were fields as flat and green as billiard tables. 'This is the Grange drive,' he told her, remembering the first time he had been driven along it, in the school minibus, having been picked up at the station with the other Manchester boys by Father Taylor – or 'Yogi Bear' as they called him. God, how innocent he had been then, at the age of twelve, he reflected with a pang, how full of idealism! All he had wanted was to be a missionary priest and go to Africa to save souls for Christ! If only he had known what lay ahead …

'This drive used to be full of potholes,' he told her, remembering that first, bumpy ride in the school minibus. 'They seem to have repaired it. About time, too!'

A little way down the drive, he stopped the car. 'You see that telegraph pole,' he said. 'That was as far as we were allowed to go. We used to go for walks along the drive during recreation, but beyond that was out of bounds. From there to the gate we used to call 'No-Man's-Land'!'

'What happened if you went out of bounds?'

'Well, if you were seen, by a prefect for example, and reported or 'sent up', as we called it, you'd get six of the best from Father Director. He was the priest in charge of us. We used to call him 'Greg', because he looked like Gregory Peck.'

'With a cane?'

'No. He had this special strap, made of leather, with whalebone inside and weighted with lead. It was actually more like a cosh. In fact, it was more like an offensive bloody weapon! Apparently, the Dean of Studies, Father Egan, who was Irish, brought a whole arsenal of them with him from Ireland. *He* ended up teaching at Blackrock College, just outside Dublin.'

'What was he like?'

'He was a real nutter. A little weed of a bloke, but with a terrible temper. Used to fly into apoplectic rages at the slightest thing. He was as bald as a billiard ball and had this ghoulish, deathly-white skin, so he looked like a corpse! Used to go round in a long black cloak. In fact, we used to call him 'Dracula'. Actually, I think I was the one who started calling him that. He didn't like *me* from day one, for some reason.'

'Why not?' she asked, in her innocent way.

'I don't know,' he shook his head. 'The veins on his skull used to swell up as if they'd burst when he lost his temper! I think he really was mentally unbalanced actually. He certainly had anger management issues, as they say these days. He was a rabid Irish nationalist into the bargain. Used to curse the English, especially Oliver Cromwell, in class. That's about the only thing I can say in his favour!'

'Did *you* ever get the strap from Father Director?'

'Just once.'

'What for?'

'I was sent out of class by Father Haynes, the priest who taught us English. He gave me two of the strap, one on each hand. This was just a few weeks after I arrived. I remember feeling really upset. In fact, I was so upset, I tried to run away. I turned back at the gate though. Sometimes now I wish I hadn't!'

'Why did you turn back?'

'Why? Because I was only twelve years old, I was a hundred miles from home and I had no money – we weren't allowed money. And it was bloody cold! It must've been November. Remember, we only had short trousers on. Plus I was starving! It was nearly dinnertime, and even though the food was crap, it was better than nothing.'

'I'm sorry, love,' she said, putting a hand on his cheek. It was the first sign of affection he had had from her that day, yet it made him feel uncomfortable. 'I wish you had run away.'

'Why?' he asked, driving on slowly.

'I might have met you earlier.'

'I don't know about that,' he laughed, embarrassed. 'Anyway, when I got to the gate, I suddenly realised I couldn't face my family, especially my mother, if I ran away. I couldn't face the thought of going back to my old school – I would've felt like a failure. And I couldn't face the thought of not being a priest. I still wanted to be a priest, despite everything.'

'So, what did you do then?'

'I went back and joined the others going for dinner.'

'Did you get into trouble?'

'No, I don't think anyone noticed. It was a miracle really, because you were always being watched. It was like a bloody concentration camp!'

He stopped the car again. 'You see that embankment over there?' He pointed across the level green fields, in some of which sheep were grazing. 'That's the railway line. It runs from behind that cliff there, which we used to call the 'Bluff'. That's the way we used to go home and come back. We used to dread coming past the Bluff, because that's when you get your first sight of the school. You knew you were back then and it was real! Anyway, the embankment was built in the last century to carry the railway across the bay. Apparently, all this land you see here, on both sides of the drive, was reclaimed from the sea. That's why it's so flat – and fertile. Apparently, the sea used to come right up to the house then.' It was weird – as he explained all this to her, he remembered how Gyp, the old boy who had accompanied them on the train, had given them the same spiel in the minibus.

He drove on till they came to a sharp bend in the drive. 'We used to call this bend 'the elbow', he informed her, feeling like some sort of tour guide, as they drove slowly past a high redbrick wall on the right. 'That used to be the farm,' he said, stopping to glance through an open gateway in the wall and noticing a Land Rover parked in the 'farmyard'.

'Who looked after that?' she asked.

'Brother Healy. He was Irish too. A big, fat fellow with a ruddy face. We used to call him 'Bacon Chops'! But we used to work on the farm, too. Mucking out the cowshed, for example. Most kids hated it, but I quite liked it, because it reminded me of Ireland.'

He glanced to the left. 'Oh, look, the horse chestnut trees are still there,' he said, pointing to a line of trees in bright green livery opposite. 'We used to play with the conkers off them, just after going back in September. God, how we dreaded September!' The memory of going back to school in September, with three long winter months to endure before going home again, sent a shudder through him. 'Let's carry on.'

After a short distance, he stopped again, next to a fenced-off plot on the right. 'Let's just have a look in here,' he said, getting out. 'We'll have to climb over the fence.'

'I don't think we should, Fran,' she objected nervously, to his irritation. 'Somebody might be watching.'

'There's obviously nobody around. Anyway, who gives a damn?' he said, vaulting over the barbed wire fence. He was being a bit cheeky, he supposed, but he almost felt as if he had a right to go wherever he liked – after all, he had spent six years of his life here!

'I can't climb over that,' she said, timorously.

'Don't be silly – of course you can,' he insisted, holding out a hand to help her, annoyed – he knew she had a bad leg, but suspected she was just using it as an excuse, because she was afraid of 'trespassing'.

He helped her over, catching her in his arms. 'You see,' he said, giving her a hug. 'You can do it if you want.' He had always had to encourage her to overcome her 'handicap'.

'This used to be the rose garden,' he told her, leading her in by the hand. 'It was really impressive, with roses of all kinds. It looks like a vegetable garden now. There used to be a statue of Saint Theresa over there in the middle.' The statue had gone, but the plinth was still there, somewhat derelict-looking.

'We used to do manual labour here on Saturday afternoons, weeding the roses,' he told her. 'On the feast of Corpus Christi we used to have a procession along the drive and end up with benediction here in the open air. We spent all morning collecting flowers and making designs of monstrances and chalices and such like with the petals on the drive.' How mad it all seemed now, he thought, like the esoteric ritual of some crackpot cult! At the same time, he felt a certain nostalgia, as if for lost innocence, as if it had been not just a rose garden, but a Garden of Eden …

It really had been like a Garden of Eden, because there had been a snake in the grass here, too. This was the very place, he recalled, where Mark had told him, during manual labour one Saturday afternoon, what Father Director had been doing, which was the ammunition he had needed. He remembered the conversation as if it were yesterday, how they had had to whisper to each other while pretending to hoe, under the watchful eye of a prefect, because they were supposed to work in silence and had been expressly forbidden, on pain of expulsion, to have any communication whatsoever with each other.

'I think we'd better go before somebody sees us,' Mary said, nervously.

'OK, let's go,' he agreed, glad of the excuse to put the memory out of his mind, and led her back to the car.

They drove around a curve in the drive and parked in a car park with buildings on three sides. 'We used to call this the 'quad' – we used to play here during recreation,' he told her. 'That block there used to be the study hall and classrooms, with the dormitory on top. That other block used to be the washroom, with the refectory on top. There used to be some wooden huts along this side, but they've gone. They were the 'games huts', where we played table tennis and billiards and such like, but only if it was too dark or wet to go outside. This other building wasn't here when I was here.'

He led her over towards it. 'All this used to be grass, which we called the 'Oval', where we played football during recreation.' He peered through a window. 'It looks like a science laboratory. Blimey, they must've moved into the twentieth century after I left! We never did science.'

'Why not?'

'I think they were afraid it might contradict all the baloney they taught us.'

'What kind of baloney?'

'Oh, about God creating the world in six days and all that crap, for example.'

'That's not necessarily crap.'

'Come on, you can't believe all that crap! It's just fairytales! Superstitious nonsense!'

'You may think so, but I don't.'

'Well, I find the theory of evolution a bit more convincing, myself,' he said, sarcastically.

Sometimes her reactionary brand of Catholicism really got on his nerves. It was part of the problem between them. To him, this place symbolized all that was wrong with Catholicism. It was another reason why he already felt so uncomfortable here, apart from what had happened to him.

He didn't want to get into a theological argument with her, so he walked away, stood in the middle of the 'quad' and gazed around. The place seemed eerily quiet, with not a soul in sight. In his memory, though, it was filled with the raucous sounds of boys in blue blazers, talking, shouting, laughing, running around, letting off steam between classes.

'Come on, let's go inside,' he said, heading towards a door.

'Shouldn't we ask somebody?' she asked, nervously.

'There isn't anybody to ask, is there?' he said, irritated by her timidity again. 'Come on!'

He led her in through the door of what used to be the washroom. Even inside there seemed to be nobody around, but eventually, upstairs, they found a man in an office, in what used to be the refectory.

He introduced himself and Mary and explained why they had come. The man, who was the teacher in charge, explained that the place was empty because it was the Easter holiday and told them they could wander around wherever they wanted.

He decided to do what for him was the worst part, so looked at the dormitory first. It was still a dormitory, but had been divided up into separate cubicles and neatly fitted out. 'In our time this was just one big room,' he told her, 'with four rows of iron beds and a chair next to each bed – no furniture, no curtains, bare floorboards, no carpet, not even lino on the floor. We used to call it the 'Barn', it was so cold in winter, because there was no heating.'

'So you all used to sleep here?'

'Yes, nearly a hundred of us. Can you imagine?'

'Where did you sleep?'

'Well, it used to be seniors this end, juniors the other end, so I slept in various parts. You had to change beds every term, anyway. That was supposed to stop you becoming possessive, or 'attached', as they called it.'

'What were the beds like?'

'Oh, not sprung divans, I can tell you! Just plain iron beds, like hospital beds, with thin, horsehair mattresses. You had to make your bed every morning after mass, before morning study – strip it completely, turn the mattress, and leave it neat and tidy and in line with the others. If you didn't, you got into trouble. It was like being in the bloomin' army!'

'Maybe that's why you're so neat and tidy now,' she observed.

'Am I?' he laughed. 'Maybe something good came out of this place, then!'

'What time did you go to bed?'

'Oh, nine o'clock. We used to say night prayers kneeling by our beds. Then we had about ten minutes to get washed and into bed before lights out at nine-fifteen. After lights out, in the dark, the First Auxiliary – that was the head prefect – would intone the last prayer of the day.' He proceeded to recite it for her, in a melodramatic voice: '"Remember that at any moment you may DIE and enter into ETERNITY. If you die in a state of grace, you will live for ever in eternal happiness. If you die in a state of SIN, you will BURN! FOR EVER! IN THE HELL OF THE DAMNED!" What a pretty little lullaby to send children to sleep with!'

It was hard to believe he had slept so many nights in this very room. He remembered how strange it had felt at first. 'It was funny, sleeping here in the dorm with almost a hundred other boys, hearing all the strange noises: breathing, snoring, creaking bedsprings ... Sometimes you could even hear boys whispering to each other, though it was strictly against the rule, and if Father Director caught you, you'd get the strap next morning. He used to patrol the dorm after lights out, saying his rosary and shining his torch round to make sure everybody was in bed. You could tell if he was near your bed, even though he wore carpet slippers, because you could hear his rosary beads jingling behind his back – they had these special, extra-large rosaries. The worst sound of all was trains crossing the bay in the distance, especially when they gave a whistle. That was the loneliest sound in the world! It reminded you at regular intervals of the world you'd left behind.'

'What do you mean?'

'The world of home and family.' *The world of warmth, comfort, love, affection, normality ...*

'Sometimes, especially in the first few weeks, you'd hear boys crying themselves to sleep.'

He remembered crying himself once, because he had been so homesick, but Father Director had heard him and took him to his bedroom to comfort him ...

'What time did you get up?'

'Six-thirty. Father Director used to come into the dorm, turn all the lights on and shout, 'Benedicamus Domino!', to which we were supposed to reply, 'Deo Gratias' – if we were awake. Then he'd walk around, clapping his hands loudly to wake you up and making sure everyone got out of bed. If you didn't, he'd just pull the bedclothes off. You had to get dressed immediately, sitting on the edge of the bed with the sheet over you.'

'Why was that?'

'He was really hung-up about 'modesty' – ironic, really.'

'What do you mean?'

'Oh, nothing. I'll tell you later.'

'Tell me now.'

'No, later. I don't want to talk about it now. Let's have a look round the rest of the place.'

As they left the dorm through the swing doors, they passed another door on the right, which was slightly open. He couldn't resist looking in. 'Oh,' he said, surprised, pushing the door open and going in. 'It's an office now.'

'Why, what did it use to be?' Mary asked, going in behind him.

'It used to be Father Director's bedroom. God!'

'What?'

'Nothing. It's just so – different.' He pictured the room as it used to be – the wardrobe, the chest of drawers with the medicines on top, the washbasin, the bed with the crucifix on the wall above it – and suddenly he felt as if he was suffocating. 'Come on, let's go,' he said, ushering her out.

'What's wrong, Fran? What happened here?' she asked, following him.

'I'll tell you later,' he said, hurrying down the stone stairs to what used to be the study hall and classrooms.

At the bottom of the stairs, he stopped to look into another small room, which was now obviously a bedroom. 'Gosh!' he exclaimed. 'This used to be Father Director's office. This is where you had to come and see him if you were in trouble, where he used to give you the strap. He had his desk right there, against that wall.'

He remembered how, as a twelve-year-old, he had once sat in the old, brown, leather armchair in this very room, while the doctor dug a verruca out of his foot and Father Director had had to hold him down, because he was writhing and screaming with pain, even though the doctor had given him several injections. He remembered, too, how lonely he had felt afterwards, when Father Director had sent him limping back to the study hall, without a word of comfort …

He left quickly and led her to the classrooms. They were still classrooms, but looked much more modern now, with overhead projectors, flipcharts, whiteboards and wall posters, though he noticed they still had the original parquet flooring. There were also tables instead of the old-fashioned, brown, wooden desks they had used.

'There used to be partitions in here that opened up to make the study hall,' he told her. 'We had to study every evening after rosary from quarter-past five till supper at seven – including even Saturday evenings. After supper we had half-an-hour's recreation, then we had to come in here and study or read our library books from eight till quarter to nine. Then we had conference – a talk from the Director – followed by night prayer and bed. During study the Dean of Studies – Father Egan – used to sit on a rostrum here and watch us like a hawk. Or he'd walk up and down in his black cloak, like some spooky sentry, reading his breviary, checking you were doing your work. If he caught you doing anything you shouldn't be doing, he'd whack you round the head or take you out into the corridor and give you the strap.'

'Did he ever give you the strap?'

'Yeah. For dropping my dictionary on the floor one evening! He went crackers! Well, he was permanently crackers. I'd only been here a few weeks. I was so terrified when he gave me the strap that I dirtied my trousers.'

'What did you do then?'

'I went to the toilet – or 'bogs' as we called it – and tried to clean myself up using toilet paper and water from the loo. Then I tried to get rid of my dirty underpants by flushing them down the loo, but they wouldn't go. In fact, they nearly flooded the damn place.'

'How did you get rid of them?'

'I wanted to go into the boiler room, which was just opposite the toilets – I'll show you later – and chuck them in the boiler, but I was too scared, because the boiler room was *strictly* out of bounds. In the end I just hid them in my locker in the 'boot room', which I'll show you in a minute. I had to go round without any underpants for the rest of the evening though, which was really uncomfortable.' He didn't tell her what had happened later that night. He remembered it all so clearly – as if it had happened yesterday! He sometimes had nightmares in which he was back here, trapped, a prisoner. Now, he suddenly felt afraid that the present was a dream from which he might wake up and find he really was back here! He wanted to leave, but didn't, carried on looking around what used to be the study hall.

'You know, even on Sunday mornings we had to come in here for an hour and a half and do English composition,' he told her. 'Even on Sunday bloody Sunday morning they couldn't let us relax a bit!'

'Why was that?' she asked.

'Good question! I think partly because they had no imagination, couldn't think of anything else for us to do, and partly because they were too damn lazy to organise anything else.'

'What did they do on Sunday mornings?'

'Oh, they just sat on their fat arses in their common room, drank coffee, smoked their fags and read the Sunday papers. They had comfortable armchairs to sit in, of course. We hardly ever saw an armchair till we got home! Of course, we weren't allowed to read the papers. They were terrified we might find out about the real world. Or see some pictures of *women,* SHOCK, HORROR! The Director was fanatical about anything to do with women or sex. There used to be two big bookcases here, which were our 'library'. He used to go through all the books and censor anything in the slightest suggestive about women or sex, especially pictures.'

'How did he do that?'

'He'd cut it out with scissors, or cross it out with black ink, or even stick brown paper over it. Some books ended up almost twice as thick! Can you imagine the mentality?' He tapped the side of his head with a finger.

'He sounds as if he didn't like women very much,' she remarked.

'Somehow I don't think he did,' he agreed, sarkily.

'Why was that?'

'Well, he was a Catholic priest, of course, so he wouldn't like women very much, would he? But I think he was even more screwed-up than the average priest.'

'Why do you think that?'

'I suspect it had something to do with the fact that he never had a mother. At least, he never *knew* his mother. The story was that his father, who was some sort of film director in India, had an affair with some Indian woman – hence his dark complexion – and he was the illegitimate result. Apparently, he was packed off to boarding school in Scotland when he was about seven. It was all a bit shrouded in mystery, because he never spoke about his childhood – significantly, perhaps.'

'It's sad if he never knew his mother.'

'Yes, I suppose so. I do feel sorry for him sometimes. I think he was deprived of love and affection as a child. And, of course, later he couldn't get it from a woman, because he was a priest. That's why he looked for it elsewhere, I suppose.'

'What do you mean?'

'Nothing. I'll tell you later. I don't want to talk about it here.' He had said too much. He didn't know if he wanted to talk about it at all. He was already feeling faintly nauseous.

'What did you do on Sunday afternoons?' she asked, to his relief not pursuing the subject.

'That was more or less the only time we were allowed out. We used to go for walks – along the prom, where we went last night, for example – but we had to go all together, in groups of three in a long line or 'crocodile', as we called it. That was only for a couple of hours though. On feast days we'd go for longer walks, mind you, across the fells for example. We'll go on one tomorrow.'

'And on Sunday evenings what did you do?'

'We wrote letters home, here in the study hall. Listening to classical music on the gramophone.'

'Were you allowed to receive letters?'

'Yes, but only from family. And Father Director even censored those.'

'What do you mean?'

'He opened them and read them before he gave them to you. Same for any letters you wrote. You weren't allowed to seal them, because he read them first.'

'That's horrible.'

'It was like living under a bloody totalitarian dictatorship, I can tell you. Eastern Europe had nothing on it. Anyway, come on, let's have a look out here.'

He led her out into the corridor. 'I had to clean this corridor every morning in my first term. That was my 'function'. We had to do 'functions' for half an hour every morning, straight after breakfast and before class.'

'What did you have to do exactly?'

'Sweep the floor. Dust the window sills and bookcases. There used to be three bookcases. At this end there was a big statue of the Sacred Heart on a wooden pedestal. On the wall on this side there were reproductions of paintings by Old Masters – mostly religious ones, mind you. I think that was the Director's idea. There was actually a spark of imagination there, I suppose. On the wall on the other side there were framed school photos and here there was a notice board. That's where they put up the Honours List and Black List every Friday evening.'

'What were they?'

'Every week, on Friday evening, the Dean of Studies read out your average mark for each subject. You got marks for 'Conduct and Deportment', too! If all your marks were seven or more out of ten, you went on the Honours List, which was typed in red. If you got two or more marks under five, you went on the Black List, which was typed in black – and you got the strap from the Dean of Studies. Some poor buggers were on the Black List every week, regular as clockwork.'

'What about you?'

'I was usually on the Honours List, luckily.'

'So were you top of the class?'

'No – I usually came second. There was a Polish kid called Zapolski who always came top. He was very bright, but a real swot, too. I did beat him once though, in the Upper Sixth Form, in the Easter exams, which were our mock A-levels, in fact.'

'How did you manage that?'

'Well, I just thought, I'm going to beat the bugger once, just to prove I can, so I pulled out all the stops and did it. I was as chuffed as hell when the Dean of Studies read my name out during exam results, followed by 'first'. I felt as if I'd won an Olympic gold medal or something!' He didn't tell her the real reason that had spurred him on to this moment of glory ...

'How did he take it?'

'Zappo? He couldn't take it. He was so used to coming top of the class, he had a nervous breakdown and left – they found him huddled in the toilets afterwards, sobbing and shaking uncontrollably. He was a bit of a neurotic character, anyway. I felt sorry for him, to be honest. I'd never've done it if I thought that was going to happen! I still feel a bit guilty about it!'

'You don't need to feel guilty. You just did your best and beat him.'

'Maybe.' She might not say that if she knew the real reason behind his 'triumph', he thought.

'Let's go through here,' he said, leading her down some narrow steps at the end of the corridor and into a large kitchen.

'This used to be our washroom,' he told her. 'The stone floor is still the same, but there used to be washbasins all round the walls, with flyblown mirrors above them, and a big table in the middle.

God, it was freezing cold in here at half-six on a winter's morning – there was no heating or hot water, of course! You had to come all the way down here from the dorm in your vest and grab a washbasin or wait for one to be free. Over there, where those cookers are, there were baths, only two of them, mind you, in little cubicles, one on each side. Can you imagine, two baths for nearly a hundred kids? You were only allowed to have one bath a week, according to a rota on the notice board, and you were only allowed twenty minutes in the bath.'

'Why only twenty minutes?'

'I think the Director was afraid if you had longer, you might start playing with yourself!' he laughed darkly.

He left the room quickly and led her along the stone-flagged corridor to a cellar-like room full of outdoor sports equipment, such as canoes and paddles. 'This used to be the 'boot room',' he explained. 'There used to be wooden lockers all round the walls, where we kept our shoes, slippers, football boots, wellies and so on, and brush and polish.' This was also where he had come to sit, in a state of shock, he remembered, after being expelled by Father Director that day back in the Sixth Form …

'Come on, let's go outside,' he said, feeling claustrophobic, and stepped out with relief into the bright April sunshine.

Here, from the back of the buildings, a lawn sloped up to a wooded hill. He remembered standing on this lawn sixteen years before with his parents, having just received the habit of the order and taken his first vows – of poverty, chastity and obedience – before going to the novitiate, having just escaped expulsion by the skin of his teeth and having *lost his faith* …

'We used to have a fête on this lawn every Whit,' he told her. 'The lawn would be covered with stalls and crowds of people, mostly relatives. It was one of the few times we were allowed visitors. The only other time was Easter. You really looked forward to it, because you weren't allowed home between Christmas and summer. It was a long seven months!'

'Did your mum and dad visit you?'

'Yeah. They were very good – they always came. Sometimes they stayed in a B & B in Grange and made a little holiday of it. Other boys weren't so lucky though. Their parents might not be able to afford it or they lived too far away. It was strange for us, seeing ordinary, *normal* people wandering round – especially girls. Mind you, the night before, Father Director used to give us a hell-and-damnation lecture about how we weren't to talk to them or even look at them. He really had a hang-up about women!'

'What happened if you did talk to them?'

'Oh, if you were caught, he'd give you a flogging or even expel you. Or both, the bastard! It was terrible if you were expelled or even if you just left because you wanted to – the night before you were forced to sleep alone in the infirmary, as if you had leprosy or something, and in the morning you were given an early breakfast on your own and whisked off to the station, without being allowed to talk to anyone.'

'Not even to say goodbye to your friends?'

He laughed. 'They didn't care about normal human niceties or civilities like that! If you left, especially if you were expelled, you were considered a pariah. Nobody was allowed to have any further contact or communication with you afterwards either.'

'What sort of things could you be expelled for?'

'Almost anything, really, but especially anything to do with sex – 'impurity', as they called it. Touching another boy the wrong way, for example, or even looking at another boy the wrong way. Touching yourself, too, for that matter. 'Tugging your toggle', as we used to call it.'

'What was that?'

'Masturbating, silly,' he said. 'Wanking, if you want.'

'Did boys do that?'

'Of course they did. What do you expect testosterone-filled, teenage boys to do if they have no other outlet?'

'Did you do it?'

'Funnily enough, no. Not here, anyway. I think I was too well indoctrinated with the fear of Hell. Not to mention the fear of expulsion. I did have wet dreams, of course.'

He remembered the Director's pathetic attempt at sex education – he was sitting in the brown leather armchair in his office at the beginning of Form Three, when he was just fourteen: 'Now, son, you're fourteen, you'll notice that your body will change in certain ways. You'll get hair where you never had it before. You'll also notice that sometimes there's a hardness in your trousers and sometimes you'll notice that a sticky, whitish fluid comes out at night. This is nothing to worry about. It's natural. It's the way God has made us. Just ignore it, pray for purity and carry on studying and working hard as usual …' God, the man had had no idea! What a goon he was! He didn't tell Mary, because it made him squirm with embarrassment just to think of it, even after all this time.

'Some boys were expelled for reading dirty magazines once,' he told her. 'One of them must've brought them back from holiday. About four or five boys! You could be expelled just for going round with one person too much. That was called 'grouping'. In fact, you were never allowed to be with just one person – you always had to go in groups of three.' He didn't tell her that that was what Father Director had tried to expel *him* for ... 'Come on, let's go for a walk,' he said.

He took her down to the river that ran through the grounds and across the old stone bridge at the bend to the fields on other side, where sheep were grazing. 'This is where we played football or cricket, every Wednesday afternoon, hail, rain or shine,' he told her. 'It looks lovely and pastoral now, but, God, it could be cold down here in winter! The wind from the sea would cut through your football shirt like a knife and you weren't allowed to wear anything underneath. It was lovely in summer though. We used to enjoy playing cricket, lolling around in the long grass … See the bend in the river here? That's where we used to go swimming. I'm sure it used to be wider and deeper though. It seems to have shrunk. It looks positively piddly now.'

He gazed at it grimly, remembering how one summer evening, towards the end of his first year, Gerry Donnelly, who had been infatuated with him, had rescued him from drowning and Father Director, who used to supervise them swimming, had told him off for swimming instead of revising for his GCEs. Father Director, he realised now, had been *jealous*.

He remembered, too, how he had come down here after Father Director had expelled him, towards the end of the Sixth Form, intending to throw himself in rather than face the shame of going home. That had been the lowest point of his life. He didn't tell Mary about either of these memories though. Instead, he told her about John Wilkinson.

'Apparently, the very first iron boat was built on the river here in the eighteenth century by a fellow called John Wilkinson. He was an iron founder, the chap who built the house in fact. That's where the name Wilkinson Sword comes from, I think.'

'Really?'

'Yeah. Interesting, isn't it?'

She didn't seem very interested though, so he led her back along the river to the main building. This was the original house, built by Wilkinson, a square, grey, stone mansion, rather plain apart from the teak veranda, up the steps to which he led her. 'This was the Fathers' House, where the priests lived,' he told her. 'It was strictly out of bounds to us, unless you were cleaning it during manual labour. Let's have a look inside.'

'I don't think we should, Fran.'

'Come on, don't be silly. He said we could go where we liked.'

This timidity of hers annoyed him, especially as it had been her idea to come here. He wasn't sure it was such a good idea – he felt as if he was trespassing himself, trespassing on the past ...

He pushed open the heavy front door and she nervously followed him into the spacious hall. He remembered the first time he had come through this door, as a twelve-year-old boy in short trousers, on the day he had arrived at the school – he had bumped into a small, carved, wooden table from Africa with his suitcase, so that the brass dish that sat on top clattered to the tiled floor and rolled around, making an unholy din. The Dean of Studies, who had drifted in behind him in his long, black cloak, had yelled 'Eejit!' at him, scaring the life out of him.

Of course, the table wasn't there any more, but otherwise the hall looked almost exactly the same – the beautifully-tiled floor, on which the brass dish had clattered so deafeningly, the oak-panelled walls, the moulded plasterwork ceiling, the wide oak staircase that led up to what had once been the priests' bedrooms.

He took her upstairs to show them to her, enjoying the sensation of being able to go somewhere that had once been strictly 'out of bounds'. The rooms were still bedrooms, but now, like the dormitory, had been fitted with bunk beds and modern furniture. He was amused to see the name 'Father Taylor's Room' on one of the doors – he had been the 'bursar', the priest with the bushy beard and glass eye who had collected them from the station in the minibus when they had first arrived.

After looking around the 'Fathers' House', he took her down the 'back stairs' and showed her the room that used to be the chapel. It was now a library, but the ornately plastered ceiling was still the same, he noticed. It was strange to think he had spent hundreds, maybe thousands, of hours in this room, most of them on his knees! Every morning they had morning prayer here, followed by mass and 'meditation'. On Sundays they had had to attend two masses in the morning and benediction in the evening. During Holy Week they had done the Stations of the Cross here every evening and celebrated the Passion, Death and Resurrection of Our Lord.

In his mind's eye he could see the altar and the pews with lines of boys in blue blazers, juniors at the front, seniors at the back. He could hear their voices reciting the Latin of the mass or singing the hymns at benediction, hymns such as 'O Salutaris Hostia' and 'Tantum Ergo'. He could hear the swelling chords of the little organ that stood at the back. He could even smell the incense …

'Can we go now?' Mary said, interrupting his reverie.

'Yeah, OK,' he agreed, needled. 'We'd better say goodbye to the chap in the office.'

'Do we have to?'

'It'd be good manners, wouldn't it? Why are you in such a hurry to leave? You're the one who wanted to come here!'

'I'm sorry, but the place gives me the creeps.'

'What do you think it does to me?' he laughed. 'Well, OK – let's go then.'

They left the 'chapel', and he was secretly glad to go himself, feeling suffocated by the past. He led her down the narrow, stone-flagged corridor to what used to be the 'ref', but was now an office, where they said thank you and goodbye to the teacher in charge.

'I want you to tell me exactly what happened here, Fran,' she insisted, as they left the building and got back in the car.

'Later,' he said, starting up the car, not sure if he wanted to or would be able to.

'Where are we going now?'

'To Lindale,' he said, driving off.

'Where's that?'

'It's the village just up the road. We used to go through it on walks. Remember we drove through it on the way?'

'What's there?'

'John Wilkinson is supposed to be buried in the churchyard there. There's a monument to him, too.'

'I don't want to know about him. I want to know about you.'

'There's a nice pub there. Remember we saw it on the way? We could go for a drink and have dinner there.'

'Will you tell me everything then?'

'God, did you use to work for the Gestapo?'

'I know you don't want to tell me,' she said, sulkily.

'All right, I'll tell you,' he promised. 'Come on, we can go out by the Lindale drive. I'll show you where the cook, Mister Johnstone, used to live.'

CHAPTER TWENTY-ONE

'So, tell me what happened, Fran,' she insisted, after he had brought drinks and sat down in the pub.

He took a sup of his Guinness. 'Well, basically, what happened is that the Director was a pederast.' He still didn't want to talk about it, but knew he couldn't stall her any longer.

'What does that mean?' she asked.

Sometimes her ignorance frustrated him, but he had to keep cool tonight, he told himself. After all, she hadn't studied A-level Greek.

'A pederast is someone who has sex with children,' he explained. 'It comes from Ancient Greek, pais meaning child and – '

'You mean, the Director had sex with boys?' she asked, interrupting his Greek mini-lecture.

'Yes. Not necessarily sex. It depends how you define 'sex'. But he used to, you know, mess about with them.'

'What do you mean exactly?'

'Well, for example, he used to bath them.'

'Why did he do that?'

'Well, that's how he got his kicks, I suppose.'

'But a twelve-year-old boy doesn't need to be bathed!'

'No, of course not. He normally only did it if you were ill, if you had flu or something. He had this thing about 'sweating it out'. He'd put loads of extra blankets on your bed, so you sweated a lot, then he'd make you strip off and wash you all over. It was just an excuse to touch you, of course. Afterwards, he'd dry you off and rub talcum powder all over you – Johnson's Baby Powder!'

'Where did he do it?'

'Oh, in the infirmary if you were in there. That was just a special room where you had to sleep if you had something like flu. It was a kind of isolation ward, I suppose. But sometimes he did it in his bedroom. That was the room at the end of the dormitory, the one I showed you, which is an office now.'

'Did he do it to you?'

'Oh, yes. In fact, he did more than that to me. I think I was his favourite for a couple of years. I think he was 'in love' with me.'

'Why was he in love with you?'

'I dunno – I must've been quite good-looking once!' he joked, trying to do the impossible and make light of it.

'I'm sure you were.'

'You mean, I'm not any more?'

'You know I think you're handsome, Fran.'

'And I think you're pretty.' He put his arm around her and tried to kiss her, but she resisted.

'I want to know more.'

'What more do you want to know?'

'You said he did 'more' with you. What else did he do?'

He took another, bigger sup of Guinness. She obviously wasn't going to let him off the hook. Anyway, suddenly he wanted to tell her. Maybe it would be cathartic. Maybe it would bring her back to him. How ironic that would be!

'Well, one day when he was washing me – I was in the infirmary with flu or something – he told me I had a 'varicocele'.'

'You mean, the same thing you've got now?'

'Yeah. What a coincidence! It's incredible, isn't it? He told me I had this when I was twelve years old! Of course, I didn't understand what it was, so he had to explain it for me.'

'What did he say?'

'Oh, he said something about it being like a varicose vein. I knew what that was, because my mum had varicose veins, but I didn't know you could have one down there. Anyway, he said it needed treatment, so he'd tell the doctor about it. I was scared at first, because I thought I was going to have to have an operation or something.'

'Did he tell the doctor?'

'He told me he did and the doctor told him to treat it himself. Actually, I don't think he told the doctor at all. He fancied himself as a bit of a doctor, in fact.'

'So what did he do?'

'This is the really ridiculous part – he used to rub Germolene on it!'

'Germolene?'

'Yeah, you know, the pink ointment you get in the chemist's for cuts and grazes? As if Germolene could do anything for a varicocele! He used to use it for everything though. If you had a boil, he'd put Germolene on! If you had a sprained ankle, he'd put Germolene on! If you had a bloody broken leg, he'd put Germolene on! He was obsessed with the stuff! Some doctor!'

'He rubbed it on himself?'

'Yeah. Every night! In his bedroom. After lights out. He'd make me stand in the middle of the room, take my pyjama trousers off, wash me with cold water, then rub Germolene on! Of course, it was just an excuse to, you know, fiddle about.'

'How did you feel when he was doing it?'

'At first, I felt as embarrassed as hell.'

'So why did you let him?'

'Well, it might be difficult for you to understand, but at the time he was like God to us. You would never dream of questioning him or disobeying him. Remember, it was a boarding school, in the middle of nowhere, and he had virtually total control over us – we had no access to any other adults, apart from our teachers in class. In fact, he made sure he was the only one who had any close contact with us by keeping all the other priests away from us as much as possible. I think one or two of them were the same way inclined actually, so he didn't want any competition. He was quite a control freak, when I think about it. Of course, that was so he could indulge himself. You couldn't even tell your parents, because he censored your letters. As I told you, it was like a police state.'

'Couldn't you have told your parents when you were at home on holiday?'

'I suppose so, but I would've been too embarrassed. Anyway, it would've been too much of a shock for them, especially my mother – she thought the Director was the bee's knees. I mean, she was a bit of a priest-worshipper at the best of times. That's why she wanted *me* to be a priest. If she knew anything like that was going on, she'd've been devastated.'

'What about your father?'

'He'd probably have gone there and beaten the bastard up!' he laughed, though it was no laughing matter. 'Anyway,' he carried on, taking another sup of Guinness – he was starting to relax and enjoy himself now – 'the Director was a really manipulative character, as well as being a control freak – not that it was hard to manipulate a twelve-year-old, I suppose. He used to tell me it was all a secret between me and him, just like between a patient and doctor, or just like in confession. So I didn't tell anybody. I didn't want to anyway. The point is, I didn't really think it was wrong at the time. I was embarrassed at first, but after a while I started to enjoy it.'

'Did you have an erection?'

'Well, a sort of semi-erection, I suppose. I was only twelve or thirteen at the time, you know! I remember trying not to let it happen, because I thought it was a sin to enjoy it, so I used to try and think about something else while he was doing it – like my irregular French verbs or Latin declensions or something. He used to tell me to close my eyes and say my prayers. Sometimes he'd even make me hold his rosary beads. There I was, standing half-naked in the middle of his bedroom, with my eyes closed and my arms outstretched, holding rosary beads, saying my Hail Marys, while he was playing about with me! It'd be funny if it wasn't so sick!'

'So he did this every night?'

'More or less. Sometimes during the day as well, if he felt like it.'

'Really?'

'Yes. Sometimes he did more than just rub Germolene on, too.'

'What do you mean?'

'Well, for example, I remember once we were on our way down by the river to the playing fields to play cricket, when I got a message that he wanted me. At first, I thought the kid who told me was 'jossing', as we used to call it, but he wasn't, so I went back. I was worried, because I thought I was in trouble.'

'Were you?'

'Not at all. He just wanted to have a bit of fun with me. He must have been feeling really randy that afternoon. Or lonely. Or something.'

'Why, what did he do?'

'You don't really want to know, do you? It's pretty sick.' He suddenly felt disgusted by the memory ...

'Yes, I do. I want to know everything, Fran. You can tell me. I love you.'

It was the first time he had heard those words from her for a long time. Maybe this story had a positive side to it!

'Well, he made me lie on the bed, on a towel, took my trousers and underpants off, and told me he had to wash me with cold water, because of my, you know, problem, and because the weather was so hot. It was a hot summer's day, I remember. He'd closed the curtains, too.'

'Why?'

'I don't know. It wasn't on the ground floor. I suppose he wanted total privacy. Of course, he always locked the door.'

'So what did he do?'

'He gave me his rosary beads to hold, told me to close my eyes and say my prayers.'

'And?'

'Well, he brought a basin of water and a flannel over, sat on the bed and washed me. I mean, you know, down below. Took his time about it, too.'

'What did you do?'

'I just lay there trying to say my rosary. I couldn't concentrate though. Anyway, he kept talking to me, asking me questions.'

'About what?'

'Oh, about my family, classmates, what I was reading, cricket, football … He sounded different from usual. Usually he was very stern. He sounded quite soft and solicitous, almost fatherly. I suppose it was his way of giving and getting some sort of affection, perverted as it was. That's the main problem for people in that way of life, I think – it's not the lack of sex that gets to them, because you can solve that yourself, it's the lack of affection, of human warmth. Of course, you were trained to extinguish all feelings of affection, whether for people or animals or anything.'

'That's sad.'

'Is it? Why?' Of course, he agreed – he just wanted to hear it from her, because she was so real, so normal ...

'It means you didn't *get* any affection, either.'

'Yes, that's true.'

'I think that's why you are as you are.'

'What do you mean?'

'You're not very affectionate.'

'Aren't I?'

'No. You're quite hard. Outwardly. '

'Am I?'

'Yes. Didn't you realise that?'

'No, I didn't. I show you affection, don't I?'

'Not enough. Not as much as I show you.'

'Oh, I'm sorry,' he joked. 'I'll try harder. I'll show you some affection tonight, if you want.'

'You know what I mean, Fran.'

'Yes. Well, it's hard when you've been brainwashed and conditioned a certain way, as we were. You're lucky. You had a normal, family upbringing. We were removed from our families at the age of twelve and institutionalised. Cut off from all normal human sources of love and affection. We weren't even allowed to have particular friendships, because they were so terrified of homosexuality.'

'I understand, Fran. I'm not blaming you. I'm trying to understand you. That's why I wanted you to bring me here.'

'So do you understand any better now?'

'I think so. I wish you'd told me all this before.'

'I told you some of it.'

'Not so much. Not so clearly.'

'Well, it's difficult, you know. I hate talking about it, actually. I spend a lot of my time trying to *forget* about it, in fact. Not just the abuse – the whole bloody experience.'

'I think you need to talk about it, instead of suppressing it.'

'Now you sound like a psychiatrist! How much are you going to charge me?'

'Don't be funny.'

'Well, you can either laugh or cry. I prefer to laugh.'

'I think you just try to avoid the issue. You always try to avoid the issue.'

'Do I? So what else do you want to know?'

'Well, first of all, I want to know what else happened.'

'You mean, that afternoon?'

'Yes. And afterwards.'

'Well, nothing really. That was it. He washed me, dried me with the towel and then rubbed Johnson's Baby Powder on. He had a thing for Johnson's Baby Powder!'

'Is that all?'

'Yes. What more do you want? Oh, actually, when he'd finished, just as I was about to go, he asked me to do something for him.'

'What was that?'

'He asked me to rub some liniment on his shoulder. He said he'd strained it bowling. He used to play cricket with us sometimes.'

'Did you?'

'Yes. I didn't want to, but he took his shirt and vest off and made me. You couldn't disobey him anyway. I was as embarrassed as hell! Besides, all I wanted to do by that point was go back down to cricket and join the other kids.'

'He didn't make you do anything else?'

'No, funnily enough. He didn't make me touch him anywhere else, if that's what you mean. I'm sure he wanted to, but I don't think he had the nerve. He couldn't delude himself that it was medically necessary, I suppose. That was always his big cover story, that it was all for medical reasons.'

'So how long did all this go on?'

'Two years exactly.'

'Then it stopped?'

'With me, yeah. I'm sure he carried on with somebody else though. In fact, I know he did.'

'When did it stop?'

'When I came back after the summer holiday – or 'vac', as we used to call it – and went into Form Three. I'd just turned fourteen by then and, of course, I'd started to, you know, grow. I think he only liked young, pre-pubescent boys – children, in other words. He was a pederast in the true sense of the word. Or a paedophile if you prefer. Same difference. Of course, he could manipulate and intimidate them easier at that age too, I suppose.'

'So he never touched you again?'

'No, never. He stopped just like that. The funny thing is, I remember feeling really unhappy about it for a while.'

'You felt *unhappy*?'

'Yeah, as if I'd been rejected or something. I mean, sick as it was, it was the nearest thing to affection I got. Remember, there was no mummy or daddy around. He made me feel special, as if I was his favourite – his pet, I suppose you could say. I didn't think of it in those terms, but that was the feeling, I think.'

'So how long did that last?'

'Oh, I don't know – a few weeks, I suppose. I got over it.'

'You've never told anyone about this?'

'No. You're the first person I've ever told, actually.'

'Maybe you should've done.'

'Why?'

'He should be arrested for child abuse.'

'Yes, I suppose so.' He didn't mention that he was dead. That he had committed suicide. He'd save that juicy titbit for later, he thought. 'Actually, I can almost forgive him for the sexual abuse.'

'How can you say that?'

'Well, I know it was sick and perverted and disgusting and all the rest of it, but at least it didn't *physically* harm the kids. And I suppose you could say he was something of a victim of the stupid system he found himself part of. It doesn't excuse what he did, but maybe it mitigates it slightly. What I find impossible to forgive is the way he flogged kids with that bloody strap. He should have been locked up for that if nothing else. And flogged himself.'

'You say it didn't harm them physically, but it must've harmed them psychologically.'

'I'm sure it did in some cases. It probably screwed some kids up sexually. The whole place probably did.'

'What do you mean?'

'I mean, I think it turned some boys into homos. Because there were no women around, it was all male, so there was no other outlet for normal feelings. Boys fell in love with each other all the time.'

'You mean they had sex?'

'Not necessarily. Sometimes maybe, for all I know. I think it was usually platonic though. Actually, one of the older boys was in love with me, as well as the Director.'

'Really? Who?'

'He was an Irish bloke, actually. From Northern Ireland. His name was Gerry Donnelly. I wonder what became of him.'

'How do you know he was in love with you?'

'Well, he was in Form Four and I was in Form One, so he was about sixteen, I suppose, while I was twelve. He was a big, well-built lad, not tall, but stocky. Anyway, he took a real fancy to me, for some reason. It's funny when I think about it now.'

'What did he do?'

'Oh, he didn't do anything sexual. He just befriended me, even though you weren't supposed to have 'particular friendships', as they were called. He followed me round, gave me little presents, such as sweets, made my bed for me, polished my shoes for me, cleaned my football boots for me, even cleaned my comb for me, helped me with my function ... Sometimes, he even left sweets under my pillow! He was totally infatuated with me! Wouldn't let anybody else near me. If anybody tried to pick a fight with me, he'd defend me. It was like having my own private bodyguard! If anybody else tried to become friendly with me, he'd chase them away. And if I became friendly with anybody else, he'd go into a big sulk and freeze me out, not talk to me or have anything to do with me for a few days, till I stopped. Then he'd come back to me, give me a little peace offering of some sort, leave a sweet under my pillow, start following me round again. It was just like two lovers! In fact, the other kids noticed after a while, of course, and started calling us by each other's name – that was what they used to do if they noticed you were very friendly with somebody. They used to call me 'Gerry' and him 'Frankie', which was quite embarrassing. They even used to sing that song, 'Frankie and Johnnie Were Lovers' about us, but changing the words to 'Frankie and Gerry'. That was really embarrassing. That was when I started to get worried, because if you got done for 'grouping', as it was called, you were in big trouble.'

'Didn't you get caught?'

'Well, yes, of course, eventually the Director noticed or got wind of it – some prefect probably reported us. I'd still like to know to this day which tow-rag it was!' The Guinness was getting to him. He was well into his pint by now – and they hadn't eaten.

'So what did he do?'

'He called me to his office, gave me a big bollocking and told me to stay away from Gerry or he'd put both of us on the 'nine forty-three' – that was the train you caught if you left or were expelled. Of course, I realise now he was just jealous – he wanted me all to himself. It was better than any TV soap opera!'

'So did you stay away?'

'I tried to, but Gerry turned really nasty. He went into a massive huff and deliberately avoided me, then started giving me dirty looks, making sarcastic comments and playing spiteful little tricks on me, like pinching my comb or my toothbrush or one of my books. It was like a war of attrition and in the end I gave in and started being friends with him again, even though I was terrified of getting into trouble for 'grouping' and being expelled. I knew the Director wouldn't really expel *me*, though, because I was his favourite. In the end, the bastard expelled poor old Gerry, just before his O-level exams, too. I can never forgive him for that.'

'You mean, he didn't let him take his exams?'

'That's right. He just kicked the poor bloke out, after four years of sweat! I remember the morning it happened – Gerry didn't go to mass, because if you'd been expelled or were leaving, they kept you in the infirmary the night before, gave you an early breakfast on your own and took you to the station. I wasn't sure till I went to the dorm to make my bed after mass and Gerry's bed was stripped bare. That meant he'd gone. They were bloody ruthless, didn't let you say goodbye.'

'How did you feel?'

'I felt really sad. I mean, I'd lost my best friend! That night, while the Director was doing his usual pervy thing with me, he asked me if I was upset about Gerry leaving, the hypocrite.'

'What did you say?'

'I had to pretend I wasn't. I just said I didn't care about it. I still feel guilty about that, even to this day, as if I'd betrayed Gerry or something. I was only twelve years old though and didn't understand what was going on.'

'What did he say?'

'Oh, I'll always remember what he said. He came out with one of his favourite expressions. 'That's a good boy,' he said, 'you *paddle your own canoe*.' What a hypocritical, twisted bastard he was, in retrospect! I'd really like to know what happened to Gerry, actually. I hope his life wasn't completely screwed up.'

'Did anyone else fall in love with you?'

'There was another one actually, a chap called Gordon Lewis in the Fourth Form, but the Director got rid of him too. He was really good at Greek, I remember, and really into Greek culture. I think he took it a bit too seriously – the Greeks were into homosexuality apparently – so he imagined he was in Ancient Greece.'

'He never did anything, did he?'

'Oh, no. I wouldn't have let him, anyway. He used to try to put his arm round me, but even that wasn't allowed. I remember the Director caught him once and gave him a right bollocking. That was in Hampsfell Hospice, which is just an old stone shelter on top of one of the fells, with a Greek inscription over the doorway. It was one of our regular walks over the fells. It's desolate, but beautiful. We'll go for a walk there tomorrow, if you like.'

'You seem to have been popular.' She ignored his suggestion – he knew she was worried about her bad leg.

'Yes, well, I still am, aren't I? I mean, Seamus fancies me, doesn't he?' he joked. 'Not to mention one or two of the others, like whatsisname who played James Joyce that time.'

'And what about you?' she asked, straight-faced.

'Actually, I think I fancy Perry more than Seamus,' he said, deadpan.

'I do sometimes wonder about you.'

'What do you mean? You don't think I'm a closet homosexual, do you?'

'Sometimes you give the impression you like men.'

'Do me a favour! You can accuse me of liking women, if you want, but not men! I can't help it if they like me. I'm just friendly to everybody, that's all. No, I don't have the slightest interest in men sexually, I assure you. In fact, I find the idea revolting. Mind you, I did fancy somebody at school.' He immediately regretted saying it, but alcohol had loosened his tongue as always and, anyway, he decided, he might as well tell her the whole story.

'Really? Who was that?'

'Can we leave that for later?'

'No, tell me now.'

'You'll have to buy me another pint then.'

'I thought you were treating me tonight.'

'What, I'm giving you all this information and you can't buy me one pint?'

'All right. You have to tell me when I come back though.'

She went to the bar and came back with another pint of

Guinness and an orange juice for herself as usual. 'Go on then,' she demanded.

'What do you want to know?'

'I told you, I want to know everything.'

'Why?'

'You know why. I want to try and understand you better.'

'Do you?'

'I think I'm starting to. Now go on. Stop stalling. Who was it?'

'It was a boy called Mark Brown,' he said, taking a sup of the black nectar. 'He was a new boy when I was in the Sixth Form, but he started in the Second Form, because he was thirteen. However, he hadn't done any Latin or Greek, so the Director appointed me to give him private tuition. I was doing Latin and Greek for A-level, you see, and I was quite good at them. Anyway, he developed a crush on me.'

'What about you?'

'I developed a crush on him too, I suppose. He was quite a pretty boy – blond hair, smooth skin, a bit girlish. It only happened because there were no girls around, you know.'

'Yes, but not everyone had such an experience, did they?'

'What are you suggesting?'

'Well, maybe you had those feelings because of what Father Director did to you.'

'Oh, I don't know. Maybe. Who knows?' It sounded simplistic, but he knew it might well be true.

'Where was he from?'

'South London, actually. He had a rather posh accent though – I think that was one of the reasons I liked him. Anyway, we became very friendly.'

'What do you mean, 'friendly'?'

'I just mean, we were always together, even though it was against the rule. I didn't *do* anything with him, if that's what you're thinking. It was platonic.' In fact, that wasn't entirely true. 'I remember I used to write him poems. Anyway, inevitably we got done for 'grouping', as it was called.'

'What happened?'

'The Director gave me a big bollocking, stopped me tutoring him and warned me to stay away from him, threatened to expel me if I didn't. This was just a few weeks before my A-levels!'

'Did you stay away from him?'

'No. Looking back, I was crazy, but I suppose I was infatuated.'

'So what happened?'

'One afternoon the Director caught us together. We were in the games hut, playing table tennis. We must've been mad – I was supposed to be revising for my A-levels and Mark was supposed to be playing cricket. Anyway, suddenly the door flies open and the Director bursts in, like a bloody SAS man or something. Caught us in the act! We were actually mucking about, wrestling, which was just an excuse to touch each other really.'

'So what did he do?'

'He went absolutely ballistic! Ordered Mark down to cricket, said he'd deal with him later, and expelled me on the spot. I'll never forget what he said: "Francis Walsh, you have disobeyed me! You have defied me! You have persisted in this unhealthy 'liaison'! You will leave this seminary tomorrow! You will not take your examinations! You will not receive the habit of this order!" Can you believe it? Just like that – after six bloody years! This is the guy who had fucked around with me for two years, who fucked around with other boys all the time! What a fucking hypocrite! What a fucking bastard!' As always, alcohol made him lapse into the vernacular.

'What did you do?'

'Well, I was devastated of course – I couldn't face the thought of going home after being expelled and facing my family, especially my mother. She would've been totally devastated. I couldn't face the thought of not being a priest either – I still wanted to be a priest. I felt like committing suicide. I actually went down to the river to throw myself in, but couldn't bring myself to do it.'

'So what did you do?'

'I went to see him that night. I more or less begged him to at least let me do my A-levels.'

'Did he let you?'

'Yeah. I had to bloody grovel though. He said he'd think about whether to let me receive the habit. So that's how I did my A-levels, with a sword of Damocles hanging over me. That's why I didn't get quite as good grades as expected.'

'You got good grades, didn't you?'

'Good enough to get into university, thank God.'

'So then what happened?'

'Well, I found out, just by chance, that the Director was doing with Mark Brown what he used to do with me – you know, washing him and so on.'

'How did you find that out?'

'Mark told me himself. It was lucky, really, because we'd been forbidden to speak to each other. It was mad to take the risk, after what had happened, but I'm glad I did. It gave me a weapon.'

'What did you do?'

'After A-levels, I asked him if I could receive the habit, and he said no. In other words, he still wanted to expel me. So I had a big row with him – I told him if he didn't let me, I'd inform the Superior all about his activities.'

'What did he do then?'

'He went absolutely ballistic. Tried to hit me! Then he sort of collapsed. I just ran out of his office. The next day the Superior called an emergency 'conference' and told us he'd been found dead in bed. Died of a heart attack. But in fact he'd taken an overdose.'

'You mean, he committed suicide?'

'Yeah. Took an overdose. He always had loads of tablets around. His bedroom was like an apothecary's shop.'

'It's sad.'

'Yeah. I suppose you could say it's tragic. Because he was an impressive fellow in some ways. Even though he was sick.' He took a quaff of Guinness.

'Anyway, you received the habit?' she asked, after a solemn pause.

'Yeah. Sometimes I'm sorry I did now.'

'Why?'

'Well, then I went to the novitiate for a year. That was in a village called Upton, in the Midlands, a nothing place in the middle of bloody nowhere. That was a total waste of a year of my life.'

'Why was that?'

'It was like being in a monastery for a year. I mean, all we did all day, every day, was meaningless religious exercises, read rubbishy religious books and do manual labour. All in silence! It was like being on retreat for a year.'

'Weren't you allowed out?'

'Once a week, on Sunday afternoons, just for a walk, all together. In black suits with clerical collars and shaven heads. We must've looked like a bunch of cons! Or mental patients! It was as much like a mental asylum as a monastery actually. Some of the blokes did go mental, I think, and left. They were the sensible ones, in retrospect! I wish I had. Christ, what a waste of time!'

'What did you do after the novitiate?'

'Went to the senior seminary. That was a huge old ex-convalescent home in the Midlands, even deeper in the middle of nowhere.'

'What did you do there?'

'We were supposed to study philosophy and theology, but I spent most of my time reading novels – and playing table tennis. I became pretty good at table tennis, actually! I didn't mind the philosophy too much, but I couldn't take theology.'

'Why not?'

'It seemed like a load of baloney to me.'

'So why did you leave? Was it because of celibacy?'

'Not at all. I'm quite capable of being celibate if I want to. I left because I just couldn't believe in it all any more.'

'Couldn't believe in what?'

'I couldn't believe in any of it – God, Catholicism, the priesthood, the religious life, all that claptrap.'

'Why couldn't you believe in God any more?'

'I think we'd better not go into that now or we'll be here all night.'

'We've got all night.'

'Yes, but you don't want to spend it discussing theology, do you?'

'No, but I want to understand you, Fran. Anyway, what happened to Mark Brown?'

'Oh, that's very sad too. He left the seminary the following year, when I was in the novitiate, and I never had any more contact with him for several years. Then I met him in London a couple of years ago, completely by chance.'

'How?'

'Just bumped into him in a pub near the private school I used to work in, in Soho. He was with his boyfriend, a Greek-Cypriot boy.' He didn't tell her he had been with his Yugoslav girlfriend – she didn't know about Marina.

'How did you know it was him?'

'I thought I recognised him, but I wasn't sure, so I went up and asked him and it was. Of course, he was a lot older – I knew him when he was thirteen, but by then he was twenty-two or three. He was teaching EFL just like me, but in another school.'

'So what happened?'

'Well, I couldn't really talk to him properly then, because he was with this boyfriend – he'd turned out to be gay – and, anyway, I was meeting someone, so we arranged to meet another day.'

'Did you?'

'Yeah. We met a few times, talked about what had happened and so on.'

'You didn't still fancy him, did you?'

'No. I told you – I'm not gay! The trouble is, he still fancied me – which caused a problem with his Greek-Cypriot boyfriend, of course, who left him – but I wasn't interested in him in that way any more. For me, what had happened at school had just been an aberration, because of the unnatural conditions we were in. I tried to tell him this and sort of stopped meeting him, but he couldn't accept it. In the end, he committed suicide.'

'That's awful! How?'

'He threw himself under a tube train. At least, I think he did. He may just have fallen, because he was usually drunk. He'd become an alcoholic as well as a homosexual. He was really screwed up actually. It was tragic. And it probably all goes back to that bastard at school, messing him up. I'm just glad he didn't mess me up the same way. It could just as easily have been me.'

'Don't say that, Fran.'

'Well, it's true. Sometimes I think it's a miracle I'm even half-normal.'

'Did you go to the funeral?'

'Yes. That was hard, because I met his parents. He was their only child. They actually asked me if anything had happened at school.'

'Did you tell them?'

'I couldn't. I still feel guilty about it, but I just couldn't bring myself to. How do you tell a parent something like that? That their child was sexually abused at school – at a *seminary* – and that's why they became a homosexual and probably an alcoholic, too, and were so screwed up they killed themselves? I chickened out. I thought I might write a letter to them one day and tell them, but I haven't. Maybe it's better if they never know.'

'Maybe. But at least they could confront the order about it.'

'What good would that do? The Director's dead.'

'It might give them closure.'

'I don't think 'closure' as you call it is possible after something like that.' Suddenly he felt unutterably depressed. 'To be honest, I don't want to talk about it any more.'

'I'm sorry, Fran.'

'Sorry? About what?'

'About bringing you back here, reminding you of all these things, making you talk about them.'

'That's all right. I'm glad, in a way. Especially if it helps you to understand me better.'

'It does. You've been through a lot. I never knew. I just wish you'd told me about it all before.'

'Well, now you know. So, never mind the past – what about the future?'

'What about the future?'

'Are you going to come back?'

'Yes. You know I love you.'

'I love you, too.' He tried to give her a kiss, but she pulled away.

'There are a couple of conditions.'

'What are they?'

'No more women.'

'No more women.' Ironically, there hadn't *really* been any other women, but he didn't say so.

'Promise?'

'Promise. What's the other one?'

'Will you have the operation?'

'Yes. You still want a baby?'

'You know I do, Fran. Don't you?'

'I suppose so. All right, I'll book myself into the hospital as soon as I get back. It might not work though.'

'There's only way to find out.'

'No, there isn't.'

'What do you mean?'

'We could try tonight.'

'Try what?'

'Try to have a baby.'

'Do you want to?'

'Of course I do.'

'Let's go now then.'

'Now? What about dinner?'

'I don't want dinner. I'm not hungry. Are you?'

'Not really.'

'Come on, let's go back to the hotel then.'

'OK. I'm ready. Let's go. Let's do it.'

'I love you, Fran.' She put her arms around his neck and kissed him, kissed him properly for the first time in months.

'I love you, too,' he whispered in her ear, hugging her close, stroking her hair, caressing her back. And suddenly, for the first time in many months, he felt happy again, felt as if he had been released from prison, as in a way he had.

'Come on, let's go,' she said, breaking away.

'Yes, let's go – we'd better not do it here!' he joked.

'You're still wicked!' she laughed, the way she used to laugh at his little jokes, and suddenly he knew everything was all right again, the nightmare was over.

CHAPTER TWENTY-TWO

'Mister Jenkins, you're exposing yourself!' the nurse remonstrated with the old man who was shuffling about the ward in his pyjamas, using walking sticks. She tied his pyjamas up properly for him.

'Got to exercise me artificial 'ip,' the old codger said, to Frank's dismay shuffling towards his bed. 'What you in for? Prostrate? It's prostrates today, ennit? I'm in for stones. They used to cut you right across the belly. Now they do it by laser. Stick a wire up your prick and burn 'em out. I got Paget's disease too. That's a lack of calcium in the bones. I got everything! I even got asbestosis! You don't need to worry – I'll share it with you if you like! Didn't like the wire up me prick! I like it when the nurses come round and wipe your knob off though! Mind you, I think we'd a been better off born without one o' those, all the trouble they cause. Don't you?'

Frank forced a grin and thankfully he shuffled off. He didn't feel like humouring the dirty old bugger – he just wanted to sleep. That was difficult though, even after the lights went off – there were too many noises in the ward and he was too tense. Earlier, the surgeon had come around and explained the procedure: 'This is the plan. We make an incision there or there, about an inch and a half, two inches, go in, find the vein, tie it off and stitch you up. Any questions?' This was it – there was no turning back now!

They had offered him sleeping pills, but he had refused them. He managed to sleep fitfully and finally was woken up at five in the morning by the noise of vehicles outside – there was a post office depot next door. For one ghastly moment he thought he was back in the dorm at the junior seminary. All the more reason to get the operation over with and get out of hospital, he told himself grimly.

'Since you're awake, you might as well have a bath,' the staff nurse said, coming over to his bed. 'I'll come and give you your jab at seven.'

'I had a bath yesterday,' he protested feebly – a bath was the last thing he wanted. He just wanted to get it over with!

'Well, go and have another one,' she ordered.

God, she was a real bossy-boots! She had a posh, RP voice, too, which made her sound even more annoying. He wanted to argue, but was afraid she might take revenge, so he went obediently to the bathroom, pretended to have a bath and returned to the ward, where she was making his bed.

'I didn't realise you were going to be so quick,' she said.

'Speedy Gonzalez, that's me,' he quipped and noticed she was putting a plastic sheet on the bed. 'What's that for?'

'We put this on because sometimes you're a bit, er, you know, bloody, when you come back from theatre.'

Christ, that's all I need to hear, he thought, noticing the NIL BY MOUTH notice above his bed as he got back in. This was the worst part, waiting, and you couldn't even have a cup of tea!

A little later she came to give him his 'pre-med' injection. 'This won't make you sleep, just dopey and a bit high,' she said, telling him to turn on his side and jabbing the needle painfully into his buttock, making him wince. He was glad he hadn't crossed swords with her earlier!

A few minutes later, a man in a white coat came into the ward. At first he thought he was a doctor, but he turned out to be a barber. Well, they used to be one and the same, didn't they?

'Anyone for a short, back and sides?' the white coat announced.

This turned out to be a joke. He hadn't come to give haircuts, but to shave off body hair pre-operation – in his case, pubic hair. He felt put out, because none of the nurses or doctors had warned him that this would be necessary, though he supposed he might have guessed it.

The barber came over to his bed first and sprinkled talcum powder on the target area. Then, to his horror, he produced a cut-throat razor!

'Shall I take that off and solve all your problems?' he quipped, pointing the razor at his willy.

Frank laughed nervously and flinched as the cold steel kissed his skin. 'Don't be nervous,' the barber joked. 'They can stitch 'em back on these days, if I make a mistake!' It was 'hospital humour', he supposed, but he wasn't really in the mood for it.

When the barber had finished, he lay back and closed his eyes, waiting for the injection to take effect, just wanting it all to be over, wanting to be left alone. However, he felt more and more tense as the minutes ticked slowly by and then another man in a white coat came to disturb him. This time it was the anaesthetist, who asked him lots of questions and also seemed to fancy himself as a bit of a comedian. 'Anything false?' he asked. 'False teeth? False eyes? False leg?' Frank shook his head and forced a smile – it was hard to laugh when you were about to have your belly slit open.

After the anaesthetist had gone, he lay back and tried to relax again. The injection seemed to make no difference – maybe he was immune to whatever was in it. At last, to his relief, a porter in a blue coat came in and with the help of a nurse pulled his bed out.

'Good luck,' the chap in the next bed said, as they wheeled him out of the ward and down the corridor.

However, they didn't seem to know which operating theatre to take him to. 'No, not this one,' the nurse laughed, whenever the porter stopped. They seemed to think this was funny. Finally, after doing what seemed like a scenic tour of the whole hospital, they arrived at the correct theatre. The fun and games weren't over though.

'We have to wait for the surgeons to come – they're not here yet,' the anaesthetist told him. 'Now, I'm just going to test this needle on the back of your hand.'

Oh, God, he thought – was this another sick joke? It didn't exactly inspire confidence! He felt like jumping out of the bed and making a run for it. He couldn't though – he was only wearing an operating gown. Besides, Mary would be shattered if he didn't go through with it. He was well and truly trapped! Anyway, a few minutes later, thank goodness, the surgeons arrived and started scrubbing up.

'This will send you off to sleep,' the anaesthetist said, picking up his hand and slipping a needle into a vein …

'Mister Walsh! Mister Walsh! Wake up! Your operation's finished! It's over! It all went very successfully!'

He opened his eyes. A nurse was leaning over him, tapping his face. He immediately felt a violent, throbbing pain deep in his groin. It was as if he had been stabbed and the knife was still stuck in the wound. He closed his eyes again. He just wanted to sleep, but they wouldn't let him. Anyway, the pain made sleep impossible.

'It all went very successfully.' *God, I hope so*! The theory behind it was that a varicose vein 'overheats' the sperm in the testicles and kills them, thus causing you to be infertile, or 'subfertile', as the quacks called it. It sounded better, but it amounted to the same thing – you couldn't have children. By performing what they called a 'ligature' of the vein – in other words tying it off so that the blood couldn't get through – his sperm count should rise and, hopefully, one of the little devils should get through to one of Mary's eggs.

God, the whole business of conception was mind-boggling, he thought! It was so complicated, dependent on so many factors being right – the quantity and quality of the sperm *and* the eggs, the temperature, the angle of penetration, the timing ... It was a bloody miracle anybody ever got conceived! Well, that was why there were millions of sperm in each consignment. *Except in my case, apparently!* Apparently, you needed twenty million per millilitre to have any chance, whereas his was down at fifteen million.

For the past few weeks, based on this theory, he had had to put a packet of frozen peas on his balls for twenty minutes before having intercourse. That would be fine if you had a fetish for frozen food, he supposed, but in his case it only served to cool his ardour. Sometimes he just couldn't 'do' it. *It'd be funny, if it wasn't tragic!*

It certainly would be tragic if they couldn't have a baby. Their marriage depended on it. It had become an obsession with Mary and every month she got out her thermometer, charts and the frozen peas. He just hoped to God the operation worked! Whatever happened though, he'd never eat frozen peas again ...

The funny thing was, now that he had been told he *couldn't* have children, he wanted them himself! The thought that he might never be able to depressed him, because having children was part of being normal – he just wanted to be *normal*. He hadn't left the 'loony bin' to be childless! He hadn't stopped being celibate to be sterile! He hadn't chosen not to become a 'Father' only to find that he couldn't be a 'father' either! What a cruel irony that would be! It would almost be as if they, the Ghosters, had won after all!

This was an irrational way to think, he knew, but sometimes he couldn't help feeling irrational, just as he couldn't help feeling sorry for himself, especially now, with the relentless, throbbing pain in his groin. One of the books he had read about infertility was called, 'Why Us?' 'Why Me?' more like it! Why did he have to suffer this pain and indignity, just to be able to do what most normal men did naturally?

The nurse came to take his temperature and check his blood pressure again. 'How's the pain?' she asked.

'Bad,' he groaned.

'Do you want an injection?'

He hated to give in, but it was unbearable. It was like a red-hot knife deep in his belly. 'Yes, please,' he gasped.

'I'll bring you something in a minute,' she said.

Thank God for morphine, he thought, a few minutes later, after she had given him the injection, and he drifted off into a fitful sleep.

'How are you feeling?' Mary asked, when she came to see him later.

'The pain's bad,' he said, with a grimace – actually, it wasn't quite as bad since the nurse had given him the morphine injection, but he wanted her to know how much he was suffering for her sake, as well as his own!

'I'm sorry, love,' she said, giving him a peck. 'It'll be worth it though.'

'I hope so,' he grimaced.

'If we can have a baby, it will, won't it?'

'If we can, yes, I suppose so.'

'You don't sound very enthusiastic,' she pouted.

'You wouldn't sound very enthusiastic if you felt as if you had a dagger stuck in your belly.'

'I'm sorry, love. I know you're in pain. Haven't they given you anything?'

'Yes, but I think it's starting to wear off. Don't worry – I'll survive.'

'I know what it's like – I've had two operations.'

'I know you have.'

'And I'm the one who'll have to suffer the pain of childbirth.'

'Well, at least I can say I've suffered in the cause, too.'

'I know you're in pain, love, but it can't be worse than the pain of childbirth.'

'Hey, let's not argue about pain. Let's just hope you *do* have to suffer the pains of childbirth!'

'When will you know if it's been successful?'

'I have to give them a sample next week.'

It was funny, having to masturbate into a specimen bottle and hand the proceeds over to a nurse – not to mention embarrassing. It wasn't always so easy! Was it a mortal sin, he wondered? Was he liable to go to Hell for wanting to have a child? What would the moral theologians say about it? Not that he cared any more!

'Of course, we won't get the result for a week or two after that. Anyway, the real test is if you get pregnant, isn't it?' he said to her.

'When can we start trying again?'

'You want to get into bed now?' he joked.

'I wouldn't mind!'

'You must be joking! The slightest movement makes it feel as if the knife is twisting in the wound. It's the very last thing I could do now!'

'I'm sorry, love. It's just that I can hardly wait. I want a baby more than anything in the world. From *you*.'

'I know. That's why I'm here.'

'Thank you for doing it, Fran. I do love you.' She took hold of his hand.

'I love you, too.'

'I know. I know you wouldn't do it, if you didn't.'

'I wouldn't do it for anybody else, I can tell you!' He squeezed her hand weakly.

'Have you thought about names?'

'Names?'

'Names for the baby!'

'God, let's see if this works first.'

'Don't say that. It will. I'm sure it will. If it's a boy, I want to call him 'Francis'.'

'Actually, I think I'd prefer a girl.'

'Oh, no. I want a boy! Just like you!'

'You mean, intelligent, handsome and charming?'

'Yes.'

'Flattery will get you nowhere!'

'I'm not flattering you. It's true.'

'Let's just hope it's healthy, shall we?'

'Oh, I'm sure it will be, coming from you.'

'And let's hope this bloody operation works.'

'I'm sure it will, Fran. I can feel it. You have to think positive, you know.'

'I *am* positive. I'm here, aren't I?'

'You do want a baby, don't you?'

'Yes, I do actually. I suddenly quite fancy being a dad.'

'I think you'll be a good dad.'

'It makes me feel old though.'

'You are thirty-four, Fran.'

'Yes, I know. I suppose it's time to settle down. Can I ask you something?'

'Yes?'

'Will you be the mother of my child?'

'Of course I will!' she laughed, hugging him.

'Aaargh! It hurts!' he groaned, putting an arm round her.

'Oh, I'm sorry, love!' she said, trying to let go, but he pulled her close, even though it hurt.

'Ah! Mister Walsh. Come in. Have a seat,' the consultant said, standing up and shaking hands with him.

He sat down in front of the desk, behind which sat the consultant and two other doctors, while a nurse sat to one side. It was like being on trial! Well, it was a kind of trial – he had come for the verdict.

'How are you?' the consultant asked.

'Fine, thanks,' he said.

'Good Now, let's see, how long is it since you had your op?' He opened a file, put a pair of specs on the end of his nose and read.

'Hmm. Six months. Have you been having regular intercourse?'

'Yes.' He still felt a bit embarrassed about admitting in public that he had been having sex! Once a Catholic ...

'Still no result?'

'No.'

'Hm. I've got your thermography report here. I'm afraid the temperature is still too high, so there's been no change there.'

'But the thermographer told me it was normal now. I don't understand.'

'I don't understand myself. I'll tell you what – let's have a look at you, shall we? Would you mind popping into the cubicle, just drop your trousers and underpants and we'll be with you in a minute.'

He went into the cubicle, dropped his trousers and pants, and waited, feeling self-conscious. The temperature was still too high? Then why had the thermographer told him differently? It sounded bad.

The medics all trooped in and the consultant crouched down to examine him. He tried not to blush, but it was difficult, because there were so many people in the room and because it reminded him of what had happened all those years ago in Father Director's bedroom …

'The varicocele is still there,' the consultant said. 'In fact, it's a classic. A real bag of worms.' He stood up. 'Come and have a look,' he invited the student doctor.

The student doctor crouched down to have a look, then the other doctor. By now he couldn't stop himself blushing. Even worse than any embarrassment, though, was the growing suspicion that it had all been in vain. *In vein, ha ha.*

'Thank you, Mister Walsh. If you'd just like to get dressed and come back into the consulting room.'

They all trooped out. He got dressed, went back into the consulting room and sat down in front of the desk again, feeling like a condemned man waiting for his sentence.

'So, you say, the varicocele is still there?' he asked the consultant.

'Very much so, I'm afraid.'

'And the temperature is still too high?'

'Yes.'

'What about the sperm count?'

'Have you given a specimen?'

'Yes, I gave one a couple of weeks ago.' *What a wanker I am!*

'Let's have a look and see if we've got a result for that then,' the consultant said, shuffling through the notes. 'Ah, yes. Here we are. Your sperm count was twelve million per millilitre.'

'*Twelve* million? But it was *fifteen* million before the operation!' His heart sank.

'Yes. It was. It's gone down, I'm afraid.'

'So what you're telling me is that the operation was a complete failure?'

'To put it bluntly, yes.'

It hit him like a bullet in the chest. He sat in stunned silence, staring in disbelief at the consultant, struggling to fight back waves of despair and anger.

'What you're saying in effect,' the consultant resumed, 'is how could we have been so bloody stupid as not to do it properly? Well, here's a short anatomy lesson.'

He walked over to an anatomical chart on the wall and proceeded to deliver a little lecture about veins, the scrotum, the kidneys, missing valves, tying veins off, blood forcing itself through another channel that might be too fine to see … but he was too stunned to take it in.

'We can see everything all right when we open up the tummy, but sometimes the vein is just too fine,' the consultant concluded, sitting down. 'What we really need to do is have another look at you.'

'What do you mean?' he said, suddenly registering what he was saying. 'Another operation?'

'Yes.'

'I'd have to think about that,' he said, shaking his head incredulously. Was the man serious? Did he really think he'd go through another operation?

'Why?' the consultant asked, genuinely surprised.

'Because I don't feel like having my belly slit open again by a bunch of bungling butchers!' he thought, but didn't say it. 'I just find the whole business very – unpleasant,' he said instead. 'Anyway, there's no guarantee it'd work a second time, is there?'

'There's no guarantee, no, but either Mister Hendry or myself would do it. In fact, Mister Hendry. I think it's only fair if you have to have a second operation, it should only be done by the best available. Not that I wouldn't do it properly myself. We would do it at your earliest, too.'

'I'll have to think about it and discuss it with my wife,' he said. The thought of telling Mary the bad news sent a wave of anguish over him.

'Please do,' the doctor said, standing up and offering his hand. 'Are your wife's tests under way, by the way?'

'Yes,' he replied, standing up, shaking the doctor's hand quickly and making for the door – all he wanted to do now was escape.

'Oh, could I just ask you one thing?' he turned and asked at the door. 'Would you send me the thermography report in writing and let me know about the thermography discrepancy?'

'Why?' the doctor asked. 'There's no point. The varicocele's still there.'

'I would appreciate it.' He wanted it as proof for Mary. 'If it's not too much trouble,' he added, with a flash of sarcasm – the consultant's evasiveness irritated him.

'OK, if you like,' the consultant agreed, reluctantly.

'Thank you,' he said, and fled the room.

He decided to walk home by Regent's Canal. It would take an hour or more, but he needed some fresh air and exercise. Besides, it would delay the dreaded moment when he had to tell Mary the bad news. She'd be devastated, but he knew what she'd say – have the operation done again. There was no way though – he wasn't going under the knife again, even if she left him!

The thought that she might leave him again filled him with despair. It would be like a 'double whammy': no children and no wife! He tried to distract himself from thinking as he walked along the towpath by observing the scenery – the sycamore and plane trees along the bank of the canal, a lilac bush reeking of perfume, the surface of the water rippled by playful breezes, barges negotiating the locks at City Basin, Gordon's gin factory ...

It was all very interesting, but he knew there was only one way to distract himself properly. So when he came to a Young's pub by the side of the canal, he stopped and went in.

CHAPTER TWENTY-THREE

'You're drunk!'

'I'm not drunk! I've had a couple of pints, that's all!' In fact, he had ended up having five pints of Young's Special.

'It's not fair, Fran. I've been waiting here for two hours.'

'I know it's not fair. Life's not fucking fair. It's not my fault. I didn't design it.'

'You're drunk. Go and sit down. I'll make a cup of tea.'

'"Aargh, if a man were dyin', you'd offer him a cup o' tay",' he declaimed, quoting from 'Juno and the Paycock', the O'Casey play they had both appeared in at the Sugawn.

He staggered over to the stereo to put some music on, wondering what might be suitable. Mozart's Requiem, perhaps, for the death of his unborn children? But he didn't have that, so he put Van Morrison's 'Astral Weeks' on instead and collapsed onto the settee.

'So what did he say?' Mary asked, bringing him a cup of tea and turning down the music, to his annoyance.

'He said my fucking sperm count has gone down. If you'll pardon the pun.'

'You don't need to swear, Fran! Gone *down*?'

'Yes. Gone down! It's now twelve million per millilitre. It was fifteen. Fucking incredible!'

'So the operation was no good?'

'A complete balls-up, if you'll pardon another pun.'

'Can't they do it again?'

'Oh, yes. He said I could have it done again, at my earliest convenience.'

'What did you say?'

'I said you must be fucking joking. Not quite in so many words.'

'Why not, Fran?'

'You must be fucking joking!'

'There's no need to swear at me, Fran.'

'I'm not swearing at you. But do you really think I'm going to go through all that again? Let those cowboys cut me up? I don't think they know what they're doing. Anyway, there's no guarantee it'd work a second time either.'

'It's our only chance, Fran.'

'No, it's not. How do you know it's not you?'

'We've been through all that, Fran.'

'What about your tests?'

'I won't get the results till next week. I don't think it's me, anyway.'

'Oh, so it's my fault?'

'It's nobody's *fault*, Fran.'

'That's what you seem to be saying.'

'I'm not saying that. I'm just saying, if you have to have another operation – '

'Well, I'm not having another fucking operation! It's as simple as that! I don't care if I can't have children!'

'I do. What about me?'

'What about you? Go and find somebody else, if I can't give you what you want!' He knew that was the wrong thing to say, but he couldn't stop himself – it was the alcohol talking.

'Just like you do, you mean?' He could see she was on the verge of tears now. 'Who's Cinzia?'

Christ! How did she know about Cinzia?

'Cinzia? What are you talking about?'

'I found this in your jacket pocket,' she said, passing him a piece of paper. It had the name and address of one of his students on it, yet another Italian girl. It was true, he liked her, had even had a date with her, but nothing had happened …

'Oh, you've been snooping again, have you?' he accused, snatching it from her.

'I was looking for that letter from the solicitor's about the house, actually.' This was the house they were trying to buy.

'I've told you before not to go in my pockets.'

'Why have you got her address?' she demanded, ignoring what he had said.

'That's none of your business.'

'You've been fucking her, haven't you?'

This infuriated him, because it was both gratuitous and untrue. He would *like* to 'fuck' Cinzia, as she so crudely put it, but had resisted temptation, even though Cinzia had made it clear she fancied him. He had resisted, because he really wanted to make his marriage work, really wanted to give Mary a child, really wanted a child himself. Yet she accused him of infidelity! He might just as well have been fucking unfaithful!

'Yes, I've been fucking her!' he shouted angrily. 'She's a much better fuck than you, too, I can tell you that!'

Mary burst into tears, ran into the bedroom and shut the door. He followed her and shouted through the door: 'She's much prettier and much more intelligent than you, too!' Then he grabbed his jacket and stormed out, slamming the front door behind him.

He had already had too much to drink, so resisted the temptation to go to the pub. Instead, he went down to the Marshes for a walk by the river, since it was a pleasant spring evening. He was enraged at being falsely accused, but as always, walking helped to calm him down. He walked up the slope to the top of the park, admiring the trees and flowers, and sat on a bench to take in the view of river, marina, reed beds, railway viaduct and reservoir with its little wooded islands, from which herons flapped to and fro. It was one of his favourite views and as always helped to soothe him.

It had been bitchy of her to accuse him of being unfaithful, he thought, but he could understand. She was shocked by the bad news, just as he had been himself. He'd go back home, tell her he was sorry for the things he had said and tonight he'd make love with her. Who knows, maybe they'd conceive the baby they both wanted tonight? It would be great to prove the doctors wrong! He stood up to go.

But when he got back, she was gone. He guessed she had gone to Lisa's. Lisa was a college friend who lived in Walthamstow, but he didn't know exactly where. He didn't like her, because she was a rabid feminist and was always encouraging Mary to leave him. Worse still, she was a lesbian and he suspected that she fancied Mary. He couldn't imagine Mary ever having a lesbian relationship, but the thought was enough to antagonize him.

For the next day or two he was worried sick, because Mary made no contact. For all he knew, she might have thrown herself under a train. Teaching was an almost impossible strain, but somehow he managed. *You have to be professional!* It made him angry though – she had no right to do this to him again. It was cruel and selfish! He felt like 'fucking' Cinzia, just to get revenge. It would serve her right for accusing him, then leaving him in a state of high anxiety like this.

Funnily enough, he bumped into Cinzia at the bus stop outside college a couple of days later. He suspected she was waiting for him, because he knew she liked him. A couple of weeks before, he had found her waiting for him outside his classroom door and Hassan, one of his students, said to her: 'What are you doing here? Do you like him? He is married!' Joyce, a Nigerian girl, ticked him off: 'Hassan, you talk too much!' It didn't put Cinzia off, though, for here she was, waiting at the bus stop, and not just for a bus, he suspected.

'Hello,' he said to her, stopping. She looked pretty, in a black, glittery summer dress which revealed her nicely tanned skin.

'Ees thees the righta stopa for 123?' she asked him.

'Yes,' he said. 'Where are you going?'

'Woodforda,' she said.

'You don't live in Woodford, do you?' he asked.

'I 'ave moveda,' she told him.

'Oh. This is the right stop then. Are you still an au pair?'

'Yes. Where are you goinga?'

'I'm going to the pub,' he said, on the spur of the moment – he didn't normally go in the afternoon.

'Do you go to the pub after class every daya?' she asked.

'Yes. I'm usually thirsty after teaching!' he laughed. 'What about you? What do you usually do?'

'Nothinga. I never do anythinga.'

'Do you want to come for a drink?'

'I 'ave no money.'

'That's all right – I'll treat you.'

'Thank you!' she said, her dark-brown eyes lighting up. 'Where are you goinga?'

'Just down the road, to the Bell. Come on.' He walked off and she walked beside him.

'Ees eet true you are marrieda?' she asked, in the pub.

'Yes, but my wife's left me,' he said, taking a sup of his Guinness. It made him sad to say it, because it was true, but it also gave him a certain vindictive satisfaction.

'I'm sorry,' she said. 'Why 'as she left you?'

'Problems,' he shrugged, taking another sup of his Guinness. She was drinking orange juice.

'Do you 'ave children?'

'No,' he said, sadly. 'That's one of the problems.'

'I'm sorry,' she said again.

'What about you? Have you got a boyfriend?'

'Yes,' she said, but with a sigh.

'Tell me about him. Is he Italian?'

'Yes. 'e is a sailor. 'ees name is Luciano. 'e is quieta. 'e don'ta talka. 'e ees too quieta. I 'ave changed 'eem a bita, but eet's not gooda.'

'You don't sound very happy with him.'

'I only see 'eem every three monthsa.'

'That could be a good thing!' he laughed.

'Eet's no gooda,' she said. 'If 'e gets a job on dry landa, I weel marry 'eem.'

'What about children? Do you want children?'

'I only wanta one childa. More would be too mucha trouble and expense.'

'With your husband?' he teased.

'Of course weetha my 'usbanda! 'ow otherwise?'

'Do you love him?'

' 'Love'? What ees 'love'?'

'Good question!' he laughed.

The following Sunday morning, as he was reading the papers, the phone rang. He picked it up quickly, hoping it might be Mary, but it was his father. He told him they had sold the house in Manchester, because they were retiring to Ireland, and were giving all the children, including him, £1000 as a gift out of the proceeds. Touched, he thanked him, but typically he said he didn't want any fuss about it, gave him some more family news and then asked the question he was afraid of: 'How's Mary?'

'Oh, she's fine,' he fibbed. 'Studying hard.'

Afterwards, when he had put the phone down, there was a lump in his throat and he had to fight back tears from his eyes – he felt touched by his father's generosity, but guilty for lying to him – and more worried than ever about Mary. He tried to carry on reading, but couldn't concentrate, couldn't stop wondering where she was, what she was doing, whether she was safe, whether she was even still alive …

Later, the phone rang again. He picked it up quickly. It was Lisa, who told him Mary was staying with her. So at least she's alive, he thought, with relief! 'Can I speak to her?' he asked.

'She doesn't want to speak to you,' Lisa said.

'Why not?' he asked, irked.

'She's still very shaken up by the whole business,' Lisa said.

'So am I,' he retorted.

There was a silence, which irked him even more. 'If we don't speak to each other, we'll never solve the problem, will we?' he said, with a touch of sarcasm.

'I'll see what she says,' Lisa said, and the phone went silent again, to his further irritation. Then: 'She says she'll speak to you, if you come here.'

'Can't she meet me in a pub or something?' he asked – he would prefer neutral territory, not Lisa's lair.

'I'll ask her.' There was another irritating silence, then: 'She doesn't want to go out. She's too nervous.'

'All right,' he agreed, reluctantly. 'I'll go there. Can you give me the address?' She did so.

'I'll be there about eight o'clock' he said, putting the phone down before she could object – that would give him time to have a couple of pints first.

That evening, he took a train to Walthamstow. He had a pint in Flanagan's, opposite the station, another one in the Victoria, next to the cinema, and a third one in the Rose and Crown on Hoe Street. By then he felt sufficiently fortified to confront both Lisa and Mary in their den.

When he went in, they were in the kitchen, washing up, having just eaten. Pork chops. He had passed a couple of Indian restaurants on the way and thought of inviting Mary out for dinner – she loved eating out – but now that idea was thwarted. He resigned himself to staying there, but he really wanted to speak to Mary alone.

Lisa had short hair like a man and was dressed like a man, too, in a dark-blue shirt and green tie with jeans. Mary, by contrast, was wearing a pink sweater, short grey skirt and tights. She looked so pretty, so feminine, so vulnerable, he wanted to hug her, but she wouldn't even let him kiss her on the cheek. He noticed with a shock that she had removed her wedding ring.

They sat in the tiny living room, on wooden chairs – his seemed like something from Tudor times. Lisa offered to go, but Mary, to his annoyance, insisted she stayed. He tried to make small talk for a few minutes, looking around the room as he did so. There was a piano, with a cloth over it, and on top two speakers, through which Bob Dylan was singing, a picture of Salvador Dali's praying hands and a stuffed owl. There was a book case with lots of philosophy books in it, such as Gilbert Ryle's 'Concept of Mind', which he remembered reading at university. There was a brown suede sofa and a red bean bag. Around the walls were several cards with provocative women's lib slogans, such as, 'IF THE POPE WERE A WOMAN, ABORTION WOULD BE A SACRAMENT'. That sounded bloody stupid to him, not because he considered himself a Catholic any more or was a fan of the Pope, but because he didn't believe in killing babies, or at best thought it was sometimes a necessary evil.

'So, er, how's college?' he asked Mary, trying to make conversation, wishing Lisa would go away.

Suddenly, though, Mary burst into tears, and started sobbing violently. Afraid she was going to have a fit, he half-stood up to go and put an arm around her, but Lisa, who was sitting on a chair next to her, beat him to it. Was there something between them, he wondered, jealously? He couldn't believe Mary would, but she was in such a fragile state …

'I can't make conversation, I can't talk,' she sobbed, shaking, taking her hankie out of her sleeve and wiping her eyes. 'I'm having a nervous breakdown.'

It made his heart bleed to see her like this, like a broken bird. More than anything in the world, he wanted to rush over and put his arms around her, hug her, as he had done so many times before, but Lisa had *her* arm firmly, possessively, around her thin, shaking shoulders.

'Why have you come here?' she sobbed.

'I thought you wanted me to come here,' he said, a lump in his throat. 'I thought you wanted to talk.'

'Talk about what?' she sobbed.

'About the situation,' he said, impatiently.

'What situation?'

'The situation between us,' he said, struggling to suppress his impatience. 'Why you've left.'

'All right, I'll talk if you want. I'll tell you why I've left you,' she sobbed. 'I haven't left you because I'm jealous. I'm not jealous, you know, Fran. You can fuck or screw who you like. It's the insecurity I can't stand. I love you, with your lovely legs, but I just can't stand the insecurity. Why do you need sexual variety? Why don't you come to me and say what you want, say you want it this or that way? I'll give you whatever you want! Why don't you?'

'I think you're being a bit irrational,' he said, embarrassed – he didn't want to discuss his sex life in front of a stranger!

'I *am* irrational,' she sobbed. 'The situation has made me irrational. I think I'm having a mental breakdown. I'm not irrational all the time though. I'm going in and out. It comes and goes.'

While she spoke, Lisa was rubbing her back. This really irritated him, because it should be *him* doing that. After all, she *was* still his wife! *He* was the one who had looked after her for the past nine years!

'Are you sure you wouldn't like to come for a drink or go for a walk or something?' he asked her, desperate to get her away from Lisa, from this claustrophobic little flat. Besides, he was feeling hungry now.

'No. I want to stay here. I feel safe here. Why should I go? As long as Lisa doesn't mind. I know she might want to study or something.'

'I've told Mary she can stay here as long as she wants,' Lisa said, still rubbing Mary's back. 'And I'll stay here as long as she needs me.'

Part of him was grateful for Lisa's support, but part of him resented her intensely, especially when he thought she might fancy Mary.

'You see,' Mary sobbed. 'Here I am stripping myself in front of a stranger! I'll tell Nora, but no one else. Not even my mother. I don't want anyone else to know. Just you, Lisa and Nora.' Nora was her older sister.

'I'm not going to tell anyone else,' he said.

'I'll call Nora tomorrow,' she sobbed.

'Why don't you just come home?' he suggested, annoyed.

'I've told you, Fran. I can't stand the insecurity any longer.'

'What insecurity?'

'The insecurity of knowing you might be fucking someone else. That Italian girl, for example. What's her name? Cinzia? I know you've probably been fucking her.'

'Just because I've got her address in my pocket?'

'Why else would you have her address?'

'Lots of reasons. Maybe she's asked me for private lessons, for example.' He did give private lessons sometimes.

'It's sex, you mean. You've had sex with her. Or you want to have sex with her. You're obsessed with sex! Why? Sex is not important! Love is important – care, concern, affection.' She was crying copiously now.

'If sex is not important, why are you so worried by me having sex with someone else?' he felt like asking her, in his adversarial way, but didn't. 'I know love is important,' he said instead, annoyed by her accusations, but moved by her tears. 'I love you. I want you to come home.' He reached out to take her hand.

'Don't touch me!' she exclaimed, brushing his hand away, then apologised. 'I'm sorry, but I'm very upset. Why do you want me to come home? Why? What for? What do you want from me? I'm angry now! I've never been angry before. I've never shown it. I've suppressed it. By God, I'll show it now! I feel so lucid, so intelligent. I've spoken to intelligent people. They say I'm not so unintelligent or inadequate! Why didn't your mother tell me before we got married?'

'Tell you what?' he asked, trying to keep cool. Why did she have to bring his mother into it? He was embarrassed, because Lisa was still here, holding her hand.

'That you weren't ready for marriage! I felt sorry for you! I knew you'd been deprived of love and affection, what you went through with the Ghosters and all that. I never felt so bad before, even when I left you last time. I feel *betrayed,* that's what I feel. I remember what you did to me in Dublin. I remember wandering around, looking for you, and all the time you were with that French whore! I remember the time you were in a bad mood, treated me like dirt, didn't talk to me for six weeks! I remember all those things!'

He felt angry now. How dare she bring all that up? What about all the love and affection and help he'd given her over the years? How dare she throw Dublin at him? The only reason she had ever been to Dublin and spent six weeks in Trinity College was because of him! Without him she would never have got anywhere near the place! And why hadn't he spoken to her for six weeks? Because she had *attacked* him in public, in front of all his colleagues, sided with *them* against *him*, the one who took her there! That was betrayal! That was infidelity! That was as bad as if she had been unfaithful to him. She was lucky he hadn't left her for good then, never mind for six weeks!

He felt rage welling up inside him, felt like lambasting her, but bit his tongue, sat in silence for a few moments, struggling to keep calm, telling himself not to say anything, not to retaliate, she was upset, she was hurt …

'I don't think there's any point dragging all this up,' he said after a while, as calmly as he could, and stood up. 'I have to go now to catch the ten o'clock train. All I want to say is I love you and I want you to come home. Come home tomorrow. I'll be waiting for you.'

'Why put the onus on me?' she cried. 'I'm not able to make any decisions!'

'I'm not putting the onus on you,' he said, going to the door. 'I'll come here for you tomorrow, if you want.'

'Why do you want me to come home?'

'Because I love you,' he said, opening the door – he just wanted to get away as quickly possible now. 'Good night.'

'What about Lisa?'

'Good night,' he said to Lisa, and left.

The next morning, he woke up with a hangover. He had come home the night before feeling depressed and guilty about Mary and drunk himself unconscious. He didn't feel like going to work, but did so and somehow struggled through the morning. *You have to be professional!*

It was a sunny afternoon, and he needed some fresh air and exercise, so after work he walked home across the Marshes. On the way, he sat on the grass in the middle of one of the meadows and wrote her a letter, telling her he was sorry about everything, telling her he loved her, telling her he wanted her back, telling her he would be faithful, telling her he would do anything to make her happy, even have the operation again …

Later, in mid-afternoon, arriving home, he was surprised to see her, in her blue anorak, leaving the estate with a suitcase in her hand.

'Where are you going?' he asked, fatalistically.

'I'm going to Ireland,' she said. Her parents had retired there, like his own.

'Shall I help you with that suitcase?' he offered.

She gave it to him and they walked to the station together in strained silence.

'When are you coming back?' he asked her, as they waited on the platform.

'I'm not coming back.'

'Oh, I see,' he said, shocked.

Just like that! After all we've been through together, after all I've done for her, she's going to walk away from me, just like that!

'I've written you a letter,' he said, taking the envelope out of his pocket and handing it to her, but she declined to take it.

'You don't want to read it?' he asked, offended.

'No, it would just upset me,' she said.

'I see,' he said, putting it back in his jacket pocket. 'Why are you leaving?'

'I told you last night, Fran – I just can't take the insecurity any more.'

'I see. Is somebody meeting you?'

'Yes. I'm being met by a Samaritan.'

'Oh.' He was shocked again. 'Why?'

'I need help. I need counselling. I need therapy.'

'I see.' He was too shocked to say anything else.

The train came in. The door opened and a few people got out. She picked up the suitcase.

'Don't go,' he said.

'Why not?' she asked.

'If you go, it's the end of us,' he said.

'Is that a threat?'

'No, it's just a fact,' he shrugged.

'I have to go,' she said, getting on the train.

'Bye then,' he said, as if unconcerned. He even blew her a kiss as the train pulled out!

Afterwards, he stood on the platform for a few minutes, in a state of shock. Then he looked at his watch. He felt like going and getting plastered again, but had an evening class to teach. He could phone in sick, he supposed, but his students had an oral exam the following week. He couldn't let them down, he decided. He'd better go back to work. *After all, you have to be professional*, he reminded himself, turning to go.

For information about Eugene's other books,

please see over.

GHOSTERS

GHOSTERS is the prequel to Opposite Worlds. At the age of twelve Frank Walsh leaves home in Manchester and goes to a Roman Catholic seminary in the English Lake District to fulfil his dream of becoming a missionary priest. At twenty-one, having lost his faith, he makes an unsuccessful attempt to commit suicide, leaves the seminary and returns home. With the help of Sally, the girl next door, he slowly manages to recover from depression and starts to feel 'normal' again, especially sexually. After finishing university, he leaves home yet again – and Sally – to go and live in London. There he tries to escape the ghosts of his past and fulfil his dream of being a writer, while teaching English to foreign students in a private school in Soho. He has a passionate love affair with one of his students, Marina, a vibrant, eighteen-year-old Yugoslav girl. They plan to marry, but a chance meeting with a ghost from the past threatens to destroy this dream too. Yet Frank refuses to be beaten, because he still has one dream left …

'I like it ... imaginitively strong ... I was riveted ... sensitively worked out ... intelligently written ... powerfully presented ... this heart-felt painful re-creation of a central hidden part of our culture.'
Kate Cruise O'Brien, Poolbeg Press Ltd.

VENICE AND OTHER POEMS

VENICE AND OTHER POEMS is Eugene's first book of poetry. It includes poems written when he was a teenager to poems written recently. In other words, it covers a span of nearly fifty years, from his schooldays in the early sixties to 2011. However, the poems are in alphabetical not chronological order. Each poem expresses a state of mind or emotion at the time, an observation of a scene or a reflection upon some experience. So in a sense the poems are autobiographical, though not necessarily an exact mirror of the author's life – there may be some 'poetic licence'. Perhaps it would be better to describe each poem as a prism. As well as reflecting his own life-experience though, the author hopes that in at least some of these poems readers may catch a glimpse of their own lives, past, present or even future …

VENICE AND OTHER POEMS is available from Amazon

You may contact Eugene at:
eugenevesey@ntlworld.com

3648074R00197

Printed in Great Britain
by Amazon.co.uk, Ltd.,
Marston Gate.